SHEMLAN

A DEADLY TRAGEDY

D1518424

Alexander McNabb

The Levant Cycle

Three roughly contiguous books set in the contemporary Levant but by no means a trilogy.

Olives – A Violent Romance

Beirut – An Explosive Thriller

Shemlan – A Deadly Tragedy

More at www.alexandermcnabb.com

For Sarah.

ONE

Jason Hartmoor has been alive a little over an hour. He has recovered from his recurring nightmare and turned the damp side of his pillow to face the mattress. He luxuriates in the bright light streaming through the window overlooking the sea. It takes up most of the length of the room.

The bed sheets are white and crisp. Every opening of the eyes is a bonus, a thrill of pleasure. Sometimes he tries to stave off sleep, lying and fighting exhaustion until the early hours. It is becoming increasingly hard to push back the darkness. These days he's lucky to hold out beyond midnight.

Throwing the lightweight duvet aside, he pauses for breath before sliding himself into a sitting position, looking out over Newgale's glorious sandy mile, the breakers cascading. The dots of shivering early surfers bob in the glistening waves.

The pain starts to creep back, like a slinking dog.

He stands by the window, gazing out over the hazy beach, the fine misty spray thrown up by the incoming tide. His face in the morning light is lined and wan, pain etched into his still-handsome features, a face that would seem haughty but for the humour in the blue eyes nestled in the bruised-looking shadows. His hair is white, his forehead prominent and his nose aquiline.

He draws himself up unconsciously; the slight puff of his chest brings a twinge of discomfort.

The beige folder lies on the kitchen table. Hartmoor reaches for it, his pain dulled by the tablet he took before his enzymes, tea and toast. He slides one of the dark blue-grey transparencies out of the folder and turns to present it to the light, his reward a ghostly image of a skeletal torso. Peering, he picks out each one of the little tumours that cling like grains of rice thrown at his bones.

He remembers the first diagnosis, the nervous young doctor whose eyes gave away the news before his mouth did. The shock of it and the dullness of the hospital noises as he sleepwalked out of the little office into the brightly lit corridor with its shining floor and rubber-wheeled gurneys. He returns the x-ray to its folder and takes it to the dustbin. He presses down on the pedal and folds the bundle of plastic sheets to fit them into the round steel cylinder. The lid clangs shut.

Hartmoor signs the note for Mrs Paternall, the woman who 'does' for him. She was to visit the house regularly, clean weekly. A deposit directly to her account would settle business matters. He would telephone whenever he felt it appropriate. He doesn't leave her a contact number, but does tell her he will be in Beirut for the foreseeable.

The cap of the pen snaps shut as the horn sounds outside, two irritating beeps. The Stick is by the front door. He debates whether to take it with him. Reason prevails. His black overcoat folded over his forearm, The Stick in hand, Hartmoor drags the wheelie bag behind him into the grey morning light.

For some reason the snick of the closing door fills him with a feeling of closure, of optimism and even excitement. Someone nearby has been cutting grass. Rolling the bag behind him down the path, he cherishes the journey into his past. It was just as well, he reflects as Bert The Taxi hefts the bag into the boot and Hartmoor settles into the back seat, because he doesn't really have that much of a future.

Bert's gaze flickers in the mirror. 'Heathrow, then Mr Hartmoor? Terminal five?'

'Yes, Bert. Terminal five. Thank you.' Hartmoor settles back in the black leather seat to watch the countryside roll past in the soft rain. The motorway's long, sulky curve around the belching smoke stacks of Port Talbot is, as ever, the journey's low point.

*

The doorbell interrupted Elsie's puzzled scrutiny of Mr Hartmoor's letter.

'Mr Hartmoor in, please?' An English accent.

'No,' Elsie snapped, looking the stranger up and down. He was a gingery-looking fellow, stooped by his height and whiskered. His pale, freckled features were bland but his mobile green eyes were nervous. 'He's gone away.'

'Mind if I come in, then?' The gingery man waited, his hands held loosely by his side.

Elsie frowned. 'I don't know who you are. Who are you?'

He reached into his inside pocket, getting his hand stuck on the way out. He finally pulled free his wallet and showed her a shiny ID card in the name of Nigel Soames. He beamed at her. 'Sorry. Foreign and Commonwealth Office. Mr Hartmoor used to work for us.'

'Before he retired.'

'Yes,' Soames' head bobbed. 'Before he retired. He was very ill, I understand.'

She stood aside. 'You'd better come in. But you can take your shoes off and leave 'em by the door.'

Soames' schoolboy gratitude was disarming. He held himself steady against the wall as he kicked the heel of one shoe off against the other's instep then held the remaining shoe down with his brown-socked foot as he pulled. He turned right down the corridor into the living room with its picture window overlooking Newgale beach, a mirror of the bedroom window above.

'Nice, this.' Soames ran a finger along the sideboard, studied it and nodded at her. 'Know if he'll be long?'

Elsie realised she was holding a duster and wearing a pinafore. She felt dowdy. 'I said, he's gone away.'

Comprehension dawned on Soames' face. 'Oh, you mean properly away. Where to?'

Elsie smirked, imparting her secret knowledge. 'Beirut. In The Lebanon, it is.'

Soames' eyebrow shot up but his face remained impassive otherwise. He stared at her a second then turned to face the sea. 'And why not? Leave a forwarding number, did he?'

He was looking at Mr Hartmoor's writing table. Elsie shook her head. 'No, just a note letting me know what he wanted me to do with the house. He says he'll call if he needs anything.'

'Did you know he had cancer?'

She nodded. 'Yes. He's been ill a long time. My Jim says it's a miracle he's made it this long.'

'Your husband? Jim?'

Elsie's mouth tightened and she lifted her head. 'Yes.'

'Look, if you don't mind I rather think I'd like to look around.'

'Well, I'm not sure I—'

'This is official business, Mrs?'

'Paternall.'

'This is official business, Mrs Paternall. You can check with London if you like, but Mr Hartmoor was one of ours and I have full authority to search these premises.'

Elsie gauged him for a second, pulled up to his full six feet and more. She nodded. 'Go on, then. I'll be in the kitchen making some tea.'

His smile was brilliant. 'Thank you.'

Elsie sat listening to Soames moving deftly around the house, opening drawers and cupboards before he padded down the corridor to the kitchen. He snatched Jason Hartmoor's note from the table, glancing up at her standing by the kettle. 'Yes, please. Two sugars.'

She poured hot water into a mug. Mr Hartmoor preferred leaf tea, but kept bags for her when she came to clean. She squeezed the bag with the back of the teaspoon.

Soames sat at the kitchen table, waving the note. 'Did you know him well?'

'No, I just cleaned here once a week.'

'Been doing it long?'

'All of five years. He was a good man. Respectable.'

'Did you know he caused a scandal? That he had to retire early?'

She poured milk into the cup and handed it across the table. 'That doesn't sound right. Like I say, he was a quiet man.'

'It was little girls. In the Sudan.' Soames' eyes glinted. She shuddered. Soames handed a card over to her. 'Here. If you hear anything from him, call this number. Don't tell anyone else, just call me. It's important, you understand?'

The undecorated card read 'Nigel Soames' and underneath in italics, 'Foreign and Commonwealth Office.' It was a London number. Elsie nodded, looking down at the card.

'He was a good man.'

Soames stood and smiled. 'I'm sure he was. But now we want to speak to him again. I'd rather you didn't tell him, just let me know if you hear from him. I'd not want you in a position of *danger*, see?'

His gaze alighted on the dustbin, its lid slightly raised. He pressed on the pedal to open it. He glanced over at her with a tight grin. 'Find a lot of things in dustbins.'

'If that's where you like looking.'

Soames pulled a cream folder out. He laid it on the table. Elsie glared at him. The petrol sheets slid out with a little hiss and Soames held one to the light from the window. He peered at the boxed text to the bottom left of the x-ray. 'Jason Hartmoor,' he said, gazing back at the image of a man's skeletal torso. 'I'll take these if you don't mind.'

'I can't hardly stop you.'

Elsie followed him up the corridor and watched his little dance putting on his slip-on shoes. He took his jacket from the telephone table where he'd flung it down. She stood at the door and stared at Soames walking down the street gripping the cream folder. She wondered where he had parked his car.

TWO

The interior of Beirut's Le Gray Hotel was as chic as it was luxurious, vases of single stems and brushed steel surfaces, dark woods and artfully matched colour contrasts soothed and cosseted those willing to pay the stiff room rates. Hartmoor, exhausted despite sleeping on the flight, was willing.

The bellboy was fussing. Hartmoor tipped him before he could start to introduce the delights of the television controls and other features of the room. As the door closed, he paused and took in the ambient silence, the susurration of the busy traffic in Martyrs' Square beyond the double glazed window. He sat on the bed and took his wallet out of his jacket, riffling through the notes to find the slip of paper he had carefully folded there. He lifted the phone handset and dialled the number, peering at it over his half-rims.

'This is the Embassy of the United States of America. I'm Stacy, how can I help you today?'

Hartmoor winced at the brightness of her voice. 'Good morning. I would like to speak with Frank Coleman, please.'

'Frank Coleman? I'm sorry but… one second, please. Umm, who is on the line?'

'Tell him it's Jason Hartmoor.'

'Okay. P-please hold, caller.'

Hartmoor waited, gazing around at the purple curtains and carpets, the mushroom walls and halogen-lit dark wooden surfaces of his suite. The line was fumbled and she came back, her voice more confident.

'I am sorry, Mr Hartmoor, but Mr Coleman is not available at this moment. Would you like to leave a message for him?'

For some reason, Hartmoor hadn't expected Coleman not to

be there when he needed him. But of course Coleman would have no inkling of his arrival, or expectation of a call. He sighed.

'No, no thank you. I will call back later.'

'Could someone call you back? I can take a number and have someone call you back. It's really not an issue to do that. Where are you calling from, Mr Hartmoor?'

'No, it's okay. I'll call back later.'

'We could have someone call you within the next few minutes, I'm sure.'

'Thank you but—'

'Mr Coleman would never forgive me if I didn't have a number or something for him, I mean really he's such a stickler for these things. Are you here in Beirut, Mr Hartmoor, or calling from overseas? The line is really good if this is an overseas call. You know what the network here can be like, I'm sure.'

Hartmoor quelled his irritation at her babbling and said 'Thank you, firmly. He cut the line, feeling guilty she was still talking as he did so.

Hartmoor replaced the handset with a sigh and walked over to open the window overlooking Martyrs' Square. The traffic was heavy, the cars glittering in the bright sunshine of the cold February morning. The cool air refreshed him, a whiff of wood smoke from somewhere. The distant peal of church bells rang out.

The city had been so different when he had first flown in from the rain-swept greyness of Heathrow, back in 1978. It was the first time he had flown in his life, escaping the windowless little office off St James' Park. Hartmoor had inherited a chipped metal filing cabinet and a fading poster for Lebanon Tourism featuring a 1960s open top car motoring through these very roads, the hillside green with spring's bounty. With rainy skies outside, he had often glanced at the poster, sipping his tea from the chipped green Foreign Office cup and imagining those cedar-rich mountain valleys. Landing in Beirut, the city back then teetering on the brink of all-out civil war, he had peered out of the scratched plastic window and caught a glimpse of dark smoke, a building off the runway with its windows smashed. For the first time in his life, he saw hints of true violence.

He had slept through the landing this time, strangely incurious about this city he first arrived in as a young man. He had never returned, despite the years of longing. Now he was actually here. *Beirut*. He wanted to wave regally from the hotel window to the traffic below. Look at me, I have returned. Finally.

He closed the window and went back to the bed. He dialled again, a different number from the same slip of paper. Another receptionist.

'I'd like to speak to Lance Browning, please.'

'Connecting you.'

'Lance. Good morning. It's Jason Hartmoor.'

'I'm sorry, I don't… Oh, hang on, hang on. Hartmoor. Jason. Bloody hell! God's truth, that's a voice from the past if I ever heard one. Jason bloody Hartmoor. I thought you'd gone to ground with the fuzzy wuzzies or something. Bloody hell. I'll be damned. What have you been up to, old thing? Where are you? Surely you're not back here after all that time? Not back in the big shitty, are we?'

'I am, yes, Lance. It has rather been a while, hasn't it?'

'Over thirty years and more, I'd say. The Prodigal Son. Well, we'd best fatten a calf. Where are you staying?'

'The Le Gray. I just arrived this morning.'

'Marvellous, bloody marvellous. What say we visit the trough together then? There's a decent place there on the rooftop level, *Indigo* it's called.'

'That would be very good, Lance. At eight?'

'Bugger me, Jason Hartmoor. I'll be damned. Yes, yes, old boy, eight's just fine. I'll see you there, then.'

Hartmoor kicked off his shoes and lay back on the bed, exhausted. He closed his eyes and relived the journey he had made from the battered airport up into the hills, back in 1978 before the Civil War had spat him out of Beirut. Spring had given way to summer and the warmth was just out of the hillside, autumn starting to brown some of the trees lining the road. The air was rich with pine, lavender, myrtle and juniper, the midday sun brightening the villages clinging madly to the precipitous hillsides. They passed a group of women bustling up the road, cloaked in black *kandouras* with white headscarves, small girls dancing around them…

Hartmoor woke, disoriented by the room around him, the memory of where he was returning along with the sly insistence of pain. He took a painkiller and made his way creakily to the shower, where he luxuriated for a while in the warmth and scent of hotel shower gel. Shuffling around the room in his white bathrobe and the towelled slippers he had wrenched from their cellophane wrapper, he unpacked his bag and put his things away.

He dressed, pulling on a light cardigan over his blue checked shirt, fussing with the belt of his brown slacks. His jacket was crumpled from the flight and having been slept in, but linen has no memory. He took more pills, the enzymes he needed before a meal. They hadn't left enough of his spleen for him to be able digest food for himself.

He took the lift up to the rooftop, steadying himself on the handrail, having decided to leave The Stick behind. The sun was fleeing the day, the Mohammed Al Amin Mosque already lit by floodlights, its four minarets seeking the deepening sky. The glass-walled terrace restaurant was almost empty, eight being early by Beiruti standards. Browning was already sitting at the table clutching his drink and playing with a mobile phone. The years had thickened him; a double chin now framed the face of the man Hartmoor had known back in Shemlan. Browning's hands were pudgy, his arms stretching the material of the black suit jacket, his red tie dropped over a belly that pushed at the white shirt, opening it in between buttons.

Browning looked up, caught Hartmoor's eye and clearly tried to hide his evident shock at Hartmoor's appearance. If the years had thickened Browning, the last few had certainly thinned Hartmoor, he knew.

'Hello, Lance.'

Browning shot to his feet. 'Bloody hell. I mean, bloody hell.'

Hartmoor submitted to the awkward embrace and its accompanying waft of gin. Browning was already sloshed. The high points of red on the man's cheeks and overly confiding tone as he leant across the starched linen rather gave the game away.

There was a hint of violence in Browning's body language. 'So you came back. You'll find nothing's changed really. It's still a madhouse and you still can't get anything done for love nor money. I'm due to retire in five years and it can't come soon enough, I can tell you.'

Hartmoor smiled to hide the wave of distaste that passed over him. This meeting had clearly been a terrible mistake.

'It's not bloody funny, you know.' Browning was querulous. 'This place is a bigger dump than it was during the bloody war. They haven't had a government for months. Hezbollah's all over the bloody place.' He glanced around the glittering tables. 'Look at this place. Shower of shits. The country's falling to pieces and all they care about is where the next million's coming from.'

Browning broke off to glare at the waiter who came to the table and presented them both with menus, a little flourish for each and a tight smile. Hartmoor ordered a Perrier.

'What, off the sauce are we?'

Hartmoor found himself unwilling to explain. 'Just thirsty, really, Lance.'

'Right. Take the edge off it. Wise man.' Browning wagged a fat finger. 'Never do to go at it too hard, eh?'

Hartmoor nodded. 'Quite, Lance. So you're still with the bank?'

Browning fiddled with his menu. 'Same old same old. Keeping my head down and my nose clean.'

Hartmoor's Perrier arrived and they ordered, both taking the foie gras starter. Browning ordered a half bottle of Tokay and another G&T.

'Make it a double,' Browning called as the waiter turned away.

The man nodded and bowed slightly. 'The same as the last one, *seer*.'

Browning turned to Hartmoor, his gaze darkening. 'Cheeky bastard. Mind, they all are. No service culture. So what about you, then? What's your news?'

'Nothing much, really, Lance. Much like yourself, I have spent a fine life in the service of my country.'

'Not me, old man. I've been serving bloody Mammon, me. The country can go to hell, my masters' attachment to Sterling is hardly the stuff of patriotic legend.'

The waiter brought Browning's drink and took away his empty glass. 'Here,' Browning lifted the clinking tumbler. 'To her Majesty's Royal Britannic Middle East Centre for Arab Studies and the year of '78, the last-ever students to grace the bloody place.'

Hartmoor raised his glass.

'Mind you,' Browning paused to gulp at his drink, 'I can remember throwing those bloody word cards away and swearing never to read another one of the things. You remember them?'

Hartmoor did, clearly. He had struggled with the daily allotment of words, the vocabulary seeming utterly irrelevant given he could barely string together a sentence in the language. What use the Arabic word for blanket when you couldn't even introduce yourself? Like other students, Jason felt himself wrestling with the demands of this new life and language, thirty new cards issued every day with words on them, Arabic one side, English the other. His room, Spartan but not uncomfortable, was soon strewn with tiny white stacks of words.

They were a funny little bunch. The intake was mostly Foreign and Commonwealth Office with a handful of students from commercial companies. There were also, unusually apparently, a couple of Americans. The commercials, taking a shorter course than the FCO people, ranged from a pair of British Airways types and a strange, pebble-glassed little man from the computer company ICL through to a trio of salesmen from Rothmans. The salesmen were worldly and mildly contemptuous of the course. The Americans, despite having more in common with the salesmen than anyone else, kept their distance. Browning had been a commercial.

The starter arrived. The waiter fussed over the wine, Hartmoor relishing the silence as Browning focused on the man's movements. The waiter put no foot wrong: the food served and Browning's wine poured he retired, bowing slightly. Ironically, Hartmoor rather thought.

Browning glowered after the departing figure. 'You ever meet the SIS guy here? Lynch?'

Hartmoor's humour was thin-lipped. 'I never made it back here, Lance. I had many reasons to return, but never the opportunity. Not until now.'

'Unfinished business, is it, then?' Browning leered, sitting back. He drank deeply from the frosted glass of Tokay. Hartmoor raised an eyebrow and waited.

Browning's face screwed up in frustration. 'Oh, come on, you know. Back then. The popsie from the restaurant. Scandal of Shemlan, that, you and her. What was her name now?'

'Mai. You were telling me about the SIS resident here, Lance.'

'That's it. Mai, Khoury wasn't it?' Hartmoor dipped his head. Browning was owlish for a second. 'SIS chap. Northern Irish. Cocky bastard. Bog Irish. Lynch. Gerald Lynch.'

Browning stabbed morosely at his foie gras, slicing into the pink-centred morsel.

Hartmoor smiled. 'I've never met him. Talking of our *intelligent* friends, how is Frank Coleman these days?'

'Coleman? Dead. Didn't you know? Died in disgrace. Killed himself after the Freij affair.'

Hartmoor was glad to be sitting down. He swirled the water in his glass. Gazing into the clear liquid, he composed himself before glancing up with a rueful smile for Browning. 'Sorry, old thing, not sure what the "Freij affair" is.'

'Long story.' Browning wiped his moist lips on the napkin, leaving a brown streak of reduced balsamico on the linen. 'Coleman was a bad apple, see? They say he went wrong after his famous Russian source dried up on him. He started doing *private* work. Retirement, see? That pressure to make a little extra to line the nest. They say.'

Hartmoor paused in the act of cutting into his foie gras. 'I honestly don't understand a word of what you're telling me, Lance. Sorry.'

Browning reached out to the ice bucket and refilled his glass, startled staff rushing up too late to intervene. Browning waited until they backed off. 'Frank Coleman had a source, a Russian Ministry of Defence official who ran a number of agents, they say. The wonder of the secret world. It was a treasure trove and Frankie's career went stellar in the '80s and '90s. He was the Democrats' golden-eyed boy, got called in to consult at Camp David, Geneva, the lot. Then Bush gets in and Coleman acquires a load of right-wing buddies, neo-con think tanks couldn't get enough of our Frank's views on the Middle East this and the Middle East that. His starship crashed sometime around when the Yids pulled out of South Lebanon. Whatever happened, Coleman's source went to ground in the mid '90s and he couldn't keep it all going.'

Throwing down his knife and fork with a satiated grunt, Browning licked his lips. 'Frank's career hit a brick wall then, without his precious source. He was due to retire last year. He was still in with the neo-con crowd and the boys down south. He got wrapped up in an attempt to smuggle two nuclear warheads here from Czecho, his big chance to get back to the top table. It was Lynch, the SIS paddy, who busted the whole operation and, of course, Coleman got outed, too. A little bit too much private enterprise, a little more co-operation with the boys over at Mossad than Washington had sanctioned. All backed by these neo-con groups Coleman was running with.'

Hartmoor carefully laid out his cutlery at six o'clock, half of the foie gras still on the plate. Despite the enzymes, he'd found it too rich. 'I had no idea. I was rather hoping to see him while I was here.'

Browning snorted, a theatrical glance around the empty room to share the joke. 'Like I said, you'll be lucky.' He drank again, licked his fat lips. 'He shot himself. He fucked it up, took half his skull off but left most of his brain intact. It was the infection that killed him. It took three days of raving for him to die, they say.'

'Do they?' murmured Hartmoor. 'How very much they have to say, Lance.'

'Good riddance an' all.' Browning leered. 'He was always the wrong side of right, that bastard.'

Hartmoor pushed back his chair. 'Frank Coleman was a good man, Lance. I am sorry but I do so disagree with you. I think I had best leave. I don't have much time left and I rather think we are both wasting what little I do have. Goodbye.'

Hartmoor walked out of the restaurant without looking back and without putting out a hand to steady himself. He Browning's outraged 'I say' rang out as he turned the corner to the lift. He took it down to the ground floor, striking out left towards the sodium lights and reconstructed sandstone walls of the *Solidere* district. Quick to tire, Hartmoor slowed as he reached the cobbled streets, leaning against a wall to recover his breath from his straight-backed march out of the restaurant.

Walking out tall and straight like that had been an expensive gesture his tired body could ill afford. He slowly regained his breath, but the pain was dragging him down. Damning Browning with every step, he was visited by the irrational urge for a cigarette, something he hadn't felt in thirty-odd years. He pulled up a chair inside the first street café he came to, a wooden-panelled traditional French style place, warm and full of people's chatter and the clatter of crockery. He asked for a double espresso and stayed for a second one before making his way back to his hotel.

Hartmoor woke in pain. The weather had turned. The window onto Martyrs' Square was spattered with raindrops, the tarmac shining and buildings streaked. He popped the painkiller through the foil backing and washed it down with water from the bottle at his bedside. Waiting for it to take effect, he replayed the encounter with Browning. When he had calmed, he got up to face the day.

Despite having eaten little the night before, Hartmoor skipped breakfast and waited in the lobby for the hotel car he had ordered. The porter, showing him out to the waiting Mercedes, gave Hartmoor a hotel umbrella against the inclement weather, for which the man had apologised as if the hotel took full responsibility.

As they climbed up into the hills above Beirut, Hartmoor gazed out of the car window at the buildings around them. No scent of spring for this trip, he reflected, the February rain greying out the scenery. Misty tendrils snaked around the treetops. He remembered his first journey on this road, past the sprawling village of Bchamoun at the foothills then the road winding through the villages clinging to the plunging gorges of the Chouf Mountains. Now, as then, the houses in the villages seemed stacked up on top of each other, densely packed on the steep hillsides.

To the side of the road ran a concrete storm drain that crossed the tarmac as the camber and direction changed, the grating covering it clanging under the taxi's wheels. The taxi hit a pothole hard, the engine note jumping and a dark cloud left behind as the driver changed down a gear. The rosary hanging on his rear mirror jangled.

They passed the village of Ainab, Hartmoor marvelling at the number of new stone-clad villas, gated developments and building sites overlooking Beirut spread out far below. A blue sign proclaimed 'Shimlan.' He leaned forward and asked the driver to slow down, '*Shway, Shway.*'

He tried not to look at the restaurant as they passed, merely glad it was still there. Time enough for that. They drove on and then there it was, the little turning from the *Rue Philip Hitti* up to the School. Hartmoor directed the driver to turn right and sat back in the cool softness of the seat, his heart hammering in his chest. There was nobody to man the little whitewashed guard-post at the gate. The Mercedes scrunched to a halt in front of the imposing building, a piece of pure 1970s architecture, the balustrades around the car park painted the same institutional green as the lampposts, each balancing a little white globe. The window-frames above the stonework facade were painted the same green. A set of steps led up from the car park to the entrance level. The worn white paint covering the wooden pergola was curled and cracked.

Hartmoor left the car and stood at the balustrade, staring down over the hazy city far below. The air was cool and damp. The trees rustled. He turned, sighing, away from the city and surveyed the school building. A sign in Arabic read 'Social Care, Shemlan Institute.' There was nothing to show this had once been the famous MECAS – the Middle East Centre for Arab Studies, over thirty years of students hurrying up the hill to learn their Arabic here before shuffling off to their careers in the diplomatic service, the FCO or even in commerce.

Somehow the 'commercials' managed to keep in touch with

the 'dips'. It was good for business, after all.

He tapped the cold green railing, a momentary impatience grabbing him. The pooled raindrops shuddered and the hollow ironwork resonated down its decorative length like a railway track anticipating the oncoming train. He turned back to the car and peremptorily urged the puzzled driver to take him back down the hill. At the main road, he asked the driver to stop and got out again. He spoke in Arabic, to the driver's surprise. 'Wait for me back at the school, please.'

'School, *sidi*?'

Hartmoor tutted. 'The orphanage.'

Hartmoor hated using The Stick, but the exhaustion was gnawing at him. He wanted to walk along this little stretch of road, to feel again the anticipation of his journeys as a young man.

They had passed it on the way up; he knew it was still there. He was gasping for breath by the time he reached it, leaning heavily on the hated cane with its stupid rubber foot. He regretted sending the driver away. The logo outside the restaurant was modern, but it said the same as the sign on the stone wall always had: '*Al Sakhra*' - The Cliff House.

For a moment, Hartmoor lost control; the sense of himself in his time. It was strangely disorienting, more so than standing in front of the school. He struggled to control his breathing before walking in between the two giant verdigris-stained Arabic coffee pots that guarded the entrance. It was subtly different, reassuringly unchanged. The vaulted ceiling arched above him, the same window seat with its *argileh*, the same table layout, the covered terrace to the right. The furniture had changed and there was a modern till with a touch screen.

The sound of a footstep stilled him with a feeling of awful trepidation. He found himself bitterly regretting this long-awaited journey into his past. He had played this moment over in his mind for months and now he had arrived at it, he found the ghosts threatening to overwhelm him.

He gripped The Stick with both hands.

She walked in, patting her hands on her apron, a black skirt and a white blouse underneath. She smiled, welcoming. '*Sabah Al Khair*.'

He had the Arabic this time, but his mouth betrayed him. He was back in 1978, looking at this very girl as she walked out of the kitchen onto the restaurant floor that first time they had met. She had stood by that very doorway, wearing a black skirt and white blouse exactly like the ones this ghost was wearing. Hers had been slightly too tight across her chest. Her hair had tumbled down over her shoulders. The curls caught the light. Her hair had been longer, richer. Or perhaps that was memory embellishing the past. She had smelled of jasmine.

He tried to gather his thoughts, to find some way of managing this apparition. He left her behind a lifetime ago, yet here she is standing in front of him as she had that first day.

Panic set in making his heart pound. Shaking his head, he averred he was still alive, an effort of will. He staggered to the nearest table, leaning heavily on The Stick and clawing weakly at the chair-back to drag at it. He sat, his chest heaving as she brought a glass of water, biting her lip as her big brown eyes searched his sightless features.

His voice was a hoarse whisper of hope, 'Mai?'

Her smile broadened and she laughed lightly, Mai's laugh. 'That's my grandmother's name. I am Estelle.' Her face clouded. 'And you are?'

'Jason Hartmoor. I… knew your grandmother. Is she here?'

Estelle shook her head. 'No. Wait, I shall bring my mother.'

He tried to tell her no, don't bother her, but the words stuck in his dry mouth. She reached out to support his arm as he grabbed at the plastic-covered tabletop.

THREE

At the back of the wooden church building, Dennis Wye, dressed in a charcoal greatcoat, stood listening to the ethereal voices echoing from the high roof and icon-hung walls. White hair marked his temples, his coat open in the warmth of the packed church. He was perhaps in his late fifties, clean-shaven and straight-backed. The harmony rose and fell, dying notes enriching each wave until the massed voices rose to their crescendo. He listened attentively. Slowly, with great grace, the waves of sound rolled gently to a last, long note.

As the final note from the congregation died, he turned and made his way out of the church into the freezing exterior, his breath misting as he buttoned the coat and puffed a red scarf around his neck. He waited to the side as the double doors were pulled open, the Estonian Orthodox priest smiling and bobbing as he bade farewell to his ageing congregation shuffling out of the church, hunched against the cold.

Wye's gaze flicked over the snow-covered pale green building, its slatted wooden walls capped by a tiled roof. He waited, luxuriating in the sharpness of the cold on his face. The first shuffling rush out of the church had died as the man Wye was waiting for appeared, a distinguished figure in a dark suit and heavy woollen overcoat. He was big even now, in his seventies, his peppery hair cropped short. He, too, wore a red scarf and his broad features were only barely lined. He looked young for his age. Wye felt a pang of jealousy.

Jaan Kallas bent to kiss the priest's hands and wheeled to face Wye. Kallas smiled a welcome. Wye had never seen Kallas looking so peaceful. Transformed by his weekly religious experience, no doubt. He stepped forward, his hand held out to meet the big Estonian's.

'Dennis. We are honoured.'

Wye beamed, reaching out to pat Kallas' arm as he pumped hands. 'I'm pleased to be able to come back to this amazing country, Jaan. I only wish I were the bearer of better news.'

Kallas' hand on his back propelled Wye towards the black Mercedes waiting at the side of the church, its exhaust smoking. 'You are always welcome, Dennis.'

The car's interior was warm and smelled of leather. The driver waited for the heavy doors to close, light glinting off the man's shiny peaked cap as he glanced back. The car pulled away smoothly, the wipers clearing the windscreen of the big flakes drifting down from the granite sky.

Kallas sat back in the grey leather, his shucked overcoat across his knees. 'What is the problem, Dennis?'

'There's this British guy, a diplomat called Jason Hartmoor. He was… *involved*, in the past. He retired and we'd written him off, pretty much. We thought he was out of the picture, nicely sidelined. Frank took care of that, years ago. Now he's on the move and we believe he's potentially dangerous to us. He's gone back to Beirut.'

Kallas chuckled. 'Retired? So he is an old man, no, Dennis? How is he so dangerous, this old man?'

'He's the only guy on earth who can link you to the '70s and Operation Dmitri.' Wye wriggled on the seat, popping the buttons on his coat under the seatbelt. 'He doesn't know that, but he can. We, Frank that is, arranged that he retired in disgrace. Any testimony he gives up is flawed. But all the same, we don't need any loose cannons around right now. We've got a tight ship. And this guy knows way too much. If he starts poking about in Beirut waking up ghosts, we're in trouble.'

'Why?'

'It doesn't matter. We're just in trouble.'

Kallas grimaced. 'So remove him.'

Wye turned from peering out at Tallinn's snow-dusted

rooftops. 'That's an option. I'd rather we put him under close surveillance. We understand he's not well. It might just be a storm in a teacup.'

'No.' Kallas shook his head. 'Remove him.'

'We don't do that, Jaan. Not offhand like that. We can put him on watch, we can escalate if necessary. I just thought you needed to know about the issue. We can handle it.' Wye shot his cuffs.

Kallas barked at the driver in Estonian and sat back to glare out of the window. The driver made a call, closing the connecting window as it was answered.

'Do you have a file on this man?'

'We do.' Wye fumbled in his pocket, then proffered a memory key.

Kallas pulled a tablet from the seat pocket and plugged the key in. He sat back reading and swiping at the screen. Wye admired the snowy scenery.

The black car pulled into the garage, cameras tracking its progress down the concrete ramp. Halting in the neon-lit area, it was met by big men wearing earphones. Wye followed Kallas across the shiny grey non-slip garage flooring to the lift lobby. At the top, an efficient blonde secretary in a dark dress and burgundy blouse met them and led the way to Kallas' office. Wye was disconcerted to find two men waiting on the black leather sofa. They stood, their movements oddly synchronised, as he and Kallas entered.

They were both dressed in black trousers and jackets, wearing black polo-neck jumpers. Both men were blond to the point of whiteness, their pale skin and blue eyes flawless and neutral. There was something waxen about their pallor and unnatural stillness. Wye shivered and didn't quite know why. Kallas gestured for all to sit. The secretary brought little black coffees to Kallas and Wye.

'You would like a drink?' Kallas asked Wye, who shook his head. 'Two vodka, Elena.'

Kallas twisted in his high-backed leather chair to gesture at the black-clad figures. 'Dennis, meet Persson and Loewe.'

The two nodded as one man. Wye beamed, nodding back. A lifetime of realpolitik and expedient killings had given him a very good sense indeed of danger, but these guys went beyond Wye's experience. They scared him; something of the bitter Baltic cold had made its way into those neutral eyes.

Elena returned. The drinks came in little frosted glasses. Kallas held his up to Wye, who reciprocated the gesture and tossed back the vodka. It had never bothered him, this bolt of cold, harsh spirit hitting his throat. He spoke clearly, '*Terviseks.*'

Elena took the glasses from them.

Kallas turned to the waiting men in black. 'You will travel to Beirut. Elena has made arrangements. There is a man called Abbas Ali who will give you any local support you need, particularly hardware. His representative will meet you at the airport. He will be holding a sign with the company name Horus Travel. Here,' Kallas passed the tablet to the two men in black. 'This is the man. He is to be eliminated.'

Wye leaned out of his chair, his hand raised. 'Jaan, surely we—'

Kallas' voice was sharp. 'Not now, Dennis.'

Wye settled back into his chair and his role of passive observer.

'You are deniable, of course. You have no link to me or to this man sitting here, whom you have never met. Your expenses and fees will be met as usual plus a bonus of twenty thousand dollars for rapid completion. If you are apprehended, you will remain silent and the agreed compensation will be arranged. Any questions.'

The left-hand one spoke. 'No questions.' They stood, nodded and wheeled around as if they had choreographed the movement.

As the two left, Kallas turned to Wye with a tight smile. 'So, it is done. And you can be assured your government will not be implicated in the *accident*. It is better this way.'

Comfortable in the warmth of his hotel room, Wye carefully composed his report to Hilton Polson. His finger hesitated over the Enter key for a second before he sent the message on its way.

He had just made a coffee when his mobile rang with the different tone of the encrypted VPN application installed on it. He tapped the screen to answer the call. Polson's New England drawl belied the lateness of the hour in Washington. Wye was impressed; he'd expected maybe a mail back in the morning, but not a direct call back.

Polson's voice was measured. 'Dennis, can you manage this situation? It feels to me like it's getting out of hand.'

Setting down the steaming mug, Wye cracked two of the tiny plastic pots of creamer into it. He held the mobile between his cheek and shoulder and opened the minibar, cracking a miniature of scotch and pouring it into the coffee. 'As I said in the report, Kallas has sent two men to Beirut to find and eliminate this Hartmoor guy. We can ring fence him, but I'm not sure how long we could keep two trained *Ühiskassa* killers at bay for. Hartmoor is a British citizen; we can hardly take him into protective custody.'

'No. It's imperative the Brits don't find out we have an interest here. We're already getting requests from them about this case.'

'Requests? What's their interest in Hartmoor?'

'We're not sure. It looks like they've been digging around in his past. I hope to God it's nothing to do with Frank Coleman and Operation Dmitri. Because if it is, we have a problem.'

'So what do we do?'

'For now, nothing. Kallas might just have the right idea

about this. Let me know the second anything develops. You sure these guys are deniable?'

'Totally. There's no link.'

'Good. Let me know how it pans out.'

'Sure, Hilton. Thanks.'

'Take care, Dennis.'

'Yessir.'

FOUR

Gerald Lynch tensed, feeling the figure behind him move left. He kept his eyes on the man in front, a simian little bastard with the strength and cunning of an orang-utan. Lynch advanced on the smaller man, his hands at his sides. He felt his muscles loosen for a second as he smiled, weaving slowly and fixing his eyes on Monkey Man's little black orbs. He tensed and lunged forward, sweeping his arm left to parry any blow, his right fist driving for the ape's face.

Lynch's fist found air. Unbalanced, he tried to turn his momentum to his advantage, but he was too late. The blow to his shoulder was massive. He felt muscle tear. A second smack to his side drove him earthward. Trapped for a split second in stasis, Lynch watched the ground rise, his mouth a rictus of frustration and pain. The world came crashing back as he hit the wooden floor hard, his head bouncing painfully off the thin matting. He rolled, using his last strength to lurch to his feet just in time to meet the second man's foot driving into his exposed guts. Lynch went down hard. Monkey Man kicked him in the kidney. Darkness claimed him.

Lynch came to his senses painfully, his body bruised and taut. He inhaled the rubbery stench of the mat under his cheek. Sergeant Coates stood above him holding a clipboard.

'Open to it, you were. No sense of balance, see? You've been marked unfit across the board, bar your marksmanship which was exceptional.' Coates peered down at Lynch over the clipboard. 'Don't let that go to your head, you'd be lucky to get in position to shoot anyone the way you run.'

Lynch pushed himself onto his back, wincing at the waves of pain the movement brought. He let his Northern Irish vowels thicken. 'Coates, would you ever just fuck off?'

Coates made a few scratches on the clipboard and tore off a form, tossing the pink copy down to Lynch. 'There's your assessment. Apparently there's a car to take you to London, so you need to get your things together sharpish. You've been overseas too long, you drink too much and you're in no shape to be an active SIS asset. In my *humble* opinion.'

Coates turned smartly and walked across the shining wooden floor of the gym, pausing at the door to share a quiet laugh with Monkey Man and his companion. They left together. Without a glance at the pink form, Lynch staggered to his feet and limped out of the gym.

Brian Channing's door was frosted glass, a brushed aluminium plaque etched in black text: '*Brian Channing. Deputy Director for Security and Public Affairs.*' Underneath, a smaller plaque: '*Director, European Joint Intelligence Committee.*'

Lynch knocked and peered around the door. Channing's office was male beyond reason, brutally minimalist with a glass-topped desk to frame his tablet stand, a Bauhaus angle-poise lamp to the side.

There were no cupboards or shelves, but a steel-framed glass coffee table sat by a buttoned cream leather sofa, a high-backed chair at each end. A brace of Taschen hardbacks lay at a precisely casual angle on the glass. Behind Channing's desk was a large piece of Modern Art. As usual, Channing was impeccably turned out, a slightly noisy pinstripe, Jermyn Street shirt with black thread detailing and a tie just loud enough to murmur expensive without screaming gauche.

Channing rose from his desk, beaming genially as Lynch entered. Lynch hated when he did that. It always struck him as sharkish. Channing waved at the coffee table and sofa.

'Welcome home. Have a seat, dear boy, have a seat. Drink?'

Lynch breathed in sharply. 'On the rocks. Thanks.' He peered idly around the office, seeing the pieces on the walls for the first time as individual objects. They were similar, daubs and sploshes of primary colours. Modern Art.

Channing handed Lynch a tumbler and clinked his own against it. 'Cheers. To the marvellous bloody Middle East.'

Lynch raised his glass and drank. 'Cheers.'

'How's the old quarterly review been going?' Channing settled back on the sofa.

Lynch snorted. 'First one I've done in five years, for a start. Sure, it went well enough. They failed me in fitness and I told that snooty wee bitch from HR to stuff her questionnaires.' Lynch sipped. 'A result all round, really.'

'You can't go on being such a wilful maverick, Gerald.' Channing's forefinger stiffened as he waved his tumbler at Lynch. 'We have processes and procedures to follow. I know you've had some remarkable successes in your time, but intelligence in Europe is changing and we need team players, people who'll knuckle down and really work with the gang to deliver exceptional results to our stakeholders.'

Lynch sipped his whisky. A decent enough malt, slightly peaty. 'Berry's?' he asked.

Channing inclined his head. Lynch waved his glass. 'You won't get by in the Middle East with process and well you know it.'

Channing's handsome, florid, face clouded. 'The Americans do.'

'Do they fuck. The most volatile and complex place on earth, so it is. And they just blunder around it doling out aid dollars and wondering why the guys with their nose in Uncle Sam's trough still hate them.' Lynch leant forward. 'And the whole Arab revolution thing totally threw them. They didn't know which way to turn. It took them completely by surprise. We had consistently good intel to work with precisely *because* our operations are more unconventional. Look at Bin Laden – ISI was all over the Yanks with that for years until they got lucky. The Pakistanis owned the *ground*, just like the Lebanese do. And the Iranians. Which is how Syria got so messy so quickly. And how they found they couldn't just un-mess it with a truckload of CIA cash.'

Channing waved Lynch down. 'Look, that's not really the point. I wanted to talk to you about the changes we're making. We're streamlining, cutting unwanted assets. The recession, you know. We've had to make some deeper cuts than we'd like, including headcount. HR wanted you on a slab and I wouldn't give it. But you really need to help me out, Gerald. Stop behaving like you don't have any responsibility to hierarchy, because you do. And I can't, I won't, go on protecting you forever.'

Lynch nodded. 'You mean be nice to the wee bitch from HR?'

Channing leaned forward, his face earnest. 'Gerald, they're talking about cutting out your role entirely. You really don't want that, unless you want to retire and open up a butchers shop on the Falls Road. I believe we need dedicated resources in the Levant. EJIC believes that too, which is why I have funding to keep you on. But the French are baying for blood because they want to own EJIC's operations in Beirut and the bloody Germans are baying because they like baying. I really could use at least an attempt at co-operation from you. That, or I'll just cut you loose.'

'So it's conform or die, so an' it is?' Lynch drained his glass.

Channing stood, holding his glass out for the refill. 'Not quite. We have a small problem.'

Lynch watched Channing splash scotch into both glasses. He couldn't remember Channing drinking in the office before, despite the well-stocked trolley he kept. He settled back, the chair leather creaking.

'We've been working on a new system here, digitising

archives and linking to current sources, to GCHQ and other inputs.' Channing handed back the clinking tumbler. 'The technology is American. It's based on smart analysis of data based on fuzzy language algorithms. We can derive a new level of linkages and causality from data that was previously effectively static.'

'No shit,' Lynch murmured into his tumbler.

Channing frowned. 'We've backtracked some interesting leads as a result of the new searches, a range of connections based on previously circumstantial data that didn't add up to any big picture. Now it does. One of the great big red lines that came up in that analysis regarded a tip-off from a low-level KGB operative based out of Syria regarding a major Russian hood code-named Dmitri. Dmitri was a high-ranking KGB officer who claimed to control a British mole. There was a major internal investigation and Dmitri was dismissed as Russian chaff at the time, back in the '80s. We had a big tiff with the Americans over it – they insisted the whole story was rubbish, bought out the KGB guy and that was the last we heard of him. They pulled rank. The file was closed until this new data analysis system started to throw up links. Now it looks like Dmitri did indeed own us, Gerald. Lock, stock and barrel. The little bastard knew our every thought in the Middle East and either he or his masters seem to have sold that information left, right and centre.'

'Our thoughts in the Middle East? Little enough there to know, sure.'

Whisky splashed out of Channing's glass as he banged it down. 'Stop being so fucking smart, Gerald. I can send you to Siberia. I might just enjoy it, too. You are not the only one with a boss.'

'Okay, okay.' Lynch held his palms up.

'The new search algorithms threw up a set of coincidences we hadn't been aware of before. Mapping the two snippets of Dmitri product we had got our hands on before the Americans clammed up threw up fifteen possible identities for the mole. We put in a request to the Americans for more of Dmitri's little gifts, just a couple of the non-British references so we could narrow down the list, but they went very coy on us. The KGB man died in America in 1999. He had taken American citizenship, changed his name and been rehoused as part of a witness protection program. That caught our analysts' eye, actually. One of the list of fifteen retired from the FCO that very year, in some considerable disgrace. He'd been caught fiddling with the local bints in the Sudan. Our analyst felt someone had been cleaning up.'

Lynch finished his drink. 'Do I know him or something? This mole?'

'No. No, you don't,' Channing said, taking the glasses and putting them back on the side table by his desk. He returned with a memory key. 'Here. Jason Hartmoor. He retired to Pembrokeshire. We sent a chap out to talk to him, but we missed him by a whisker. It would appear he's returned to Beirut. He studied at Shemlan in the '70s. He hasn't been back there since, at least not to our knowledge. You would likely never have crossed paths.'

'Shemlan? Up in the mountains? What was it, the Centre for Arabic Studies or something? Wasn't George Blake arrested there?'

Channing drew himself up. 'Arab, not Arabic. The Middle East Centre for Arab Studies. A language school funded by the Foreign and Commonwealth Office. Hartmoor was there, Gerald, in your neck of the woods and now he's gone back. We don't know he is our rotten apple for sure, but we have the opportunity to backtrack what appears to have been a major sleeper operation and we're keen to take it. Find him for us. And no rough stuff. Hartmoor has cancer. He's a very sick man and a distinguished former diplomat. He's to be treated with respect.'

'What when I find him?'

'*If* you find him, you are to report back and await orders.' Channing held his office door open.

Lynch got up. 'Thanks for the scotch.'

'You're welcome. One more thing. This operation is the only thing stopping Resource Management from closing you down, Gerald. Be a good chap and don't fuck it up.'

The death of Sister Helena Mary O'Rourke had two consequences for Gerald Lynch. The first was a bequest that reached him in Beirut six months after the news she had passed away in her sleep, her laboured breathing finally failing her. The little, neatly wrapped parcel contained a cheque for ten thousand Euro, a holy medal and a letter from the old nun who had stood by Gerry Lynch, the tearaway orphan from the Falls Road who'd been brought to them as an abandoned baby left outside a church door. The letter was an apology for something she had tried, but failed, to stop. It had been written in 1976 and sealed back then. He marvelled that she had kept it for him until the occasion of her death. Lynch read her words, picked out in her precise hand in blue fountain pen. He had closed his eyes for a second and then had burned it, letting the carbonised flakes rise into the warm air above the street his balcony overlooked in Beirut's busy *Ain Mreisse* district.

The second consequence was social services' rehabilitation of Darina Tynan, his wet nurse and the nearest thing Gerry ever had to a mother. On the rare occasions he found himself travelling back to London, Lynch invariably hopped over to Belfast to visit the people who had passed as his family. Now only one of them was left.

On this trip, he visited a gravestone, onto which he laid a small bouquet of bluebells, Sister Helena's favourite flower. He drove in silence to his second stop. When Lynch arrived at the Denham Hall Care home and got out of the car, Darina was walking with an attendant in the grounds. She waved to him with a childish chuckle of sheer joy. He held her in his arms as she laughed and cried. Later, he sat with her gazing out over the shining terrace and emerald lawn, drinking tea from flowery cups. She shifted in her armchair. 'One day, Gerry, I'll leave here and find my man, you know that?'

'Sure you will. Sure, it's only a matter of time, ain't that the truth, Darina?'

She settled back, smiling. 'You know yourself.'

He massaged her hand. 'Are you keeping well here, Darina? Do they look after you proper, like?'

'They do, Gerry. They're very kind. I'm happy, am't I?'

Surrounded for much of her adult life by implacable rules of law, certitudes and days of dreary work in the laundry that were only enlivened by punishment and prayer, Darina had given in and surrendered herself to dumb compliance, her only escape the cheap little romantic novels she scraped together the pennies to buy.

Sister Helena Mary had Darina taken from the laundry to nurse Gerry but afterwards she had gone back and then somehow it had been too late to save the girl's mind. Institutionalised all her life, Darina's time in the laundries robbed her of her spirit and left her simple.

They sat in companionable silence, listening to the rain on the windows, Lynch massaging her blue-veined hands and Darina smiling warmly at him with her happy, empty eyes.

Lynch stayed too long with her and missed his flight to London from George Best International. They made him buy another fare.

Lynch, beyond fury, paid without demur.

FIVE

Sitting down on the balcony of the restaurant he had once known so well, Hartmoor sipped the cool water, recovering. He took a pill. He was swallowing it as Mai's granddaughter Estelle returned with an older lady, perhaps in her early forties and elegant, a cream blouse and wooden necklace, navy blue slacks.

She held out a cool hand. 'It's nice to meet you. I am Dana, Mai Khoury's daughter, Estelle's mother. Please, don't get up on my account, better that I sit. It's my age, you know,' she confided.

He sat back, the colour returning to his knuckles that grasped The Stick. 'I'm sorry. The resemblance...'

Dana sat, her necklace clacking. 'It's amazing isn't it? I always had mum's eyes, but Estelle is the absolute image of her. Of course, she's her nana's favourite. Estelle told me you knew my mother?'

Hartmoor took another sip of water. 'Yes, yes, I did rather. During the war, back in the '70s. I studied at MECAS.'

Dana's puzzled gaze cleared. 'Oh, the spy school? They had a reunion here once, years ago back when I was at university. I missed it. Were you a spy? How very exciting.'

She wore an expensive-looking solitaire. A slim, gold watch adorned her wrist, her hands crossed casually on the table. Estelle brought a cup of Turkish coffee, medium sweet. Looking up at her as she turned away, Hartmoor saw her brush an unruly strand of hair back behind her ear. The gesture, so familiar to him through the years, made him want to cry.

Hartmoor fussed over the cup, aware of Dana's cool, amused regard. 'No, not really a spy. I was just a diplomat. I worked for the Foreign and Commonwealth Office. Embassies and all that.' He looked up to find her smiling at him. There was something familiar about her he couldn't quite place. Her eyes searched his face, concern reflecting in them as he shifted in his chair and winced with pain.

'Is your mother here?' Hartmoor's voice faltered.

Dana sipped her drink. 'No. She lives in America now. They moved some fifteen years ago. They gave the restaurant over to Elie and I. Dad came into a lot of money from over there, a relative in California.'

Hartmoor nodded. 'Elie is your husband.'

'Yes. We have two daughters, Estelle and Lara. Elie works in Beirut.' She smiled. 'The restaurant doesn't make as much money as architecture.'

He looked across at the blue expanse of the city below them, the glittering sea beyond. 'We used to write. I didn't know she had moved. I wouldn't have come.' He smiled. 'No offence.'

Dana laughed, her necklace and bangles clattering as she tossed her head back. 'None taken. I can understand you have come a long way to visit your past, is it not?'

Hartmoor gazed up at the trees towering on the hillside around them, the rich blue sky above. He listened to the buzzing of the insects, the sun warm on him and the smell of his little cup of coffee strong in his nostrils as he sipped.

'Yes,' he said, getting to his feet with a decisive movement that cost him dearly. Unusually, he welcomed the pain's sharp focus. 'Thank you for the coffee. You have been very kind, but I should get on with that journey.'

She rose with him, her arm outstretched to offer him support but he leaned on The Stick. 'You're not well.'

Hartmoor turned to walk through the cool shade of the restaurant. Dana followed him. He paused to speak to her, his breath insufficient for walking and talking. 'Oh, I wouldn't go worrying about me. Do please tell your mother I passed by and give her my regards. We kept in touch for many years, but eventually our correspondence died out.' He turned on the doorstep. 'I rather missed her, you see.'

Her face was puzzled, her mouth open to remonstrate with him. He took her cool hand. 'No, I should never have come. I realise that now. I always promised I wouldn't. It is best I go. Thank you again.'

Dana watched the Englishman walk away. There had been something strangely endearing about him, his formal manners and attractive features. He was a visitor from the past, a time-traveller from before the Civil War had torn Shemlan, all of Lebanon, apart. He had obviously been close to her mother, but Mai had never mentioned an Englishman in her life. Come to think of it, she had never really talked about life in Shemlan before the Civil War. Dana stood in the doorway, playing with her wooden beads and puzzling at how little she knew about those she loved. It intensified the feeling of loss in her. Her eyes pricked, she felt silly to be so affected but there really was something about the man that was, well, familiar.

She closed the door behind her. Her mother was indeed living in America, but was due to visit in the coming week. She had withheld the information from the stranger, but he had been so fragile she had regretted her reticence. It quickly became too late, she had let the moment to tell him pass and afterwards it would have seemed strange to have mentioned it. Dana couldn't understand the affinity she felt for the old *ajnabi*, foreigner. An Englishman from the spy school, from before the war. She wondered about what he had meant to her mother and, indeed, she to him. Was he an old flame? He must have been. Her father would be furious.

No, Dana was right not to have told him. She could tell mum about the man and then Mai could decide whether to call him or not. Estelle came into the room and Dana pushed herself away from the door. 'Here, call your dad and tell him we're going out for dinner tonight. I feel like a treat. Bilal can look after the restaurant.'

She handed her mobile to her daughter, the phonebook entry already highlighted, *Elie*. Estelle's face was troubled. 'What about the old man?'

Dana shook her head. 'It's nothing. We can tell mum about it when they come next week, *bass khalas*.'

'But he was so sad. He had so much hope inside him and yet so much pain. Did you see his face, the lines? He was so disappointed. It was if he had lost his life.'

'Forget it,' Dana's voice was rougher than she'd intended. She kissed Estelle on both cheeks. 'Come, call dad and we'll go out. Enough troublesome strangers.'

'You don't even have his number. What if mum did want to see him? You should have told him.'

Dana thought of the lone Englishman wobbling up the Rue Phillip Hitti on his stick and she felt a wave of anger at him she immediately regretted. It was unfair to be angry at him because she had avoided telling the truth.

'Call your dad,' she threw at Estelle and whirled to pull the door open.

Dana strode purposefully up the street, catching up with the Englishman as he turned uphill towards the Islamic Orphanage that had once been the spy school. She called out to him, ashamed because she didn't even know his name. He turned and Dana halted, horrified by his red-rimmed eyes. He wiped his cheek with the back of his hand and tried to smile.

Dana rested her hands on her thighs as she caught her breath. 'I thought you should know. The past has a way of catching up with us, *monsieur*, when it wishes to. We have just heard. My mother is coming to visit us from America. She will arrive next week. On Friday. Will you still be here? Can you make time? Shall you see her?'

His relief was tragic to watch. His shoulders sagged, he

collapsed into himself and looked grey and haggard, a man old beyond his years. His features screwed up, his mouth working to contain his emotions. Dana was certain he was feeling at least a little shame to be caught like this by a stranger. She reached into her sleeve and pulled out her handkerchief, offered it to him and put her hand on his arm. 'Here. Please, take your time. I know this must all be a shock. You have come so far.'

So she had lied a little, so what? The relief she was feeling told that she had done the right thing in the end.

SIX

Le Chat Botté had long been one of the more notorious bars in the Monot district's roster of drinking establishments. Monot was starting to show its age. Its younger competitor, Gemmayze, was the more vibrant and echoed nightly to the sound of shot glasses on wood and laughter. Monot was a little more frayed at the edges, its older establishments perhaps attracting a slightly wearier clientele and coming to life later at night. Eclipsing them both, Hamra was the new place to be, a cycle of fads that led back to before the war, Hamra, Monot, Gemmayze, Hamra...

It was early, the sun had barely set and the bar area was empty save for three figures. Sitting at the bar on adjacent red-leatherette stools were Gerald Lynch and Marcelle Aboud, *Le Chat Botté's* proprietress. Standing a respectful distance away from them was a young barman, whose pale goatee-bearded face was watchful and nervous as he polished glasses.

Marcelle sipped her Cosmopolitan and studied Lynch warily. She was a remarkable-looking woman, long waves of hair tumbling over her bare shoulder and brushing against her full breasts. Around them was a lace-lined burgundy silk wrap that cascaded carelessly down her torso and flared out from the tie around her flat tummy. It dropped down caressingly along her long, brown legs to the golden straps of the high-heeled shoes she hooked into the chrome struts of the barstool. She was in her early fifties, little more than a tiny crop of lines around her eyes and perhaps a little inflexibility of the skin on the back of the hand holding the cocktail glass belying her true age. She radiated languorous warmth, her deep brown eyes half-lidded with a lazy sensuality that veiled her ability to flare into all-consuming rage.

Lynch drank beer, Almaza, from the bottle. He was lugubrious, tearing up a beer mat with slow pulls of his strong, dark-haired hands. Marcelle lit a cigarette, throwing her head back to blow out a confident plume of blue-grey smoke.

'*Shou*, Lynch? Someone die or something?'

He glanced across at her. Marcelle's full, red-painted lips fellated the white-filtered Marlboro pinioned in her long fingers. He dropped the shreds of paper onto the bar top. 'They want to shut me down. Bastards.'

Marcelle snorted. 'What, the big spies in London?'

'Spies? No, fuck no. These bastards are bean-counters...' He caught her puzzled inclination. 'Accountants. Cutbacks, see?'

Marcelle shook her head. 'So they send you home, little spy? Poor Beirut, we can't even be important for the British to spy on us anymore? *Yallah*, then, Lynch. Who will you spy on? The Afghans, the Koreans?' Her chuckle was a low, viscous incitement. 'You won't fit in so good in Korea, Lynch.'

'Ha fucking ha, Marcie. I'm serious. They'll take their,' Lynch craned his fingers into speech marks, 'bloody "Input" from GCHQ's new-fangled social media monitoring services. Shit, they'll take the fucking Yanks at their word. Anything, other than spend a penny on the ground. There's no need for "intervention" in Beirut, see? It's a case of the inconvenient truth, perhaps. Whatever, they want a nice, cheap truth.'

Marcelle stubbed her cigarette out. 'You trying to tell me I'm not getting paid any more, Lynch? Our little spy camera has worked well for you in the past.'

'Sort of. They're reducing your retainer.'

Her soft brown eyes flashed. 'To what?'

Lynch took a deep pull of beer, savouring the sour-wheat taste of it. 'To nothing, Marcie. You can be an ideological recruit, but you're not to be corrupted by emolument.'

She drained her glass. 'Corrupted by what the fuck was that, Lynch?'

He grinned. 'Emolument.'

'Fine. Get your damn camera out of my room then.' She signalled to the barman, who leapt forward to take her glass. He retreated to fuss over the cocktail shaker.

'Can't even be arsed to do that, Marcie. Just switch it off. I've got an errand to run for them but I can't see me sticking around here for long after that. There's no future in the Middle East, just a load of new semi-governments and messy activists. My road is run, girl.'

She lit a cigarette and regarded him through half-lidded eyes. 'Jesus, Lynch. You after sympathy, is it? You looking for a freebie?'

'No, Marcie. I'm not after any freebie, just like you're not after being loved.' He stretched and signalled the barman for another beer. 'We both do what we do for money, but we're getting too old to be in the front ranks anymore, that's the shape of it.'

The barman's hand shook as he delivered her Cosmopolitan. She signalled to Lynch with the glass. 'Speak for yourself, Lynch.'

His mobile rang. 'Hey, Tony. No, just having a swift one with Marcie, I've some men to meet in a while. What's the craic?'

'Your man's in Beirut alright. Arrived into the airport bold as brass. He flew first class BA. He's staying at the Le Gray under his own name, no attempt at anything that looks remotely like tradecraft. He had dinner with that arsehole Browning last night.'

Lynch took the beer from the barman and nodded his thanks. 'Lance Browning. The HSBC bloke? What's he to Hartmoor?'

'Hartmoor's your mark, so you tell me. He stormed out on Browning, my tail said he was furious about something. We weren't listening.'

'No, fair enough. Thanks though.'

'So what's the deal? You get bored of spying on the Lebanese now? Starting on your own lot?'

'Funny, Tony.'

'Anything we should be taking an interest in?'

'No, not right now. I'll let you in if he's interesting. You know that. But thanks for the tip.'

'No problem. Let's do beers sometime.'

'Sure, it's been too long. See you around.'

He placed the mobile back on the bar and lifted his beer. The bottle was against his lip as he caught Marcelle's eye. 'What?'

'Lance Browning. You interested in him, Lynch?'

Lynch swigged at the bottle and smirked. 'Might be.'

'It'll cost you, you English bastard.'

Lynch moved fast, his left hand twisted in her flowing hair to wrench her head back. His right found her breast, twisting her nipple and making her cry out with surprise and pain. His rough cheek grinding against hers, he whispered in her ear. 'You know it, Marcie. You know I'm Irish. You're just being bad and I won't have it. Do you hear me?'

A long pause, a further pressure on her sensitive flesh then her restrained nod straining against his grip on her hair. He stepped back. 'You'll have your money. But I need him fast, not next week.'

Marcelle rearranged her wrap, her face flushed. 'He's due later.'

Lynch pulled away. 'Call me, so.'

Lynch picked up his mobile and nodded to the barman as he left.

SEVEN

The driver stole a peek in his mirror at the men he'd picked up at the airport. They both wore black. They watched incuriously from the back of the car out at the tatty streets. They were pale-skinned, with piercing blue eyes and short-cropped blond hair. The driver shuddered, glancing away quickly as one of them caught his eye.

He concentrated on driving, taking them deeper into Chatila, the refugee camp that had solidified into a ramshackle township over the years. A place where hope had been crushed, where dirty-faced children stood glaring sullenly at strangers against a backdrop of cinder-block houses capped with rusty corrugated sheeting. A place people didn't go unless they belonged there or had someone looking after their backs. The *azan* sounded from close by, a call taken up by other mosques around. The driver slowed by a large whitewashed compound wall and leaned on his horn, two short blasts and one long one. The roller door creaked and juddered up its rusty runners. They drove in.

The compound was paved with terrazzo tiles, single-story buildings all around the perimeter and netting stretched out above them dulling the sunlight. The large courtyard area was strewn with automotive junk, battered cars, wheels and oil drums. As they halted, leather-jacketed men bustled forward to open the doors. They stood back to let the two pale men straighten up. The driver lit a cigarette.

'This way.'

They followed him towards a long building, the windows barred and an aluminium railing running up the steps to the doorway. The driver rang a bell and a suspicious-looking man opened the door. His eyes flickered between the two visitors. He stood aside to let them in and the driver led them into a large room with dark wood bookshelves lining the walls and rich rugs on the floor. There were tatty leatherette-covered sofas with carved wooden scrollwork decorations all around the room, a coffee table in the middle bearing an overflowing ashtray, a plastic gold Arabesque flask and tiny cups next to a green plastic bowl of water. A garish box of pink tissues had been placed next to the bowl.

'Wait. Abbas Ali will come soon.'

The two men sat on a sofa together. The driver stood by the door and watched them. They were motionless, straight backed, both of them sitting like showroom dummies, their piercing eyes impassive. The ceaseless electronic tick of the gold-enamelled wall clock was relieved by the haphazard buzz of a fat bluebottle.

The driver felt physical relief at the sound of the door and the rasping voice berating the guard. He turned, his hand on his chest as Abbas Ali burst into the room followed close behind by two men carrying AK47s. Abbas Ali was a giant of a man, his luxuriant brown hair, great soup-strainer moustache and clear unlined skin belying his years. Only the puckering around his eyes gave away the fact he had lived well over six decades. He stood over the two pale men on the sofa, his great hand held out. 'Welcome to Beirut, gentlemen. How's Mr Kallas these days? Keeping well, I hope.'

They stood politely, each taking his hand. The leftmost one spoke, his voice so quiet the driver had to strain to hear him, 'He is well, thank you, sir and sends his kindest regards.'

Abbas Ali grunted, opening his heavy jacket and pulling out a packet of cigarettes. 'Nobody offered you coffee or anything?' He swept his hand around him. 'By the Prophet, but these people forget we are Arabs.'

Abbas Ali sat, his strong features creased in a benign smile. He flicked the bottom of the soft pack and slid a cigarette out, lighting it with a Zippo.

The left-hand marionette, for the driver had decided that is what they were, spoke again. His dry whisper was like a winter wind. 'You have made the arrangements for us, sir?'

Abbas Ali's face lit up in surprise. 'Of course. For Jaan Kallas, anything.' He plunged his big hand into a pocket, delved around and tossed the bunch of keys he found at the skinny young man standing near him. 'Here, Abed, take our friends to the armoury and give them everything they need.'

Abed hooked the keys on his finger. He licked his moist lips. 'Sure, boss. This way, gentlemens.'

The two men each paused to bow slightly to Abbas Ali as they passed him. He beamed after them.

He spoke to the driver. 'What of them?'

'Nothing boss. Not a word, I swear. They just walked up to me at the airport and the lippy one said "Take us to Abbas Ali" and not another word did they say. They're like showroom dummies.'

Abbas Ali grunted, rubbing his gold signet ring with its red stone. 'Know who they work for?' The driver shook his head and Abbas Ali pointed his nicotine-stained finger at him. His nail was split, the driver noticed. 'Death, that's who. They're two of the most dangerous passengers in the world, *ya* driver. Many men have looked into those blue eyes for the first and last time before death came to claim his reward. They're machines. Killing machines.'

The driver forced a smile. 'As long as they're not looking for me, boss. I pity the poor bastard they're here for.'

'Don't waste your pity. Take them up to the guest flat in Manara, give them keys. Stay there for the evening. Record it. I want to hear what they're up to.'

The driver nodded.

Abed returned, ashen faced, with the two colourless men behind him. 'Two desert eagles, two Uzis, two AKs, four tear gas grenades, two concussion and six HE. Two thousand rounds. Two Heckler and Koch SL8s, two Laserlyte sight. Two knives.'

Abbas Ali raised an eyebrow. The two men bowed again. The driver realised the one who spoke always stood to the left. 'Mr Kallas will be grateful to you, Mr Ali.'

The big man sighed and dropped the little coffee cup into the plastic water bowl. 'Driver. Take them to the guesthouse. Make sure they have everything they need. Abed, get those things bagged up for them.'

The drive out of Chatila was uneventful, dusk masking the details of the slum, the jagged outline of the buildings like broken teeth against the dying sun. Driving in silence, he took them down to Manara, the street vendors readying for the evening rush, streetlights flickering hesitantly into life. He stopped outside the apartment building.

'Tenth floor, number 1018,' he said. He handed the key over his shoulder without turning to them. Cold fingers took it.

They got out and he waited as they pulled the heavy sports bags from the boot. He felt eyes on him and turned to see one of the men squatting by his window. He wound it down, trying not to appear scared, but his nuts tightened as the unblinking stare caught him. 'Don't wait up for us, driver.'

The driver twitched a smile and nodded, his tongue rasping on the roof of his dry mouth. He watched them walk up the steps to the apartment. He drove around the block to the gloomy little car park behind the building, switched on the radio and settled down to listen. Nothing happened. The car was warm and the driver tired. Soon enough, he nodded off.

'Wake up, driver.'

He jerked awake, fear consuming him. The voice had come from the wireless. He felt sweat prickles all over as he cast around. The rear door banged open. He grabbed for the handle but caught air as his own door was snatched open. A fist grabbed his hair from behind, pulling his head back to the side of the headrest. Another hand reached in and slid a knife across his exposed neck, a cold blade that burned his flesh. The driver spasmed. He strained against the seatbelt, his back arced. He gurgled, trying to claw air into his heaving lungs. His chest burned agony, iron in his nostrils.

The rear door banged shut. A pale hand tossed a tangle of wires and tiny microphones into the driver's sodden lap.

EIGHT

The room upstairs at *Le Chat Botté* was glorious faux Victorian, rich burgundy and mahogany, pelmeted velvet curtains and gold tasselled tie-backs, a four-poster bed open at the top to allow a clear view of the heavy gilt-framed mirror on the ceiling. Lynch sat quietly as the white panelled door opened towards him, the little scrolled gold handle dropping with a click. Fat fingers pulled the door shut behind the man's wheezing bulk.

Lynch waited for the stranger's sixth sense to kick in, driving him to turn and stare with horror at the unexpected presence of a slightly shabby Irishman, hands steepled in front of his handsome face, the blue urchin's eyes dancing as Lynch exulted in the fat man's confusion.

'Hello, Lance. Fancy finding you here of all places.'

Lance Browning paled. He reached for the handle but it didn't give to his pressure. He snatched his hand away, staring as if it burnt him.

Lynch beamed, lifting the glass of scotch from his side and raising it to toast Browning. 'Cheers, Lance. Lovely to see ye. Drink?'

The fat smile was wobbly. He reached for his collar. 'Don't mind if I do, actually, old thing.'

'Pull up a seat, why don't ye?' Lynch gestured to the Lloyd Loom chair in the corner as he stood, pouring a generous measure from the Tyrconnell bottle at his side. Browning didn't quite cower, but his eyes lowered as Lynch stood over him, handing him the glass.

'Here. Take this.'

Browning drank then breathed in heavily. He gazed down at the tumbler in his hands.

Lynch sat back, enjoying the sip of his iced whiskey as much as Browning's sweaty discomfiture.

'So business good is it, Lance? Enjoying the new wealth of Lebanon's oligarchs are we?'

Browning drank again, cleared his throat. 'We're not involved in the whole telecom thing, you know.'

'You did that deal with the Misrati boys, didn't you? The property one. It went through.'

'Someone has to provide backing for commercial risk. Even in Lebanon. Even for controversial projects that nevertheless create wealth and benefit. It was just an old harbour. Nobody cares about history here when there's long term economic *value* at stake.'

Lynch waved the argument away. 'Sure, whatever. Of course. Just a few Phoenician walls. Now, tell me about Jason Hartmoor.'

Browning glanced around. Lynch smiled into the ice in his glass. 'In your own time, Lance.'

'He just turned up, out of the blue. Not even an email, he called the bank. I don't even know how he managed to get through. The call centre usually keeps them contained.'

'What did he want?'

'To meet. He's staying at the Le Gray. I suggested dinner. We knew each other before, in Beirut. During the war.'

Lynch studied his nails. 'You both studied at MECAS.'

Browning nodded. 'Yes, yes we did. I was what they called a commercial, not quite in the pale. He was FCO. I didn't know he was ill until we met. He looked ghastly. It was like he came here to say his last farewells. I thought him rather distant, to be honest. He was very concerned about Frank Coleman.' Browning stopped talking, his mouth drawn tight as he realised he was gabbling.

Lynch leaned back, his voice slow and gentle. 'Concerned? Why would he be concerned about Coleman?'

'I don't know.' Browning shrugged. 'He just said Coleman

had been a friend to him. He didn't know about, you know. That stuff.'

'What, Michel Freij getting busted and Coleman's suicide?'

'Err… Yes. That. Your *little triumph*.'

The man's flushed forehead was a shiny arc in the orange light, glinting sweat.

'So why did Hartmoor come to Beirut, Lance?'

Browning's laugh was a sharp bark. 'To see his Lebbo bint. Why else?'

'A girl? Here? Why didn't he come back for her before?'

'Search me, Lynch. But Hartmoor had a girl here back then. Well, not here precisely, but up in the mountains, in Shemlan. Where the school was. A real popsie. Her family owned the restaurant there. It was something of a scandal, the way they carried on back then. They say he broke her heart when he left. But we all had to get away, it was just too bloody dangerous to stay around. These boys were starting to rip each other to shreds, you understand.' Browning smiled. 'You were here too, in the war, weren't you, Lynch? At least, that's what they say.'

Lynch was silent. Browning gazed down into his empty glass. He held it out and Lynch, recognising the need in the man, refilled it for him with a generous hand. 'So how did the reunion go, Lance. Did you hit it off after all these years?'

Browning's gaze flickered to the four-poster bed and the mirror above it before he answered. 'He walked out on me, the bugger. Left me with a bill for two starters and a half bottle of Tokay. I told him what I thought of Coleman and his precious Russian source and Hartmoor lost the plot altogether. It was bloody rude of him.'

'Source? What source?'

'You know bloody well, Lynch.'

'Humour me. Take me through it.' Lynch smiled. 'For old times' sakes.'

Browning licked his lips. 'They say Coleman had a Russian source, a high ranker in the Ministry of Defence based out here.

Apparently he ran an agent in the FCO, among others. Coleman's career got a nice little kick-start from the operation. Coleman was the blue-eyed boy for a few years in the '90s. They never found the British agent. Dennis Wye did quite nicely for himself by hanging onto Coleman's coattails. The dutiful deputy finally comes good. And Wye did even better by distancing himself from Coleman over the Freij affair, they say.'

'But we don't know who this source was, let alone his agent, do we Lance?'

'You tell me, Lynch. You're the SIS man. I'm just a banker.'

Lynch stood. 'That you are, Lance.' He walked to the door, the bottle in his hand. 'Don't get up. I'll have them send your girl in.'

On the way out, Lynch slid the bottle onto the bar. 'Film him,' he snapped at Marcelle, who flipped a languid, glittering middle finger at his departing back.

Keenly aware of the irony, Hartmoor had too much time on his hands. He wandered through the Solidere district the Beirutis called *Sodeco*, the reconstructed heart of the city that was somehow grander and more ordered than it had ever managed to be before the Civil War's relentless tide of destruction. He pottered, never far from the forbidding walls of the Ottoman Grand Serail perched up on its hill. He took his time, The Stick, a hated companion. He tired all too easily these days. The elegant sunlit colonnades and café awnings sheltered their chattering clientele. The sight of café society at leisure amused him and lightened his mood. He carefully picked his way to one of the sunnier tables, took his seat with as little fuss as he could manage and ordered a double espresso, speaking English. He called the waiter back. 'Oh, do you have a newspaper I could borrow?'

The waiter's shrug was almost comical. 'Not English, sorry *monsieur.*'

Hartmoor smiled thinly and said, in Arabic, 'Arabic or French would be fine.'

The waiter was guppy-faced for a split second before relaxing into a broad grin, bowing a little as he turned. 'But of course.'

With care, Hartmoor propped The Stick against the chair next to him. A shadow fell across him. He glanced up sharply. The man standing at his table was smiling, an urchin's amusement that didn't quite reach the blue eyes above the snub nose. He was perhaps in his early fifties, his dark hair receding to form a widow's peak. Elegantly shabby in a plain shirt, a blue cotton jacket and jeans, he held out his hand.

'You'd be Jason Hartmoor. Welcome to Beirut.' The accent was Northern Irish, softened by years abroad, Hartmoor guessed.

Hartmoor took the man's firm grip. He moved to rise but the stranger gestured him to stay. 'No, please, don't put yourself out on my account.'

Hartmoor glanced around as the man hunkered down. He was talking quickly and Hartmoor, interrupted in an otherwise peaceful and serene moment, struggled to keep up.

'I hope you don't mind me joining you like this, but I was awful keen to have a little tête-à-tête, you see. And you know, I thought it perhaps best if we did so away from here because you've been tailed by a squad of three CIA goons all morning and I would, to be honest, love to know quite why you're quite so important to them and, indeed, to our own lot. My name's Gerald Lynch, by the way. I'm from the Embassy.'

Hartmoor gathered his wits. He frowned. 'You're the SIS man here.'

'Top marks, Mr Hartmoor. Can you tell me, have you talked to anyone else since you arrived in Beirut? Made any calls?'

'I tried to have dinner with an old colleague, but it didn't work out very well. I called the American Embassy yesterday morning. I hardly see what—'

Lynch leaned forward, his urgent tone at odds with his relaxed smile. 'What did you say to them?'

'Nothing. I called for Frank Coleman but they messed me around. I understand Frank is dead. I knew him from… Before.'

'Can we leave together now? I have a secure location and we can try and work out quite why your call resulted in this level of surveillance.'

Hartmoor hesitated, searching Lynch's earnest face and marshalling his thoughts as best he could in the growing sense of confusion. 'I hardly…'

Lynch stood. It was only as he spoke into thin air Hartmoor realised he was wearing a hands free earpiece. The line must have been open all the time. 'Okay, Hassan, now.'

A battered white Mercedes pulled out of the side street above the café and slid smoothly to a halt alongside them. Lynch reached out to Hartmoor and helped him stand, handing him The Stick and propelling him gently but firmly towards the car in a fluid movement. He heard a shout and the screech of tyres before the door slammed on him and the Mercedes shot forward and raced down the cobbled street. Hartmoor glanced in the wing mirror at the stunned pedestrians glowering after them.

They reached the army checkpoint on the seaward side of Sodeco. The soldiers had already opened the barrier and were stood back to let them pass, despite their breakneck speed. They joined the traffic, the car slowing to blend in among the jostling, honking melee.

Lynch, sitting next to Hartmoor in the back seat, reached forward and patted the driver, a silver-haired man wearing a tweed jacket, on the shoulder. 'Nice one, Hassan. Thanks.'

Hassan wove through the traffic towards the looming black mouth of a tunnel.

Lynch leaned into Hartmoor, his voice raised about the noise of the traffic. 'You left here in the '70s, didn't you? Never came back?'

Hartmoor nodded. 'You won't have had the pleasure of travelling in the Selim Salam tunnel, then. They didn't finish it until after the war.'

Hartmoor shrugged, avoiding Lynch's direct gaze. Lynch chatted on. 'It's a case study in how not to build a tunnel, actually. See what they did, is they dug a nice long passage for traffic out of the city towards the South and the airport. But they followed the contour of the hill, so it rises in the middle, creating a natural air lock. It's not ventilated, so it fills with the exhaust. Genius, eh?'

Lynch paused as Hassan drove them into the tunnel. He waited a moment for his eyes to adjust to the gloom. 'It's the most polluted place on earth. Official.'

The slow-moving glut of traffic hesitated, hazard lights flashing and headlights casting ghostly swathes of light in the roiling smog of exhaust fumes. Lynch twisted around, noting they were followed closely by a red BMW. He leaned forward to Hassan as the traffic shuddered to a stop in the dark grey air.

'Now. Thanks Hassan.' He turned to Hartmoor. 'We're getting out here, taking the car behind. You need help?'

Hartmoor shook his head as horns started to blare. He pushed the door open, the filthy air choking him. He struggled to stand, racked by coughs. Lynch took his arm and propelled him back to the BMW. Hartmoor tried to hold his breath, but the coughing forced him to gasp for air, taking more of the dirty cloud into his lungs. Lynch yanked open the rear door of the red car and pushed Hartmoor in. He whipped the door shut and raced around to the other side.

Hassan pulled away ahead of them as the traffic started to move again. Lynch gestured toward the two crew-cut figures in the front of the car.

'Jason Hartmoor, Meadows and Henderson. Meadows and Henderson, Jason Hartmoor.'

Hartmoor's eyes stung. He wiped the tears from his cheeks, his breathing slowing. Turning to Lynch, he snapped. 'Was that really necessary?'

'Sure it was. You've been under close surveillance. I don't know why on earth the American Embassy's interested in you, Mr Hartmoor, but right now I'd rather they didn't have the luxury of knowing where we are. Hassan's going to take them on a goose chase to Sidon and we're going to a nice, safe villa north of Beirut. I assume you won't mind staying with us a little while. It's entirely for your own protection. You are, obviously, at any time free to leave.'

'Is that correct?'

They looped back to drive north out of the city, uphill towards the snow-capped peak of Sannine, the great mountain that overlooks Beirut's Mediterranean littoral.

The villa's entrance was set back from the road, a dusty little track leading to the stone gateway, bougainvillea bushes beyond. The single-story stone-clad building was simple but modern inside, tastefully furnished. There was a pool in the garden. Hartmoor stood at the window watching the dappled sunlight glinting on the water. Gerald Lynch studied the man's face. Lined by pain and prematurely old, it was enlivened by sardonic blue eyes. His black polo neck made him look even paler. There was a certain bearing to Jason Hartmoor, old-school FCO to the core, Lynch thought.

Lynch cleared his throat. 'Can I get you a coffee or a scotch or something?'

Hartmoor walked over to the white cotton sofa and lowered himself, his hands wobbly on his stick. 'Water, please.'

Lynch tipped his forelock and headed for the kitchen, where Meadows and Henderson were busy making tea. He returned with a glass of water and a mug of tea.

'Why were you following me, Mr Lynch? Because they

were?'

'Not in so many words. We were going to ask you for a chat anyway. The FCO people tried to pick you up over in Newgale but just missed you. So you got passed on to me. Do you mind helping me out?'

Hartmoor's eyes were closed. 'No, no. Not at all. I have nothing to be scared of.'

'Sure, I'm not threatening anything.'

Hartmoor opened his eyes to watch the Irishman place the tray down on the glass-topped coffee table. 'It wouldn't make a difference even if you did, Mr Lynch. I am terminally ill. There's nothing you can do to me. Nothing at all.'

'Me, I'm on the side of the angels here, Jason.' A thought struck Lynch. 'It's okay if I call you Jason, yes?'

Hartmoor smiled thinly. 'It hardly matters...?'

Lynch smiled back. 'Gerald.'

'...Gerald. Call me what you like. I am beyond formality.'

Lynch raised his tea mug in a toast. 'Can we just go through some details from the files, if you don't mind? I realise this is all, well, very *irksome*, but there are some leads being thrown up by new computer systems in London that we think you might be able to help us with. Details that seemed insignificant thirty years ago that our new age of data mining and the like make suddenly, oh I don't know, terribly important to some analyst in a little grey room.' Lynch flashed a grin. 'Is that alright with you?'

Hartmoor lowered his head in a gesture Lynch thought, uncharitably, was intended to be regal. 'Of course.'

He had duly read his briefing notes from Channing. Hartmoor had gone on from the interrupted long course at MECAS in Shemlan to finish his Arabic studies in Jordan and London and then carve out a perfectly respectable career in the Middle East, first a stint in Iraq where he married, then Israel with his new wife in tow. The marriage had been a disaster, a great deal of excruciating detail on the record. From Israel he had gone on to Saudi Arabia where his marriage eventually blew apart. He had gone back to Tel Aviv and then onto Sudan and disgrace. Lynch had enjoyed the details of the disgrace but now, looking at Hartmoor, he found himself somehow doubting it was as simple as it had seemed. The man's career hadn't survived the incident and he had been pensioned off with indecent haste just in time to celebrate the millennium with a nice Foreign Office Annuity.

A few years afterwards, the file had said, Hartmoor had first been diagnosed with cancer.

'You went to Balliol?'

'Yes, I did. I studied modern languages there.'

'When did you enter the Foreign and Commonwealth Office?'

Hartmoor was icily amused. 'The role or the building? 1973 for both. It was a horrible place full of files and stern secretaries in horn-rimmed glasses as I recall. I was given a small office to share with four others.'

Lynch was ticking off notes on a pad, taking down details. 'That's good, thanks. Let's try and stick to straightforward answers for now, we can get more detail later if you don't mind?'

'Not at all.'

'What was your father's name?'

'Byron.'

'Where were you born?'

'Southwold. It left me with a lifelong restlessness assuaged only by proximity to the sea.'

'Have you ever betrayed your country?'

Hartmoor sipped his water. He placed the glass carefully back on the coffee table. 'No. Have you?'

Lynch paused. 'When were you married?'

Hartmoor's face tightened, his face lit by the sun from the window. He cast his eyes to the pelmets. '1979. December. Iraq.'

'December?'

'Yes. The second. It was a Sunday.'

'Her name?'

Hartmoor raised an eyebrow. Lynch nodded.

'Lesley.'

Lynch waited. The silence weighted heavily. Hartmoor glared, capitulating. 'Ainsworth. Lesley Ainsworth. Her father was the ambassador.'

Lynch leaned back. 'Was he, now?'

'Yes, he bloody well was. You likely know it, too.'

'She was a tennis player,' Lynch stated.

'Yes, she was. We were the best players in Baghdad, we made a good couple.'

'On the court,' Lynch quipped. Hartmoor's mouth tightened.

'As your file will have told you, our marriage was terminated during my tenure in Riyadh. You have the details, I cannot see why we have to go over the whole thing.'

'It's all about details, though, isn't it Jason.' Lynch sipped his tea. 'Have you ever had relations with a known terrorist group or a person affiliated with such a group?'

Lynch sat back, surprised at Hartmoor's explosive bark of laughter and intrigued to see he man struggle to manage the spasm of pain his outburst triggered. Calming himself, Hartmoor wiped his eyes.

'Me, oh, my. In my day, Mr Lynch, they used to ask about affiliations with the Communist Party of Great Britain or even Russians. How things have changed, no?'

Lynch smiled. 'Have you?'

'No. Let's get to the point, Mr Lynch.'

'Khartoum. An African girl called Aaliyah. Sudanese. Very beautiful from the photo I have.'

Hartmoor was stilled. The silence was absolute. Hartmoor looked down at his hands, white knuckled and age-spotted. He wore a Longines watch, Lynch noticed belatedly. Hartmoor looked up.

'And so she was. What has that to do with you, Mr Lynch?'

'Were you set up, do you think?'

Hartmoor was confused, his eyes casting around the room. Lynch saw the pulse on the man's temple.

'Set up?' Hartmoor's thin wrists were like taut cables. 'Of course I was set up. It would have been blindingly obvious to a schoolgirl I was set up.'

Lynch chuckled, despite himself. 'Bad turn of phrase there.'

Hartmoor was on his feet in an instant, no effort and no stick. He wobbled, though, Lynch noticed.

'She was eighteen. But fuck you, Mr Lynch. And fuck the government that sent you.'

NINE

Lynch stood in the kitchen of the villa, his mug of tea in hand, waiting for Jason Hartmoor to calm down before going back into the living room. He gazed at the two big men sitting at the table drinking their tea. They had been seconded to him from the SAS without a murmur from Channing's bean counters. They had been in Beirut before and knew their way around, worked seamlessly together and had quickly gained Lynch's respect. Meadows was the older of the two, a merry-eyed, stocky man with a moustache and high hairline. Henderson was taller, fair and freckled, with a Scouser's wit and ironic perception. He jerked his thumb towards the living room.

'So how's he doing?'

'Fine,' said Lynch. 'But this will take a while yet. You might want to get some scran together.'

'Sure,' Henderson replied, standing to rinse his mug out. He glanced raised his chin over his shoulder at Meadows. 'Muddy's a gourmet chef, so he is. What do you fancy? Spag bog or cottage pie?'

Lynch placed his mug on the red-checked tablecloth. 'I'll take the pie. No rush, though. We've got a lot to talk about.'

Strolling out of the kitchen, Lynch paused and turned. 'Muddy?'

Henderson grinned. 'Meadows. Muddy fields.'

'Right.'

It was Lynch's turn to gaze out of the living room window. Hartmoor sat on the sofa behind.

'You were here at the Arabic place, weren't you? Shemlan.'

'I was, yes. The Middle East Centre for Arab Studies. In '78. We had to leave in a hurry. The Civil War. I was in the last class there. It had been going thirty years. It was established during the Second World War in Jordan, but moved to Shemlan.'

'You never came back, though.' Lynch turned, shielding his eyes from the cool sun to read Hartmoor's wary features.

'No, no I didn't. I always went where I was told to go and didn't go where I was told not to go. I regret that compliance now.'

'You were told not to come back?'

'Initially, yes. The Civil War meant Lebanon was effectively off limits for years. Afterwards I told myself I didn't want to see the bombed-out shell of a place I had loved so well. Or disrupt the lives of the people I had known here.'

Lynch folded himself into one of the armchairs and placed his mug carefully on the coffee table. 'So here's the question you wanted me to ask. Did you know any Russians in your time here?'

Hartmoor frowned. 'Russians? No, we were hardly on speaking terms back then, were we? There were some Americans on the short course at the centre, but of course no Russians.'

'I meant outside the school.'

'God, no. We were rarely out of there, in any case. We made it down for a few trips to the West of Beirut. The East became pretty hard to get to. I used to drive a Mini-Moke, if you know what they are.' Lynch nodded and Hartmoor continued. 'We went over to Damascus once. It was actually easier to get to Damascus towards the end.' Hartmoor checked his reverie, blinking. 'Sorry. Rambling. No. No Russians.'

'Does the name Dmitri mean anything to you?'

Hartmoor paused, his eyes veering to the left, recalling. 'No.'

'Did you know Frank Coleman well?'

'Relatively. We tended to go to the same conferences, working in the same region you see. We sometimes helped his people out, as they, I am sure, helped your people out.'

'And Mai Khoury?'

Hartmoor raised his hand to point a trembling finger at Lynch. 'Nothing to do with you. Keep away. That's nothing to do with you.'

Lynch raised his palms. 'Okay, okay.'

He sat back in his armchair and waited for Hartmoor to calm. 'So, back to Reds under the bed. Did you have contact with any members of the Russian armed forces?'

Hartmoor's face flashed irritation. 'No. I told you. I once spoke to an Estonian at a reception in Tel Aviv to remark on the amusing coincidence that our careers appeared to have run in parallel. He agreed. That is the full extent of my contact with anyone from the Russian embassies in the countries in which I worked. I am not a spy, Mr Lynch. I was a diplomat.'

'What was his name?'

'How the hell would I know? It was over twenty years ago.'

Lynch sighed, lifting his teacup and staring into its emptiness. 'Would you mind staying here overnight? We've bought you fresh things.'

'Is that necessary?'

'Desirable.' Lynch put the mug down.

'Then yes, but only one night. I have a life to be getting on with and precious little of it left.'

'How long you stay here may be dictated by circumstances out of our control, Jason.'

'I will not be held against my will, Mr Lynch.'

'I have already assured you we do not have that intention.'

Hartmoor's hands shot to his jacket pockets, he patted them, then checked the inside pockets. He pulled out a foil strip of pills, a single white tablet left. 'I don't have my medication.'

Lynch stood. 'We'll get your things from your hotel room. You can eat with Meadows and Henderson in the meantime.'

Hartmoor shook his head. 'I can't. I need to take enzymes to digest food.'

'Okay. I'll pick them up now.'

Lynch walked into the kitchen. 'I need to go into town. Look after our friend. You guys want to leave me a plate?'

'Sure,' said Meadows, stirring a sizzling pan of mince. 'Might not be a lot left on it, mind.'

Lynch was still smiling as he hooked the car keys from the table by the front door, sliding his finger into the fob. He turned at the open door as Hartmoor called out to him. 'Mr Lynch.'

'Sure, what is it?'

'His name. The Estonian. It was Jaan Kallas.'

Lynch snapped his hand closed on the keys. 'Thank you.'

Brian Channing's voice on the phone was tired. 'You found him.'

Lynch glanced into the rear mirror. He generally avoided driving in Beirut, the constant jostling chaos was too much for him, cars slipping past to create second and third lanes, honking and creeping by to edge in front. Preferring the anonymity of the city's plentiful and cheap *servees* shared taxis, he only drove *in extremis*. He tried to keep a lid on his temper as he was bullied along the road.

'Yes, we found him. He was being followed.'

Channing's tone picked up. 'Oh?'

'Yeah, you're gonna like this. By the CIA.' Lynch leaned on the horn as a four wheel drive cut into his lane.

'Are you sure?'

'Your friend merits a whole profiling team, at least three watchers at any given time. We got him away, but they're not going to be happy.'

'Where is he now?'

'Safe house, with Meadows and Henderson.'

'I wish you'd consulted before acting. Have you talked to him?'

'He says he's never been in touch with any Russians. I

believe him. He's got little enough reason to lie now. He's a very sick man indeed. He did mention an Estonian, apparently their careers had run in parallel, no significant contact. I didn't have time to go into that further, but I have his name.'

'Go on.'

'Jaan Kallas. That's it.'

'Okay, we'll look into him. Meantime don't do anything else to annoy our friends. I'll talk to Hilton Polson over in Washington and let you know what happens, right?'

'Sure. I need someone looked into as well. Hartmoor's here to look up an old girlfriend, name of Mai Khoury. She lived in Shemlan, her family owns a restaurant there called The Cliff House. I have a contact looking into her background here, but can you run her through your fancy machines?'

'Mai Khoury. Do we know anything else?'

'Nope. That's the lot for now.'

'Okay, I'll have one of the guys send you whatever we've got. Don't go making any waves, Gerald.'

'Fine.' Lynch cut the line and dropped the handset on the passenger seat.

Lynch pulled up outside the Le Gray and took the tag from the valet. Armed with Hartmoor's card key, he took the lift up. Glancing around as he strode up the empty corridor, he noted the little black bobbles of the security cameras on the ceiling and turned away instinctively. He slipped into Hartmoor's suite.

Lynch froze, puzzled, by the bedroom door. The cupboard doors yawned open and clothes were strewn untidily across the bed. Little foil strips of pills gleamed in the halogen light, boxes scattered on the floor. He found a laundry bag and stuffed all the pills he could collect into it. He pushed this, along with the clothes, into Hartmoor's wheelie bag.

Taking a tissue from the holder in the bathroom, Lynch picked up the handset of the bedside phone and dialled zero.

'Operator.'

'Reception, please.' Lynch gazed around the room. He

disliked funky chic as a rule.

An efficient female voice. 'Reception.'

'This is Jason Hartmoor. I was just wondering if anyone had called for me earlier.'

'Yes, sir. Two gentlemen. I called up but there was no answer from your room. They didn't leave any message sir.'

'I was out. Did they say who they were at all?'

'No sir. They were very,' she paused as if troubled. 'Well, distinctive.'

'Really?' Lynch raised an eyebrow. 'How so?'

'They looked like twins. They sounded, well, Russian. They were very white.'

'White?'

'Yes. Their hair. But their clothes were black.'

'Nobody I know from the sound of it. Well, thank you anyway.'

'Thank you, sir.'

Lynch replaced the handset. His mobile rang. Tony Chalhoub.

'Tony. What's the big occasion?'

'We need to meet. Do you know where Lance Browning's house is?'

'As it happens I think I do. The old British Bank of the Middle East villa in Ashrafiyeh, isn't it?'

'Can you meet me there right away? It's urgent.'

'Sure. I'll be there in about ten.'

Lynch was planning to wait outside for Chalhoub, but as he pulled up outside the tree-lined compound wall of the old house, the flashing lights of the squad cars and men in Tyvek overalls moving about inside told him he was at a murder scene. He clicked the remote and strode into the lush, long-established garden of the Ottoman villa.

Chalhoub met Lynch at the front door of the main house,

his face set. 'Come in. It's not pretty.'

Browning's body was in the living room. It was tied to the frame of a chair; the base of it had been knocked out. His trousers were around his ankles. There was a lot of blood, the air reeked of it. A figure in white Tyvek straightened up as they entered the room.

Chalhoub gestured at the figure. 'Gerald, this is Elias Habib, head of my forensic team. Elias, Gerald is from the British Embassy.'

Habib was in his sixties, balding and sallow skinned. His pebble glasses accentuated his bulbous eyes, the curved sweep of his nose capping a bushy moustache. Lynch thought he looked like those Groucho Marx disguises you buy from joke shops.

Elias Habib nodded to Lynch, displaying his silicone-gloved hand. 'You'll understand if I don't shake hands, Mr Lynch.'

'Sure, no problem. What happened here?'

Habib took off his glasses, leaving a red welt on the top of his nose. He rubbed his forehead with the back of his wrist. 'He has been dead something like three hours. He has been tortured. They beat him quite badly around the head and chest, there is evidence of bruising to the genitals and anus which, you can see, are exposed by the way the straw base of the chair has been cut away. It was cut while he was sitting on it; there are a number of lesions from this. The blows to his nether region were likely kicks with a pointed shoe. They cut his throat, the cause of death I believe. We will have to verify this assumption in the laboratory. He is missing two fingernails and one tooth. The fingernails, they have been extracted. I believe the missing tooth to have been the result of a blow to the mouth.' Habib pointed to a little evidence tag at the corner of the room. 'It is over there.'

'They? You said "they" cut his throat.'

Chalhoub answered. 'The neighbour saw two men enter here this morning at around 8.30. Both were pale-skinned, blond and wearing black clothes. One carried a holdall.'

Lynch turned at the sound of raised voices by the front door, running footsteps as policemen joined the fray. A woman's voice cried out. He followed Chalhoub out of the living room. In the hallway, two burly policemen held back a mousy woman in a green cardigan. She was pummelling the chest of one officer. Her lined face was reddened, her tortoiseshell glasses awry.

'Let me see my husband. This is my home. You have no right.'

Chalhoub barked an order in Arabic and both policemen stepped back. The woman tottered momentarily, her chest heaving. She gained her composure, straightened her glasses and smoothed the front of her blouse, her breathing slowing. She blinked at Chalhoub. 'What has happened here?'

'I am sorry, *Madame*. Your husband is dead.'

'I know that, they told me that at the school. Where is he?'

Chalhoub gestured, 'In here,' he raised a hand to stop her. 'But I think it best you don't go in. It is not…' Chalhoub cast about for the word. 'Pleasant.'

'Nevertheless, it is my right.'

Chalhoub stepped aside, glancing at Lynch. 'It is, *Madame*.'

They followed her into the living room. She stood stock still. Lynch slipped to the left of her, Chalhoub to the right, standing ready to support her. Lynch watched her expressionless face, her eyes darting around the room, taking in the scene. Lynch followed her gaze to the bloodied corpse, its head lolling. Even in death, Lance Browning looked stupid. A high-pitched staccato barking noise came from Mrs Browning. Turning, he realised she was laughing. Chalhoub's horrified eyes were on her as well. She walked around the corpse, stepping around Elie Habib, who had stopped his scraping at the floor to look at her giggling and smiling, her hands over her mouth, patting her cheek and pulling on her chin.

She walked up to Chalhoub, her eyes shining. 'Thank you. I

shall go and stay with a friend now while you clean up. I suppose you think me a little mad, but you see Lance has been forcing me to do things like this for his sexual gratification for over twenty years now. I did so hate him.'

They watched her leave the room, the clatter of her heels on the wooden stairs punctuating the silence.

They stood together in the villa garden, breathing in the fresh air. Inside smelled of rust and faeces, but here the air was cool, clean and carried a hint of jasmine. The stuccoed walls were green with vines, trees threw their shade over patches of roller-striped lawn. There was a wrought iron table and four chairs in the middle, painted white. Behind them, the crime scene team was making a racket, radios barked and someone called Adel was being rebuked for parking in the wrong place. It made an odd soundtrack to the English country garden ahead of them.

'Here. Take a look at these.' Chalhoub handed a tablet to Lynch, who pulled a face at the sight of a hand poking out from a car door. He swiped to bring up the next shot. 'Nice.'

Chalhoub nodded. 'There's a lot of it around. Browning is the second messy murder in two days. These were taken yesterday in Manara. The body in the car is Ahmed Assad, known in criminal circles as simply The Driver. His throat was cut. We found four highly sophisticated listening devices on his lap. All had been torn out of a flat in the building behind this parking lot. The concierge at the apartment building was very forgetful but after some pressure was applied remembered two foreigners dressed in black and carrying holdalls. And now we have an eyewitness report from a neighbour of Browning's. Two pale men in black.'

Lynch winced as his swipes through the sequence of pictures started to move to close ups, blood-spattered windows and soaked upholstery, the shapeless body, its head pulled back, the huge, gaping wound in its neck.

'The concierge. She mention they sounded Russian?'

'Yes.' Chalhoub took his tablet back. 'Care to tell me what's going on?'

'I don't know myself, Tony, and that's the truth. So who's this Ahmed Assad guy?'

'That's the thing, Lynch. That's what's got me worried. He was Abbas Ali's driver. Abbas Ali owned the flat the bugs were torn out of.'

Lynch whistled. 'The Uncrowned King of Chatila? A drug baron? What is this, a gang war? Why would Lance Browning be involved in a gang war?'

Chalhoub searched Lynch's face. 'You tell me. You seem to know more than I do at any rate. Because I don't have a clue. So what do you know about Russians?'

'Nothing, Tony. Honest Injun.'

'And what about your old man, this Hartmoor?'

'That's the funny thing, Tony. I get the feeling he knows even less than I do.'

TEN

Dennis Wye, not one of nature's most patient creatures, hated being stuck in Tallinn while so much of what was happening in Beirut threatened to jeopardise his operation. Worse, outside of hanging around in his hotel room, admittedly luxurious compared to the usual dosshouses they found for him, there was little to do other than try and co-ordinate things remotely while they waited.

Wye loathed waiting. It was action he lived for. He clipped his nails, showered twice a day and watched too much porn on the hotel adult channel. He went out for long walks through the old walled city, but his mind was furious with thoughts of Beirut and he passed the museums and galleries by as he walked his frustrations away.

He sat in a café overlooking the square drinking beer and looking at the winter tourists shuffling around the cobbled streets in ordered lines behind umbrella-toting guides, Baltic cruises in for the day. The snow was still on the rooftops. The main roadways were clear and shining wet, the weather was cold but the sky was gloriously blue and if you found a corner sheltered away from the breeze, you could actually warm up.

His mobile rang, the encryption app's tone sounding. Wye fumbled for it, standing and walking out of the café as he stabbed at the screen. Clancy Goldman calling from Beirut.

'Clancy.'

Goldman's voice was constricted. 'We lost the old guy. He got lifted from a café by the SIS guy, Lynch. We tried to block them off but they seem to have had help from the Lebanese somehow. They pulled a swap on us, we ended up following the wrong car to fucking Sidon.'

Wye balled his fist. 'So what about satellite?'

'That's what I mean. We tracked them to Selim Slam, then ended up with the wrong car. We pulled the guy at Sidon, a random security check. He's a driver for some go-go bar in Monot, swears to God he doesn't know anything other than some hood hijacked him out of Solidere. We're running a back trace on proximate cars, but all they had to do was hang back in that tunnel for a few minutes and they could have been any one of thousands of cars. We lost the trace, Wye. They're gone.'

A tourist blundered into Wye's path. Wye elbowed him and ploughed on along the snowy sidewalk. The red brick wall alongside him reflected the sunlight, the snow was half-thawed and crackled under his feet. 'So trace Lynch, where does he live? Known haunts. Don't let that driver go, he's an associate of Lynch's. The go-go bar's a place called the Puss in Boots, it's run by a friend of his.'

'We had to let him go, Wye. Come on, we got no jurisdiction. He started kicking off and there was a crowd building up. You know how things can get ugly fast around here.'

Wye slammed his palm into the wall. 'Dammit. Go for Lynch, his apartment, known hangouts, associates. Nail his mobile.'

'We're on it. He doesn't have much of a footprint, I'll give him that.'

'Find it, Clancy. Find whatever footprint you can. Before this blows up in our faces.'

Wye cut the line and picked up pace, headed back to his hotel. He contemplated flying back to Beirut. He could get the evening Lufthansa through Frankfurt. He'd be as well waiting there as here.

Back in his hotel room, Wye switched off the TV he'd left on, which was muted and displaying two enthusiastic young ladies and their paramour. He called Polson, who answered almost immediately.

'We lost Hartmoor. He got picked up by the SIS guy in

Beirut, Lynch.'

'Damn game. I just had a call from his boss, not two minutes back. Brian Channing. Guy's in charge of European Joint Intelligence. Sometimes you kinda wonder if there really is some sort of co-ordination to the universe. He was asking me why we had a profiling team sicced on a British national. I made some shit up about mistaken identity and asked why SIS wanted to lift the guy and he made some shit up about needing to question him about some old diplomatic paperwork. Not the most comfortable conversation.'

'You could have just denied it.'

'He'd emailed me photos of our people. Don't underestimate Lynch, Dennis. Frank Coleman did and look how he ended up. If your guys lost Hartmoor, how are your Estonian friends gonna find him?'

'I got Goldman chasing Lynch. He's clearly involved now. Which I have to say does not make me feel secure. I was thinking of going over to Beirut.'

'No way, Dennis. Stay where you are. Kallas is important to us and we need the distribution end of things properly managed when this next load comes in. The last one was too sloppy and I do not want to be caught holding this particular baby, kapisch? Leave it to Clancy, he's a big boy and he'll manage things that end. Between our technological assets and your Estonians, I don't fancy your British friend will hold out long.'

'I hope you're right, Hilt. Because this Hartmoor guy couldn't have picked a worse moment to turn up.'

ELEVEN

It was dusk by the time Lynch left Tony Chalhoub to his crime scene and drove over to Marcelle's club. He pushed open the stage door and headed down the dark, burgundy-plush corridor to her office, pushing past a girl wearing a black basque and little else, her purple lipstick curled around a Marlboro, her dark eyes contemptuous in her milky-white face. The place smelled of cigarettes and booze, the dark walls were scratched. Someone had scored an arrowed heart into the plaster. Lynch pushed the door at the end of the passageway open and went in.

She was chatting on her mobile, her husky voice dropping as she glanced up at him. He waited for her to finish the call, wandering over to the picture window set in the far wall.

'*Shou*, Lynch. Why you never knock?'

The angled windows looked down onto the club's stage, the darkness alleviated by the waves of yellow-green light strobing with the pumping music. Two girls stood back-to-back, running their hands up their thighs, around to their bellies and over their breasts, synchronised with the music and each other. It was the first show of the night. They licked their lips and pulled on sullen nipples, their green-splashed buttocks swinging together in a lazy arc, mechanical grinding, a camshaft made flesh. Gerald Lynch looked down onto the smattering of heads watching the show. About half of them glittered in the slow lurid beats of light.

'Why the fuck are you still putting this cat show on, Marcie?'

Marcelle wore a crimson ball gown cut down her back to display the fine curve of her gorgeous spine as it plunged into darkness. 'Because it still brings in punters, Lynch. Here, you wanted this.' She tossed a little slice of plastic at him.

He caught the memory key. 'What's this?'

'A dead man fucking, Lynch. You'll enjoy watching it, I'm sure.'

'Lance Browning? You heard then?' Lynch pocketed the key.

'Jesus, Lynch, all of Beirut's talking about it. He was a fool and a pervert, but he didn't deserve this.'

'You've had no visitors, then.'

Marcelle stood at the drinks cabinet sparkling on the wall opposite the one-way window down to the public part of her writhing little emporium. She turned, curiosity mingled with contempt on her rich features. 'Visitors?'

'The people who killed Browning are looking for a man. They might look here. Browning would have given them this place while he was begging for his life.'

'Which man?'

'You don't know him.'

'But you do.'

Lynch nodded.

'So the reason they've got a link to here is you used my room to hassle Browning. Thanks, Lynch.'

Lynch shrugged. 'That's the way things play out sometimes. Like I say, beef up your security. They're not nice boys.'

'Who are they?' Marcelle lifted a bottle from the fridge.

'I don't know and that's the truth. I'm hearing people talking about two pale Russians dressed in black. But that's about the long and short of it. And whoever these two are, they're making a mess. They killed Abbas Ali's driver yesterday, over in Manara.'

Marcelle frowned, a frosted champagne bottle in her hand. 'What's that old crook got to do with them?'

'I wish I knew. What's with the champagne?

'We're celebrating.'

She popped the cork and handed Lynch a flute, filling it from the green and gold-labelled bottle. She poured, twisted the neck with a finishing flourish. 'Santé, Lynch.'

'So what's the occasion?'

'We're moving the club. I found a new place in Hamra. Monot is last year's thing. I missed out on Gemmayze because I stuck with here, now I've got somewhere lined up where the young crowd is going.'

Lynch gestured at the bald heads below. The intertwined girls on the stage were tonguing each other, the lights had turned into reds and pinks. 'You sure you want a young crowd?' He sipped the champagne. 'What is this stuff?'

'Lamiable. It's rare, an extra brut. Michel Freij used to insist on drinking this and no other champagne. I had to ship it in especially for the bastard. This is the last of his stock.'

Lynch tilted his flute. 'To Michel Freij.'

'No. To the future.'

Lynch caught her earnest expression, a rare thing to find in Marcelle. He nodded. 'To the future, then. A nice, simple future would be nice.'

They clinked glasses. Her scent was heady, her skin glowed. The champagne was dry, a fine treat and Lynch sipped again, viewing the little dancing bubbles against the halogen lights.

His mobile rang.

'Tony.' Lynch poised, his head cocked to the side. 'Okay, understood. At Marcie's. Right. See you in ten.'

Lynch tossed back the champagne. 'I have to go. Marcie, tell Hassan to go heavy on security tonight, those two Russian bastards tortured Lance Browning and I can guarantee he gave them this place.'

She sipped the champagne, a waxy red imprint on the fine glass. 'I'll take care, Lynch. Remember who has always wiped whose nose around here.'

Lynch smiled and handed back the flute. Marcelle stood and darted forward to kiss him on the lips. '*Yallah*, go, Lynch. Take care.'

*

They drove along the empty Corniche road, the streetlights picking out a few shadowed pedestrians. It was getting late, the traffic was sparse. Lynch slumped in the passenger seat, wordlessly gawping out of the windscreen as Chalhoub raced to their rendezvous in *Ain El Tineh*, the seaside area of West Beirut near the popular Raouché Rocks, as much a symbol of Beirut as the Cedar.

The two great rocks of Raouché loomed to their right, arcing out of the moonlit Mediterranean, the white-stippled waves surrounding them. Chalhoub punched Lynch's shoulder.

'Wake up, we're nearly there.'

Lynch shifted, snarling. 'I wasn't asleep, you fecker. I was thinking. You should try it, does wonders for the mind.'

Chalhoub glanced across his mirrors, his mouth tightening with wry amusement. 'Have you ever met Abbas Ali before?'

'Not in person, so to say. But I know of him. The man's a complete bastard altogether.'

'Oh yes,' said Chalhoub, steering left away from the Corniche and into Ain El Tineh, 'he is most certainly that. He started out in the Civil War, a family business growing cannabis. None of the militias could be bothered with him, he was small fry and by the time any of them had thought to check out how well he was doing, he already had hooks into them all. He sold heroin to the Israelis, coke to the Saudis and hash to the Europeans. By the end of the war, he owned pretty much every politician in the country. There's a testament to what you can achieve if you can get over the sectarian divides.'

'What about the Syrians?'

Chalhoub laughed. 'It's a legend, you know. The one time they sent Lebanese army troops to trek up to his village in the Bekaa and close him down, they were headed off by a Syrian army unit. There was total confusion, of course.'

'And his bag is still drugs, right?'

'Oh, he's bigger than that now. He's got investments in property here and abroad, a chain of clubs, a few hotels. His company's even got an office building downtown, all smoked glass. But he stays in Chatila. They love him there, Lynch, he's like the uncrowned king of the place.'

'What about Hezbollah?'

'They leave each other well enough alone. He's been known to do favours for them. They don't mess with Abbas Ali. He's done more for the people of Chatila than the government ever did and possibly even more than Hezbollah. Like them he recognises grass-roots popularity begins with helping poverty. It's very Lebanese. From his badness and the misery he spreads, he does good and alleviates misery. We're complicated like that.'

'Yeah, right. So we've got a proper Robin Hood, then.' Lynch reached over to switch on the car's air conditioning. He was feeling drowsy and wanted a clear head for their encounter with Abbas Ali the criminal philanthropist.

Abbas Ali was jerked out of his reverie by one of his men stepping into the room, his voice urgent. 'They are here, *sidi*. Will we bring them up?'

He mooned around. The place had belonged to a professor of English at the American University of Beirut and was furnished in a slightly fussy imitation of what the man, a Palestinian, had thought an English country house should look like. It had a rose patterned sofa set around a mahogany coffee table, a mock-Edwardian dining table with a gold plaster chandelier above it, a teak dresser and a reproduction Victorian carving table. There were shelves of leather-bound books. Above the marble fireplace hung a copy of Millais' drowned 'Ophelia' in a massive gold frame.

He lit a Marlboro Light and grunted at his man. 'Yes, bring them.'

He had barely settled in the armchair before the door opened and two men waved the cop Anthony Chalhoub and the Englishman into the room. Abbas Ali had come across

Chalhoub in the past. He always looked like that dog, what was it called? The English one – a beagle, that's the one. Chalhoub looked like a beagle, those big, doleful eyes and the bags around them. Abbas Ali was amused by the beagle reference. The Englishman was interesting, something violent about the man. He was around six feet, maybe a little less. Blue eyes in a snub-nosed face that belonged out on the street kicking footballs around, but something about the set of him that said the ragamuffin would turn into something altogether less pleasant. Abbas Ali didn't like the smell of this one.

Chalhoub was smiling, his hand held out. 'A long time, *ustaz*. This is a friend from the British Embassy, Gerald Lynch.'

Abbas Ali waited until his men closed the door behind them before taking Chalhoub's hand. He turned to Lynch. 'Welcome to Beirut, Mr Lynch. Is this your first time?'

He sensed Lynch's pause before the man took his hand, smiling. 'Yes, thank you. It's a pleasure to be here.'

'Please, take a seat. This flat used to belong to an English, I thought you'd feel comfortable here.'

Lynch sat, smiling, smoothing his trouser leg. 'I'm Irish, but the thought is appreciated.'

He turned to Chalhoub. 'What can I do to help you, Mr Chalhoub?'

'We wondered why you were involved in a gang war with the Russians, actually.' It was Lynch who had spoken and he turned to the man, blinking at the unexpected directness. The ash fell off his cigarette onto his trouser leg. Abbas Ali brushed at it.

'*Shou*? A gang what?'

Lynch leaned back on the sofa. 'A gang war. You know, your driver getting his throat slashed outside one of your safe houses and his corpse decorated with your microphones. That's what they called him, wasn't it? The Driver?'

Abbas Ali flicked his cigarette into the ashtray. 'I heard he had been in an accident.'

Chalhoub leaned forwards. 'And Lance Browning?'

His glance flicked between the two of them. 'Lance *meen*?'

Lynch was smiling. 'Browning. Don't fuck about, Abbas Ali. Your men were spotted near his home this morning. The same knife killed both your driver and Browning. You don't need to see the forensic report to know that. Your driver was killed cleanly, but Browning took hours to die. So what was this, your revenge?'

He laughed, taking a last deep draw of his cigarette before stubbing it out. He placed his hands on the arms of the chair.

'I am sorry you gentlemen have the wrong end of the sticks. I do not know this Browning. I am think maybe my driver die in unfortunate accident. I have no reason why there is any warfare like you describe. *Bass*, I do not like to waste more time on this.'

Lynch snapped forwards, his hand chopping the air. 'Who are the Russians, Abbas Ali?'

Halfway to his feet, Abbas Ali's triceps tensed to take his weight. He turned to face Lynch. 'Russians? What Russians?' He tried to slow his thumping heart. He waited, glaring, for Lynch to say something. He pushed himself to his feet. He held out his hand to Chalhoub.

'Thank you for your visit, *ya shorteh*.'

Lynch wouldn't stand. 'Let me try a story on you, Abbas Ali. The two men who killed your driver are Russians. You were going to put them up in your safe house, but they found you had bugged it. The police have the bugs on the driver's body and they checked the state of your apartment in the building next to his body. The concierge talks too much. They always do.'

'I do not know these men, Mr Lynch. Goodbye.'

The door was open and men waited. Chalhoub left, Lynch lagged behind.

Lynch's bright eyes were laughing. 'You know what I think Abbas Ali?'

Abbas Ali flicked a glance at his men and they moved into the chintzy room.

Lynch stood his ground. 'I think you're in the crap, my old son. I think you're way out of your depth. And you're running fucking scared right now.'

'Get this piece of shit out of my house.' Abbas Ali snapped in Arabic at his men, the veins in his neck pulsing.

'Just drop me in town, Tony. I got some errands to do.'

'Sure. Sodeco do you?'

'Gouraud, if that's alright.'

Chalhoub chuckled. 'You wanna party now?'

'Just some errands.'

'So what did you make of Abbas Ali?'

Lynch shrugged. 'Like I said, he's out of his depth. He rattled too easily.'

'I don't get it, you see,' Chalhoub muttered. 'His men were at Browning's house, but they weren't part of the house party, so either they were guarding these two Russian nutters or they were following them. His driver's dead, so I'd say they were following. He'd have had them killed if they were encroaching on his territory, so he must be scared to act or perhaps biding his time. For sure Abbas Ali's involved with this, but we don't know how.'

Lynch peered out of the window at the shadowed streets. 'But he's in over his head.'

They reached Martyrs' Square as it gave into Gouraud Street and Lynch clapped Chalhoub on the shoulder. 'Thanks Tony. I'll let you know if anything else happens my side, okay?'

Lynch slammed the door and stood in the shadow of a lamppost, watching the Audi's taillights consumed by distance. He turned and started walking uphill towards his favourite late night bar. He tossed back a brace of whiskies and left a few dollars on the bar-top rather than wait for the barman, who'd disappeared to change the music.

He took a *servees* to Bourj Hammoud, paying the driver off

before walking across the road and flagging another after a short wait in the shadows. He headed to Monot, picked up the parked BMW and drove North through the deserted streets, taking the road up into the hills and a villa at the end of a gravel drive that snaked up from the winding hill road.

Two dark figures detached themselves from the shadows near the villa. Both carried pistols. They flanked Lynch who twisted left and right to shake hands. They entered the house together wordlessly.

Hartmoor was playing patience in the living room. It was well past midnight. The villa still smelled of cooking. He glanced up as Lynch entered, distaste on his drawn features. Lynch, acutely aware Hartmoor hadn't had his enzyme pills, held his palms out. 'I am sorry for this inconvenience, Jason, but I have reason to believe your life is in terrible danger.' Lynch ignored Hartmoor's dry, barking laugh and pressed on. 'I brought the clothes and pills from your hotel; they're on the bed in your room. Your suite had been pretty comprehensively ransacked. We believe there are two extremely dangerous men looking for you, quite apart from the CIA's unhealthy interest in you. Lance Browning has been tortured to death. Whatever you have become involved in is obviously a deadly affair. We have to keep you under protection until we know more. I hope you understand.'

Hartmoor gazed up. 'I am of no conceivable interest to anyone, Mr Lynch.'

Lynch shrugged as he placed a bottle of whiskey and two tumblers on the coffee table. 'I'm sorry to disagree, but you're very wrong. Everybody and his uncle seems interested in you.'

Lynch sauntered through to the kitchen returning a few seconds later with a glass filled with ice cubes and a little jug of water.

Lynch held the jug, his little finger raised and a smile on his lips. 'Water?'

Lynch waited. Hartmoor's lips tightened, then he relaxed and sighed. 'Just water. I can't drink alcohol. The painkillers.'

Lynch placed a recorder on the table. 'Are you too tired?'

'No, you're fine.' Hartmoor sipped his water. 'I snoozed earlier.'

'Did you eat?'

'Yes. Not bad for army food.'

'Do you need your enzymes now?'

'No, no it's too late. But I can eat well enough in the morning now. Thanks. Better late than never.'

'This will be a formal interview. Are you still sure?'

'Yes,' Hartmoor's voice carried a hint of weariness. 'I am quite, quite sure.'

Lynch nodded and spoke into the device. 'Interview with Jason Hartmoor, formerly of the Foreign and Commonwealth Office. Can you please confirm your identity, sir?'

'I am Jason Charles Hartmoor.'

'What brings you to Lebanon after such a long absence, Mr Hartmoor?' Lynch sat back.

'I am not a well man and wanted to catch up with some of the places and people I had known in my past. I have not had the opportunity to visit Lebanon since the outbreak of the Civil War, when I was stationed here.'

'You recently returned to Shemlan, the former site of the Middle East Centre for Arab Studies. May I ask why?'

Hartmoor passed a hand over his brow. The gesture left a smear of moisture from the glass on the blue-veined skin. 'For that very reason. Catching up.'

'With Mai Khoury?'

Hartmoor glared at Lynch. He leaned forwards. His voice was barely a whisper. 'What do you know about Mai Khoury?'

Lynch had picked up the file waiting for him on his tablet when he'd returned to the house. There was little enough there, but enough.

'I understand she's living in America and she's coming home for a visit. She's expected here soon, isn't she? Are you waiting for her? Why don't you tell me about it all?'

Hartmoor glared at Lynch, his aloofness punctured by naked hatred. 'How dare you poke about in my—'

'Past, Mr Hartmoor? Isn't the past the key to all this?'

Hartmoor stared at the glass in his hand. His shoulders sagged. 'Very well. Mai Khoury and I were lovers.'

Lynch tried to keep his voice gentle. 'You left Beirut. Can I ask why?'

'Because they closed the school, MECAS. It shut in November 1978 and I was one of the last students to leave. It was just as well, really. They were about to throw me out anyway.'

'Throw you out?'

'Our affair was something of a scandal. You weren't supposed to fraternise with the local women, it was the great taboo. Shemlan is a Christian village in a Druze area. The sheikhs of the village are Druze as well. There are five big families of Shemlan, the Hittis, Tabibs, Jabbours, Farajallahs and the Khourys. Mai used to joke that her family had lived there since the Middle Ages and were still considered blow-ins. It's a very insular community.'

'And they ran the restaurant there, the Cliff House.'

'*Al Sakhra*, yes. There was some unpleasantness with a cook there who had fancied his chances with Mai, a surly young man called Fadi. He was threatening to get physical but Frank Coleman stepped in. That was in our last week there, in fact.'

'Coleman?'

'He was a student on the short course. It wasn't normal for there to be Americans there, apparently, because MECAS was run by the FCO, but it did happen occasionally.' Hartmoor pulled a wry face. 'Funding, you see?'

'More than you can begin to guess. So you had to leave.'

'Looking back on it I'm surprised they ever let us go there.

The Civil War effectively started in 1975, although everyone always believed it would settle down again, but by 1978 it was getting pretty hairy. They used to post a list of roads that were open day by day, there were Syrian tanks stationed in the village and we regularly heard rocket fire from above us aiming down into the city. The final straw was a bomb that was set off against one of the school's walls. So halfway through his speech to me about how I'd ruined thirty years of the villagers' trust, Probert lets me know it doesn't matter because he was sending us home anyway.'

'Probert being the director of the Centre.'

'Yes. He never liked me and I can't say I liked him either. Not since I arrived three days late and got a dressing-down in my first minute there.'

'So did you not want to go back for this girl? You loved her, right?'

Hartmoor gazed down at his hands. 'I did, yes. Did love her and did want to go back. Initially I couldn't because there was an FCO travel ban. Then I was posted to Baghdad. We wrote to each other all the time. And then her letters just stopped.' Hartmoor shrugged. 'I met Lesley.'

'And moved on.'

Lynch felt sorry for Hartmoor, then. The man looked utterly lost, his wan face bleak and those washed-out blue eyes gazing unseeing into the past. He opened and closed his mouth a couple of times. His shoulders slumped. 'I suppose. I held out, but it seemed as if it had all been a dream. Unreal, somehow. Life moved on and when her letters stopped I…' Hartmoor's hands were together. 'I wrote and wrote, you see. But nothing. So I let… I tried…'

Lynch let the silence ride for a while. He tried to keep his voice gentle. 'Going back to Frank Coleman…'

Hartmoor's pallor was waxen and there were beads of sweat on his forehead. 'I was just about to. You see, I met Frank at a conference in London and he explained the postal system had broken down. He agreed to take a letter to Mai for me and so I wrote to her, explaining I had married. Frank had told me so had she; he occasionally went up to eat at the restaurant. I told her…' Hartmoor paused and Lynch remained very quiet and very still. 'I told her I thought we had both made a mistake marrying, but that we could stay in touch by post at least. She replied and agreed. We used a post box in Syria. Deliveries over the mountain were pretty reliable. We kept in touch for many, many years.'

'But you never came back.'

'No. I wanted to, God knows I wanted to.' Hartmoor straightened, his voice strengthening. 'But she had a family. What would I achieve other than breaking up her family?'

'And when your own marriage broke down?'

Lynch sat back in his chair and sipped his whiskey, waiting for Hartmoor's glare to subside.

'Lesley was drinking. Rather too much latterly and it all became de trop. I realised I had married the wrong woman, I should have known that from the start. There was a scene at a French embassy reception in Riyadh, where I was vice consul. It was the final straw.'

'She claims you hit her.'

Hartmoor flinched as if he had been slapped on the face himself. His glance at Lynch was part anger, part horror. He put his head in his hands and swept them back over his hair. His eyes met Lynch's again. 'And so I did. I put her to bed and she got up again, found me writing to Mai in the study. She was still drunk. There was a scene. And I hit her. Once. Never before, never again.'

'I have to admire your candour.'

'If not my morals.'

'I can understand. That must surely have been the time to go back to Beirut.'

'No,' Hartmoor shook his head. 'No, not then. I met Frank and he talked me down off the ledge.'

'You were seeing an awful lot of Frank Coleman, surely?'

'We moved in the same circles. It was the Cold War. We were on the same side.'

'Unlike Jaan Kallas.'

'I didn't know him at all, Lynch. I met him once at a reception, I told you. I only remembered the name because he was an unusually striking man, very Teutonic. Cold and haughty.'

'Did you know any other Soviets?'

'No, none.'

'Ever contact any Soviets?'

'No, none.'

Hartmoor's head was back in his hands and Lynch watched him shuddering. Seeing moisture seep between the pale fingers he realised, with horror, Hartmoor was crying.

Lynch's mobile was ringing. He clicked the recorder off and left the room to answer it with relief. Meadows and Henderson were playing cards in the kitchen over mugs of tea. He returned their enquiring glances with an upraised thumb on his way out to the dark cool of the garden.

Channing was urgent. 'How's it going, Gerald?'

'I've been talking to him on the record just now. It's one o'clock here and the man's exhausted. This guy is totally clean, Brian, I'd swear it.'

'Every piece of compromised information obtained by the Americans from source Dmitri, and sent to us back then for corroboration was contemporaneous with him, Gerald. Nobody else could have established this pattern of leaks. Nobody else was in those right places at the right times. He's got a controller somewhere. He's toxic. Press harder. As hard as it takes. You understand me?'

'No. I'm stupid, Brian. Tell me in words of one syllable. In fact, preferably, put it in writing that you want me to rough-house a distinguished former member of the diplomatic service who has terminal cancer.'

Lynch savoured the mildly fragrant night air. Frangipani. He desperately wanted a cigarette. Channing was silent, which suited Lynch fine. He waited, pulling one of his two remaining cigars out of his jacket pocket. He bit the end of one with a twinge of regret for treating a Cohiba so. He reached in the kitchen door for the little book of matches by the cooker and went back outside to the evening air. He lit up gratefully.

Exhaling, he gave Channing the little victory of breaking the silence. 'He vets clean, Brian. I swear he's clean.'

'The Yanks say he makes Aldritch Ames look like a schoolgirl. They're baying for Hartmoor's blood, but they're being very coy indeed about Dmitri. They don't know for sure we've got Hartmoor, so do keep it that way, would you? They wanted to know what your business with him was and I told Hilton you had merely picked him up for a routine chat and left him back at his hotel. They suspect, of course, but they can't be sure. They have offered their full co-operation in finding Hartmoor. I've never known them so evasive and yet so demanding.'

Lynch drew on the cigar, its tip glowing against the vague corona of light pollution from Beirut below to the South. 'I'd be worried for his life, Brian. First thing he does when he gets into town is try and contact Frank Coleman and the Yanks put a profiling team on him, so he hits some sort of red button for them. Second thing he does is take an HSBC staffer called Lance Browning out to dinner and now Browning's been tortured to death by two Russian hoods. A lot of people would appear to have a distinctly unhealthy interest in Mr Jason Hartmoor.'

'Hang on. Browning.' A patter of keys. 'Yes, got him. British Bank of the Middle East. He'd have been at MECAS same time as Hartmoor. He's HSBC now. What do you mean, Russian hoods?'

'According to eyewitnesses, the men that did Browning are Russians. Browning had dinner with Hartmoor on Tuesday. He was tortured to death yesterday morning. It wasn't pretty. Hartmoor's hotel room has been turned over. Reception IDs the same pair. This location's secure, but I'm starting to wonder how long for.'

There was a long silence from Channing. 'Are your escorts doing well?'

'Fine. We're okay for the moment, but it's heating up around here and I do not trust Dennis Wye and his merry men from Langley one jot, Brian. Not one jot. So, yes, I'd actually be truly grateful if we continued not to tell our friends that Mr Hartmoor is staying with us.'

'Well, you may have to leave him with the SAS boys. We have a lead on Dmitri, which may explain why you have a Soviet angle developing there. We're relatively certain he was a Russian Defence Ministry officer seconded to Syrian Intelligence as an advisor during the Lebanese Civil War.'

Lynch coughed. 'Christ, Brian, there were thousands of the bastards.'

'Yes, but there's one thing that makes him stand out. According to the analytics people, of all the things Dmitri was, he wasn't a Russian. Which makes him a rare animal given he was a high ranker in the Russian military. He was Estonian.'

'Same as the guy Hartmoor mentioned. Kallas.'

'Quite. Jaan Kallas is a former Soviet official and currently one of the most powerful oligarchs in Estonia. He's serious money. We've been talking to the Estonians. He's marked high-grade untouchable, whiter than white. There are strong political links all over the place. Getting anything out of him is going to be a long game. If Kallas and Dmitri link, it means a major Estonian businessman has longstanding links to American Intelligence. Which hardly seems interesting, unless he's bent.'

Lynch whistled. 'But it might explain why two hoods have suddenly turned up here and shown a distinctly unhealthy interest in our man. Everyone thinks they're Russian, but they're not, are they? They're Estonian. Which makes your major

Estonian businessman a hood too, doesn't it? So what next?'

'We rather thought it was worth asking the Syrians. There's been a change of guard, as you know. Your old friend has retired. He's one of the very few people who could make that link.'

'Junaidi? What's he doing?'

'Festering in Aleppo. We booked you on tomorrow morning's flight. Details are on secure mail to you, including an e-ticket as if you had booked yourself. There's a visa in your cover name on their system. Have a nice trip.'

'You're a pretty highly paid travel agent, aren't you Brian?'

'Find out what Dmitri's protecting before I lose your funding, you hear?'

Channing cut the line. Lynch shivered and went back into the warmth of the kitchen. In the living room, Jason Hartmoor sat staring sightlessly out of the window. He turned as Lynch came in, his red-rimmed eyes filled with a terrible desolation that stopped Lynch in his tracks. Hartmoor tried to smile, but failed.

'I'm sorry. I'm too tired. I have to go to bed. Maybe we could continue tomorrow. I want to help, really. But I'm not terribly strong these days.'

Lynch tried to modulate his voice, to keep his tones gentle. 'It's okay. I have to go away tomorrow, anyway. But please tell me you will bear with me as we progress this enquiry. Your life is genuinely in grave danger and yes, I know it is forfeit anyway, but I would actually, believe this or not, like to see you meet Mai Khoury and if I can't work out what is going on here, you may not have that opportunity.'

'I'm indebted to you, Gerald. Truly. No sarcasm.'

'Meadows and Henderson will look after you. They'll protect you until I get back. I'm sorry to cause you all this upset, but you're safer here.'

'I quite understand. At least, I think I could possibly come to understand.'

Lynch held out his hand and, after a second's hesitation, Hartmoor took it.

Hassan was waiting outside the villa at seven in a cheap hire car to take Lynch to the airport. Meadows and Russell were already watchful. Channing had thoughtfully booked him the early morning flight to Amman. The Aleppo flight didn't depart from there until past five in the afternoon. Lynch stared darkly out at the passing countryside as they sped towards Rafiq Hariri International, wishing he could spit in Channing's coffee.

Hassan interrupted Lynch's brooding. 'The Russians, they come last night to the club.'

Lynch shifted in his seat. 'Did they so? How come you're still in one piece?'

Hassan shrugged and brushed his white moustache with his smoker's yellowed forefinger. 'They are not so good, these people. We are ready for them. They ask about this Browning. Then they ask for you. Marcelle she tell them get lost. They have gun, but we have more. I bring Ali, Jad, Faisal and Shukri, all. They cry a little, they leave. *Khalas* Russians.'

Lynch was urgent. 'Listen, old friend. They're not Russian, they're Estonian and they'll be back. They're very, very bad news those two. Take care of yourself, bring extra muscle. Do not for one second think that's the end of it. Look after Marcelle, get her away from there for the next few days. Send her to Hamra to play with her new place, whatever. Just keep her away.'

Hassan laughed. 'Marcelle? As she would do like I say?'

'Ask her, beg her. Whatever it takes, Hassan. I'm dead serious.'

'*Shou*, Lynch, you are scared of them?'

Lynch pondered the question. 'Yes, Hassan. Yes, I am scared of them. They're evil little bastards and they like to hurt people. They're psychopaths. Please, take me seriously.'

Hassan nodded. 'Okay, Lynch, Okay. We take care too much, okay?'

Lynch scanned Hassan's face, satisfied he'd been taken seriously. 'Sure, okay.'

TWELVE

Hartmoor opened his eyes. The receding confusion of dreams still in his mind clashed with the familiar feeling of relief. A dog being chased had run to him, turned into a bird, a dove. Where had that come from? Dreams so often eluded him, the wisps of sleepy memory departing as he assembled his routine and brought it to order. These days, he tried to bring them back, to relish them. Especially when he dreamed of the girl in the little room above the street in Khartoum. Each time the recurring dream left Hartmoor in a state of horror, but underneath the duvet was the truth, a reaction he rarely encountered these days.

There was a knock on the door.

'Come,' Hartmoor called, his voice throaty. He took a sip of water from the glass on the bedside table. The room was pleasant, plain and white with wicker furnishing.

Meadows peered around the door and stepped in, a cup of tea in his hand. 'We didn't know if you took sugar or not, sir.'

Hartmoor smiled. 'I don't as it happens. Thank you very much, that's very kind of you both.'

Meadows retreated. 'We reckoned a spot of breakfast in about half an hour, sir?'

'You don't have to go to any bother on my account.'

'It's no trouble, sir. We're sort of making hay, if you like. This isn't one of the toughest jobs we've ever had. Our last tour was Kabul.'

Hartmoor wanted to laugh. 'I quite understand. I'll be there in precisely thirty minutes, sergeant.'

'Right you are, sir.'

The door closed and Hartmoor pushed himself up in the bed. He reached for the glittering foil strip of Roxanol capsules, popping one out and swallowing it with a sip of water. He was always tempted to crush them all in his teeth and go out in a blissful head-rush, but never quite tempted enough. He took a second sip of water to wash down his digestive enzymes.

The tea was strong and reminded him of school for some reason. He flopped back onto the bed and waited for the drugs to drive away the burgeoning ache. The past flooded into his mind as he lay back, the taste of the tea fresh in his mouth. He closed his eyes and travelled back to 1978, those last hours in Beirut.

Jason had drunk tea that last morning too, before leaving MECAS and Shemlan. Mai had insisted on taking him to the airport. He sold his Mini-Moke for a few pounds to the village butcher's son, who had wasted no time in spraying the little jeep-like car in dun-coloured camouflage. Mai had borrowed her father's Mercedes, a magnificent car that the constant fuel shortages kept garaged for at least twenty-eight days of each month. Jason and Mai sponged two precious gallons of diesel from the Syrian tank crew installed in the village in return for English cigarettes. Jason's Arabic, reasonably fluent by now, wasn't quite up to the task of negotiating with soldiers over black market fuel. And he didn't quite have, he admitted ruefully as the soldiers pretended to be gallant but devoured Mai with greedy eyes, the charm.

It was a misty, damp morning but already the August sun was starting to chase the blueness away from the mountainside. The city below was silent, but as they slowed for a Syrian checkpoint outside Aley they heard the distant crack of small arms fire and the deeper concussions of a mortar. Neither they nor the soldiers reacted to the percussive sounds, part of the daily routine. As they drove along the quiet road through Bchamoun, a Katyusha launcher high on the mountainside roared defiant fire into the blue sky, the grey vapour trails of multiple rockets arcing overhead to drop far away in West Beirut. They heard the detonations, the car's wheels clanking against the storm drain grilles traversing the road. More small arms fire, then a tremendous explosion closer by. Jason reached over to steady the wheel in Mai's hand as she flinched.

'Don't worry, now. We'll be fine.'

She laughed. 'You, perhaps. You are leaving this place, no?'

He gripped the wheel, knuckles white and his voice urgent. 'So can you be. Come with me. I love you. Come away with me.'

She shot a cool glance across at him, picking his fingers off her steering wheel. 'You know I cannot do this, Jason. I have to stay with my family. These are not good times.'

Exasperated, Jason clenched his hands in his lap and looked out on the passing stone-clad houses and bright shop-fronts as they reached the bottom of the mountain road and passed into the highway. There was little traffic, a combination of the early hour and the raging tide of civil war. Machine gun fire tore out a tattoo nearby.

The buildings around them were pockmarked with bullet holes, smooth concrete riddled with crazy patterns, a head-sized hole in a building surrounded by the odd splashy shape of shrapnel, a little sculpture preserving a moment of unfolding steel destruction and white heat. Windows were shattered, cars abandoned by the roadside, their windscreens gone and tyres blown out.

This was the detritus of war and it shocked Jason. He had seen it before coming down to the city, but they had been too safe and cosy in their mountain. Only now he was leaving did he appreciate the danger they had come to accept as a minor everyday convenience.

'Are we all mad?' He asked himself. His hand was on Mai's thigh, he could feel her muscles flex as she worked the clutch. In that instant he wanted her, all the more because he knew it was impossible. Jason was going to the airport, the black holdall in the back seat packed with his clothes, a wet bag and thousands of white word-cards, bundled together in precise hundreds with elastic bands.

He could stay, he thought. Resign the FCO. To hell with

them. He could make his living in the mountains. He could live wild, do maintenance work, be a waiter in the restaurant. Teach English to the spoilt children of the rich studying at AUB. Those who were staying, at least.

There was a checkpoint ahead, a big one. The Israeli invasion of the South had driven the Palestinians north and now they were asserting themselves over the Western suburbs, while the Syrians were fighting the Christian militia deeper in the heart of the city. Sure enough, the checkpoint was PLO.

'Papers,' in Arabic. A bored young man in a shabby camouflage uniform, his palm held out. Jason handed his passport and the man riffled through it. Jason doubted he read English, it was just an indifferent show. 'Who is she?'

'From Shemlan. She is taking me to the airport.'

'*Shou*? She is a taxi?'

'A friend.'

'Papers.'

Mai handed her passport across to Jason, who offered it up to the PLO man.

'Wait here.'

Jason turned to Mai. 'What do we do? He has our passports.'

'It's okay, Jason. We just wait here, like he said. Are you scared you might have to stay behind?'

Jason looked up at her but she was smiling, her eyes warm and sad. He took her hand. 'There's nothing I want more. Maybe I can pay him to keep them?'

Mai glanced out of the window. 'He's coming back. He has company.'

A PLO officer, silver-haired and running to weight. His eyes were too close together and his fleshy nose dominated his heavy-jowled face. He leaned into the car, a smell of sweat and pomade.

He spoke in English, waving Jason's passport. 'You are English?'

'Yes. I am just going to the airport.'

The fat face was comical. 'Why? You don't like Beirut?'

'I do like Beirut very much. But everything must come to an end.'

'Oh yes, English. That is true. *Bass*, I don't like Beirut. These people,' he waved towards Mai, 'they think we are cockroaches, like the Israelis do. Too many feet wanting to stamp on us. What you think, English?'

Jason was sweating too now, the sweet smell of the man's perfume and stench of his body cloying. 'I think there are too many people fighting in Lebanon today against each other when they could be fighting together. Israel has made fools of them by invading their country.'

The officer's chuckle was throaty. 'Israel made fools of us Palestinians too, didn't they, English? After you gave them our country. Here, *Ingleezi*, go and run away with your *sharmouta* to the airport.'

Jason's instinctive grab for the door handle was halted by Mai taking his arm on the one side and the AK47 in his face on the other. *Sharmouta* – whore. The distinctive clacking of the Russian machine gun being cocked rang out.

'Leave it, Jason. We must go. He's only trying to provoke you.' Mai put the car in gear and inched away from the checkpoint, speeding up as they got clear. The tension left Jason. He turned to her to see the tears streaming down her cheeks.

'Mai. What is it?'

'This. All this. This stupid war. You leaving. Everything is changing and nothing for the better. It's... oh, just forget it. I'm being stupid. Pass me a tissue would you?'

Jason plucked tissues from the ornate little box on the passenger-side dashboard and handed them to her and she dabbed at her eyes. The look she gave him was heart-rending, the sadness in her a desolation that he felt himself.

They kissed at the airport, kissed and kissed until a security guard tapped Jason on the shoulder and mumbled an admonition. The tannoy called out Jason's flight and he tore himself away from her, the ink coming off the BA ticket to stain his sweaty hand as he waved goodbye to her and shouted out that he would write, he would be back, he loved her, he would call. He would return to her quickly, get their permission so he could travel.

Meadows' gentle knocking startled him. Hartmoor called out, surprised at how feeble his voice sounded. 'Sorry. Coming.'

He slid out of the bed and into the bathroom where he showered as quickly as was decent, shaved and dressed. His face in the mirror was drawn and his skin was acquiring an unhealthy grey pallor.

He walked into the kitchen to find Henderson reading a newspaper at the kitchen table. It smelled of breakfast, fried bacon, toast and coffee. The extractor was humming over the cooker. Henderson stood, folding the paper. 'Nice to see you sir. Question of the day – fried or poached? And do you prefer 'em runny or cooked to death?'

'I rather think poached and runny, Mr Henderson. This is very kind of you.'

'Nothing, sir. It's a lovely morning, why don't you take a seat outside? I'll be with you in just a tick.'

Hartmoor picked his way out to the sunny patio behind the villa to find a cast iron garden table bedecked with a red-checked cloth, laid for breakfast for one. It was cool but the little suntrap took the edge off the freshness. Meadows appeared. 'Coffee, sir?'

He smiled. 'Coffee would be splendid, thank you so much.'

Meadows disappeared and Hartmoor sat at his table looking out over the garden and, beyond it, glimpses of faraway Beirut below them. It was a different angle down to the city from that of Shemlan, seeing the city from above to the East rather than the West. An odd mirror image of his memories, the city was so much bigger now.

He shook his head, the late winter sunlight warming him and the growing dull pain in his throat turning into shameful tears. He reached out for the napkin to dab at his eyes.

Meadows reappeared with a cafétiere in one hand and a plate in the other. A perfect poached egg, two rashers of crisp, streaky bacon, mushroom, sausage and beans. Behind him, Henderson balanced a glass of orange juice, a rack of toast, a butter-dish and a jar of Oxford marmalade. The two men were chuckling at Hartmoor's reaction as they placed everything on the table.

'Tuck in, sir,' said Meadows. 'We've had our scran already and we need to do a bit of patrolling around, but if you need anything just whistle and we'll hear yer.'

Hartmoor shook his head in wonderment. 'No, this is just beyond belief. Thank you so much.'

Henderson squatted, one hand on the table, one on Hartmoor's shoulder, his gaze direct. 'It's nothing, sir. We said already, this is a cushy job for us but we know you're having a hard time and anything we can do, you just ask us. We'll leave you to it now, sir.'

He met the kindly eyes, his own watery and weak. He tried to say something to the two of them but he was too late. They were gone.

He washed a Roxanol down with orange juice and started to eat. For the first time in months, he found he truly had an appetite. He chased the final mouthful around the plate with a piece of toast, mopping up the egg yolk and tomato sauce from the baked beans.

Sitting in the warmth, bathed in contentment, he cherished life.

THIRTEEN

Gerald Lynch blinked at the transition from the late afternoon sunlight to the cool darkness of Aleppo's covered souk. Wearing jeans and a plain white t-shirt under his leather jacket, scuffed sneakers and with a slim bag slung around his neck and over his shoulder, Lynch felt like a tourist as he caught curious glances from the crowds around him.

The souk was noisy, a bustling tide of people packing the narrow flagged street, a motor scooter welded to a trailer forging its way through the press. The stalls were brightly lit from inside, neon strips hung crazily from twisted wire stays. Broken fittings, sacks of flour, wheat, herbs and charcoal lined the way. *Poor* stores sold charcoal, tobacco, spices and sweets butted up against collections of pans and kitchen implements. Every available surface was used to store and display goods; ancient rusty nails driven into door frames held bags of candy floss, great bales of sponges or tied-together bundles of shower pipes.

Lynch slipped through the throng feeling lost as he tried to recall his way around the Ottoman labyrinth. He passed a man butchering a lamb, the carcass hanging from its back legs on a great hook, its blue-veined viscera shining as the knife slashed at it. He turned left off the busy street, passing shops stacked high with bolts of cloth, tailors working on ancient-looking sewing machines whirring away, their voices raised in cheerful conversation.

There it was, just as it had been all those years ago, the little shopfront hung with sequinned belly-dancer costumes and kandouras decorated with dangles of little brass coins.

Lynch stepped into the shop, pushing aside the clothing in

the doorway. The clamour of the souk was muffled by the dresses hanging on the walls. Towards the rear there were shelves of gold-decorated bottles, packets of solid *bakhour* perfumes and *mabkharas*, the little jars used to burn incense. Sitting behind a glass-topped tin desk was a thin man with bulbous mouse eyes. They flitted around the room, settling on Lynch then slipping away in an instant. The man sniffed, wiping the back of his hand under his nose. '*Salaam Aleykum affendi.*'

'Cut the crap, Selim. I want to see The General.'

The moist brown eyes danced around Lynch's face for a second. Selim cleared his throat, his hands raised to steeple in front of his reedy lips, which he licked constantly. He bobbed his head. 'It has been long time.'

'It has. The General.'

'Is not available. Times they have change.' Selim's features were screwed up in an exaggerated moue of regret. He shrugged. 'So sorry.'

'He will see me. Tell him I want to talk to him about Dmitri. Don't make me have to look for him, Selim. I'll only break things.'

Lynch slipped his hand into his leather shoulder bag. Selim's eyes flashed wide open.

'Wait,' Selim urged. He dashed into the tiny storeroom at the back of the shop. Lynch watched the man's profile highlighted by the mean orange light from the ancient bulb as he argued in an urgent tone on his mobile. Lynch ran his finger over a row of beads sewn onto a chemise and waited, amused by a crystal-studded bra glittering on its display stand.

Selim's hands were clasped together as he slid past the storeroom door. He stood behind his desk, his ceaseless eyes on Lynch. 'Come back tonight after eight.'

'Thank you, Selim.' Lynch waited for a response, but Selim stood silently glancing around his shop, his thin lips pressed together so hard they whitened.

Lynch shrugged and left.

The souk was busier at night, glowing with orange and blue light, voices raised as stallholders called out to customers and each other. Lynch retraced his steps, this time wearing a leather jacket against the cold night. He glanced around and entered the clothes shop.

Selim's rodent eyes would dart no more. He was slumped in his chair, his head lolled to one side. The room reeked of rust and Lynch marked the path of the great red stain from Selim's slit throat from the splashed glass top down to the dark pool under the desk. Lynch could imagine the arterial gouts, the terrible gurgling of a man held fast as he choked to death on his own blood.

Lynch was still lost in his macabre flight of fancy when the storeroom door swung back and a figure turned to face him. Pale faced, blond short-cropped hair and piercingly blue eyes, the man was wiping blood from his hands with a cloth. He grinned at Lynch, a diamond glittering on his right dogtooth. He threw down the cloth and whipped out a combat knife.

'*Sa oled surnud liha.*'

Lynch snatched at a handful of clothes and flung it at the killer. He wheeled around and fled out of the shop. He cannoned into a stout woman wearing an *abaya*, sending her flying and smashing his shoulder painfully on the wall. Outraged voices shouted at him as he ran as fast as he could in the crowds, colliding with people and pushing back at the heroes putting out their hands to try and stop him.

Snatching a glance behind, he could see his pursuer struggling to make his way through the livid wake. For a moment he struggled with the possibility the other Estonian was waiting up ahead, but the souk was too complicated for games like that. Lynch's breath rasped in this throat as he jinked through the laneway, caroming off a spice display and upending it as his arms flailed to stay upright against his own mad momentum. He regained his balance, his legs pumping as he saw the opening of the Antakya Gate. With a last surge of desperate energy, he jumped for the ledge that ran along the city walls from the gate, scrambling to find footholds in the pitted, ancient walls.

He pulled himself up to stand, his back pressed against the cold stone, to the side of the gate and looking down on the people entering and leaving the souk through the great ancient portal. His pursuer had lost ground to the chaos Lynch had left behind, precious seconds for Lynch as he watched the blonde man in black clothes burst out of the gate below him and slide to a halt. The man scanned the open streets around. Lynch dropped from the ledge, hitting the Estonian hard from above and behind, his hands looping around the pale man's neck as they fell together to the ground. Lynch wrenched with all the force at his command as they hit the flagstone street. He heard and felt the snap of the man's neck breaking a second before the crack of skull against stone.

The knife skittered across the flags into the shadows. Winded and in pain, Lynch forced himself to his knees, patting down the man's pockets. No documentation. A semi-circular tag of some sort on a silver necklace. He yanked it off.

Lynch pushed himself unsteadily to his feet. A crowd was gathering. Screaming, he ran at the collection of curious faces, the pack parting, hands held up in defence against him.

Lynch ran along the old citadel wall, his lungs heaving, finally giving up and collapsing against the stonework. He was alone, but the mob would soon send company his way. He flagged down a passing yellow cab.

'The Baron Hotel.' Lynch glanced behind to see some of the men had started to follow him. They stood, uncertain, watching his taxi. He checked his watch and winced in irritation. He'd have to go back into the souk at ten for the fallback meeting.

*

Lynch slipped into the ancient Armenian Church. He stood by the door and scanned the gloomy space, taking in the rich icons; ceiling fans dropped from the vaulted shadows, the complex altar area bathed in the warm light from two massive chandeliers. It was quiet in here, the hubbub of the souk forgotten in an instant. The cool air smelled faintly of frankincense.

Lynch stole to a middle pew and sat. He bowed his head, reflecting piously on the gun in his holster and the bottle of scotch in the carrier bag he had put down beside him. He waited, listening to the occasional creak of wood, the sandy shuffle of feet on marble and the odd echoed whisper.

The girl in front of him crossed herself and rose, walking past him toward the door. She paused, turned and spoke.

'Are you a friend of Bashar's? I seem to recognise you.'

Lynch looked up. Perhaps in her late twenties, she was raven-haired with skin so pale her blue veins showed. Long lashes framed dark eyes. Her full lips were generous but she was clothed meanly, her shoulders wrapped in a threadbare shawl.

'Bashar Junaidi? Yes, I am.'

Her smile was fleeting. 'Then you must surely follow me.'

Lynch slipped out of the church behind her as she led him into the darkest recesses of the old souk. They clambered up a stone stairwell to the upper level. She set a smart pace and Lynch, still aching, winced frequently as he tried to stay alongside her.

Finally they stopped by a doorway. 'Here,' she said. 'Please, don't excite him too much. It has been too long for him since these days of wars and spies.'

There were tears in her eyes. Lynch realised, damning his own stupidity, who she was. He had listened to her childish babble, watched her playing as he and The General had walked and talked. Aida. She had been a pretty child but her flowering had been spectacular, her beauty shining through her drab clothes.

'Thank you.'

He wondered if she recognised him. She opened the door. 'Be gentle. Be good. Please.'

It was the 'please' that told him. Yes, she remembered. Lynch gazed around the room. It was barren, stone floors and rough-hewn walls. Ahead of him was a great hewn windowsill, some three feet deep. The windows were shuttered, the wood ornately carved in oriental whorls and intertwined leaves. The General sat in the middle of the room next to a pot-bellied stove, a dull metal table to his side carrying a bottle of whisky and an overflowing ashtray. There were two glasses, one half-empty. The table was scattered in coins as was, Lynch noticed, the windowsill. The General sat in a wheelchair, his twisted legs covered in a beige woolly blanket. He had withered, his great frame shrunken inside clothes that were too big for him.

The Sandhurst English voice was still strong. 'Come in, damn you, you Irish bastard. There's a chair over there.'

Lynch lifted the bottle out of the bag and onto the table. He pulled up the battered wooden schoolroom chair, its scrape echoing in the empty room. The General nodded appreciatively at the Green Label. He unpeeled the foil, pulled out the cork and poured Lynch a stiff drink. He fumbled for the pack of cigarettes and lit one, puffing smoke from grey-blue lips under his great yellowing white moustache. There was an unhealthy sheen on his forehead and he started to cough, a rumbling noise that ended in a great walrus bark.

'Cheers,' said Lynch, tipping the glass at the old man. 'You want to give those up. They'll kill you.'

The General took a great draught of whisky and wiped his mouth with the back of his hand. 'Go to hell, Lynch.'

Lynch waved at the table. 'What are the coins for? The meter?'

'Pigeons.' The General's shrewd brown eyes examined Lynch. His hair was white and sparse above his age-spotted forehead.

'You bet on them?'

The General's laugh turned into a hacking cough. He drank again. 'I throw the coins at the bastards. By day Aida opens the windows for me to let in the light, but the pigeons scratch and flap on the ledge. Rats of the sky, they are. Only way I can scare the bastards away, see? Can't jump up and down like I used to.'

Lynch raised his chin at the wheelchair. 'So what happened?'

'Rebels. Bastards, worse than the pigeons. After a lifetime at war, you imagine? I survive the Israelis. I survive a life of Baath party politics. Then some kid gets me with a homemade pipe bomb and there I am, rogered. Give you a hint, Lynch. Don't ever get old. It's not a pleasant experience.' Draining his glass, he refilled it from the Green Label. 'What brings you here, anyway? I'm no use anymore.' A wave around the room. 'As you can see, I'm out of it all now. I'm a creature of the past.'

'Selim is dead.'

'I know. The whole souk knows. You always were a messy bastard, Lynch. Who was the guy with the missing tooth?'

It took Lynch a second to realise. 'It wasn't missing when I left him. It had a diamond set in it. He was Estonian.'

'He killed Selim.' The General grunted at Lynch's nod.

'He worked for an old friend of yours'

'I don't have friends, Lynch. Only enemies. Friendship is for the weak.'

'Dmitri. His workname. He was based here as a Russian military advisor in the '80s.'

The General lit a cigarette; the first drag triggering a fit of coughing that wracked his body. He grabbed the table for support, the coins slithering and rattling noisily on the tin surface. Aida rushed in, dabbing his foam-speckled lips with a cloth. He waved her away. 'Leave. You don't want to hear this talk. Get me more cigarettes. Here.' He dug into his jacket and thrust a grubby banknote at the girl. She hesitated, glared at Lynch and strode away.

The door slammed behind her. Lynch waited for the old

man's breathing to calm.

'Dmitri, eh? There was a character.' The General sat forward, his face grim. He puffed at his cigarette, blowing up into the air. Lynch's fleeting urge for a smoke was dispelled by the wet rattling cough. 'He's ancient history Lynch. Another ghost.'

'Tell that to Selim.' Lynch waited as the old man's eyes closed on his memories.

'He wasn't much of a son, was he? Eh? He was never going to be a soldier like his father. Why would Dmitri want Selim dead?' Ash fell from The General's cigarette and he brushed his leg, his voice quiet in contempt. 'He sold women's clothes.'

Lynch kept his voice gentle. 'Dmitri was different, wasn't he? He was a bigwig, for an Estonian. The Russians must have loved him. What did he have they wanted so much, General?'

The General drank before answering. 'Why does it matter now, Lynch? That was all years ago. In the past. Like me. It doesn't matter now. We're old men now, put out to pasture. Our secrets may as well die with us.'

'Except the past has a way of catching up.' Lynch pushed himself to his feet and walked over to the window. He started to pick coins from the ledge. 'You want to know what I think?'

'I don't particularly care what you think.'

'I think the dead man in the souk was Dmitri's man and he killed Selim because he was on his way to you. I think Dmitri might be tidying up his past.'

'You think too much.'

'Did you ever know his real name?' Lynch paused in the act of picking up a coin and turned to The General, who stared back at him. 'Jaan Kallas ring any bells? He's quite a famous boy these days.'

The bottle clinked against The General's glass. He waved it at Lynch, who nodded. He splashed whisky unsteadily into Lynch's glass, spilling the amber liquid onto the metal table top. 'By God he was a greedy, devious bastard. He was good, Lynch. Very good. He didn't have a heart, he had stone there instead. A heart of Estonian, we used to say. Ha. Even our *mukhabbarat* boys were scared of him.'

'So what sort of product was he selling your lot, Bashar? What was Dmitri selling?'

He twisted in his chair. 'Where is that damn girl?'

The door opened and the girl padded in to the room, her sandaled feet swishing on the cold stone. She placed the cigarettes on the metal table. She emptied the overflowing ashtray into the paper bag she had brought the cigarettes in. She whispered, 'You shouldn't be smoking so much. You're straining.' She turned at the door. 'There are police arriving at all the souk gates.'

Lynch's heart quickened. 'What are they after?'

'A murderer. Two men have died in the souk today. They say the same man killed them both.' She smiled. 'An *ajnabi*.'

Lynch felt sweat prick his armpits as the door closed behind the girl. He turned to The General, who was watching him with those yellowed eyes over the glass at his lips. Lynch leaned forward. 'I don't have much time. So what did Dmitri sell you, General?'

The General nodded, sipping. He held his glass up. 'For Selim.'

Lynch suppressed his grim smile, understanding. He watched The General, noting the sweat on the grey skin, the knuckles on the chair.

The General gasped for breath. 'He tipped us off about that bastard Saddam and his purge of the Baath. He was our eye on the Israelis. He forewarned us of Mole Cricket 19, not that it did us any good. He gave us everything the Brits could see. Dmitri turned your people inside out for us. Mind, a lot of his product we used as corroboration, you understand? We had our own sources.'

Lynch murmured, 'Of course.'

'He gave us a lot of good stuff on Iraq but his most valuable product was on Israeli movements around Oslo. He always had accurate assessments of the Israeli and Palestinian positions, the Americans' intentions and so on. His product was sound, right up to just before the Israeli pull-out from South Lebanon. We knew everything the Brits did and we knew their strategic focus, too. He pulled your people inside out, Lynch. But then Dmitri died.'

Lynch tensed. 'Died?'

'Sure. Died. One minute he's selling us gold and bitching for more money every time, next minute he's on a plane out of here and fallen silent as the grave. Early 1991, just before the Sovs fell apart.' The General considered his glass, his chest labouring. 'We reasoned he'd been recalled to Moscow to be there for the fall. He never spoke to us again.'

The door slammed back against the stonework. The girl was framed against the rooftop by the light pollution from the city around them. There was a faint corona of drizzle around the bare bulbs strung on the battlements behind. Her face was grim. 'The police. They are here and many.'

The General turned to Lynch, his hand held out with an effort that made his whole frame quiver. Lynch took it. The febrile grip tightened and Lynch felt an echo of the iron. 'He got drunk once. The infallible Dmitri. Just before he left Syria. I was with him. We ended up in one cathouse in Damascus. The stuff he sold us was just business on the side. He was on his way up the ladder, fast. And it was the Americans helping him climb it. They owned him, not the Sovs.'

Lynch froze. He searched The General's face but there was only age and pain there, no guile. He nodded. 'Thank you.'

'And yes, his name was Jaan Kallas.'

Doors slammed outside, boots sounded on flagstones. The General spoke urgently to Aida. His wheezing voice was reduced to a whisper. 'Take him away, over the roofs. Keep him safe.'

The old man dismissed Lynch with a tired hand as he slumped back into his chair. 'Go, *Ingleezi*. Go with God. Take care with Dmitri. He's an operator.'

Lynch followed the whirling skirts of the girl running into the soft drizzle falling on the miles of darkened rooftops covering the Aleppo souk. He struggled to keep up with her as she leapt over the uneven surfaces, stonework battlements giving way to lead flashing. They climbed over a section of tiled roof. She ran gracefully and he lumbered, his heart battling in his chest. Below them, Lynch caught sight of an alley and heard shouts as two uniformed men advanced into the souk brandishing nightsticks.

In the open street beyond them, the corona of orange-tinted damp around the sodium streetlights was tinged with rapid coruscations of blue from the squad cars' lights. Lynch pushed himself over the rooftop and slid down the wet tiles to the rusty gantry below, glancing at her elfin face taut with fear as she waited for him to catch up. She was away in an instant without giving him a second to catch his breath, sliding down a slate tiled roof, jumping over a long-abandoned revetment and curling herself around a pillar that joined two ancient buildings, the rough curved surface stretching down into the souk below. Lynch scrabbled around the curve, following the girl into the shadows beyond. She stopped him with an upturned hand and a hiss and he doubled up, breathing as deeply and quietly as he could.

'You're not very fit,' she scolded him in a whisper.

There were more shouts from below, urgent voices berating pleading voices. He let slip his brat's grin, his breath still coming hard. 'No, not very.'

She was off again, dancing across the dark rooftops. Lynch lurched after her, the shadowed darkness softening as the moon broke from behind the clouds. The stonework and tiled roofs glistened; Lynch's shoes skittered and clattered on the wet surfaces. Ahead of him, the running girl barely made a sound as she hopped between obstacles. Lynch marvelled at her, balancing now on a ledge, jumping across deep stairwells that veered down into the warm depths of the souk and dancing around the assorted rubbish that decorated areas of the roof-scape, bedsteads, bicycles and twisted car parts, looming shapes under tarpaulins and, here and there, little shanty dwellings.

She paused again, watching him as he struggled to get his breath back, supporting himself against a chimney. The stonework was warm. Lynch was drenched from the outside and in, rain and sweat combined. He wiped his forehead.

'We are nearly there. It will be close; there are too many police. Look.'

She swept her arms across the rooftop and Lynch saw the flashing lights picking out the shape of one of the great gateways to the souk. Sirens near and far filled the air. The girl shot him a glance of amused contempt. 'Are you ready now?'

'As I'll ever be. Where are we going?'

'To the wall. Come.'

He followed her once again and this time she set a slower pace, taking care to flit between the cover of the shadows. Lynch caught glimpses of the souk below, the neon-lit trays of spices and strings of garish sweets hanging in doorways. It was eerily quiet. Lynch guessed the police were evacuating the souk through each of the gates.

The girl stopped by a broken-down portion of wall. 'Here. You must go down here. Stay in the shadows. Go down backwards. There is a ledge below you, drop down to it. Go to the left. Then you will see the hand holds down. Go left again and there will be a car. It will be blue.'

Lynch smiled at her. 'And what if I drop and there's no ledge?'

Her tight little grimace in return gave him little solace. 'Then I have killed you.'

Lynch walked to the breach in the wall and glanced down but there was only darkness. Taking a deep breath, he crouched, gripped the wall as best he could and pushed away, letting his arms straighten and take his weight. Looking up he saw her pale face above him.

'You'll look after him?'

She nodded. 'Godspeed.' And was gone.

Lynch let go and dropped into the darkness.

FOURTEEN

For a moment Lynch felt pure fear as his body found weightlessness and plunged into the void. He hit the ledge hard, unable to tell when to bend his legs to cushion the landing. He flailed at the wall for a grip as he felt himself falling outwards. His fingers found a small cavity in the cold stone but it was too little to halt his outward momentum and he pivoted on the ledge, straining to pull himself back in, feeling his fingernails breaking as his grip loosened. Slowly, his muscles screaming, he pulled himself around to lie flat against the wall again, his other hand finding a grip on a piece of sharp rock.

He inched left, scraping along the wet wall. His foot dislodged a pebble from the ledge and he waited for the noise of its falling, counting. One Mississippi. Two Mississippi. The clatter told him he was at least forty feet above the stone below. His breath was laboured and shallow with fear, his body betrayed him on the instant, freezing. He willed himself to move, his teeth gritted. He let go with his right hand and brought it closer to himself, found a purchase and inched forward to his left, his left hand seeking a hold on the slippery rock face.

His left foot stepped into space. A split second of all-consuming panic loosened his grip. He tried to find his balance again, stretching his foot in the darkness to seek a clear foothold. His left hand found cold iron, a rung set in the wall. He dragged himself over to it. He found another rung. Inching downwards, he moved from grip to grip. It started to rain again, more heavily this time, the drops spattering off the rock, the water running down its sheer face. Lynch's harsh breaths came out in cold puffs.

His feet touched ground. He wanted to lie down and kiss it. Bathed in the shadow, he glanced along the wall. He was in a quiet side street. He could see the great Citadel floodlit at the head of the street to his right. He turned left and walked as quickly and as quietly as he could, pausing by a great gnarled tree that had grown up through the flagged walkway, parting the stones over the centuries to make way for its twisted roots. Lynch strode towards the blue car parked by the corner into the main road, his head down and his sodden collar jacket turned up. He slipped into the front seat.

'Where to, *Sidi*?'

Lynch kept his head down. 'Yarmouk Street. The Hotel Al Faisal.'

'Sure.'

The driver set him down at the Hotel Al Faisal and Lynch waited for him to go away before turning and walking back onto Yarmouk Street and turning right to The Baron Hotel.

Lynch ordered a bottle of Black Label, a bucket of ice and a glass from room service and headed for the shower, where he gingerly soaped his bruised body. The hot water was a blessing and Lynch luxuriated in it until the bell sounded and he wrapped himself in the threadbare bathrobe to let the room service girl in. She was pretty and flustered by the loosely tied bathrobe. He flirted with her and she blushed before taking his generous tip and leaving with a glance behind as she closed the door.

Lynch pulled on dry clothes and packed his wet, dirty clothes into his wheelie bag. He slid his toilet bag and his other dry clothes into a carrier bag. He poured himself a generous scotch and plopped ice into it, draining the tumbler in a single gulp, holding the glass to the light. Lynch pulled on his leather jacket and slid the bottle of whisky into the carrier.

He left down the fire escape, treading quietly. Reaching the bottom, which gave out onto the hotel's service yard, he hefted his wheelie bag into a skip and slipped out into the side street. It was quiet, the traffic sparse and he had to wait over twenty minutes before a taxi passed. Lynch flagged it down.

'How much to Latakia?' said Lynch in Arabic.

The driver leaned across to Lynch. 'Latakia? Are you crazy? At this time of night? We wouldn't reach there until the morning.'

'I'm in a hurry, my aunt's ill. How much?'

The driver's face was calculating. He scanned Lynch's features, his eyes flicking down to Lynch's hand on the windowsill; the white knuckles and the broken nails. 'A hundred. US. Cash in advance. You buy the petrol and leave me with a full tank for the way back.'

'You're kidding. Who's got that kind of money?'

The driver shrugged. 'Who wants to go to fucking Latakia at two in the morning?'

Lynch straightened up. The dark streets around were empty, only the occasional car flashing past. The faint sound of sirens carried in the damp night air from the direction of the souk. The taxi was a relatively new car, a Mitsubishi. Lynch shrugged. 'Okay, deal.'

He got into the car, slinging his carrier bag into the back. He counted out the notes and handed them to the taxi driver, who counted them again and shoved them into his inside pocket. The driver licked his lips then grunted. 'Okay, let's go.'

Lynch settled back into the seat. The taxi was warm. The driver pulled out into the main road, his head swivelling as he evaluated his best route. He was in his early fifties, grey-haired and weather-beaten. There was a cedar wood crucifix hanging on the mirror. Cigarettes and a lighter were stuffed into a nook in the dashboard. There was a scattering of sweet wrappers in the central console recess. The driver reached for his cigarettes.

'You smoke?'

'No.'

'You mind?'

'Would it matter if I did?'

'Not really, no.'

'Then go ahead, why not?'

With a laconic shrug, the driver flicked out a cigarette and lit it. He half-opened his window, the gesture just laborious enough for Lynch to know this was a major concession to a difficult customer. He turned the radio on.

Lynch sniffed the smoke, as always the aromatic tendrils gave him a momentary pang, a tiny thrill and denial. 'So what's your name?'

'It's on the license, there.' The driver flicked his cigarette toward the dashboard. 'Assad. George al-Assad. No relation. Call me George. You?'

'Michael Sfeir. Mike.' Lynch's fake Lebanese ID had been a major expense Channing had balked at and grudgingly borne several months ago. This had been Mike Sfeir's first border crossing and Lynch was mildly relieved when he passed through Aleppo's airport unchallenged. Passports, as Channing was quick to remind him, were complex things to fake these days and expensive even when procured direct from the FCO.

'Where are you from?'

'Beirut. Before you tell me I don't look or sound Lebanese, my father was from Beirut but my mum was *Circassi* from Anatolia. I was brought up mostly in London.'

The driver raised an eyebrow at Lynch. 'Exotic.'

'I like to think so.'

They settled down into a companionable silence as they left the city behind, taking the south-westerly M5 highway, the four lanes of bumpy blacktop bisected by a concrete barrier not quite living up to the designation of motorway. The big street lamps flashed past, the floodlit green boulevard giving way to sparse vegetation and meagre lighting as they left the outskirts.

The driver flicked his cigarette out of the window. The tiny spark arced into the darkness beyond the pale lights dotting the central reservation. Soon the lights petered out and they drove through the night down the two-lane highway. The music on the radio stopped. The news came on.

Realising the danger, Lynch's mouth was open to ask him to turn it off as the announcer's barking Arabic filled the car. 'The police are searching for a foreigner on the run who is suspected of killing two men in cold blood in *Halab* today. One of the victims is Syrian. A spokesperson has described the murders as bloody and incomprehensible. Police have launched a nationwide manhunt for the man, believed to be in his fifties with dark hair and blue eyes. Reports say the man is likely armed and dangerous and he should not be approached. A nationwide hotline is open for anybody who can assist police with their enquiries...'

Lynch hit the off switch. There was a silence.

'Well, my friend,' the driver said. 'That just tripled your fare.'

A second later, before Lynch could respond, the driver wrenched the wheel right and took them off the highway onto a newly constructed filter road. There was no lighting and no road marking as the car slid onto a roundabout above the main highway. The driver veered right, the Mitsubishi slid for a second before the wheels bit tarmac. He switched the headlights off and drove away from the highway into farmland.

'You were lucky, *khawaja*. Look at the next intersection. You can see it now.'

Lynch saw the roadblock, the squad cars and flashing lights and, behind them in the semi-lit area below the cloverleaf exchange, the army warthogs.

He nodded. 'No problem with the fare. I guess you earned it.'

The driver lit another cigarette. This time he didn't bother with the window. 'We'll go across country. It'll take longer.'

'Fine by me.'

The driver held out his hand.

'No,' said Lynch. 'You got an advance. The rest is cash on

delivery.'

'And if I decide to take it from you anyway, *ya khawaja*?'

Lynch smiled in the darkness, his teeth reflecting purple from the dashboard lights. 'I'll shoot you, donkey.'

Lynch had the driver drop him on the street in front of the Le Meridien hotel. He handed over the fare and grabbed his plastic bag from the back seat.

'Don't spend that all at once, now.'

The driver folded the notes and tucked them into his shirt pocket and lit a cigarette. 'Glad to see the back of you, to be honest. You're trouble. I can smell it.'

Lynch grinned and turned away, walking towards the hotel. He was exhausted, despite sleeping for the last two hours of the cross-country drive and he knew he must look dishevelled. He would have given thousands for a coffee, but he stood out too much, the man with the greatcoat and the plastic bag: a dosser in a five-star hotel. However, the Le Meridien was one of the few places in Latakia where a call from a Lebanese mobile number wouldn't stand out.

Lynch called Meadows' secure mobile but there was no response. As calmly as he could, he tried again, standing in front of the big hotel, the early morning sunlight glinting off the revolving doors. He called a third time and the line rang out. He slipped the mobile back into his pocket and strode towards the taxi waiting by the hotel's front entrance.

Lynch got into the back of the car. Again, he spoke in Arabic. 'Take me to Al Sewar Restaurant. It's on the southern corniche, off Orouba Street. Five hundred lire and not a penny more.'

The cab driver glanced at him in the mirror, a matchstick between his lips. 'I know it. Six hundred and not a penny less.'

Lynch shrugged. 'Fine.'

He sat back and watched the drab city go by as the streets

started to come to life. He closed his eyes.

The taps on his leg woke him. 'Hey, I said we're here. Come on, this is a taxi, not a dosshouse.'

Lynch shook his head to clear it. The restaurant was in front of them, a stone-clad monstrosity with painted plaster tree trunks either side of the door and a vine-strewn pergola along its frontage. Under the canopy were tables; to one side were rows of *argileh* pipes ready for the lunchtime service.

'Here,' he scowled, throwing a ten dollar bill at the driver. 'Keep the change.'

Lynch walked away from the cab and towards the little dock nearby, cursing himself for the impetuous, silly gesture that rendered him even more memorable than the plastic bag, greatcoat and tramp's blue chin.

Walking along the dock, Lynch spotted the lone figure, stretched out on a plastic chair in front of a fishing boat, basking in the early sunlight, a roll-up between his lips and peppery stubble on his chin. He was wearing a shabby t-shirt and torn jeans, his hair flecked with grey and receding under the blue cap. Lynch pulled up the plastic chair next to the supine figure and sat himself down. He pulled out the whisky and took a deep pull from the bottle. The boat behind them was a typical small fishing smack. On its bow was a painted nameplate with flowery decorations. "*Bride of Smyrna.*"

The voice was a sandpaper-throated growl. 'Lynch. Fuck me. What brings you here?'

'Morning, Saif. I need a coffee and a boat, in that order. I'll pay for the boat, the coffee's on you.'

'Where to?'

'Anywhere north of Beirut. Jounieh, ideally.'

'You in trouble?'

'Yup.'

Zaidi nodded. 'Nothing changes. Usual price. Two thousand US. Cash.'

'Done.'

'Come on, then. We'd best get going.'

Zaidi shaded his eyes to squint up at Lynch. 'You in that much trouble?'

'Yes.'

Zaidi sighed. 'Fine. *Yalla.*'

As they chugged past the coastal smudge that was Tripoli to their left, Lynch raised a tin mug of whisky poured from the bottle in his pocket in a toast to Lebanon. The sea was calm, the bow wave of the *Bride of Smyrna* casting a creamy wake behind them. The powerful engines concealed in the little smack's hull had taken them straight out to sea, beyond Syrian territorial waters. Zaidi had announced when they were clear and Lynch's relief had been considerable.

The long loop around took them out towards Cyprus before they headed south and back in towards land, coming back in close to the border crossing at Aarida. As they sighted land, Lynch checked his mobile signal and placed a call to Brian Channing in London.

'Lynch.'

'Brian.'

'What the fuck have you been playing at? They're playing ping pong with my reputation all over Whitehall! The FCO's throwing fits, we're issuing D notices as fast as we can write 'em and I've got the Syrian government moaning to their new best friends the Americans who are in turn asking us why we're not taking action to rein in our, and I quote, "murderous operatives" unquote.'

'I'm sorry Brian, it kicked off when one of the Estonians turned up. They were after Junaidi. They're cleaning up for Dmitri.'

'I know how they bloody well feel, don't I? Do you know how much those cover IDs cost? Have you any idea how many favours I had to pull to get just one of those things issued?'

'Like I said, Brian, I'm sorry but it was unavoidable.'

'What, murdering two people?'

'One. The Estonian killed Selim.'

'Who the fuck is Selim?'

Lynch cast his eyes to heaven. The sky was a marvellous, rich blue. 'Selim was The General's son, Brian. The Estonian was close to finishing his mopping up act when I found him. I got out as best I could. And I got what I wanted. Junaidi confirmed Dmitri was Jaan Kallas. He also claimed Kallas was a double. The Americans were pulling his strings and feeding him information to pass on to his masters to earn him fast track promotion. Kallas sold intel to the Syrians on the side.'

'That's not working for me, Lynch. Write it up and I'll have the analytics people assess it, but it sounds unlikely at best. Junaidi must be losing his marbles.'

'No, he's good, Brian. He's old and sick but he's most definitely got his marbles.'

'We've been talking with the Estonians. We have sources who claim Kallas is the head of the Ühiskassa, the Estonian Mafia. Thanks to that particular link we got an ID on your two killers. Your blond twins aren't twins at all, they're an item. A pair of white supremacist lunatics, Karl Persson and Piotr Loewe. They're two of the most feared killers in the Baltic.'

'Were.'

'Oh, yes. Sorry, Lynch, I was forgetting your indiscriminate and unjustifiable killing spree.'

Lynch was weary. 'Look, thanks for the info, Brian. I'll pick the files up later. Right now I want to check out the villa, Meadows isn't picking up calls.'

Channing's voice was sharp. 'No more cowboy stuff, Lynch. I can't hold off the FCO if we get another howl from the diplomats, you understand me?'

'Sure, Brian. Sure.'

Lynch cut the secure line and the mobile screen dulled to quiescence. He sniffed the clean sea air and tried to shake off the cloying sense of death, the sunlight on his face warming him. He slid the mobile into his pocket and climbed up to the bridge to find Saif Zaidi puffing on a roll-up and steering the *Bride* in towards Jounieh harbour.

'Saif, I need a car. The second we land.'

Zaidi nodded, reaching for his radio handset. 'Sure, anything can be arranged. Extra five hundred including driver.'

Lynch threw Zaidi a black look, took a deep breath and nodded. He brightened as a thought came to him. 'Sure. But you pay for the petrol.'

FIFTEEN

The Toyota's tyres crunched along the gravel driveway. A chill ran through Lynch – there was no way the two SAS men would have let a strange car approach like this.

He got out of the car, waving down the driver. 'Wait for me here. Don't move, whatever you do. You understand?'

The bearded, pale face nodded. Lynch approached the villa, slipping his revolver out of its holster and thumbing the safety off. The front door was ajar and Lynch felt himself breaking into the familiar sweat of fear as he pushed it open with his toe, staying back and hugging the door jamb. The silence was absolute. Lynch broke the tension by calling out. 'Meadows?'

His voice was flat in the lifeless air. Lynch caught a faint, familiar smell that took him back to a villa near Sidon and the day he had discovered the body of his young charge, Paul Stokes. It was the smell of the charnel house, the faint sweetness of death. At first it was almost attractive, a richness, hints of caramel and then something else underneath, something tropical like ripe papaya that soon strengthened and became durian – cloying, sticky and corrupt. As he inched into the house, Lynch's gorge rose as the stench intensified.

'Henderson?' He paused. 'Hartmoor?'

The living room was empty. Lynch opened the connecting room to the kitchen and recoiled at the smell. A gourmet of death, even as he turned away from its smell, he recognised it as relatively fresh, the fatty, rich iron smells of the abattoir rather than the miasma of liquefying corruption.

Lynch held his breath and re-entered the kitchen. Meadows was tied to a chair, his throat slashed. He had been treated appallingly, his hands a pulpy mess and his face mottled with contusions. One of his ears had been cut off.

Lynch went through to the master bedroom, overlooking the rear of the house. The French window was smashed, bullet marks were traced across the walls and Henderson's body lay sprawled on the floor. At least he had died cleanly; a spray of bullets across his chest had torn his shirt into strips, exposing bone. The flies had wasted no time.

Lynch walked through the rest of the house calling out to Jason Hartmoor, but there was no sign of the man other than the clothes and neat stack of blister-packed tablets. The driver was standing by the car smoking as Lynch walked out of the villa. 'Give me one of those, would you?'

Lynch took the cigarette and lighter the driver offered him and turned so the man wouldn't see his hands trembling. He handed the lighter back, exhaling a grateful plume of smoke. 'We're going back to Beirut. As quick as you like.'

The driver nodded and flicked his cigarette into the bushes. Lynch kept his, opening the window to let the smoke out, luxuriating in the forbidden pleasure and letting the smoke clear the stench of death from his airways. Only as they neared Jounieh did he flick the butt begrudgingly out of the window and pick up his mobile to call Tony Chalhoub to report the murders.

Chalhoub wasn't interested. 'Later, Gerald. I'm at Marcelle's. Get here, fast.'

Lynch's feet crunched on broken glass. Lengths of plastic crime scene tape stretched out around the club's main floor. There were dark splashes across the bar's fascia, bottles strewn across the shelves. Drab sheeting covered mounds on the floor. Lynch gazed around, taking in the destruction. Stuffing poked through the wrecked furnishings. The remnants of mirrors clung to the walls, crazed with impacts. Lynch followed the policeman up the stairs and along the corridor. The door at the end was hanging from its hinges.

He recognised the girl, one of Marcelle's flock. She was red-eyed, tears streaked her pale cheeks. She was smoking, the cigarette shaking in her fingers. Lynch desperately wanted one. *No.* Tony Chalhoub turned to him. 'Lynch. You look like shit. You're late. Your Russian friend beat you to it.'

'He's not Russian. He's Estonian.'

'Same difference.'

Chalhoub's face was grim. Usually possessed of a baggy-eyed lugubriousness, now those eyes were bruised and his skin was pallid. He rubbed his eyes. Lynch surveyed the room, following Chalhoub's bleak regard. There was another huddled shape draped in sheeting on the floor to the side of Marcelle's desk. Lynch pushed back the edge with his toe.

Chalhoub was too slow, his restraining touch on Lynch's arm came as the fold of cloth flipped over. 'No, Lynch, don't…'

Lynch realised the potential consequence of the casual gesture too late. It was *her.* Under that. All these years. Those eyes. Her smell. Marcelle. The cloth rippled, revealed the broken flesh of a face turned sideways.

Lynch, inured to death and the instinctive urge to retch at its unveiling, felt the bile burn his throat. Hassan's dead eyes glared up at him. The lined face was frozen marble, a rictus. Of hate? Fear? Triumph? Lynch tried to read the dead man's expression even as his hand flew to his mouth to stem the acrid tide.

It wasn't her. He lurched aside blindly and puked.

Lynch returned from the bathroom. Tony Chalhoub put a hand out to his shoulder. 'Sorry, Gerald. It gets you sometimes no matter how many… you know.'

'Sure, Tony. Thanks.' Lynch cast his hand around helplessly. 'So where's Marcelle?'

'She wasn't here when we got here. A patrol was sent here to an apparent altercation. They had a flag on her address to call me. I sent my guys as quick as I could but there was nobody here alive. I know you and Hassan go back. I'm truly sorry.'

'How'd you know it was the Estonian?'

'Look around you. How often have you seen this kind of damage? Your friend got to your protection then came down here to get to Marcelle.'

'How did you know I had…'

'I know things. It's my job, no? You had two SAS men up in that villa near Jounieh. The two dead men you tried to call in to me.'

Lynch acknowledged the point with a dip of his head. 'So now I've lost Hartmoor and Marcelle both.' He glared around at the ransacked office space. 'What a mess.'

A mobile ringtone, a Haifa Wehbe song. The iPhone was on Marcelle's desk. He reached out for it, glanced at Chalhoub enquiringly and got a nod. He picked it up. It was an unknown number, nothing displayed on the screen.

'Hello?'

The voice was an insidious whisper. 'You have thing I want. I have thing you want. Listen.' A cry, then, a woman. 'Bring me the Englishman, the old one. Or she die. It will not come quick. Slow. Very slow. Believe.'

'I don't have him.'

'Then you find to him. Not time.' Another cry, choked in a sob. 'Morning. I call this telephone. No answer, she die.'

Lynch thumbed the phone off and pocketed it. Chalhoub lit a cigarette.

'Well?'

Lynch rubbed his forehead. 'The Estonian. He's got Marcelle. He wants to swap her for Hartmoor.'

'I thought he'd taken Hartmoor?'

'Me too. But it looks like he got away. God knows how, that Estonian's a machine. He took out two SAS men. He took out Hassan and Marcie's security boys. They're good, probably the best private security in Beirut. This guy did that single-handed.

What the fuck is he up to?'

'Ask Abbas Ali.'

'Like that old bastard would tell us a thing. Right now I'm more worried about how you find a dying Englishman in Beirut.'

'Look in the hospitals.'

Lynch threw a caustic glance at Chalhoub, who blithely stubbed out his cigarette on the desktop.

The answer hit Lynch with a beautiful clarity. He smacked his fist into his palm. 'You know, you might even make a copper one day. Roxanol. That's what we want. Bloody Roxanol.'

'Roxanol?'

'Hardcore painkiller, used for terminal cancer patients. Wherever Hartmoor is, unless he's lying in a valley somewhere above Jounieh, he's going to need Roxanol. Quite a lot of it. And he takes enzymes for his digestion. Any pharmacy sold that combination to a stranger recently, you've got your man. Can you trace it?'

'Every pharmacy from Jounieh to Beirut? Are you crazy? I don't have sanction for those kinds of resources, Gerald.'

'Come on, Tony. You know you can do it. Make something up. Blackmail someone. Call in a marker. A *wasta*. If you don't, she's dead and you know it.'

Chalhoub nodded. 'I'll call you in the morning. Now get out of here. My people have work to do.'

Lynch, weary, felt close to tears. He punched his friend on the shoulder. 'Thanks.'

'*Yalla*, go.'

Lynch went.

The driver Saif Zaidi supplied had been silent and efficient throughout and it was only when Lynch came out of *Le Chat Botté* and told him to drive to Chatila that he showed any emotion. It had been fear.

Now, as the car sat outside Abbas Ali's compound in the heart of the camp, the driver was sweating and glancing around nervously. The naked light bulbs hanging outside the cinder-block houses drew fat moths and lit shadowed, sullen faces.

Lynch poked his head back into the car before closing the door. 'Just be here when I get back, you hear?'

Lynch didn't wait for the answer. The thud of the door started a dog barking somewhere nearby. He strode across to the compound gate and rang on the bell. He waited amid the sounds of night; cicadas, a television, voices raised in argument far away and the clatter of pots and pans from nearer carried on the cool breeze. Car tyres screeched far away, an engine racing. Feet shuffled behind the gate.

'What is it?' A gravelly voice, a lifetime of cigarettes. Guttural street Arabic.

'Gerald Lynch. I am here to see Abbas Ali.'

'I don't know any Abbas Ali.'

'*Kazzab*. He will see me. Tell him I have a message for Jaan Kallas.'

There was a muffled conversation behind the gate. Younger feet set off away across the courtyard. The old man's breath rasped on the other side of the iron door. Lynch waited, trying not to reach for his gun. He turned and checked on the driver. The car was in the shadows.

More steps on the other side of the gate, urgent whispers. Lynch jumped at the shriek of metal on metal. The flat clackclack of AK47s being armed rang out as the gate opened.

Lynch slipped his hand to the Walther P99 in its shoulder holster. He froze at the drawl behind him. 'Don't move, mister. Raise your hands and turn, real slow.'

Lynch twisted around to face the square black shape of a pistol, the hands gripping it steady and the calm face behind them incurious. The heavy-set young man was wearing a combat jacket and jeans, his feet placed apart squarely in line with his shoulders. Lynch raised his hands slowly. The gate's screeching stopped and Lynch heard jabbering from the guards behind him. He guessed there were three or more of them. They were excitable, shouting. One of them shoved Lynch's shoulder from behind. Lynch stepped forward with the blow. The young man with the pistol paced back to accommodate Lynch's movement, waving the pistol in negation.

'Shut up,' he snapped. 'Take the gun from under his shoulder. Take him inside.'

Lynch was wheeled around, the Walther dragged clumsily from the silicon holster. The old man stood by the gate, waving them in. 'Come on, hurry.'

Lynch was shoved forward into the compound, the door screeching on its rusty rails behind him and clanging shut. One of the guards walked in front of him, two behind. The young man with the pistol brought up the rear. Lynch looked around at the compound, the wide-open terrazzo tiled courtyard with rooms leading off all around it. In one doorway a veiled woman stood watching his progress, her hand on a tousle-headed child's shoulder. It was dark; only dull light from windows in the buildings edging the compound threw bars of light across the courtyard.

They were walking towards a double-story building to one corner of the walled space, the guards crowding him in their excitement, chattering to each other about how they were going to beat the *ajnabi*. Shoved forward by an over-enthusiastic clap on the shoulder, Lynch stumbled, hesitated a second and wheeled around, his foot lashing out at chest height. His left hand struck out in a straight-shouldered punch that caught the guard squarely in the face. He felt his foot connect, the second guard crashing to the floor as Lynch dropped to a crouch to spring at the third man, who had been behind him. As Lynch had hoped, the young man had holstered his pistol once they were inside the compound. He was reaching for it now, panic on his face.

Lynch moved fast, his leap forward taking him crashing into

the youngster, yanking the camouflage jacket, throwing the man and pinning his arms at the same time. Lynch's knee hammered up to connect with the shocked face. He found the pistol and pulled it out of the leather holster.

The night became day in an instant, powerful floodlights snapping on all around him. Lynch straightened up, trying to locate the sound of a powerful pair of hands clapping slowly. The big figure walked into the light, a group of some twenty men stepping forwards behind him, arrayed to each side. Every one of them was carrying an AK47. Abbas Ali beamed as he stood regarding Lynch panting above the groaning figure of the young man.

'Bravo, Mr. Lynch. You are a very dangerous man. But this is my home and you are behaving too badly. I should have you shot.'

'I asked to speak with you,' Lynch snarled, 'not to be hit by gun butts.'

Abbas Ali tutted. 'They were maybe too enthusiastic, then. Let us talk, Mr Lynch. Put this gun down first, though. Guns make me nervous.'

Lynch wiped the back of his hand across his mouth. The pistol clattered on the floor. He stepped forwards, noting the increased tension among the men around him.

'Steady, Mr Lynch. I have little reason to love you and these men have less.'

Lynch nodded and walked after Abbas Ali, the gunmen closing behind him. He followed the great figure as it lumbered down a corridor. They turned left into a large office, upholstered chairs set all around the walls, a large desk to one end of the room. The desk was dark, battered and topped with a thick panel of smoked glass. One corner was chipped, the glass starred. Abbas Ali sat behind it, reaching for a packet of cigarettes. He barked an order at the stooped old man in a skullcap who stood at the doorway. '*Chai bi na'ana, Abed.*' He gestured to Lynch. 'Please. A seat.'

Lynch sat, wishing fervently that everyone in this damn place didn't smoke all the time.

'As I said, Mr Lynch, I have little reason to feel any love for you. I don't like policemen in my house. It makes me nervous.'

'I am not a policeman. I work for British Intelligence. A man who has an interest in you has kidnapped someone close to me. He works for a gentleman by the name of Jaan Kallas. You may remember telling me you had no link with Jaan Kallas. I didn't believe you then and I wouldn't if you claimed it now. It was Kallas' men who killed your driver and messed up the listening devices in your safe house. Kallas is the head of the Estonian Ühiskassa. The Mafia. My guess is they have moved into Lebanon and you're in their way. Would I be right?'

Lynch searched Abbas Ali's face but the heavy features were expressionless. 'Go on, Mr Lynch. Let me to have all your cards, please.'

The shuffling figure of Abed arrived in the doorway bearing a tray with two decorated custard glasses of tea. He placed one by Lynch, one by Abbas Ali. Lynch nodded his thanks, waiting until the man had left to sip the hot, sweet drink.

Lynch's glass clinked against the saucer. 'Kallas was here during the Civil War. He worked for the Russians, for the Russian Ministry of Defence. He was unusually trusted for an Estonian. He worked out of Syria, where he was a liaison for the Syrian Defence Ministry. You knew him back then. You knew him then as *Dmitri*.'

A tightening of the big man's lined face was Lynch's reward. 'He's a powerful man these days. Too powerful, perhaps. His thugs have gone on a rampage in Beirut. Your home town. Killing people. Damaging businesses. Why? Are you with him or against him? I'd sure hate to be against him, wouldn't you?'

Abbas Ali shrugged. 'You tell me, *Ingleezi*. I know nothing of this Kallas man. I have told you this.'

The phone on the big man's desk rang. His face flickered with irritation. He reached across to the handset. He spoke in

Arabic. 'Yes? What is it? Are you crazy? I have a damn cop here. Tell him no, to come back tomorrow.'

Lynch gazed in boredom at the bookshelves behind the sofas, seemingly unconcerned by Abbas Ali's urgent whisperings into the handset. 'What the fuck is going on out there? Secure the gate now. He is not to come in, do you hear me?'

Lynch turned at the sounds of an altercation outside. Abbas Ali sprang to his feet, dropping the phone. Striding past Lynch for the door, he cried out in Arabic to the guard who had leapt to his feet at the sound of shouting. 'Stop this pig from going anywhere. Shoot him if you have to.'

Lynch stood looking confused. He asked the guard, 'What's happening?'

Getting a shrug in reply, Lynch peered through the slats of the blind on the window. It looked out onto the courtyard, still brilliant in the floodlight. The gate was open, a shouting press of men around it, surrounding a single pale figure dressed in black. A shot cracked and the group of men moved back. Abbas Ali strode across the courtyard, his hands in the air. His bellows carried across the courtyard, although Lynch couldn't make out what he was saying. The blond man stepped back under the impetus of Abbas Ali's advance. There was a short exchange. The blond man nodded curtly and wheeled away.

Lynch drew back from the blind and sat down. He slipped out his mobile and called the driver.

'You see a guy with white hair, dressed in black, just left this place?'

'Yes, he has motorcycle.'

'Follow him. Keep your distance, he's dangerous. Understand?'

'Yes. Understand.'

Lynch cut the line and slid the mobile into his pocket just as Abbas Ali crashed back into the office. He gave the big man what he hoped was an incurious glance. 'Some problem?'

'No, just a misunderstanding. There are too many

136

misunderstandings tonight, Mr Lynch, including yours that I have something to do with this Kallas. I cannot help you.'

Lynch stood. 'You understand Jaan Kallas is a very dangerous man, Abbas Ali. I know your operations are extensive, that you are well protected. But Kallas heads a fearsome organisation and if it is his intention to move into Lebanon, nothing will stop him.

'Your concern is touching, Mr Lynch, but you are meddling. I don't like it when policemen meddle. Now get out before I change my mind and have you shot.'

Lynch made his way down the corridor, two guards following him at a cautious distance. He glanced into a side-room and caught the profile of a big-framed man, standing with his arms crossed, waiting Lynch assumed, to see Abbas Ali. The profile was undoubtedly that of a bald man, a man Lynch had known as Marwan Nimr, who had died in a conflagration up in the mountain of Kalaa, in the north of Lebanon. Battered by a massive cruise missile strike, the mountain and the huge military complex it housed had literally boiled. It was impossible Nimr had survived. Although, Lynch reflected as he managed not to break his step, he had himself endured that same onslaught. As had Marcelle, held in his arms as the blasts and concussions had smashed against the shielding rock.

Lynch was past the doorway in an instant, striding down the steps to cross the courtyard of Abbas Ali's compound. He reached the gate, the two guards behind him calling to the old man to open the door. Lynch stood outside the compound wall in the middle of the Chatila camp in the dead of night. A flat metallic clatter rattled on the ground. He turned to see his pistol lying in the dust. The unsmiling guard held out a handful of bullets and snapped his hand shut on them. He tipped his chin dismissively, turned and walked into the compound. The door clanged behind him. Lynch picked up the pistol and checked it was, indeed, empty and holstered it. He set off down the shabby, dark street without looking back.

SIXTEEN

Dennis Wye stood at the big picture window overlooking Tallinn's port area. The red tiles and coloured renders of the old town stood to his left, coated in a light dusting of snow so only glimpses of the colour below showed. There were two big cruisers in, one making smoke. The choppy sea stretched out smoothly under the Wedgwood sky to find its infinities beyond the curving horizon.

Wye was feeling reflective. He glanced around Kallas' penthouse office, the black leather sofa and coffee table, the showy glass desk with its Bauhaus anglepoise lamp and the two chairs set in front of it facing each other over a little glass table with a single red flower in a black glass vase. It wasn't to his taste. He wondered what Frank Coleman would have done. He had been Frank's protégé for years, a role he had gladly accepted. Frank, anyone would tell you, was an operator. Nobody knew the Middle East like Frank, God knows the place had complexities nested in complexities. Coleman had lived his life there, been stationed in Beirut throughout the whole Civil War, the good times and the bad – especially the bad. It was Frank creamed the files when the suicide bomber took out the embassy, pulling out equipment while others worried about the dead and dying in the pancaked rubble.

And then suicide. Who'd have thought it? Frank hadn't deserved to die like that, deserted by his country just because he'd called a shot everyone in the US knew was good – the Iranians and their nuclear program were the biggest threat to peace in the Mideast since Gamal bloody Abdel Nasser. Wye sighed and turned away from the picaresque Baltic. He wanted desperately to be back in Beirut right then, making sure Frank's legacy was safe despite the interfering Brits.

Jesus, but those guys bumbled around. Without American technology and firepower, they'd be out of the game. Wye snorted. The only people in the world who didn't know it were the Brits themselves, of course.

The big office door opened, Kallas' secretary Elena in the usual miniskirt and tight blouse. Her nipples were erect, Wye noted with prurient satisfaction. Kallas strode in. He was wearing a dark single-breasted suit with an open-necked white shirt and carrying a sleek black attaché case.

'Coffee please, Elena. For Mr Wye too.'

Kallas shook Wye's hand and slid the case onto the desk. He gestured to the black leather office chairs set in front of it as he sat, relaxing into in his high-backed seat. 'What is the news, Dennis?'

'Your man's dead. The one you sent to Syria to kill Bashar Junaidi.'

Kallas was good, but then Wye knew that. The lined face was impassive, the cold eyes watchful. Kallas' nod was almost imperceptible.

'So.'

'He had a bullet scar in his right shoulder blade. Not recent.'

'That would be Loewe. Piotr Loewe. How?'

'A British intelligence officer from Beirut, guy called Gerald Lynch.'

'I have one man left on the ground and local support. Did Loewe reach Junaidi?'

'No. But Lynch did.'

'How do you know this?'

'We had a chat with Junaidi ourselves. It's a shame about his weak heart.' Wye's snapped grin earned him another infinitesimal inclination of the head from Kallas.

Elena came in bearing a small tray with two espresso cups. She set them down, paused for an instant and left. Wye picked up his cup. Sweetened as he liked it. 'We have to pull out, Jaan. We need to wrap up the operation now. We've gone far enough, now it's getting messy. With the Brits involved it's just going to get messier.'

'No. We can manage this. It is clear this Lynch, was it Lynch?' Wye nodded. 'Should go too.'

'No can do, Jaan. We can't take offensive action against a British intelligence officer.'

'I'm not asking this of you. I shall take care of this.' Wye's cup clattered. 'No way. We do nothing. You're on your own if you take it further now, we can't get involved in this. It's going fucking pear-shaped!'

'Do not swear at me, Wye. Keep your cool. You know what this is worth.'

'Fucking it up is worth a whole lot more.'

Kallas stood. 'We see this through. I have decided. I will take care of these men in Beirut.'

Wye rose reluctantly. He was going to have to handle Hilton Polson very carefully over this. He already knew what the order from Washington was going to be when they heard the news about Kallas' man. Damn Lynch to hell. They'd been told he hadn't taken an active role, he'd just talked to Hartmoor and dropped him back at his hotel, but that was horseshit. Lynch was all over this and that meant trouble, Wye knew. And then there was the issue of Bashar Junaidi blowing their link to Kallas. It was all too dangerous for Wye's liking. He wondered what Frank would have done.

Wye switched on the smile for Kallas, who wouldn't have cared less whether he was happy or not, but you go through the motions. He pumped flesh and swiped his greatcoat from the back of the sofa where he'd dropped it. He passed Elena's desk on the way out and thanked her, earning a tight little professional smile in return. In the lift down, his mind pulsed with possibilities, most of them unpleasant.

The street was quiet, the wet tarmac glittered. The sidewalk was packed snow, pressed with casts of a thousand footsteps. As fat snowflakes drifted in the air and his breath misted in front of his face, Wye came to his decision. Frank would have kept it local, he'd have sat it out and let Washington know as little as possible until he had to. The stakes were too high to apply arbitrary judgements from afar – Wye was the man on the ground and he had to call it as he saw it. He almost heard Frank's voice rasping in his ear, smelled the cigar smoke. Keep *stumm*, Dennis. Ride it out.

The people in Syria reported to him, not Polson. He was going to try a little 'need to know' out on the situation. Wye's car pulled up, a black Lincoln. As they drove out of the port area, he felt a frisson of excitement. They were playing the Game again.

Wye winced at the sharp crackle of IP artefacts on the secure connection to Washington as he waited to be 'placed in conference' as the canned voice on the line had advised him. CNN was muted on the TV in his hotel room, his greatcoat slung over the armchair. The bowl of fruit and the letter of welcome from the general manager were undisturbed on the wooden table to its side. They had made the room up while Wye had been out, the bed covered with a quilted throw.

'Polson.' The robot voice again. 'Has joined the conference.' The line came alive.

'That you, Dennis?'

'Here. Is anyone else joining?'

'Couple of the guys from the analyst team.'

'Levitz.' Robot voice 'Has joined the conference.'

Wye knew Bernie Levitz well, he was head of the Middle East analyst team and a well-respected man with a prodigious memory and a knack for constructing links the computers missed.

'Hey, Bernie.'

'Dennis. Good to hear you. How's Estonia?'

Wye gave that one a little thought. 'Cold, Bernie. Colder than you'd imagine.'

'Parrish,' another voice. 'Has joined the conference.'

'Okay,' said Polson. 'All present. So we appear to have some issues with our partnership in Beirut. Everyone on this call is fully briefed. Dennis, start us off. What's the situation there?'

'Thanks, Hilt. Kallas is getting nervous but I think we're fine.'

'An Estonian national was killed in Aleppo two days ago, the Syrians say by a British national travelling under a false Lebanese ID. We got an airport scan from the Syrians and Bernie reckons its Lynch, the SIS guy.'

Wye tried to stay calm. So much for Frank's need-to-know strategy. 'Kallas sent one of his guys to close off Bashar Junaidi.'

Levitz' husky New York drawl broke in. 'The General? So Lynch was after Junaidi too?'

'He didn't get there in time, Bernie. Kallas' guy did. We're still secure.'

Polson snorted. 'Secure? I'm not feeling secure right now. Bernie?'

Levitz drawled. 'No, not feeling secure here, either. Dennis, what about this Hartmoor guy?'

Wye winced. 'We don't know where he is. We suspect Lynch is babysitting him, but we can't get a fix on his location. Kallas' men have been making a hell of a mess looking for him, too.'

'So rein Kallas in.' Polson said.

'That's not really an option right now, Hilt.'

'Listen, Dennis. I got the Brits placing information requests on Operation Dmitri daily. Now I got an SIS guy involved on the ground. I'm not feeling good about this. You have a major operation running and if this Lynch guy looks like he could blow it, I want it shut down pronto.'

Levitz again. 'What about getting Brian Channing to pull his guy out?'

'Not an option. He's going to need very good reason and I haven't got one to give him. It's his people are badgering us for information on Dmitri.' Polson's voice was tight. 'Dennis, you have to get Kallas to wind it up before this escalates.'

Wye wanted to punch the cupboard. 'I hear you Hilt. Leave it with me.'

'Good man. You're a good man, Dennis. See us through this.'

'You got it.'

Wye cut the line and tossed the mobile onto the bed. He was beginning to feel like he was running out of options. He didn't like that feeling one bit.

Kallas' car and driver were waiting at Pärnu airport, parked up outside the sleepy little terminal building. His helicopter flight from Tallinn in his Puma AS332 had been uneventful, the countryside rendered uniform by the snow, a glittering wonderland shining in the morning sunshine. It was a short drive to the house in the woods outside Valgeranna, so he didn't bother removing his greatcoat. They turned off the road into the wooded driveway, gravel crunching under the Mercedes' wheels. The trees parted and the house came into view, an imposing country chateau, its red roof dusted with snow.

There were five big cars parked in front of the house, two Jaguars, a Mercedes and two BMWs. The car halted and Kallas pulled on his black leather gloves. The driver opened the door and Kallas got out, the cold, pine-scented air sharp in his nostrils. He pulled his attaché case from the seat and started up the steps to the great front door. It opened as his foot touched the top step.

'Good morning, sir.'

Kallas shrugged off his greatcoat and it was taken from him. He peeled off the gloves and they, too, were taken. He followed the footman across the wooden floor into the drawing room. The vaulted walls were lined with wooden bookcases, the windows out over the rear of the house and its frozen-over fountain bathed the room in light. There was a fire blazing merrily in the hearth. They walked through into the dining room. Around the big table sat five men and a woman. Behind them tapestries covered the high walls and two chandeliers dropped from above to lend their glittering reflections to the polished mahogany table-top.

The group stood. The chair at the end of the table was empty. Kallas placed his attaché case by his chair and rested his hands on the knurled decorations breasting the chair back. He let his gaze travel around the group. They were serious-faced and calm; two of the men were in their sixties, the woman was strong-jawed with long, black hair trailing her shoulder. She was in her mid-forties, handsome with blue eyes. Another was of an age with her, his hair flecked with grey at the temples, a handkerchief tucked into his jacket pocket. And then two younger men, serious-faced and nodding as Kallas caught their eyes. They were his boys, would back him to the hilt. But the rest of the leaders of the Ühiskassa were not to be taken for granted, they would vote with their wallets every time. Particularly Annika Kapp, who returned his regard with her direct gaze and smiled, a reflex that lit her face and didn't reach those blue eyes. Kapp dealt in people, mostly women. Few who met her remembered the encounter with anything other than revulsion.

Kallas spoke in Estonian. 'Good morning. Please, let us sit.'

The doors to the dining room were closed by invisible hands. In front of each of the delegates was an ice-filled glass bowl with soft drinks, a leather desk-set with a blotter and pen-holder. All bar one of the young men had tablets on the table in front of them.

'I am honoured you could join me today. It is an important time for us as we contemplate a new era in our organisation's history. We have returned to profitability and have now significant gains following the recent operation we have been conducting from Beirut and the subsequent management of the

145

product into the Russian market, Klaus' significant achievement if I might say.'

One of the older men smiled and nodded his head, his hand raised in a small self-deprecating gesture. Kallas gazed around the room and continued. 'I note this is my second year of stewardship of our organisation. When I arrived, the Ühiskassa was on its knees. The post-Tarankov era saw unprecedented falls in revenues, a number of arrests of our associates and the effective closure of a number of lines of business.'

'Are you trying to soften us up for bad news, Jaan?'

Hillar Mark! Kallas kept his features neutral with effort. He smiled gently. 'By no means.'

Mark leaned forward. 'But you do have bad news for us, don't you? The Beirut operation is unravelling fast and I can only imagine you are here today,' Mark gazed around at the group at the table, 'to ask our advice on how you can extricate us without any further damage.'

Kallas managed to keep his hands resting on his legs. 'I am here to ask you nothing, Hillar. The Beirut operation continues to be successful and profitable.'

'Except British intelligence killed one of your men in Syria, didn't they? Piotr Loewe, wasn't it? Unusual that, Loewe was a very well-known operator. Very capable. Careless, such a man getting killed.'

'It was necessary to stop some information leaking that would have been prejudicial to us.'

'What information was so important?'

Kallas' smile would have silenced a more sensitive man. 'Mind your business.'

'But this is,' Mark spread his arms, 'our business.'

Kallas rose out of his chair. 'It does not concern you, Hillar. That is the end of the conversation. I will let you know when you need to be concerned, you can trust me on that.'

The two young men took to their feet. Kallas reached for his attaché case and strode out of the room. They followed him.

Kallas slid the cufflink in, twisting it to secure it against the white cotton. He picked the other from the sideboard. The bedroom was one of ten in the chateau. Cream and gold floral patterns adorned the curtains, rucked and held back by golden ropes, each side curving to meet high up under tasselled pelmets. The wallpaper was exuberant Chinoiserie, the cabinets against the walls carved from dark wood. The four-poster bed sat opulently on a rich rug covering most of the room's panelled floor.

Lying on the bed, Annika Kapp stretched luxuriantly, her obsidian hair flowing around her pale, heavy breasts. She ran her hand down her still-flat belly and teased the little tuft below it with her red-nailed forefinger.

'You fuck best when you're angry.'

'I am not angry.' Kallas stabbed his cuff through.

'The Ühiskassa is with you. Hillar Mark doesn't matter.'

'He has challenged my authority at the last two meetings we have held. He's argumentative and inquisitive. He insists on questioning matters that don't concern him. He should concentrate on his nightclubs and casinos.'

Annika flicked her hair back, exposing a dark nipple. 'So he scores little points. It hardly matters, Jaan. He speaks out but when it comes down to it, he does as he's told.'

'For now. But he's pushing all the time. And, between us, his information's too good. I don't like being spied on. He went too far this morning.'

Her teeth were white and even. Her laughter filled the room. She twisted out of bed and pranced to the bathroom. Running water splashed. She stood in the doorway, her hands flat on the wood, displaying for him. 'Jaan, you can be very funny with your serious face on. You've spent your life spying. Why shouldn't you taste your own medicine?'

Kallas slipped his feet into his black shoes. 'I guess I'm one of life's givers, not takers.'

'You think he's got people inside your circle?'

'Either that or Wye is grooming him for the succession.'

'You decided to do business with that American devil. You'll just have to pull his tail.'

'I might just do that.' He pulled his suit jacket from the back of the ornate chair. 'Did Mark ever mention he knew about the connection with Wye?'

'No, never. God, Jaan, I'd tell you the second I knew that. I understand what it means if that gets out. Your secret's safe with me. You should know that.'

Her face was earnest, the smile gone. He nodded. 'I do. I will see you at dinner.'

She wheeled around and he caught the flash of her firm ass, the black hair swinging against the canvas of her pale back. 'Don't forget I don't eat fish.'

Kallas shook his head as he closed the door behind him.

Hillar Mark didn't join the company for the excellent dinner, his voice missing from the murmur around the clink of cutlery and glass, Annika Kapp's sultry laughter and clacking heels on the wooden floor contrasted the heavier pace of Kallas and the light footwork of the two young men. The older men moved more cautiously. There were low outbreaks of laughter, less muted as the evening progressed. Liqueurs were served with coffee on the soft chairs by the great fireplace. Cigars were smoked. Later, in the master bedroom, there were soft moans followed by urgent cries.

The next morning they left after an early breakfast. It had started to snow as the party gathered in the hallway and made its way down to the cars. The drivers had warmed them up. Each one of them noted, as their cars scrunched down the drive past the stone walling between the snow-covered lawn and the dripping woodland, the bundle by the gate. It was crowned with the pale dead face of Hillar Mark, turned up to the sky.

Dennis Wye was a bemused man. In all the years he had known Jaan Kallas, he had never been invited to join him at a nightclub. And yet that was precisely where he was headed in one of Kallas' cars, a black Mercedes had picked him up from his hotel and was now speeding through Tallinn on the way to the Kilimanjaro Klub. The invitation had come late in the afternoon in gruff tones that brooked no refusal. Wye had acquiesced with grace and gone easy on the drinks with his dinner purely because he wasn't comfortable with the setup.

They pulled up outside the club. The driver yanked open the car door and Wye, who had settled on jeans, a jacket and a plain t-shirt as the evening's most appropriate wear, stepped out onto the snow-packed pavement. There was a long line of revellers. A bouncer in a dinner jacket and bow tie was waiting for Wye and walked him through the head of the queue into the club.

The music pumped. The staff at the front desk shouted to be heard as they dispensed wristbands and collected cash. The bouncer led Wye past the desk. A huge shaven-headed man in a jacket at least two sizes too small pushed open a doorway for them and Wye was led up a flight of black-painted stairs. Their footsteps echoed off the carmine walls.

There was a sofa and two chairs with a coffee table in the large room, little else. It was dominated by two floor-to-ceiling screens. One displayed the nightclub proper, a heaving crowd and strobing purple lights picking out the dance floor and DJ booth. To its right was a quieter room, a large lounge bar with a two-piece band playing. Punters sat around tables drinking cocktails and picking at bowls of nuts.

Jaan Kallas came in with two shaven-headed men in dinner jackets behind him. He was wearing his greatcoat, underneath was a pale mauve jacket, jeans and an open-necked shirt.

'Good evening, Dennis.'

'Jaan.'

Kallas turned and muttered something in Estonian to his men. He stood by Wye, their faces bathed in the flickering blue light from the nightclub. The mesmerised throng of dancers swayed, hands in the air, heads thrown back.

One of the men handed a remote to Kallas, another handed them both clinking, heavy-based tumblers.

Wye sipped his drink and turned his attention to the lounge bar as Kallas clicked the remote and the view changed to show the door. The movement on such a big screen was disconcerting and Wye had to make an effort not to step back. He sipped his drink watchfully.

'There,' said Kallas.

A group entered the lounge, two men and three girls, all perhaps in their twenties. The first of the young men was dark-haired, a genial face on a big man's frame, pumped biceps and a broad chest stretching his green t-shirt. The other man was smaller, curly-haired and slight. He glanced at the Rolex on his wrist as they walked in, the girls playful behind them.

Wye glanced around at a movement in his peripheral vision. One of Kallas' men was bending his head and touching his ear, nodding and talking in a low voice. A few seconds later, the door opened and a portly man in his fifties walked in. He was smoking a cigar, clenching it in pudgy, jewelled fingers.

Kallas took his hand. 'Arno, meet Dennis Wye. Dennis, this is Arno. This is his nightclub as of this morning. He has inherited it. Death brings some of us fortune, does it not?'

'Nice to meet you, Arno.'

He was thin-haired, a moustache that looked smeared over his weak lips by a careless face-painter's thumb. He grinned back at Wye. 'Likewise.'

'So who died?'

Arno looked away. Kallas ignored Wye's question. He decided not to ask it again.

On the screen, the little group sat around a cocktail table and were ordering drinks from a nervous Filipina in a maid's uniform. The girls were looking for attention. A dark-skinned brunette in a sheer lace top sat between the two men. The other two, blondes both, moved to the music. The big man patted a chair and one of the blondes moved to sit by him. Her hair was wavy with dark roots while the other's was ironed, dropping straight down her curved back. She curled into the seat, beaming but her face turned haughty when she talked to the waitress. Her eyes were blue, her brilliant smile slightly gappy and her mouth, at first generous-seeming, was sensual. Her upper lip curled back a little. She was wearing white jeans and a bare-backed top which showed off the Chinese characters tattooed down her lithe back as she twisted in her seat to call to the other blonde, who was standing.

She's showing off, the other one. Wye admired her Slavic bone structure, the long fingers running through that straight hair. She was looking for attention, dancing to the two-piece and laughing as she checked the room around her. A few people were on the dancefloor, moving to the music. Wye wondered what they were playing. Tattoo girl beckoned to the other blonde, a two-handed come hither as she rocked to the music, her strappy dress twirling.

They had the big guy's attention now as they danced together, holding each other's thighs. The wavy haired girl liked to wiggle and run her hand through her hair. Wye licked his lips. Now they're closer, rubbing and laughing. They constantly checked the big guy was watching, breaking apart as the tray of drinks arrived and they lost his attention. They returned to the table, the slight man whispering to the laughing brunette.

'Who are they?' Kallas broke into their silent perusal.

'Jonnie's girls.' Arno puffed his cigar. 'He's pimping them out at a thousand bucks each a night. That's hostessing. Extras is extra.'

'Expensive.'

'Word is they're worth it.'

'Word is they're ten a penny. Bring him in.'

The two shaven headed men left the room, one touching his ear and chattering in Estonian.

Wye raised his glass to Kallas. 'So it's kind of you to invite me, Jaan…'

'I wanted to show you something, Dennis. A demonstration, perhaps. I like to have us understand each other always. With close relationships over many years, sometimes we become careless in a way because we are so close, so long. You know what I mean?'

'Sure, but…' Wye felt the first stirrings of fear. It was like having a pet tiger, dealing with Kallas. Frank had always said he could feel the man licking his lips when he was caught in that unrelenting, Baltic stare.

On the screen a bouncer was approaching the big guy. He turned in his seat, smiling. The smile died and he looked up, straight at the camera. His eyes were wide. The girls were still playing, one put her hand on his arm and he shook her off, snapping. She turned to the curly-headed man, who shushed her with a wave of his hand. He asked something of the big guy, who barked back. His bleak gaze was still on the camera as he stood. The bouncer took his arm and led him to the door.

The girls were concerned now, clustering around curly hair and badgering him. His arms were open as he shrugged and they started to argue with each other.

The door burst open and the big guy came into the viewing room, his arms pinioned by the two bouncers. He was grey-faced. They stood him up in front of Kallas. Arno moved back a couple of paces.

'Hillar Mark is dead.'

The young man was silent, his scared eyes watchful. Wye fought the urge to ask Kallas what the fuck was going on here. He'd search the files for Hillar Mark later. The young man shook his head, his voice a whisper.'

'I don't know who he is.'

'Liar. You've been feeding him information. My own son, giving up my household to my enemies. Selling us out. What for, Erik? What was worth betraying your own father?'

The pale chin rose. 'Money. He gave me money.'

Kallas gestured to the screen where the girls were glowering in their chairs. 'To spend on whores?'

The young man was mute, his eyes flickering around the room to avoid Kallas'. His gaze found Wye, who stared back impassively, waiting for the next move.

Kallas strode to the coffee table and put down his glass. He pulled off his greatcoat and threw his jacket over the chair to lie on top of it.

'So what was your price, Erik? What I am worth? More than few hookers, am I not, son?'

The big frame sagged. The bouncers held him up. Erik shook his head slowly and said something in Estonian.

'Speak English,' Kallas barked. The young man flinched. His lips twitched.

Kallas stepped forward quickly and lunged to land a sweeping punch into the young man's stomach. The movement was shockingly fast and Wye stepped back a pace. Erik cried out, doubling up. The bouncers lifted him and Kallas hit him again in the gut. He drew a shuddering breath. His drawn face was sweaty as they pulled him up again. His eyes closed and his mouth clenched. He struggled against the two men but they held him tight. Kallas reached back and drove his fist into Erik's face. The punch split his lips and Wye heard the crack of bone as a second punch to the face landed and the young man's nose flattened. Kallas shook his hand and rubbed his knuckles. Erik's head was on his chest, his t-shirt streaked with drool and blood.

'Take him and kill him. Now.'

Wye stepped forward. 'But Jaan, he's your—'

'Shut up.' Kallas snapped back to Wye. 'Take him.'

The men wheeled, lifting the deadweight between them. Arno pulled open the door for them and left with a fearful glance at Kallas.

The room was silent. Kallas picked up his drink from the coffee table and drained it. He stood, his back to Wye, in the flickering light from the screens.

'He was your son.'

Kallas' voice was low. 'I am aware of this, who he was. He was my youngest son. The son who betrayed me. If your own son betrays you, Dennis, how can you trust him again? There is only one way for this and I have taken it. He made this, I did not.'

'So who is Hillar Mark?'

'You truly do not know?'

'I've never heard of him, Jaan.'

Kallas padded up to Wye and peered into his face. He extended his hand to hold Wye's chin between his thumb and forefinger. Wye held the intent gaze for an eternity.

Kallas stepped back and nodded. 'I believe you Dennis.' He raised his glass to clink against Wye's. 'Frank chose well.'

'So who is he?'

'He was the owner of this nightclub until this morning. He was not faithful to me and not honest. Like my youngest son, the playboy. They had become a problem and you must remove problems, Dennis. There is no room for sentiments. Like this I will remove our problem in Beirut, your Hartmoor and this Lynch. We will work together for success, Dennis. There can be no room for mistakes or careless actions.'

'I think we understand each other.' Wye beamed at Kallas and felt the sweat from his armpits soaked into his shirt, making it clammy. He finished his drink. 'Well, I'd best be going. It's late.'

'Godspeed.'

'Take care, Jaan.'

Wye put his glass down on the coffee table and left down the red-walled staircase, the bouncer at the bottom leading him out to the snowy night and the waiting car. Wye sat in the back, grateful for the heated seat as they sped through the black early morning streets snaking through the snowy city and shivered.

The roads were unfamiliar, even to Wye the stranger in town. They weren't heading up to the old town where his hotel was, but into the city itself. They passed a dark Soviet-era block of flats. The snow was settling, the flakes small and hard. A breeze had come up, the peaceful evening becoming more turbulent as the flakes whirled in the car's headlights.

They turned off the main road into a side street and again into an area of warehousing and industrial units. Wye tried to sound calm. 'This is not the way to my hotel. Where are we going?'

They curved round into a dark little road, industrial units looming either side of them. It was a dead end and Wye's heart started pounding.

The car drew to a halt. Framed in the headlights, standing in front of the wall at the end of the road were three dark figures. Snow pelted down from the black sky. One of them was kneeling, his hands behind his back. One stood behind him, hands held out and clasped together. Wye couldn't see the gun. The third figure stood to one side holding a mobile up, filming.

The crack of the shot was faint inside the soundproofed car. The bound figure slumped forwards and onto its side. They started to reverse, the tableau blending into the snow before it was folded into darkness.

'I am sorry. Take wrong turning,' said the driver.

SEVENTEEN

Sleep had eluded Hartmoor until the early hours and then he'd dreamed of Baghdad, his first posting after leaving Lebanon and festering in London for months while they worked out what to do about MECAS' premature end thanks to the Lebanese Civil War. In FCO parlance, the interrupted MECAS course of 1978 was the worst of all things – unfinished business, a file that couldn't be closed neatly. Instead it was passed from pillar to post. There could be a course in Jordan, things could be finalised there. The tutors couldn't be found. There were no rooms. Perhaps the students could stay in London. Decisions were deferred, delays became memos became delays. Weeks became months.

In the end someone had decided on 'do nothing' and they had posted him to Iraq instead, a junior member of the embassy staff. A part Arabist.

He woke reluctantly. He slipped out of bed and picked his way to the sofa and the strip of pills. He popped a tablet through the foil with his thumb. It skittered across the ornate glass-topped coffee table, coming to a rest by the golden base of the frilly lamp. He slipped it into his mouth and swallowed it with a tumbler of chilled water from the fridge.

The Albergo was elegant, decadent even. That the hotel's chintzy charms came at a price didn't worry Hartmoor. He had money. It was time he couldn't buy, he reflected as he felt the tablet in his throat. Another sip of icy water to dislodge it. He was taking too many of them, but he was past caring. Every time the pain started to slither back, he took a tablet. He was a little fuzzy-headed but, for the first time he can remember, he welcomed a lack of clarity.

The past two days have brought him into contact with things

he'd rather not remember. He trembled still at the memory of the screaming, the fear, his own cowardice and flight. But he had one goal now, one thing sustaining him. He was waiting for her so he can go up the mountain again and see her before the darkness finally comes for him as he knows it will. He was no longer sure which of the darknesses pursuing him it will be. But for the first time in years Hartmoor burned with the instinct to survive, not merely accept inevitability.

He had a goal.

He looked down at the foil strip in his hand. That was the last of the Roxanol. He had perhaps an hour, maybe two, to get more before the ache became agony. It was okay, he had played one of life's Chance Cards. He had a source of supply in reserve.

Hartmoor washed, his mind still back in those fateful weeks when the intense heat of summer dropped on Baghdad like a cloying blanket, rumours and alarms circulating as the city strained in the iron grip of the new president.

Saddam Hussein had smoked Cohibas. Hartmoor would always associate the smell of cigars with the strange mixture of fear and lassitude the man provoked. As the British ambassador, Ainsworth had been summoned to the presidential office and taken Jason Hartmoor for moral support. Hussein had been jocular and genial. It just made it all worse.

Hartmoor took the lift down from his room at The Albergo, almost stopping for coffee as the rich smell snaked out from the breakfast room. It reminded him of those Baghdad cigars. He hurried through the lobby and paused for breath on the front steps, leaning heavily on The Stick. The exertion had been too much and he was scared now that his hobbling pace would fail him, that the weight of the pain would fall on him before he could make it. There was a taxi, thankfully, waiting. The doorman waved him into the back seat and he duly tipped the man royally.

Hartmoor regained his breath for a second, the driver's

brown eyes quizzical in the mirror. He was young, in his thirties, pierced ears and a goatee beard.

'Clemenceau Medical Centre, please.'

'Sure thing, buddy.'

Hartmoor was distracted from his fear of The Pain by the Americanism. His first reaction, a wince of irritation - *I am not your buddy* - gave way to resigned acceptance. It really didn't matter. He sat back, feeling the coolness of the black leather, his mind drifting into the past.

He'd got out of Iraq before he went mad, but it had taken both effort and ingenuity to wriggle out of his ambassador's iron grasp. Ainsworth was a flawed man who leaned heavily on his young and brilliant colleague. He had consistently blocked Hartmoor's requests for a transfer. In the end he had gone around Ainsworth and secured a posting to Tel Aviv as a Consular Assistant.

The Ambassador's daughter, Hartmoor's wife, Lesley almost didn't come with him and, to his shock, he had realised he hadn't wanted her to. But in the end she reluctantly picked herself away from Baghdad society and her father's social cachet. To his hesitant delight, the sophisticated enchantments of Tel Aviv had brought Lesley Ainsworth back to him and, for a while, they loved again.

The receptionist in oncology looked up from her notebook computer as Hartmoor approached the desk. Her smile quickly clouded with concern. She came around the counter to offer her arm, but he waved her away breathlessly.

'No, no thank you. I shall be quite alright. Is there somewhere I can perhaps sit for a moment?'

'Here, the waiting area.' She took his arm anyway and he didn't protest as she helped him sit.

'Thank you. I'm sorry, it's just –'

'It's okay, you don't have to explain. Which doctor? You have appointment?'

'Dr Eid. Yes, for ten.'

She returned to the reception desk and made a call. He caught a faint whiff of hospital smell, antiseptic and cooking. Hospitals around the world must smell the same. Cabbage. He looked at his hands resting on The Stick. Those hands had loved once, had held life in them. They had caressed, shaped and felt the softness of her hair. Before he had become stone.

The receptionist startled him. 'He will see you now. Come, I will help you.'

'I can walk thank you, *Madame*.' Hartmoor strained to rise, following her down the corridor with jerks of The Stick.

Dr Eid was in his late fifties, already white-haired but sporting a dark moustache. He was standing, smiling a welcome as Hartmoor entered.

'Mr Hartmoor. David Evans said you may well come and see me. I'm glad you have. Please, a seat. Can I offer you coffee? We are blessed with our own machine here and it is rather excellent.'

Hartmoor nodded. 'Yes, yes that would be very nice.'

'Mariam? For me also, please. If you would not mind.'

'Of course not, *Doktor*. Mr Hartmoor, how do you like coffee?'

'As it comes, thank you.'

'It is a long time since David and I studied together. How is he?'

'Very well. He is a most diligent man. He originally made the diagnosis of my,' Hartmoor swallowed drily, 'condition.'

'And how long—'

'Almost ten years now. Dr Davies originally gave me ten months. I am profoundly grateful he was mistaken... mostly' Hartmoor smiled without warmth. 'I have come to ask you for some Roxanol. I have run out and do rather depend upon it.'

Dr Eid's face clouded. 'I can imagine. When did you last—?'

'This morning'

The receptionist returned carrying two tiny espresso cups rattling on saucers.

'Mariam, thank you. Can you please call down to pharmacy for ten boxes of Roxanol hundred? And I think,' Dr Eid peered at a sheet of paper, holding his glasses away from his face a little. 'Yes, Zenpep and Nexium. A month's worth if they wouldn't mind?'

'Of course *Doktor.*'

'Thank you, Dr Eid.'

'It's nothing. David's an old friend and it's a pleasure to be able to help one of his patients. I know he'd do the same for one of mine if they ever appeared in, where is he practising now, *Tenby* isn't it? It must be very beautiful there in Pembrokeshire. I was in Cardiff once, briefly.'

Hartmoor was taken back to the waves snaking along the mile-long beach at Newgale, the spray in the air and rolling green sward beyond the rocky margins. He tried to stem the tide of sadness. 'It is. You should visit sometime.'

'Will you be in Beirut for long?'

'I have no concrete plans. Plans seem irrelevant these days.'

Dr Eid sipped at his coffee and nodded. 'Yes. I understand. But please, if you should need anything at all when you are in Beirut, here, take my mobile number. Where are you staying?'

'The Albergo,' admitted Hartmoor.

Dr Eid whistled. 'A nice place.'

The coffee was truly excellent, Hartmoor reflected, but the little waves of hurt marred the liquorice pleasure on his tongue. Soon they would become whitecaps and then a veritable storm. He wished the pharmacy would hurry.

When the receptionist came in with the boxes in a carrier bag, he almost tore the Roxanol open, his fingers shaking. He popped a tablet from the blister pack and this time he could savour the coffee taste, its strong aroma and the burnt chocolate on his palate. The relief was instant; psychosomatic, he knew. The Roxanol would take time to come on, dulling and elephantine.

But better, anything was, than The Pain.

EIGHTEEN

Lynch held the phone away from his ear and let the tide of invective play itself out. He stood on the balcony of his fifth-floor apartment in Beirut's *Ain Mreisse* district, the street busy below him. To his left downhill stretched the Mediterranean, the stippled blue waters gleaming in the soft morning light. He sipped his coffee and placed the mug on the white plastic table, next to the Heineken ashtray stolen from some bar or another years ago. The stream of abuse turned staccato and Lynch realised he was being asked a question.

'Sorry, Brian?'

'I said, did you not have any thought of following procedure or letting anyone know what the hell you were intending to do?'

'That's how you break cover, Brian. I wanted minimal oversight.'

Channing exploded again. 'Break cover? You stupid bastard, you've caused a diplomatic incident and triggered a major murder investigation implicating British nationals in Syria. Now you've had two SAS men killed? How could you have possibly done more to break cover? I should sack you here and now, wash my hands of you. And what's this horseshit about minimal oversight? You've spent your whole life under minimal oversight. That's the problem, Lynch, because you actually need a wet nurse, let alone minimal fucking oversight.'

'Brian...'

'Don't Brian me. I've got a major shit-storm here and two good men's families have to be told they've lost husbands and fathers. We're throwing out D notices like confetti and we've had to put heads I haven't got onto trying to re-route those two deaths to Kandahar. You had two good men killed, Lynch. And you expect me to cover for you?'

Lynch took a deep breath. He gripped the mobile with white knuckles as he ground out the words. 'That's too far, Channing. They were good men who knew what they were doing and were left with a clear brief they understood and accepted. The man they were against was harder than them, that's the truth of it. It's a dangerous game we're playing here.' Lynch drew breath. 'But you're not here, Brian are you? You're sitting in your leather armchair in Millbank. So why don't you just back off? If your boy Hartmoor gets loose you'll have a hell of a lot more shit on your face than you do right now. Your whole Middle East strategy throughout the last twenty years is full of the holes Jason Hartmoor shot in it. So sure, go ahead and sack me. Tomorrow this whole shithouse is going up in very public flames indeed if you do.'

Lynch took a deep breath and held it, forcing himself to calm down. There was a stunned silence on the line. 'Look, the CIA clearly want Hartmoor very badly indeed. They don't want the past coming back right now because they're up to their necks in something here that involves this Estonian, Kallas. Hartmoor threatens it, possibly because Kallas was Dmitri back then and was Hartmoor's controller. I don't know. Hartmoor's the key to all of this and I need to find him. But the Americans are tied in with Kallas.'

'That's an extraordinary assertion.'

'The surviving Estonian was at Abbas Ali's last night. I had him tracked. He went on to an apartment in Ashrafiyeh. I confirmed the address. It's Dennis Wye's place. We know the Estonian is Jaan Kallas' man. Why's he meeting the CIA? The General pinpointed Kallas as an former American asset. What if he's still one? All these years later? What if the head of one of the most feared Russian Mafia organisations is actually working for Uncle Sam? Forget the past. Where does that leave us today, Brian?'

Lynch waited for a response, but Channing was silent. Lynch imagined him sitting back in his anthracite carbon fibre executive chair and tapping the glass desktop with his Mont Blanc pen.

Channing's voice was silky smooth. 'So what do you suggest we do, Gerald?'

'There's nothing on Kallas unless we can find out what's happening here in Beirut. There's nothing on Hartmoor unless we find Hartmoor. We're racing Kallas and the Americans to get to our man. I say we try and find Hartmoor and work out why he became the biggest traitor since Kim Philby. And that's if the bastard doesn't die on us first.'

Channing sighed. 'What do you need from me?'

'Space to work in. This is not a neat, regulated environment, Brian. I need cover.'

'You have it. But it's limited, Lynch. Anything not a hundred per cent straightforward, I want oversight. You understand me?'

Lynch fought to stop his grin projecting down the line. 'Sure. I got you.'

Lynch paid the *servees* driver and waved goodbye to the two surly Palestinian lads in the back. You never knew who you'd meet up with in the shared taxis, but then they probably didn't expect the *Ingleezi* in the front of the car to be carrying a gun. And Lynch was.

He marched through the shiny marble reception area of the building and punched the lift call button. The door opened with a soft ping and he selected the fourth floor before turning to study himself in the mirror. His reflection was pale. He had dreamed of Marcelle and woken up with her face in his mind's eye.

He rang the doorbell of Dennis Wye's flat. The door was answered by a slim younger man in shirtsleeves and denims. A white-toothed smile and frank blue eyes were crowned by a prominent forehead. 'Hi, we've been expecting you. Come in.'

Lynch nodded and entered, careful to mask his

astonishment. Behind him, the American accent was still talking. 'We've got coffee. You use some? How'd you take it now? One sugar, white isn't it. Take a seat and I'll be with you momently.'

Lynch sat on the hide sofa, gazing around at the neatly furnished apartment, arabesque prints on the walls, a chrome framed dining table with a heavy, smoked-glass top. Expensive carpet, tasselled rugs tossed artfully here and there. A show home, he thought, looking up as his host returned with coffee.

'Guess you could use this, eh? You've been a busy guy.' A hand was held out to Lynch. A firm grip. 'I'm forgetting my manners. I'm Clancy Goldman. As in Sachs, though I don't got the dollars.'

Lynch sipped the coffee. 'So where's Wye?'

'Ah, now that I am not at liberty to reveal but I can tell you he's not here. I mean obviously not here, but not in Beirut. I'm sort of heading things up here in the meantime. For the foreseeable future. Dennis has had to do a little cleaning up on account of your Mr Hartmoor. Who, if I can just be sure we can allow each other to be frank and upfront about things, we would appreciate if you would give up into our custody.'

Goldman had taken a seat and was blowing across his coffee as Lynch shook his head to clear it, placing his mug carefully on the low coffee table. 'Hang on one second here. Jason Hartmoor is a British citizen. You're going to need an awful lot of paperwork for him to be,' Lynch made air quotes. 'Given up to anyone, even if I had which I most assuredly do not.'

'I think we're talking about pragmatic on-the-ground co-operation here, Gerald, not bureaucracy. Hartmoor is a very dangerous man who has already compromised key elements of a major CIA operation and he needs to be reined in before he does more damage.'

'Hartmoor is an old diplomat with a long and mostly undistinguished career behind him who happens to be dying of cancer. He's hardly Aldritch Ames.'

'He had a lifetime working as a double, Gerald. He sold you

boys out and he sold us out through you. And now he's threatening our operation and we want him brought down, not running around wild. To be frank with you.'

'So what operation is he threatening?'

'That's classified.'

'What's the nature of his threat? He knows something from his past? How can he threaten your operation?'

'Similarly classified. And not germane. You just have to trust us on this Gerald and make like you remember the Special Relationship, *kapisch*?'

Lynch took a sip of coffee and sat back, the morning sunlight through the picture window warming him. The beam caught the soft rise of the steam from his mug. He wanted a smoke very badly indeed.

'Your operation involves Abbas Ali and the link between Ali and the Estonian oligarch Jaan Kallas, who also happens to head the Ühiskassa. Kallas was a top Soviet advisor to the Syrian government during the Lebanese Civil War. At the time, Kallas bore the work name Dmitri and scored a number of intelligence coups that advanced his career quite spectacularly. Most of these scores were at the expense of the British, a couple of smaller ones we can assume were at your own expense. The British leaks can be traced back to one Jason Hartmoor, but we can't be sure about the American ones because for some reason Langley has stopped co-operating on the Hartmoor file. Am I being germane so far?'

Goldman was immobile, his eyes watchful. Lynch pitched his voice low, making Goldman lean forwards to catch his words. 'Except Hartmoor is an innocent man, Clancy. He's no more a mole than Nelly The Elephant. So you tell Dennis bloody Wye that no, he can't have Hartmoor and unless he starts to bring us inside the tent, I'm going to set fire to it using so much fucking petrol no amount of pissing is going to put it out. I don't handle being bullied well, Clancy.' Lynch sat back with a smile and threw out his hands. 'But hey, I sincerely like you guys and want to help out. Just toss us a bone, eh? What about it?'

Lynch delighted in the fleeting tightening of Goldman's cheek muscle.

'Give us Hartmoor and we'll bring you inside. A hundred percent.'

Goldman was too old to be so young. Lynch struggled to stem the contempt before it reached his face. Bumptious, that was the word. Lynch had thought him an operator, but in fact he was just skin deep, what you see is what you get. This wasn't an act; this was Clancy to the core.

'No, I don't think so. Now if you'll excuse me, Clancy, your wee albino Estonian friend has something of mine and I need to go and get it back.'

'He's n...' Goldman halted, wincing.

Lynch pushed himself off the sofa. 'Stay lucky, Clancy.' He resisted the urge to look back as he pulled open the door, settling for imagining the American kicking himself.

Lynch's next stop was Hamra and the Princess Suites. A hundred dollar bill procured the Estonian's key from the concierge, a hunched, wet-lipped old lady in a blue dress printed with daisies that reminded him of 1970s wallpaper. The stranger had left early in the morning without a word. He never spoke unless he had to, that one. His, you know, friend, hadn't been around for days. These times, *monsieur*. These times…

Lynch had listened to her with one ear, the other gauging the sounds of the building. The creaks of the lift, the echoing tap of feet on the stairs. He thanked her with a smile, closing his fist around the cold metal key. He took the stairs to the second floor two at a time, the reek of cat piss in his nostrils. Pausing in the corridor, he listened again. A door slammed upstairs, the faint sound of a radio. He put his ear to the door of apartment 210. Lynch unholstered his gun, slipped the key into the lock and opened the door. He stole inside, pulling the door shut behind him.

The studio apartment was furnished cheaply. The cupboards were empty. The little white plastic packet of soap in the bathroom was untouched. The bedside phone rang, explosive in the silence of Lynch's disappointment. He wheeled, his gun held out. Feeling stupid, he slipped it back in its holster as he strode over to the phone. He lifted the handset.

Marcelle's voice was breathless. 'Lynch, please, please he's—' She cried out in pain.

'I could have kill you, easy,' the cold voice on the line said. Red laser light flashed on the mirrored wardrobe door. Flinching instinctively, he whirled to face the window, but his position by the bed shielded him from any direct line of sight. The Estonian was right. He had walked clearly through the field of fire covered by that laser sight. 'I tell you morning. Where is old man?'

'I don't know. I'm trying to find him. I need more time.'

'I can kill her. Slow. You have until evening. I am not patient man. You waste time.'

Lynch ground the words out. 'I don't know where he is. I swear I don't know.'

'Get him. Or I kill her. Slow.' The dry chuckle rasped like dead leaves. The line went dead. The window exploded. Lynch dived for the floor. The wardrobe mirror shattered. The room was filled with fragments of flying glass, the explosion ringing in Lynch's ears. He lay hunched foetally on the floor, listening to the silence. A voice shouted from one of the other apartments. A woman screamed.

Picking his way through the shards on the carpet as best he could, Lynch crawled to the door and, checking over his shoulder to ensure he was out of sight of the window, pulled himself to his feet. He shook himself down. Shards pattered to the floor. Opening the door, he faced a truculent-looking man in a vest.

'What's going on? What happened?'

Lynch smiled and shook his head. 'Nothing. An accident, I think. Nothing to worry about.' He locked the door and pocketed the key.

'Didn't sound like nothing to me.'

Lynch was already walking towards the staircase. 'Don't worry about it,' he called back. As he took the stairs down, his mobile rang. Saif Zaidi. His eyebrow arched as he thumbed the screen.

'Lynch.'

'Where's my man, Lynch? He's not back yet.'

'I don't know, Saif. I talked to him this morning. He did the job I asked for and paid you for. *Bass*.'

'Well, he's not here.'

'He did the job, Saif.'

'So where is he?'

Lynch strode through the lobby, ignoring the concierge's attempt to pull him back. 'I'm not his keeper Saif. He did the job, I paid you. That's it.' He cut the call and rejected the one that followed, mouthing '*shit*' as he walked into the street.

He called Tony Chalhoub.

'Tony.'

'Lynch. Your sense of timing is impeccable. We've got him. He got his pills from the cancer unit at the Clemenceau Hospital in Ashrafiyeh. You can't get them from pharmacies, only hospitals. That made things easier. He's staying at The Albergo. I've sent a team for him; I'll be there myself in twenty.'

'Can you pull them back? Please? Leave this one to me?'

'This is a murder enquiry.'

'I need Hartmoor. For Marcelle.'

'And you think you can pull off a trade with him? He'll kill her and you both.'

'I have to try.'

Chalhoub sighed. 'You've got an hour Lynch. Then we turn up with the full lightshow.'

'Thanks, Tony.'

The Albergo was Beirut's foremost monument to chintz and rococo, no surface left undecorated by scrolls and statuettes or complicated flower arrangements in elaborate vases. The corridor was richly carpeted. Elegantly framed paintings in gold filigree frames hung on the walls. There were displays of porcelain inset either side of the panelled wooden door. Any pane of glass in sight was etched with fleur de lys or floral fantasies. Lynch wrinkled his nose and rang the bell. There was a sound behind the door, a hesitant shuffle. Lynch rang again. Hartmoor opened the door.

'You.'

'Well you're lucky it's not the Estonian laddie, aren't you?' Lynch gestured into the room. 'Do you mind?'

'No, go on in. I'll order tea and cakes.'

'Now wouldn't that be nice.' Lynch sat on the sofa, flinging his arm across the back of it. 'But we don't have the time for the niceties, Jason. I need you to help me out with a little local problem we're having. And then I think we need a long chat together.'

Hartmoor sat slowly, his pale features twisting as he settled. 'What local problem?'

'Let's start at the beginning. What the hell happened up there in Jounieh?'

Hartmoor passed his hand over his eyes. 'Christ. Don't take me back there. It was terrible. He came from nowhere.'

Lynch sat forward, taking care to soften his expression. 'I can only imagine. They were good men and didn't deserve that.'

'He screamed for ages. I think it was Meadows.' Hartmoor wrung his hands. 'The other must have died instantly. The screams were all from one man.'

'How did you get away?'

'I was in the kitchen when the men sensed up a problem. They asked me to go out to the back while they handled it. I don't think they were ready for how sudden and violent the assault was. I heard the shots and hid. Like a child. In the garden. Under the bench. I listened to him being tortured, refusing to give me away. He kept insisting I had left with you. And then the screaming stopped. It just stopped. The silence was worse, in its way. He came outside, stood sniffing like a dog. I could feel him there. I stayed under that table for hours after I heard him leaving, until it started to get light.'

Lynch found the mini-fridge and poured two whiskies into tumblers. 'Here.'

Hartmoor's smile was fleeting. 'I can't. The painkillers.' He looked down at his hands bunched in his lap. 'I slunk out like the coward I am and managed to make my way to the main road. I got a lift from a farmer into Jounieh and then a taxi to Beirut. And here you find me. How did you? Find me?'

'Roxanol. You're eating quite a lot of it. There aren't many foreigners around here using the stuff, oddly enough.'

Hartmoor nodded. 'Fair cop, as they say. For what it's worth, I'm glad it was you and not that madman found me. I suppose you'll tell me I wasn't careful enough to hide properly.'

'No, no you weren't really. You didn't even look in the eyeglass in the door. You're not very good at this, are you?'

'And yet you seem to think I was a Russian spy. I'm not cut out for that life, Mr Lynch, as you correctly surmise.'

Lynch acknowledged the point with a nod. 'Just a simple diplomat, isn't that the way of it?'

'I have concealed nothing from you. Tell me, who is this Estonian murderer?'

'He works for a man you met once called Jaan Kallas. You knew Kallas better perhaps as Dmitri.'

'Dmitri? Who the hell's Dmitri?'

'It doesn't matter. Let's get my short-term problem out of the way. We'll have time to sort out the big-picture stuff.'

'And if I don't have as much time?'

'You'll be fine. You're my goat, so you are. So you can't die on me now.'

'Your *goat*?'

'Yes. I'm going to tie you to a nice tree and wait for something to happen.' Lynch pulled his mobile out and tapped at the screen. The call was answered within two rings. 'Abbas Ali. It's Gerald Lynch.'

'How the hell did you get my number?'

'It doesn't matter where I got your number.'

'I don't want—'

'No, listen to me this is important. Tell your Estonian friend I have what he needs.'

'What Estonian—'

'That's it. Pass it on.' Lynch dropped the line.

'And now?' said Hartmoor, sitting back and looking at Lynch down his nose.

Lynch placed a crystal-studded iPhone on the coffee table and pocketed his own. 'We wait,' he replied.

Lynch forced himself to take his time before picking up the mobile on the sixth ring. 'Lynch.'

The strongly accented voice was silken. 'Do you have man I require?'

'Yes. I suggest we meet and exchange. Purely four people. No associates. I am willing to give you what you seek unconditionally. But I want my…' He could almost hear her voice. '…colleague unharmed. I have no interest in pursuing my official capacity in this. It's personal. Understand?'

'Yes. Agreed.'

'There is a disused warehouse on the Daoura Road near Bourj Hammoud bearing the name Union Plastics. We meet there in one hour. Agreed?'

The line cut. He glanced across at Hartmoor, who was trying to look as if he didn't care for Lynch's conversation. God but the man was such an arrogant fucking Brit it wasn't true. And yet his courage was remarkable. Lynch shrugged off the thought and hauled himself up from the soft hotel chair. 'Come on. We'd best get moving.'

'And if I refuse?'

Lynch paused for a second. 'I'll fucking shoot you. Seriously.'

Tony Chalhoub's voice on the phone was urgent. 'Come on Lynch, just wait up. I can have a close support squad down there, we can bring in negotiators. You don't have to do this. You know it won't end well. I can't cover for you, not again. There'll have to be formal enquiries and I'll tell them everything. You can't behave like this, not in modern Beirut.'

'Modern Beirut my arse, Tony. I don't have the luxury of time here. I told you, the Union Plastics warehouse. But hold back until I tell you it's clear. You need snipers but tell them to keep a distance. He's a dangerous little bastard. He'll only do damage if your lot start letting off sirens and stuff.'

'I have public safety to consider Lynch.'

'It's a disused warehouse in an industrial area and it's past working hours. The place is deserted. Just handle it softly with some nice, distant support and I'll let you know when it's over. I can handle it. If he walks out and I don't, you get him anyway.'

'And what about the mess afterwards, Lynch? Who handles that?'

'There won't be a mess, Tony.'

The silence roared. Chalhoub spoke first. 'I can't stop you, Lynch, but listen to me. I will apply the law, I swear.'

'You're a good man, Tony. I wouldn't expect any less of you. I have to go now. I'll let you know when you can come in.'

'One last thing Lynch. Answer me straight.'

'Shoot.'

'Did you use Zaidi to get out of Syria?'

Lynch pursed his lips and nodded. 'Yes. Why?'

'They just found his driver. He'd been sliced from the groin to his neck. Awful wound. He was next to his car, just outside Chatila.'

'Interesting. Thanks, Tony.'

'Anything you want to tell me?'

'Not right now, no.' Lynch kept his voice light. 'See you later.'

Lynch dropped the mobile into the pale leather seat pocket of the Mercedes. The hotel driver was looking nervously at the gun in Lynch's lap. They had rushed to Ain Mreisse to stop outside Lynch's apartment as he dashed upstairs to pick up the squared-off pistol. Its long barrel shone, blued gunmetal in the fading orange light of the day. Lynch glanced back at Hartmoor napping. Hartmoor's eyelids fluttered open. He caught Lynch's stare and smiled wanly. Lynch tried to smile back, but it didn't really work. It was more of a wince.

'You're not going to give me up to him, are you Mr Lynch?'

'No. Of course not.' Lynch said. 'But I need to draw him out.'

'It's not death, you understand. I have an appointment I must keep. It is most important to me. You know it is.'

They pulled up outside the warehouse. Work had stopped for the day and the area felt abandoned, pieces of rubbish blown by little squalls of cold wind. The warehouse was grey, rust breaking through the paint to ooze to the ground. Lynch glanced across at the driver, whose nervous gaze was flitting. 'Wait for us here, okay?'

'Sure *seer.*'

Lynch helped Hartmoor out of the back door, saw him propped on The Stick and led the way into the warehouse. The big sliding door was open. The empty space echoed with his footsteps, the concrete scree floor resonating with Hartmoor's weary shuffle and the bump of The Stick's rubber foot. Lynch stopped a little way inside the doorway and glanced around. The waning light lengthened the shadows in the big space, girders thrusting up to support the high corrugated roof. The big fans dropping down from the ceiling were still, fluorescent lighting strips suspended between them.

Standing at the far end of the yawning emptiness, the Estonian wore black. He held a pistol loosely in each hand. His white hair stood out, even in the gathering gloom. Sitting on a chair by him, her hands pulled back behind it, was Marcelle. Her head was bowed, her rich hair tumbled onto her lap.

'Come forward,' the Estonian called out. 'Closer.'

Lynch paced the distance slowly so Hartmoor could keep up. About halfway, the Estonian waved his pistol. 'Stop here. Drop gun.'

Lynch laughed. 'Now why would I do something stupid like that?'

The Estonian moved languidly, his right hand rising to train a pistol on Hartmoor, his left pushing Marcelle's chin up with the other gun. Her face was battered, a trail of dried blood on her upper lip. She mouthed Lynch's name. One of her eyes had closed up, livid swelling around it. The Estonian put the gun to her temple, pushing her head over. Marcelle hardly looked as if she cared. Her eyes closed.

'You want her alive. I not care this man dead. I not care you dead. You want. Not me. You mistake. Stupid you. Drop gun.'

Lynch dropped the gun. It was still twisting in the air as the Estonian fired and Marcelle's head exploded. Distorted by the bullet, her face crumpled as a gout of matter flew out. Her body was flung to the side by the force of the point-blank shot. Lynch shoved Hartmoor who fell, his hated Stick flying up in the air. The Estonian's shot at Hartmoor missed. Lynch whipped his own pistol from its silicon holster and fired twice, his middle finger double tapping the feather-light trigger. Marcelle's body, tied to the chair, toppled to crash on the concrete, the remains of her head bounced once, wetly. A bleeding mass of hair and broken matter lay on the ground.

The Estonian's gun fired again, but the shot was wide and

high. He crumpled slowly, one eye transformed into an entry wound. Lynch pulled at the trigger purposefully and with great care, the bullet plucking a hole in the Estonian's chest. Advancing now, another shot to the kneeling man's shoulder. Again to throw the pale head back. Again the groin. Lynch stood over the slumped remains and emptied the magazine. The firing pin clicked as Lynch blindly pulled the trigger. He found his voice and cried out, his negation echoing from the metalled walls.

He lost track of time. Chair legs pointed at him, blood pooled beyond them. Darkness crept up around. A white-haired corpse sprawled on the floor. The sound of harsh breathing. His own. Chest pumping. Pain. Not physical. Breathing slowed. Tickly sweat ran down his face, dropped to fall on the huddle of cloth below. Rust. Muffled noises. Voices.

Flash. Light. The roof popping with light. Lynch blinked. Blinded. A touch, his shoulder. Swung round.

Tony, shouting. Lynch disconnected, watched himself from the girders in the roof, a tiny figure surrounded by bodies. He rushed back into himself, filled himself with life. He exulted in the sensation. He found laughter.

Chalhoub slapped him. The beagle eyes were furious, the man's mouth drawn in anger. Lynch's head was whipped around by the blow. He staggered. Shame washed over him. *Fool.* Chalhoub was shouting, his words still muffled by the fog around Lynch, who craned his head to hear.

He caught a phrase through the fog. 'I can manage it? Manage it?'

The words echoed, bouncing back and rising to a crescendo. Lynch's world went black.

He woke in darkness, fear in his mind. He let his heart slow, tried to be rational. He remembered. He whispered 'no' into the shadows as they resolved themselves, faint lines and shapes looming. His own bedroom. He was on the bed, clothed.

Low voices. A pencil of dim light under the door. With a rustle of cloth, he rolled over and placed his feet on the floor. He pushed himself upright. He swayed, putting out a hand to steady himself. He wasn't wearing shoes. He crept to the door and opened it. Chalhoub and Hartmoor were sitting together. Both had glasses in their hands. The lamp on the side table was providing the only light in the room. They both turned to him, Chalhoub getting to his feet.

'Gerald. You okay?'

'Get me one of those, would you Tony?' Lynch waved at Chalhoub's glass. 'Large with ice. Very large.'

Chalhoub looked as if he were going to tell Lynch where to go, but then nodded and walked over to the drinks cabinet, then into the kitchen. Lynch sat. He glanced at Hartmoor. 'Christ, you look awful.'

Hartmoor raised his glass with a grim smile. 'Not looking so great yourself, Lynch.' He sipped his water. 'I'm sorry, about your friend.'

'Sure. Thanks.'

Chalhoub returned with ice clinking in the tumbler. He lifted the bottle from the drinks tray and brought over the glass and bottle to Lynch, who took them and poured. He raised the brimming glass to the two men, drained it and refilled it.

'So.'

Chalhoub sat, wearily passing his hand through his hair. 'So, Marcelle is dead. The Estonian has been formally identified as Karl Persson. We got him coming through immigration two weeks ago. There was another Estonian national on that flight, one Piotr Loewe. Loewe left Beirut for Aleppo at the end of last week. He flew the day before you, Gerald, although he didn't use a false passport when he landed, unlike you. You underestimate our co-operation with our new friends over the border. The Syrians confirm Loewe had checked into an apartment suite in Aleppo but he hasn't been seen since. His description, they tell us, does match that of a mystery man killed in Aleppo souk two nights ago by another foreigner.' Lynch could hardly fail to detect the irony in Chalhoub's voice. 'Apparently he had a diamond in his right canine but that had been removed by the time the police got there. Whether or not it was the killer who removed it, they are unsure.'

'How long have I been out?'

'Four hours. We've been busy.'

'So who are they? The Estonians.'

'We don't know. We've got search requests for both men with Interpol and we're waiting to hear back.'

'Abbas Ali knows them alright.'

'I don't care. As far as I'm concerned, the first one is a Syrian problem and the second one is now a closed file, killed in the course of a law enforcement operation based on a tip-off. You're lucky I didn't throw you to the lions and let them charge you for murder. As it is, I'm having to fight hard to stop you being arrested.'

'Come off it, Tony. You know what that bastard did. He killed Marcelle, for fuck's sake. In cold blood. He'd have done for Hartmoor, too if I hadn't moved fast.'

Chalhoub stood. 'I'm turning in. I suggest you do the same.'

Lynch watched his old friend leave. He took a deep gulp of whisky.

'So what are you going to do now?' Lynch had forgotten Hartmoor, so still had the man been.

'How the fuck do I know?' Lynch refilled his glass. He sat back, feeling the wetness of the condensation as he held it on his belly.

Hartmoor was silent. Lynch closed his eyes and there was Marcelle, her head erupting. He fought back the urge to vomit with a gasp. He lurched forward, paddling at the air.

'Are you okay?'

'No. But I'll live.' Lynch balanced himself, fought to control his breathing. He cast around for something to take his mind off the image burned into his mind by an instant of loss. 'You mentioned you had an appointment. Before we went into the warehouse. With Mai Khoury?'

'Yes, she's coming back here on Friday. It's my chance to finally see her again, to at least meet with her. I can't put the past back, I can't make it right. But before I die I'd like just to see her and tell her…'

'Tell her what?'

'That I love her, I suppose. That I always have. That I'm a fool. That I know it now.'

'It won't actually fix anything.'

'It's too late to fix things, Gerald. I am sorry for your loss, I know what loss feels like. Perhaps not like that, not violently. But I understand, I think. You were very close, weren't you?'

Lynch sipped his whisky. 'You interrogating me now, are you?'

'I thought it might help to talk.'

Lynch laughed at that. 'Maybe, maybe not. It fills the silences though, doesn't it?' He poured another whisky and wanted a cigar.

'I arrived in Beirut in the '80s. I wasn't what you'd call a textbook SIS recruitment, they picked me up on the Falls Road and I should have been put back down there, if truth be told. The IRA and the PLO were pretty buddy-buddy in those days and there was a bomb maker called O'Brien, could have been his real name, probably wasn't. He was good, alright. But we had a lead to him and just before I could catch up with him, he ups and leaves to Beirut. There's a whole IRA training operation going on over here and so I found myself in Beirut in the middle of a bloody civil war. That's how I met Marcelle. I got a job as a barman in her cathouse, the Puss In Boots. She always insisted on it being in French, she thought it was classier, *Le Chat Botté*. It wasn't bad cover as it happens.'

Lynch stood, stretching and walked around the room. He bent down to pick up his tumbler, his face in shadow. He waved the tumbler at Hartmoor. 'You know, coming from the Falls, I thought I knew sectarianism, but we were amateurs compared to these boyos. They really tore the guts out of this country. Beirut scared me, Jason, scared me to within an inch of my life. You know what Marcie taught me back then, the "charming lady" of this little cathouse in Monot? She taught me that having death around every corner of your life gives each second you live an edge of joyful fucking brilliance. You should feel like that, in your position.'

Hartmoor acquiesced. 'Perhaps I should. It's hard to see it quite that way every day, but I see your point.'

'So I chased my IRA bucko by day and worked in her bar at night. We got on okay, Marcie and me. We never fell in love, but sometimes things just happened, if you know what I mean. Her client list was something else and I got more useful intelligence out of the girls in that place than any other intelligence operative in Beirut could get in a lifetime of baksheesh and blackmail. They're all sat in the bar at the St Georges looking at each other and I'm picking up first-hand intel from a bunch of whores. Jesus, I used to have a laugh at them all. I was providing better stuff back to London from here operating undercover than their whole formal apparatus was digging up. After the war that all quietened down of course, although when the Iraqis used to come to Beirut in the early days of the CPA the gold seam was gold again. So you see we've got history, her and me. A lot of history. She was my secret weapon. And now she's gone.'

Hartmoor's gentle snore was the reward for Lynch's confession. He shrugged, slung back the whisky in his glass and tapped the pale man on the shoulder. 'Come on, let's get you to bed.'

Blinking, Hartmoor took Lynch's hand and pushed himself up from the sofa.

Waking was the usual little ritual of disorientation, surprise and slowly building pain before the Roxanol dulled his edges. Hartmoor dressed and walked through into the empty living room. Looking around, he spotted Lynch sitting on the balcony in the sun, staring out to sea. Hartmoor went into the kitchen and rooted around until he had unearthed some cardamom-tinted ground coffee. He boiled the kettle, pulled two cups out of the cupboard and filled the cafétiere. He carried them out to the balcony, having to put down the full pot before he could slide open the French doors. Lynch didn't turn at the sound. Hartmoor put the cups on the table. He recovered the cafétiere and said, 'Shall I be mother?'

Lynch's face was drawn. There were dark stains around his reddened eyes. His face, turned to Hartmoor, was bleak. 'Sure. Pour away.'

'Did you sleep?'

'A little. Too many ghosts for now.'

There was an empty whisky bottle, not the one he had been pouring from last night, and a glass. There were four cigar butts in the green plastic Heineken ashtray and a crumpled Cohiba pack.

'Here.' Hartmoor handed Lynch a steaming mug of black coffee.

Lynch sipped at his coffee and pulled a face. 'Sugar.'

'I'll get some.'

'No, don't bother. Have a seat. The sun's only lovely.' Lynch hauled himself to his feet and went unsteadily inside. Lynch returned with sugar and milk. 'You want?'

'No thanks. You stayed out here all night?'

'It doesn't matter.'

Hartmoor glanced across at Lynch, but there was no rancour in the desolate features. The man seemed resigned, to what Hartmoor didn't know. Perhaps just beaten down. Resignation was something he felt he held a certain expertise in. 'So what's your game plan?'

'Game plan?' Lynch sipped his coffee. 'I wouldn't even begin to know right now. Look, I'm going to turn in. You'll be okay for a while?'

'I'll survive. Well, I assume.'

'You do a nice line in gallows humour, I have to say. Don't answer the door.'

'I'll try not to.'

Hartmoor sat back and savoured the cool sunlight, the coffee and the hubbub from the street below. Soon he snoozed himself.

By the time Lynch reappeared, Hartmoor had come in from the balcony, made himself another coffee and curled up on the sofa with a book on orientalist art he had plucked from the shelves after a long look through Lynch's books. It was a highly eclectic collection and considerably more intelligent than Hartmoor would have expected.

Lynch had washed and shaved. The fire was back in those blue eyes but there was a grim set to the man's mouth Hartmoor hadn't seen before. Lynch's mobile rang and he scooped it from the dining table, wandering into the kitchen as he talked to his caller. He came back out with a plastic bottle of water in his hand.

Lynch finished the call. 'That was London. They want me to bring you in. You'll be arrested at Heathrow and formally charged with espionage.'

Hartmoor placed the book down on the coffee table and sat back. His eyes pricked. 'No,' he whispered. 'No. You can't let them. I have to see her. I have to be there. If I miss her, it's all over. Everything.' He glared up at Lynch, a savage anger burning the sadness away. 'I must see her. There's no question of anything else. I just need one day. I'll come to Heathrow after. Help me. Please?'

Lynch nodded. 'Okay. You think she'll be there tomorrow

morning?'

'Her daughter said she was arriving tonight.'

Grabbing his coat, Lynch slipped the holster off the hook and shrugged it on. He pulled the coat on over it. 'I have to go out. I'll be back later on.'

'Can we do something about food? There's nothing in the fridge.'

'Food?'

'I'd rather not die of starvation and you're insistent I don't answer the door or go out.'

Lynch nodded. 'Fair enough, I suppose. I'll bring something up. Two short, two long knocks, okay?'

NINETEEN

Wye and Kallas walked along the shore of Tallin's Snelli tiik lake. Their feet scraped and crunched through the fresh snow. Both men wore greatcoats and scarves and had their hands in their pockets. Wye's breath misted. To their right, beyond the lake and the trees that lined it, rose the medieval walls of Vanalinn, Tallinn's old town. The snow-heavy sky bore down on them.

Wye had been saving this up. 'So you lost the second one, Jaan. A shooting in Beirut. Pretty messy, cops all over the place.'

'The fortunes of war, Dennis.'

'He murdered a woman. Turns out she was a long-time associate of Lynch's, runs a cathouse in Monot. There was supposed to be a trade-off, Hartmoor for the woman. Your guy jumped the gun. Literally.'

'So, one dead prostitute. Persson was killed by who?'

'Lynch.'

'I am impressed by this man, actually. Maybe I hire him.'

Wye raised an eyebrow. 'Maybe he'd kill you, too?'

Kallas halted, his face like granite in the grudging light. Wye met the cold stare. Kallas' jaw was set. Kallas shook his head. 'No.' He turned to face the lake and Wye stepped beside him. 'No, I do not think this Lynch is a threat to me. To our business together, perhaps. But not to me.'

'We have to assume that business is coming to a close, Jaan. My masters have become very twitchy indeed. I have been instructed to wrap it up.'

'I agree. It is a shame, but we must be realists.'

'I'm glad you concur. We must assume the operation is compromised. We have already started to wind down matters at the supply end, resources are being redeployed.'

Kallas nodded, turning to walk back along the lakeside path. 'We have one more flight ready. It will leave tomorrow afternoon, our friend will have it loaded in time. I will ask our friend to break down his operations in Beirut.'

'Our main concern is this end of the operation, Jaan. We need to have the cargo processed and into distribution fast. You need to close down your networks quickly and quietly.'

'Do not presume to tell me my business. It is no fault of mine this situation was permit to develop.'

Wye bit his lip and took a few silent steps before replying. 'Hartmoor coming back like that was unfortunate. We could not have foreseen the consequences.'

'We will let Abbas Ali take care of him.'

'It's a fine judgement call right now. If any more damage takes place, we will have to clean up, a deep clean. I would rather it didn't come to that, but we cannot afford for Dmitri to be compromised. There is too much water under the bridge for that. Too much at stake.'

Kallas glanced at Wye. 'You think this much danger from Hartmoor?'

'Yes. With Lynch and British intelligence involved, yes I do. They have been investigating. We have had a number of requests from them for more information on Dmitri. Lynch is hiding Hartmoor. We don't know how much he's worked out, but frankly, the sooner we get out, the happier I will be.'

'I understand.'

Abbas Ali was unhappy. This entire affair with the Estonians had not gone well and he was feeling pulled to and fro by fate. This was not something he approved of: Abbas Ali liked to be in control of his destiny and, no matter how many times a day he would piously mutter *Insh'Allah*, God Willing, Abbas Ali didn't like leaving things up to God. He much preferred to deal with them on a more temporal basis.

His mobile rang and he lit a cigarette before taking the call. Jaan Kallas.

'Abbas Ali. I hear it has gone badly with the representatives I sent. I am not pleased. It is not your fault, but I would request your help to finish this.'

'At your service, Jaan, you know,' Abbas Ali murmured, his heart sinking.

'I understand one man was responsible for both of the accidents.'

Abbas Ali took a pull of his cigarette and watched the little ember at the end burn bright for a second. 'According to my sources within the police, yes. An Englishman. His name is Lynch. He is from the British embassy.'

'I appreciate the situation, Abbas Ali. It is always difficult to find people one can trust totally. Thankfully our relationship is such that I feel able to ask you to clean up this mess for me. The Englishman is protecting another. They both must leave us immediately.'

'I understand.'

'We must assume our business together has been compromised. Tomorrow will be the last shipment. The supply chain is closing. You must break down your operations. It is regrettable, but I think we have all profited from our work together. All good things must end.'

Abbas Ali nodded. Profited? By God they had. 'Once this flight leaves, surely they do not matter to us?'

'You must not underestimate this Lynch, I think. Wrap your operations up quickly, Abbas Ali and disappear into the jungle. That is my advice.'

'And I shall take it, Jaan.' Abbas Ali stubbed out his cigarette and lit another, his hand shaking.

'Goodbye, then, old friend.'

Abbas Ali swore softly and picked up his prayer beads. He bawled out for his office manager, Ayman. The man came scampering. 'Get the boys in here fast. They've got a big job to do.'

TWENTY

Hamra Street was choked with cars. Exhaust fumes mixed with the spicy smell of cooking from the restaurants lining the packed street. The afternoon was unusually warm for late February but the air would cool quickly now the sun was low. Still, Lynch was warm in his brown leather jacket, the holstered gun under his armpit stopping him from sliding the jacket off and slinging it over his shoulder.

Lynch had spent two hours dropping into various outlets in the backstreets that branched off Hamra, asking a question here, slipping a note there. Now he had what he wanted, but he was in no rush. He dropped into a grocer's, appreciating the cool shade, and bought a bottle of water. Emerging into the traffic's noise, he stood on the street corner sipping his water and watching the world go by.

Marcelle was gone. He kept repeating the words, hoping they would hammer the reality home and release him, but he just felt numbness. She had been in his mind constantly through the long night, thoughts of her laughing, scowling, playing and being – let's face it, a hard-nosed bitch. She was a survivor. She had sailed through the Civil War playing this influencer off that. Even her first bar had been bought on the back of buttering up some randy old goat and waiting until he died. Lynch grunted as the thought hit him, he was grieving while Hartmoor was hoping. The man was amazingly resilient, but Lynch had to fight to avoid being needled by the arrogant superiority. Those supercilious, pale eyes had a way of letting you know that you really didn't matter one jot in Hartmoor's estimation.

Marcelle twisting, soft in his arms, a hot August night, the windows open and the smells of summer on the air. Hot wood and brick. Her slicked skin hot, the smell of her arousal

187

blooming as he kissed his way down to its source.

Her head exploding.

Lynch dumped the bottle in an over-full bin and strode up Hamra Street. He crossed through the beeping throng and ducked into a side street. Glancing quickly around him, he went into the open doorway of a bar, stepping down to the cool, beer-pungent interior. It was empty save for a lone drinker and the barman, who was cleaning glasses. Lynch pulled up a barstool.

'Long time no see.'

Marwan Nimr's head rose, but he didn't look around to face Lynch. He sniffed, his nostrils distending. Nimr was bald, the faint blueish shadow on the dark skin stretching to just above his ears, his crown shone in the bar's umber light. The thick eyebrows above his fleshy nose were knotted.

'Somethin' don't smell right.' Nimr had shaved off his goatee beard and put on weight since Lynch had seen him last.

Lynch waved at the barman. 'Almaza. And a Jack and Coke. Double.' He turned to Nimr. 'And there was I thinking ye'd be pleased to see me, isn't that a fact?'

The drinks came and Lynch slipped a note across the bar. He took a long pull at the Almaza before turning again to Nimr. He almost choked, battling to contain the scream trying to force its way up his constricted throat. For the first time he was looking at Nimr head-on rather than in profile.

Nimr had half a face. The right side of his features had melted, puckered welts of shiny skin traced across the mottled surface. He put a finger up to wipe the corner of his right eye.

'You did this, man. I didn't take that flying job from you, I wouldn'ta been anywhere near Michel Freij and his mountain hideaway. You left me there to die when they bombed it.'

The image of Marcelle's head hitting the concrete came to Lynch's mind. His heart beat a tattoo in his chest. He reached out for the beer, took another pull and swallowed with an effort. He opened his mouth to speak, but words had deserted him. He forced himself to look at Nimr.

'I didn't know anyone had survived that. I'm not quite sure how I did.'

'Well, I'm happy for you man. Now why not just fuck off?'

Lynch's breathing was back under control but he could feel the sweat under his armpits, the wet shirt sticking to his ribs.

'So I'll cut to the chase, will I? You're playing with Abbas Ali. Fancy telling me what game?'

'No comment.'

'So let me tell you, Marwan, given you've become so coy in your old age. You're flying again. You're flying for Abbas Ali.'

Nimr shifted. 'No comment.'

'You've got form, Marwan. You picked up a twenty stretch for flying drugs before. Why would you be stupid enough to do it again?'

Nimr tossed his whisky in Lynch's face. His powerful punch caught Lynch on the cheek, knocking him off the barstool. Nimr kicked his own stool away and lumbered over to Lynch, his foot lashing out. Lynch caught it but didn't have the leverage to topple Nimr, who landed a huge punch to Lynch's chest. He rolled away but Nimr had the advantage of momentum. Howling anger, Nimr kicked out again. This time Lynch's arm lunged upwards, pulling Nimr's leg up as Lynch whipped his foot out to catch Nimr's other leg. The man went down heavily and Lynch was on him in a flash, his hand around Nimr's neck and his gun twisting the skin between the big man's eyes.

'I don't want to take you in, Marwan. That's Chalhoub's problem, not mine. Just tell me what you're flying for him. I can help you. I can help you get out.'

Nimr shook his head, his breathing heavy. 'No way.'

Lynch stood, the gun still trained on Nimr's face. He stepped back. The barman had disappeared. Lynch scribbled a number on a beer mat. 'Here. Call me when you've thought it through.'

*

Lynch looked out over Beirut's landmark Raouché rock, the outcrop of green-capped, striated chalkstone forming a crazy passageway for the tourist boats to speed through its eye, pulling water-skiers behind them through the glittering blue-green Mediterranean waters. He scanned the restaurants that clung to the high cliffs, wishing he could be sipping a beer with the other customers enjoying their picture window view as the sun set.

He breathed in the sea and the fragrance of the wild flowers and grasses on the cliff-top. Tyres crunched as Tony Chalhoub's battered white Mercedes approached, pulling a typically flamboyant halt. The car door slammed as Chalhoub strode over to join Lynch, a cigarette dangling on his lip.

'So it's confirmed, you're officially in the clear for the Estonian shooting. The gun that fired the bullet was in the hands of a Lebanese police sergeant. He's earned himself a commendation and bonus.'

Lynch turned to walk along the cliff-top path with Chalhoub. 'Thanks, Tony.'

'Least I could do. Your tip was gold. You were right about Marwan Nimr. He is indeed flying again, for a charter company called Nimbus Aviation. They have a single 737-200 they keep at Beirut International and he's its pilot. They're owned by a Cypriot holding company, although the plane itself is leased from a British Virgin Islands held company. When you boil it all down, it spells Abbas Ali.'

Lynch whistled. 'Neat. And this 737 makes regular trips to Tallinn, right?'

'No. Kärdla. But close, it's still Estonia. It's a small rural airport on the island of,' Chalhoub pulled a piece of paper out of his pocket, 'Hiuumaa. We gave this information to EJIC liaison like you asked.'

'So what's the cargo? It's drugs, but what drugs?'

'We don't know. The plane has also flown to Afghanistan, which would spell opium or heroin. You'd need a lot of H to fill a 737.'

'Just flying it out under your noses? That's pretty brassy, even for Lebanon.'

'It's a sore point. You can always bribe your way around bureaucracy here, you know that. Try it sometime, offer me a bribe.'

'Wish I could afford it. Thanks Tony, I'll go get my instructions from Channing. Looks like I'll be taking Hartmoor home the day after tomorrow. They think he was a mole. He'll be charged with espionage. I think that's all bollocks, but I'm not paid to think, am I?'

'I'm sorry for him. Really. He's not a well man and all he wanted was a little bit of his youth back.'

'I'll look after him.'

'Right. For the airport stuff, I've sent you the contacts for our lead there. He's got access to any resources you might need, including tarmac access and he's expecting you with instructions to extend full co-operation.' Chalhoub reached out to massage Lynch's shoulder as they walked. 'Just don't decide to start any more wars, Gerald, yes?'

Lynch nodded. 'No tough stuff, promise.'

It was dark by the time Lynch reached Beirut International Airport. His liaison was waiting for him, by the front door of arrivals. Talal Abu Hosn was tall, maybe six four and obviously worked out. He held out his hand, a ready smile lighting up his handsome face. 'Good to meet you, Mr Lynch. Tony speaks very highly of you.'

'Spare me the blushes. Can we go airside straight away?'

'Sure. Here's your ID. Come along this way.'

Lynch followed Abu Hosn through security, turning right away from the check-in desks and straight into the bowels of the airport via a number of access control systems and checkpoints. They emerged airside near the baggage handling area.

'You're after a look at OD-NIM, no?'

'That's the one. A 737-200 registered to Nimbus Aviation.'

'It's in maintenance right now. Come on.'

Abu Hosn led the way to a waiting buggy and jumped in. Lynch followed suit. They turned right and sped along the tarmac past planes waiting on their stands, the little orange lamp on the back of the buggy wheeling and flashing.

They drew clear of the main terminal, leaving the traffic of catering vans, fuel bowsers and snaking luggage trains behind. The maintenance hangar area was brightly lit, the big hangar doors open. Standing outside on the apron, OD-NIM was a scruffy-looking 737, its blue and yellow paint faded.

'Here we are. I took a little time to look up its paperwork; it's an older 200 model, built in 1980. It was originally shipped to British Airways, and then sold on to Alitalia before it started to hit the Third World airlines. It got converted to cargo in 2006 and had a gravel kit added, which lets it land on airstrips that haven't been tarmacked. Nimbus leased it in 2010. They're reliable planes generally but this one's been in maintenance a lot.'

Lynch raised an eyebrow. 'Does it fly often?'

'Not really. Recently, every week or so, give and take a few days either way. Before, about once a month. Mostly to Afghanistan under a US military contract. I don't know how they're making money out of her. You need frequency to repay the lease. She's scheduled to fly tomorrow. They put a flight plan in a few hours ago. Headed for Estonia. Recently they've started more of the Estonian flights. That seems to be causing most of their maintenance problems. Other than that, they've been flying mostly to Zaranj. That's a gravel airstrip in southern Afghanistan, used a lot for both civil and military freight. Seen enough?'

'Can we look inside?'

'With their permission or a warrant. The plane's covered by CCTV, so without those it's not an option.'

Lynch's face twisted in frustration. 'Do you have a manifest?'

'Not on me. We can look it up.'

'Can we?'

'Sure. You done here?'

'Yup. It's the manifest interests me more.'

On the way back to the main terminal building, Abu Hosn called up various members of his team on the radio he carried. Lynch followed him through the warren of strip-lit corridors and staircases to a sparse, functional office with a wooden desk and a worn vinyl sofa. Abu Hosn rounded the desk and started tapping on his keyboard.

'Okay, we have an empty flight scheduled. No cargo, no passengers. Just the pilot.'

'Isn't that unusual?'

Abu Hosn swept the mouse across the desk, clicking on the screen. 'Relatively, but flights can do that, particularly if there's been a routing error or a redeployment, sometimes if they simply don't have a return cargo. The flight's scheduled for Kärdla, which doesn't support any scheduled international flights, so you'd only really see a charter plane go there. It's flown to Kärdla unladen every flight of the last six.'

'I'm amazed it hasn't rung any alarm bells. This plane flies empty to Estonia every time it goes in for maintenance and prior that flew regularly from Afghanistan?'

'We keep ourselves busy with the low-hanging fruit, Mr Lynch.'

Lynch held up his hands. 'No criticism intended. Look, what cargo did it bring back from Kärdla?'

Abu Hosn tapped again, his face lit blue by the LCD screen's glow. He frowned. 'Empty.'

'Flew in empty, out empty? Where does that make any sense? So what about the Afghan flights? What's the cargo been?'

Abu Hosn nodded and busied himself on the computer, his lips pursed in concentration. He traced a line on the screen with his finger. 'Fruit and vegetables going out. Return flights have been charters from the US military.' He whistled. 'The cargo's marked down as classified. It gets taken into bond on arrival.'

'Tell me something.' Lynch pushed himself up from the sofa. 'Planes are fuelled just before take-off, aren't they?'

'Yes. There'll be some residual fuel, but the tanks won't be full. It's too dangerous.'

'For an empty plane with no fuel on board, its tyres seemed low. I don't know if that means anything.'

Abu Hosn did some more tapping. 'So you think it might be flying to Estonia laden. That it's being loaded while it's in the maintenance area.'

'Bingo. And my money says it's heroin.'

'Hang on.' Abu Hosn stuck a pencil behind his ear, pulled a piece of paper over to him and started tapping again. He scribbled down a number, replaced the pencil and tapped. The performance was starting to irritate Lynch when Abu Hosn leaned back and laughed. 'It's fuelling for a full load over that distance. The last six fuel receipts for the Estonia flights match the requirement of a fully laden plane.'

'What's a fully laden plane?'

More tapping. Abu Hosn's face shone with wonder. 'Seventeen thousand kilos.'

Lynch leapt up and grabbed the calculator on Abu Hosn's desk. He stared in awe at the answer and did the sum again.

'Well?' Abu Hosn's eyes shone with excitement.

Lynch raised his gaze to meet the other man's. 'A billion bloody dollars.'

Lynch felt the heat of ardour in him, his loss and grief transformed into something burning and hard inside. He needed a drink, his nostrils flaring with the sour smell of stale beer as he strode into The Angry Monkey to negotiate his terms with Tony Chalhoub.

He waved down the barman, slapping Tony's shoulder. 'Two

double scotches on ice, two Almazas. What you having Tony?'

'Haha, Lynch.'

'I'm serious. They're for me. What you want?'

'Scotch.'

'Three double scotches on the rocks, then. Thanks.' Lynch took a seat. 'So. Now we know what Abbas Ali's up to with the head of the Estonian Mafia. Doesn't that feel good, Tony?'

Sour-faced, Chalhoub was hunched over the bar. 'No, it bloody doesn't. Because I know you're about to ask me to let a billion dollars' worth of heroin fly out of Beirut.'

'We've got to, Tony. We can't wrap up the European end of it if we don't. I did the footwork for you here, you've got everything you need to back track Abbas Ali's operation, get to the refinery and get your collars. But I need that plane.'

The drinks came. Lynch clinked the whisky tumbler against Chalhoub's glass on the bar and drained his first whisky in one draught.

Chalhoub shook his head. 'No. I can't let you do it.'

'Come on, Tony. We've got the biggest drugs bust in history on our hands here. They're flying in raw opium from Afghanistan, processing it in Beirut and flying high quality, cheap heroin to Estonia. They're flooding the Russian market with bargain basement smack and it's all coming from here. You've got the bust, it's all yours. Cover yourselves in glory. Just give me the plane so we can tidy up our end of this.'

'Quit playing all European, Lynch. This is personal for you. I so know you.'

It was the sort of thing she would have said to him. So Arab. He took a hit of whisky to banish her with its sharp cold tang. *It would bring her back later.* He waved to the barman. 'Two more. Cheers.' Leaning on the bar, he faced Chalhoub. 'Just let it go. That's all I ask. You have it totally in your power, Tony. Don't pretend you don't. That plane's not official yet.'

'It's not *clean*, Gerald.'

'Since when was Beirut clean?'

He'd won. He knew it. That last slump of Chalhoub's shoulders acknowledged the point. Lynch's billion dollar cargo would fly and Tony would, in time, claim the biggest drugs bust in Lebanese history. *Win win.*

TWENTY-ONE

It was a new dawn, a new day. Hartmoor woke and slowly recalled his time and place. Not Newgale's mile of sand outside, but Beirut. No cold iodine of sea air with an open window, but the sound of church bells and *muezzins*, the smell of *argileh* perhaps from the restaurant down the street or maybe a hint of fried onions wafting up on the warm spring morning breeze.

He loved this waking moment. This one of all, the one he had come all the way out here to enjoy. Hartmoor was going back to his past because his future was spent. This one moment was everything to him. The spare room in Gerald Lynch's apartment was functional, but sunny and the sheets cotton and clean.

He had dreamed of her, of course. The girl in Khartoum. *You are ebony and you are beautiful.* He often wondered if she were his mind acknowledging the joy of the cancer eating at him, exulting in its perfection as it destroyed his own unfit DNA. This morning her memory didn't leave him in a fearful sweat. He turned, feeling the sun on his face. He popped out a Roxanol and washed it down with a sip of water before the pain started to chisel its way into his mind.

He showered in the little ensuite, enjoying the warm water. Some other guest of Lynch's had left a miniature of Bulgari Green Tea, according to the little bottle, 'hair and body wash.'

The scent was heady, expensive. He enjoyed the moment to the full.

He shaved, careful not to nick himself in the misted mirror. Finally, clothed, he pulled open the door to Lynch's slightly Arabesque living room. He found himself, just for an instant, back in Tel Aviv, his second 'tour' there. It was the giddiness, the release. That was what did it. That feeling of, well, freedom. From Leslie, if he were honest. From his error.

Lynch was nowhere to be seen. Hartmoor busied himself in the kitchen making coffee, his mind back in Tel Aviv after the end of the Gulf War and, coincidentally, his marriage. Hartmoor smiled bitterly to himself, The Mother Of All Marriages. The break-up with Lesley had been a drawn out and messy affair, but the decree nisi had come through just before the chance to go back to work in Israel. The job had been a complicated and sensitive one, seconded to the embassy as a plenipotentiary and tasked with heading the British team embarking on an Anglo-French initiative to build a European agreement out of the Oslo negotiations. The Norwegians had built a remarkable degree of consensus between Israel and the Palestinians and the Americans were starting to take an interest. As Jason had explained to Mai at the time, it was vital that Europe take its place at the negotiating table or risk being sidelined in Middle East policy.

Hartmoor took his coffee back to the living room. The morning sun was shining on the balcony again and he pulled open the door to enjoy the warmth and the freshness of the spring air.

The Americans had, of course, got wind of the plan and launched a counter-offensive. Jason had travelled to Oslo with his team, but to no avail. It was Clinton who took credit for Oslo, typically planting himself between Arafat and Peres for the photo-opp.

Hartmoor had embarked on a short but torrid affair with an Israeli girl called Hannah. He hadn't told Mai about that. Later he reasoned that it had been his mid-life crisis, the loss of his capacity for moderation. He pleaded with Mai to come to Tel Aviv and join him, to spend just a few days in the bright lights and whirl of opulence.

Hartmoor heard Lynch calling him and turned to the French door. 'Here. The kettle's boiled if you want.'

Lynch was buttoning his shirt. He had a livid bruise on his cheek and a look of astonishment on his face. 'What's happened to you? You look ten years younger.'

Hartmoor couldn't suppress his smile. 'Good. It's a big day, you know.'

'Sure an' it is. Come on, then. Let's get going.' Lynch slipped on his holster and over it his leather jacket. He pulled open a drawer in the side cabinet and pocketed two dark grey ammunition clips.

'Is the firepower necessary?' Hartmoor frowned.

Lynch didn't reply, holding the front door open and padding behind Hartmoor to the lift. After a great deal of internal debate, he had decided to bring The Stick. Right now, he had no need of it, but long experience had told him no matter how well he could start a day, the tiredness would drag him down eventually. Holding it was alone an admission that this inevitability would come to pass.

They stood on the street while Lynch flagged down a *servees*, a short but sharp negotiation took place. Lynch opened the back door for him. 'Okay, get in. This is our man.'

Hartmoor got in. The car smelled of stale smoke. He wondered how Lynch did it: always picked the most decrepit specimens of a notoriously ramshackle species. Lynch's door closed with an explosive grinding of metal. The hinge appeared to be held together with a coat hanger.

'We are surely not travelling to Shemlan in this?'

Lynch beamed. 'For your big day? No, I thought we'd go to the Le Gray and pick up one of their limos.'

For some reason Hartmoor felt touched. 'Seriously?'

'Seriously. Even I've got a touch more style than taking a man to meet his nemesis in a *servees*.'

Hartmoor stilled his automatic urge to correct Lynch's misuse of the word. A motorcycle pulled alongside, unusually new-looking. Hartmoor glanced up at the rider and his passenger, both wearing black leathers and gleaming black helmets with their visors down. For some reason the sight forced a chill down his back. The *servees* driver sounded his horn, a tremulous squeak, and swerved. The motorbike pulled back as they scraped by the side of a truck, which had stopped in the road.

He craned around to try and catch the bike again, his heightened senses awakened.

'Lynch. The motorbike.'

Lynch turned to him, an irritated frown on his face. 'What motor—'

The bike was alongside the *servees* on Lynch's side this time, gunning its engine. The passenger leaned towards them. A heavy clunk sounded. The bike's engine screamed and it raced ahead of them. 'Down!' bellowed Lynch as he flung himself at Hartmoor, kicking out at his door with both feet. The battered old metal gave way easily, the door flew open hanging off its makeshift coat hanger hinge as the servees started to swerve. The driver shouted out. Lynch kicked again and the door flew off, tumbling to the street. The *servees* hit another car. Sparks flew. Behind them came a great orange flash. The windows shattered a second before the sound hit, a wave of roaring concussion. Hartmoor cried out as the car slewed to a halt with a final juddering impact.

He felt Lynch shaking him. 'Get up! Get up! Move!'

The world had gone mad. Half dragged out of the servees, Hartmoor gazed at the great column of crackling flame and smoke, the overturned cars and detritus of metal, stone and glass spilled on the road. People were howling at each other. A car horn was jammed somewhere. Lynch pulled Hartmoor off the road into a side street, forcing him to stumble past the tide of concerned-looking people.

'I can't go on,' He managed to croak, slumping against the graffiti-strewn wall, his breath burning in his throat. He could still hear the screaming and now the echo of distant sirens.

Two men ran clattering into the mouth of the side street,

silhouetted against the open sky. Hartmoor saw the muzzle flashes. He fell backwards as a hail of stone spattered over him. He managed to throw out his hand to cushion the fall and grazed it painfully. Lynch stood over him, stiff-armed, his gun extended. He fired three rapid shots.

Hartmoor noticed the street was cobbled, the uneven surface making the litter dance as the breeze blew it along. A cat was curled up under a car on the far side. He wondered what it lived on, smiling as the sight of an overflowing bin at the corner of an intersecting street provided the answer. The world was different at floor level, somehow more peaceful.

Lynch was shouting at him, pulling him up. Hartmoor, happier lying down, tried to struggle away. Lynch slapped him. 'Come on, move. There'll be more of them. This way. Oh Christ, move for fuck's sake!'

Hartmoor grunted as he was pushed against a shop front, The Stick shoved into his stomach. He reached for it. Lynch was standing in the middle of the street, his gun held out in both hands. The car in front of him stopped with a screeching of tyres and Lynch was waving the gun to one side. 'Out!' he shouted at the driver.

Hartmoor pushed himself away from the shop window and hobbled across to the passenger side of the car. Lynch holstered the gun and jammed his foot on the accelerator. Hartmoor was thrown back against the seat by the thrust. Lynch swerved right towards the sea.

They drove along the corniche. Hartmoor's heart slowed. He rubbed the dust away from his grazed hand. He pulled some tissues from the box on the dashboard. A BMW. Lynch had taste in carjacking, at any rate. They turned left.

'What are you grinning at?'

'It's a nice car to steal. Would you mind explaining what happened back there?'

'Limpet mine. It's become a favourite tool for assassination around here. The Israelis started it, the Iranians soon cottoned on. It's pretty infallible. We were lucky. They had a follow-up team, the two shooters. I recognised one. He works, err… worked for a man called Abbas Ali. Heard of him?'

Hartmoor shrugged. 'No. Should I have?'

'Just wondered. He's a major hood. He's involved in smuggling billion dollar consignments of heroin to Estonia, to a man called Jaan Kallas. You met him once, at a reception. He was a Russian advisor to the Syrians during the Lebanese Civil War. What I can't figure is why Kallas wants you dead so badly.'

'He just has to wait a little.'

'That's the point isn't it? He's not for waiting. He sent two men here to intercept you and now Abbas Ali's thugs have joined in. You know something, Jason, and you're not telling.'

Hartmoor was bewildered. 'And what if I know nothing?'

Lynch darted him a poisonous look. 'You'd be the most dangerous man I've ever met.'

They drove along the airport road. Behind them a column of smoke rose into the blue sky above Beirut. Lynch steered between the heavy trucks and vans, taking them away from the main highway. The road forked and Lynch steered them right and up into the mountains.

'How do you know she'll be pleased to see you?'

'I don't. I just know that I have to see her before it's too late.'

'She has a family of her own, though.'

'That's what Frank always said.'

'Maybe he was right.'

'Perhaps I'm beyond caring. Perhaps I think I cared about that too much twenty years ago. For all those years we have shared our hopes and fears, lived in a world together that was made of paper and ink. So perhaps now I need to see her for one last time while I still have breath left in me.'

Lynch's stare was becoming uncomfortable. Hartmoor

pointed in front of them. 'The road.'

They pulled up in front of The Cliff House, the gravel crunching under the big car's tyres.

Hartmoor's hands were shaking as he pushed a Roxanol out of the foil and swallowed it. His mouth was dry and the pill stuck in his throat painfully before finally going down. Lynch held the door open for him and helped him stand. He was wobbly against The Stick.

The young man with his pockets full of word cards was here somewhere, in this space in the past. Walking in and meeting that brown-eyed smile. Hartmoor stepped carefully over the threshold into the shade. '1936' was still there on the floor as it had been over thirty five years ago.

He glanced behind him, but Lynch had held back and was smiling encouragement. Jason Hartmoor called out. 'Mai?'

She stood in the sunshine. Her hair was flecked with white but of course it would be. She turned and her smile spun back the clock in an instant. He was plunged back to the '70s in this very place, in his awkward open-necked shirt with its ridiculously wide collars, seeing her for the very first time as she walked into her restaurant. Now she stood, an age apart from that heady memory from his youth. She had aged gracefully, was yet slim and elegant. The lines on her face were softened by the light, but her eyes were almond-shaped and deep, her mouth still full and ready to smile – in fact, a smile was lifting the corner of her lip now she regarded him. She was wearing a blouse and skirt, which tapered to just touch her knees. Her ankles, as always, were slim and she wore high heels. She wore a crucifix he didn't recognise, but then why would he? He'd last seen her a lifetime ago.

They used to sit together on that balcony overlooking Beirut, his Boccaccio unread, spread face down on the table as they talked. The city was a mauve vista glittering below them, the occasional curl of black smoke and outbreak of rocket fire or the crack of small arms reminding them their peace was fragile.

Her perfume came to him then, so faint he wasn't sure if he was imagining it. Jasmine, sweet and heady. He wanted to cry at the lifetime of love for her he'd walked out on.

'Jason? Oh, but it has been so very long.' Her face clouded. 'Are you unwell?'

'A little thing. Just a little thing.' The tears betrayed him as he tottered towards her. She opened her arms and he found her embrace. He went to kiss her, but she turned away. 'What are you doing? Jason, please, no.'

A door crashed, footsteps clattered and a man's voice rang out in fury. 'What the fuck is he doing here? Get him out of my house! Get him out or I swear to God or I'll kill him with my bare hands.'

Hartmoor whirled around in confusion, staggering as his balance left him. Lynch darted forward and took his arm, propping him up. A corpulent man in a suit stood by the door, his face crimson with rage and his fists balled. His bald head shone, the hair around his ears was white. His chins wobbled. A younger man in a dark jacket and jeans stood by him. It dawned on Hartmoor, he knew the older man.

'Fadi?' said Hartmoor in a cracked whisper. 'The cook?'

No one answered.

'Clancy Goldman,' Lynch said. 'My, my, what a pleasant surprise.'

Jason turned to Mai, gabbling. 'I'm sorry. I had to come. Before it was too late. All these years, all that has passed between us. I had to.'

Her hand was on her chest, the other gripped the table. Her face was drawn in horror. Hartmoor stepped back.

'What's wrong? What's the matter?'

She whispered. 'All that has passed between us?'

Lynch strode forward to intercept Fadi's lunge at Hartmoor. He pushed the big man's shoulder. 'Back off.'

Fadi drew air noisily through his nose, his shirt stretched across his full chest and his hand held up. 'I swear to God I will—'

Goldman's hand landed on his shoulder. 'Fadi, Fadi…'

'Mai, I love you.'

She spoke, but her eyes flashed. 'Isn't that a few decades too late?'

'I always have. Our letters, all that we've said. Surely you always knew I was telling the truth?'

Shaking her head, her eyes wide open now, Mai stepped back. 'What letters?' she whispered.

Fadi was roaring, Goldman now holding the big, red-faced man back. Hartmoor's confusion was absolute. A woman joined them. The woman he had met when he had first returned to The Cliff House. Mai's daughter, Dana.

'What's going on? What's happening here?'

Mai's chin puckered, her lips tensed as her eyes filled with tears. Hands to her face, she shook her head, glancing between Dana and Hartmoor. 'I don't know. Oh please God, I don't know.'

'There were no letters, you fool. It was a lie.' Fadi had stopped straining against Goldman's grip on his shoulders. 'I gave your stupid letters to *them* and they wrote back to you.'

Goldman shook Fadi. 'Enough,' he hissed. 'That's classified.'

Hartmoor put his hands to his ears, The Stick falling to the floor. 'Why is he even here?' he begged Mai.

'Because he's my husband,' Mai sobbed.

Hartmoor gazed wildly around. The look of comprehension on Lynch's face told its own story. The blood was rushing in his ears. He turned to Goldman. 'Frank. Frank Coleman.'

Goldman was watchful. Lynch tensed as Fadi shrugged Goldman's hands from his shoulders and sneered. 'Her husband. You hear, it, *Ingleezi*? Hear it again. Her *husband*. You left her, ruin her. I marry her. And we lived together happily a lifetime. She didn't need your stupid letters, I gave them to them,' he waved at Goldman 'and then Coleman had you send to Syria so I didn't have to pack up your filthy words anymore and give to them.'

Goldman shoved Fadi. 'Shut the fuck up, Fadi.'

'Leave him,' Lynch growled.

Hartmoor turned at Mai's wail. Dana was holding her as she cried, now she raised her head, her hair plastered to her wet cheeks. 'Why, Fadi? How could you let me believe he had just gone? That he hadn't even cared to write me?' Her face screwed up in disgust. 'The father of my child?'

If Lynch hadn't shot out a hand, Hartmoor would have fallen. It was all too much and he felt the room spinning, bile rising in his throat. He met Dana's horrified glare. His lips were stuck together. 'I...'

Fadi was shouting again. 'Why should it matter? He ran, the coward. From the war, from you.' He threw out a hand. 'Yes, and from Dana. He was gone. I protected you from the shame he leave. They made sure he never come back, this was the deal.'

There was a moment of stasis. Hartmoor glanced around the awful little scene. Mai stood propped against the table arm in arm with Dana, clutching each other for protection. Lynch stood beside him balanced on the balls of his feet. Fadi drew breath for more, but Goldman span to face him and delivered a single, precise jab to his solar plexus that folded the big man over. He collapsed, reaching for air, to the floor.

'Okay folks. Party's over.' Goldman gestured to Lynch and Hartmoor. 'You and you, move. Out of here now.'

Hartmoor hadn't seen him draw the gun. He glanced at Lynch who relaxed back onto his heels and nodded. Careful to keep his hands in plain sight and moving deliberately, Lynch picked up The Stick and handed it to Hartmoor.

Hartmoor reached out a hand to her. 'I loved you. I loved you so much. I wrote to you for over thirty five years. They made a fool of me. I am so very sorry. I tried to come back but you, they, always told me not to. That you had a life here, a family and I would ruin it all by returning. So I stayed away all this time. I only came now because I am dying. I wanted to see you more than anything. I—'

Hartmoor's body jerked at the gun blast. A shower of plaster fell from the ceiling. Ears ringing, he whirled to face Goldman and the evil little black hole of the gun muzzle trained on his face. The muzzle waved. 'Get out. Now'

Hartmoor took a step towards Goldman. It didn't matter anyway, it was only time. Lynch's touch on his arm was gentle. 'Come on Jason. Live to fight another day.'

'Very touching.' Goldman trained the pistol on Lynch. 'Gun on the floor, Lynch.'

With infinite caution, Lynch opened his jacket and slowly pulled out his Walther P99 by the butt with his thumb and index finger, crouching to place it on the flagstone floor.

'Now, go. Lynch first.'

Lynch led the way. Hartmoor turned to Mai, but Goldman jammed the gun into his kidney. His last glance was of Mai and Dana holding on to one another, crying and fearful.

TWENTY-TWO

Gravel crunched under their feet as they walked through the restaurant car park. Lynch felt the mild winter sun on his back as they cleared the restaurant's shadow. It was a cloudless day, warm for the time of year and calm. One of the kitchen staff was standing to the side of the restaurant smoking and a hint of tobacco on the air gave Lynch a momentary pang. The lights of a big Lincoln flashed as Goldman hit the remote. He gestured Lynch into the driver's seat and waved Hartmoor to the passenger seat. The metal of Goldman's pistol was cold against the back of Lynch's neck. It wasn't a sensation he had ever enjoyed.

'What now, Clancy?'

Goldman tossed a bunch of keys into Lynch's lap. 'Shut up. Just drive. Back into town.'

Lynch glanced in the mirror. Goldman had sat back and was on his mobile. 'Outcome negative. All parties present. Go option B. End.'

'Clancy's in the CIA,' Lynch threw at Hartmoor. 'They like to play soldiers.'

'Shut up, Lynch.'

'So, here we all are, eh?' Lynch spoke airily. 'What a fun ride up and down the mountain. I'm sorry, Jason, it looks like our analysts goofed up. Well, they weren't to know, were they? You must have been singing like a canary for Coleman's people without realising it. Whatever made you think the Official Secrets Act applied to everyone except Jason Hartmoor, God alone knows. But that cute hoor mined you for information for, oh, how long? Thirty years?'

Goldman hissed. 'Shut the fuck up.'

'Or what, Clancy? Come on, Jason's got a right to know what you people did to him, surely?'

'He's got what rights I say he has. That information is classified.'

'Oh, come off it. The bag's empty, Clancy. You lost the cat.'

Hartmoor's face was the colour of old linen. He stared out of the front window of the car, his lips moving. There was a twitch in the muscle by his right eye. Lynch reached across to him, a movement that earned him a jab in the neck. 'Jason?'

Hartmoor shook his head. Tears started to well up in his eyes.

Lynch opened the window to let the warm air and the scent of pine in.

'Shut that.'

'What difference does it make, Clancy? You've got the pop-pop, you're in control. Bit of fresh air never harmed anyone.'

Lynch heard it first, the faint buzzing of a small aero-engine. He flashed a glance into the mirror but Goldman's face was cold.

'Shut the fucking window.' The jab was painful. Lynch closed the window, shutting out the engine in the sky above them.

'Your Option B is pretty heavy handed, Clancy. You guys never got the hang of finesse, did you?'

'I swear to God, Lynch, I'll take you out. Shut the fuck up and drive. That's it.'

The explosion rocked the car. Hartmoor jerked in his seat, his hand flew up to protect himself.

'What the hell was that?'

'A drone, Jason. Clancy's boys have been cleaning up after them.' Lynch glanced across. 'I'm truly sorry.'

As they twisted and turned down the steep little mountain road, Lynch caught glimpses of the thick roiling cloud rising above Shemlan. Hartmoor was staring silently uphill, his face contorted in anger and grief.

A fleeting check of the mirror showed Goldman with a look of satisfaction on his face Lynch would dearly love to have wiped off. Hartmoor twisted in his seat to face the American, his face puce and his bony fist raised.

'You bastards. Why—'

'Because, Hartmoor. Turn around or I'll hurt you.'

'She was my daughter, Goldman. My daughter.' Hartmoor reached out for Goldman, but his seat belt restricted his movement. His hands scrabbled in air. Goldman hit him on the cheek with the pistol butt and Hartmoor was knocked back to slam against the car door. Lynch swerved around the sharp corner. He fought to control the car, righted it then almost immediately slammed on the brakes.

Goldman shrieked, 'What the fuck are you doing?'

Lynch raised an eyebrow at the furious face in the mirror. 'Roadblock.'

In front of them, a truck had been parked so there was just room for a single vehicle to pass. Men with AK47s were waving a car through. They weren't wearing uniforms. One broke away from the group and signalled them forward with a lazy wave of his machine gun.

Lynch drove slowly towards them. He felt the cold touch leave his neck. Goldman's voice was taut. "Okay, not a word. We're three *khawajas* out for a drive and they don't care about us, right? Any funny stuff, I shoot.'

Lynch wound down his window as they neared the group, but it was clear the men did care about them. They fanned out, jabbering excitedly.

'Now, Lynch. Gogogo.' Goldman urged.

Lynch kept his face passive. 'Are you fucking mad, Goldman? There's at least six of 'em and they're all carrying. We wouldn't get ten yards. Calm down.'

Lynch leaned out to speak to the nearest of the men. As he went to speak his door was wrenched open. Another man opened Hartmoor's door.

'Out!' yelled the nearest gunman.

Lynch left the car slowly, his hands held high. 'The passenger is ill, he needs a stick.'

Goldman's door was pulled open. 'Out! Out!'

One of the gunmen was helping Hartmoor out of the car. Lynch found that amusing for some reason. Goldman was hesitating in the car. A gunman reached in and hit him with the butt of his AK47. Goldman fired and the man fell backwards, a neat hole punched in his forehead, a second shot plucking a little burst of material from his chest.

The response was instantaneous. Three men fired on automatic, two more joined after a couple of seconds. The BMW rocked on its wheels as the windows starred then fell inwards under the pressure of the hail of bullets. Goldman was thrown back against the seat, then slumped sideways, a blaze of red trailing in an arc across the leather seat.

The shots echoed around the hills, the plume of black smoke from Shemlan still rising into the blue sky.

The momentary silence was absolute. The birdsong returned. Lynch's hands were grabbed and forced behind his back, a cable tie pulled with a loud *zip* and the stab of nylon cutting into his wrists

Lynch was led beyond the truck to a shabby Land Cruiser, the back door opened for him.

'In.'

He managed the step up, somehow. He sprawled on the seat, unable to reach out and steady himself. He wriggled to a sitting position. They put Hartmoor in front. Two more gunmen got into the back and sat facing each other on the jockey seats.

'What's happening, Lynch?'

'We are being kidnapped, Jason.' Lynch tried to keep the sarcasm from his voice, but failed. 'I think these guys work for Abbas Ali.'

A gunman got in next to Lynch. The old car smelled of cigarettes and sweat, the upholstery tatty and worn smooth in places. They set off downhill towards Bchamoun, the other gunmen following in a worn Mercedes truck. The old car's engine rattled and the gearbox whined. The gunmen chattered animatedly in Arabic.

'Yes, you're right,' said Hartmoor. 'They're taking us to Chatila.'

'Silence,' the driver barked.

Lynch shrugged.

The gunman sitting next to Lynch pulled a pair of nail clippers from his pocket and started to cut his nails with a series of slow, meticulous movements, each of which produced a little keratinous click. The driver barked, 'Cut it out, Ali. For God's sake.'

Ali grunted and carried on snipping at his cracked nail. Lynch laughed, making the man turn to him. The clippers were held over the seat. Lynch lurched sideways, bringing his head back and throwing it forward to meet Ali's face. Ali cried out, his hands flying to his ruined nose as he rocked back under Lynch's momentum. The gunmen at the back shouted out, trying to free their guns but getting tangled in the confined space. The clippers bounced on the seat. Lynch twisted to reach them, touched the metal and lost it again. His fingers scrabbled on the tatty velour as Ali pushed back at him, bellowing his fury. Lynch found the clippers and fumbled them trying to reach the nylon strip. The effort made the tight bonds cut even more deeply into his wrists. Ali was fighting to free his AK47, but Lynch was pushing against him and the big car was swerving as the driver braked too hard and lost control of the steering.

Lynch pressed down on the clippers as hard as he could but their angle was bad and they slipped on the nylon. Ali freed one hand and caught him a massive blow to his shoulder. Lynch cried out and head-butted the man again. The car slid to a stop, the brakes of the truck behind them squealed. One of the gunmen in the back was trying to reach over and punch Lynch while the other scrabbled for the door release. Lynch pressed on the clippers again, this time the cable tie gave way. Lynch brought his fist around to drive into Ali's solar plexus. He threw a flurry of hard, short punches into the man's kidney, grabbed for the gun and pulled back as Ali tried to elbow him in the face.

They fought a tug of war over the gun. Ali found the trigger and fired as Lynch pushed the barrel up, the sound deafening in the car's cabin. The gun juddered and bucked, the barrel quickly burning Lynch's hand. He held on, punching Ali in the throat with the other hand, finally wresting the gun from the loosened grip. The driver had shoved open his door, standing off from the car to try and get a clear line of fire to Lynch. Hartmoor stayed strapped in, hunched over with his head in his hands.

Lynch fired through the window, another a deafening fusillade. The driver dropped. He twisted in his seat and jabbed the butt of the AK47 into the face of the man in the back trying to clamber over the seat to reach him. He kicked his door open. The last of the gunmen had got out of the back door and was bringing his gun around when Lynch dropped to the ground, firing. The gunman's chest was plucked by bullets that knocked him backwards to crash onto the tarmac. His gun clattered on the road.

Lynch shouted into the acrid cordite smoke of the car's interior. 'Hartmoor. Jason? You okay?'

Hartmoor croaked, 'Y—yes.'

'Get down! Lie in the footwell.'

Lynch rolled clear of the car to fire back into the cab of the truck halted behind them. Hesitating halfway to the ground, one man fell immediately. Two more in the cab disappeared behind starred glass. Lynch pulled the trigger and was rewarded with clicks. He scrambled back to the Land Cruiser and frisked Ali for more ammunition, tore out the useless magazine and replaced it with a fresh one. Shots punched into the car from behind.

Lynch fired back blind, perching the AK47 on the top of the seat and crouching as low as he could. The back windscreen shattered and bullets tore through the seating, the dull impacts like angry knocks on a door. They jerked Ali's recumbent form. Blood started to gush out of his mouth. His eyes snapped open in horror and he tried to talk, choking gouts of blood down his chest.

Lynch twisted again to fire out over the wheel arch, the AK47 gripped in his left hand. Silence from behind was his reward. He peered out. Two huddles on the ground, one unaccounted for, presumably in the cab of the truck. The echoes of gunfire died in the hills, leaving birdsong and crickets. A church bell rang out from somewhere further up the mountain. The black cloud continued to rise into the cerulean sky.

Lynch gripped the AK47 in front of him and stepped out of the Land Cruiser, approaching the bullet-riddled Mercedes truck cautiously. An oncoming car stopped a few hundred feet away downhill and started reversing back around the corner.

The fifth man was lying in the truck's cab. Lynch jogged back to the Land Cruiser. Hartmoor was sitting in his seat, belt fixed, staring into the middle distance as if nothing had happened. His eyes were red.

'Okay?'

Hartmoor nodded. Lynch ran around the car and pulled open Ali's door and tugged the man's messy bulk down to the road. The rust stench of blood rose, dark stains on the leather and carpet. Lynch closed the door and jumped into the driver's seat. Lynch called in to Channing and started to make arrangements. Hartmoor stared slackly out of the window.

It was sunset before Lynch pulled up at the arranged meeting place, a small wooded road outside the village of Choueifat, the GPS co-ordinates given him by the man from the embassy he was to meet, someone new there who went by the name of Anson.

Anson's car was parked neatly in the layby, a white Mercedes 180. Lynch switched off the Land Cruiser's engine.

'You be okay for a while?'

Hartmoor nodded. He hadn't spoken since they had left the gunfight with Abbas Ali's men. Lynch put out a hand, but Hartmoor jerked his arm away as if he'd been electrocuted. 'Jason?'

'It's okay, Lynch. Do what you have to.'

'Look, I'm sorry. Really. We'll get clear of here and maybe take some time out to take stock of where we are with all this. It's a mess, there's no doubt about that, but you mustn't blame yourself.' Lynch told the lie without hesitation. Hartmoor just stayed looking out of the window and, after a second, Lynch left him to it.

Anson had got out and was standing by the car, a gangly young man with a prominent Adam's apple. His leather jacket opened to reveal a Metallica t-shirt. He held his hand out. 'Clive Anson. It's a privilege to meet you, Mr Lynch.'

'Is that right?' Lynch wiped his hand on his jeans before taking Anson's.

'I have everything you need. I'll take the Land Cruiser from here, the Mercedes is hired in your name. Your luggage is in the boot, two bags with fresh clothes. We got Mr Hartmoor's sizes from the stuff left at the villa. We tried to match the styles. There are supplies of his painkillers and enzymes. It was pretty hard getting hold of the painkillers, by the way. You can only get them from hospitals.'

'Don't I know it,' murmured Lynch.

'There are toilet bags as well, although the hotel will have pretty much anything you need anyway. You're booked into the Cavalier for the night and you're on BA to Heathrow first thing tomorrow. It's a 6.15 flight, I'm afraid. But Mr Channing appears to have gone soft, you're both booked club.'

Lynch laughed. 'No, son, he's not going soft. Channing knows which side to butter bread and you'd better believe it.

Channing's always falls butter side up.'

'You're booked into the Cavalier as Peter Smith and Dominic Jones. They won't ask for a passport or ID. The manager's a friend and the Cavalier prides itself on its discretion.' Anson held out his hand again. 'Keys are in the ignition. The bill's taken care of already, including extras. Have a nice stay, Mr Lynch.'

Lynch gripped the young man's arm as he shook. 'Thank you. You've done a good job Clive. Good luck cleaning this one up, though.'

'Oh, I rather think it's going straight to scrap, actually, sir.'

'Perhaps best.' Lynch patted Anson's shoulder and turned to the Land Cruiser. Peering in, he saw Hartmoor's eyes were closed. He opened the passenger door gently. 'Jason.'

Hartmoor didn't move. 'I'm awake, Lynch. I was just testing what it feels like to have your eyes closed for all eternity. You find you get used to it.'

'Sure, you'll have time enough for that. Come on, we're getting a clean car and night on the tiles.'

Lynch rather enjoyed the way Hartmoor's eyes snapped open to glare at him.

They had driven into the city without incident, waited patiently in Hamra's choking traffic and checked in at the Cavalier. Lynch showered, gently cleaning the scratch marks flying safety glass had left on his arms and his right temple. There was a livid bruise on his cheek and his lip had split. He looked like a bad prizefighter.

Lynch checked he had his key card. There was a pack of Cohibas in his shirt pocket and a lighter with a girl whose clothes came off when you inverted it in his trouser pocket. Anson clearly knew his customer too well. Lynch's admiration for the young man knew no bounds.

He strode down the corridor. The Cavalier had been

refurbished, but the hotel had been there since the Civil War. They'd done a nice job of it, Lynch reflected, as he waited for the lift and surveyed the dark carpets and ash wood minimalism of the refit. Hartmoor's room was two floors below. Lynch knocked four times before Hartmoor opened the door, still in the same clothes they had checked in wearing. He looked tired and crumpled.

'Do you mind some company?'

Hartmoor waved him in. Lynch noted the holdall on the bed was untouched. He called room service. 'Bottle of Johnny Walker black, two tumblers, ice please.'

They sat in silence until the whisky came. Lynch paid in cash and poured a hefty glass. He raised the bottle towards Hartmoor.

'I can't. I would dearly like to. The Roxanol doesn't react well with it, I would be reeling after a few sips, probably dead after a glass.' Hartmoor snorted. 'Actually, that has a certain appeal to it.'

Lynch sipped. 'Okay, Jason. Let's take a look where we find ourselves. For a start, don't blame yourself. It could have happened to anyone.'

Hartmoor rummaged in the minibar and pulled out a little bottle of Perrier. 'That's not true, Lynch. I have been stupid beyond belief. They're right to want me arrested. I have betrayed my country for a folly, a mirage. I consistently discussed confidential affairs with her.' He laughed. 'Her. Them. I shared our gossip, debated negotiating positions, outlined British policy even when it was at odds with our publicly stated aims and goals. I even discussed confidential defence programs and bids for defence contracts I was privy to. The more I think back on it, the more I understand a more capable man would have realised he was being led.' Hartmoor shook his head in irritation. 'No, not even led. Worse than that. Herded.'

'You're being hard on yourself. You were in love and a man you trusted betrayed you. You weren't to know.'

'Oh come on, Lynch. I'm a grown man. I should have never left her. I ran and she bore my child, a girl I was never to know. I talked with her after I arrived in Beirut, Dana. I went up there. It was Dana who told me her mother would be coming. I even have a granddaughter. It's insane. A whole family I never knew. They kept that from me.' Hartmoor shook his head. 'You know, when I went up there I thought she was Mai at first, they are so alike. Estelle, I mean, my granddaughter. I thought she was Mai's ghost. And now she's dead, because of me. My own granddaughter. My daughter. A family I never knew of.'

Hartmoor's gaze dropped to his glass. When he looked up again his eyes were shining. 'My own daughter. Brought up by that awful little man because I wasn't here for her. Oh, Lynch, you have no idea how a man can wallow in self-pity rather than face his own culpability and stupidity. It was my weakness that led me to conjure up this romantic interlocutor rather than face the awfulness of my own marriage. I escaped into writing like an author, only I wrote secrets, thinking that here I had intelligent conversation, someone whose insights would help me with my work where Lesley was just contemptuous of it.' His tone hardened. 'How many of them would there have been?'

Lynch was caught on the hop, lost in the idea of a family that had never known its true father and the man lost to them who could have found so much. 'How many of what?'

'Writers. On Coleman's team. How many writers does it take to deceive a fool?'

Hartmoor was admirable in his way, Lynch reflected. Even sitting on a hotel room bed, there was still certain poise to the man. His only possible future comprised ruin and death, things most men ran from all their lives. And yet Hartmoor, despite his red-rimmed eyes and pallor, seemed totally composed.

'It's quite a complicated operation.' Lynch sipped his drink. 'They'd have had at least a forger an author and a team of briefers. There would have been at least one committee to filter the product. And another to formulate the direction, the nature of questions she'd ask. You'd have been quite a prize to the Russians.' Lynch sipped and raised his glass to eye level. 'Which is what you became. Because I reckon boy Coleman took the product from you and gave it his pal Dmitri. Dmitri's career became quite as stellar as Frank's, his stock rose just as high, his counsel sought. Only Dmitri was buying his place at the table with British secrets, insights and briefings from his supposed "mole". Frank was being repaid in Dmitri's product, proper Russian stuff. It was a great operation, alright. At our expense. Special relationship my arse.'

There was a moment of silence.

'I have been thinking,' said Hartmoor. 'You know, every time I told her in a letter that I wanted to come back here to see her, Frank Coleman turned up in town and took me out for drinks, a meal. Whatever town I was in at the time, Frank would always pop up by coincidence. He'd ask after her, draw me out. And then he'd tell me what a bad idea it would be to visit her and ruin her family life.' There was no rancour in Hartmoor's voice. 'What a bastard he was.'

'Managing a Joe is all part of the game, whether or not they're witting.'

Asperity entered Hartmoor's voice for the first time. 'Would you stop trying to be nice? It's bloody irritating. Just treat it like work, Lynch. I don't want or need your pity. And, by the way, it doesn't suit you.'

'Suit yourself.' Lynch shrugged. 'I need you to list down the key elements you think you gave away. We'll take you back through those time and again, so try and get as many down as you can. We can try and backtrack the links, though there's going to be precious little pickings to be had these days. It's all ancient history, really.'

'So why are they so interested in me today? They've been trying to chase me, kill me. I'm a dying man, Lynch. What do they all want with me?'

'Because of who Dmitri became. Because he left the army

just before the fall and got his hands on a load of former state assets – a nice, typical oligarch. Only he was more bent than most, and he continued to work for Uncle Sam. He became Jaan Kallas, a major hood with a slick front and now he's helping Dennis Wye smuggle a billion dollars of heroin a time into Russia. The last thing those two need is someone thrashing around and dredging up the past, exposing the operation that built Dmitri's career. And proving he was always, and still is, a CIA asset.'

'It's all so neat, isn't it? But somewhere there's always a weak link for them to exploit, a sad little man they can extort or blackmail or hoodwink.' Hartmoor swirled the ice around his glass. 'It's always the men, isn't it? We're too fallible. Oh, what a waste. What a stupid waste.'

Lynch refilled his glass and plopped fresh ice in. He stood at the window looking out at Hamra bustling in the sunset's rose light.

'So what happened in Sudan?'

Hartmoor glowered. 'You've read the file, Lynch.'

'Sure I have. Tell me in your words. It hardly matters anymore to you anyway, does it?'

'Oh that's good.' Hartmoor chuckled. 'You mean I've gone so low nothing I do could possibly sink me any lower?'

'Not at all.' Lynch snapped open the sliding window and slipped through onto the balcony overlooking the street below. 'I meant telling me is hardly going to make it more public.'

Hartmoor held his glass of Perrier in his left hand, pressed down on the bed with his right and wheeled himself up to stand. He walked painstakingly to join Lynch, leaning on the concrete lip and gazing down at the street. 'So much life. It goes on, doesn't it? It's relentless.' He drank from his glass, wiping at the condensation with his forefinger. 'Sudan was late in my career, my last posting as it turned out. A colleague suggested some "relaxation" and I went there, to the address he provided. There was a girl who took a shine to me. I reasoned I had little to lose.

I had an affair in Tel Aviv after my marriage ended but beyond that I had not really indulged in, you know. *That.*'

Lynch slipped out a cigar and snipped it over the balcony edge. The cut stub spiralled down to the street. Lynch lit up with profound satisfaction. 'That? Jesus, Jason. You make it sound like a perversion.'

Hartmoor cackled. 'I'm an amateur, Lynch. You should have seen what they did with it. Love, I mean. How they could take love and twist it. That's the perversion.'

'Sure, you use what you're given in this game. Back to the Sudanese girl.'

'She was lovely, a solace and comfort to me. So I paid for her company. That hardly marks me out as unique. Mai had stopped replying to my letters for some reason, I had written and written to her with no reply. Always, of course, to that damn post office box. I wrote and vowed to fly to Beirut and, of course I didn't realise it then because I was a fool but I know it now, Frank Coleman appeared as if by magic.'

'In Khartoum.'

'Precisely. We had drinks and Frank fed me the gossip. Beirut had recovered, Hariri had rebuilt the city centre. Mai was happy with her family and I would be insane to wreck her happiness, as usual. He ate regularly at the restaurant, it was doing well.' Hartmoor paused, placed his glass carefully on the balcony's concrete edge and let his head fall into his hands. He stayed like that long enough for Lynch to finish his cigar and flick the butt to join the plug he had cut earlier, spinning to the street.

'Of course, I recanted my vow to go to Beirut. I stayed in Khartoum.'

'Dmitri had a new career by then. They didn't need you. It was over.'

'Hindsight, Lynch. It's a wonderful thing.'

Lynch went into the hotel room and emerged with the whisky bottle. He topped his glass up. 'Listen, here's the deal. I want you to help me do for them all. Wye, Dmitri, the whole thing. Take it down, smash it up. Revenge. For both of us. You might have to be a goat again. But you and I have both lost too much to this not to want to strike back at them. What about it?'

Hartmoor gazed down the street. A taxi dropped a pretty girl on the corner. She was laughing, shopping bags in her hand. Leggy in her short skirt

'Okay,' said Hartmoor. 'It's all over now anyway. The game's up.' He paused, gazing at the street. He turned to Lynch a thin smile on his face. 'What the hell. One last song and all that. I'm in. For whatever that's worth. For whatever I'm worth.'

TWENTY-THREE

It seemed a lifetime ago Lynch had last sat in Channing's minimalist office overlooking the Thames. This time there was no scotch on offer. Having availed of British Airways' hospitality in the lounge at Beirut International and slept it off on the four-hour flight, Lynch wasn't sure he could have faced it in any case.

Channing was pacing the room. 'I have to say, it's beautiful. They pay off their political pals in Afghanistan, give the Russians an endemic domestic drugs problem to keep their energies nicely focused inwards and fund their overseas operations all in one fell swoop. And by being probably the most important player in the supply chain, they've got the opportunity to totally infiltrate the Mafia as a bonus.' He smacked his fist into his hand. 'Genius.'

'Unless you take the view that they've become suppliers, corrupted by the revenue and therefore no better than the bad guys.' Lynch sneered.

Channing froze, his face a study in incredulity. He shook his head, laughing. 'Oh, Gerald. What a very old fashioned, black and white view of the world you have sometimes.'

Lynch smiled in acknowledgement, an alternative to his preferred reaction of jumping up and planting one in that smirk. Channing had undoubtedly been spending too much time at the trough recently and he was sprouting chins.

'But our masters have met and are in agreement. It is highly illegal, an outrageous invasion of European sovereignty and will be treated as any other illegal drug smuggling operation. If evidence emerges of official CIA involvement, the necessary protests will be made. Although given Frank Coleman's track record over the Freij affair, it's just as likely this will be an example of,' Channing made air quotes, 'private enterprise.'

Channing dropped down into the tall-backed chair behind his charcoal desk. 'We have a team of analysts working on Hartmoor's testimony. It's incredible how much damage he managed to do. It turns out he was the man behind Clinton getting Arafat and Rabin together for that photo call over Oslo. Imagine that? It should have been John Major, you know. Not that it matters any more, apart from putting together the charges.'

'You can't charge him. He's at death's door. I don't know how he's lasted this long. Leave him go, Brian. He was just a poor dupe.'

'Yes, it's funny how a well-meaning fool can hurt you more than an implacable enemy. I'd rather have the enemy, to tell the truth. At least an enemy cares enough to *want* to hurt you.'

'He's helping us.'

'Granted. The Estonians have reported the plane landed on schedule at Kärdla airport yesterday at midnight. They have it under close surveillance. No attempt has been made to unload; it's just parked up on the apron there. The pilot is staying at a spa hotel in,' Channing squinted at his screen, 'Haapsalu. It's a nearby town. The whole place is a Baltic sleepy hollow. It's an island, you know.' Another squint. 'Called Hiuumaa. You'll be pleased to hear that your friend Jaan Kallas has an estate there. It's huge apparently. You have a liaison in Estonian Intelligence, she will be waiting for you at the airport. Name of, hang on, Anna Jakobson.'

'And my brief?'

Channing blinked. 'Bring them down, Lynch. Bring them down.'

'I want Hartmoor with us.'

'Not an option. He's safe in custody, where he'll stay. End of.'

'No. He comes with me. I may need him. Kallas and Wye

both want him badly. He might be my key. I want Hartmoor. He's my only bargaining chip.'

'I said no. It's not an option.'

'Then you can go to hell. I'm not doing this without him. Lynch enjoyed Channing's tightening, the frustration in the man. Channing raised his fist, his forefinger extended. His mouth pursed, he seemed about to explode. Channing wheeled around and slapped his desk. Lynch exulted.

'Take him and go to hell. Get out.'

The little Bombardier struggled in the wind, their approach to Lennart Meri Tallinn Airport marked by gut-wrenching swoops, the snow dense in the air the plane was penetrating. Lynch, never a happy flier, gripped both arms of his chair. Hartmoor sat beside him peaceably looking out of the window, his pale features and washed-out eyes accentuated by his customary black clothes, the whiteness of the light and the darkness of the cloud beyond.

They came down hard, the plane swerving as the pilot brought it under control and applied the brakes. There was a smattering of applause.

They disembarked, Lynch feeling hot and uncomfortable in the uncharacteristically chunky sweater Channing's secretary had bought, thoughtfully buying the same style and burgundy colour for them both.

The airport building was warm but looking out of the glass told a different story. Apart from the black heated runway, everything was coated white. The snow was driving, gusts throwing up flurries from the ground. The Tannoy rang out as they walked towards arrivals, slowed by Hartmoor's hesitant gait. People shoved past them in their rush to stand waiting for their luggage. It was busy, the seating packed with expectant travellers and the occasional sleeping form.

They approached a group of security staff standing against

the wall wearing high-visibility clothing. Two were speaking into handsets, the distinctive triple tone cutting through the airport noise. A woman standing with them peeled away and approached Lynch. 'Mr Lynch? Mr Hartmoor? I am Anna Jakobson. Welcome to Estonia.'

'Thank you, Ms Jakobson,' Hartmoor bowed a little. Lynch held out his hand, which she took. There was to be no doubt on this one, Anna Jakobson was unmarried and was a peach. She was perhaps a shade under one metre eighty, blonde and blue-eyed. Lynch was sure she would be shapely under the big coat with the fur-lined hood that flopped over her shoulders. Her hand was as cool as her look of appraisal. Her right eye was ever so slightly cast, giving her an appealingly quirky look. She gestured ahead and they started walking again. 'We'll get you to your hotel. Your government must love you, you're booked into the Hotel Telegraaf.' Her accented English was undeniably sexy.

Lynch was playful. 'Oh, our government loves us very, very much, Ms Jakobson. Loves us to bits.' She was looking ahead, but he caught her smile.

'I'm sorry.' Hartmoor had fallen back, out of breath. Now he stopped. 'I wonder, could we take it a touch easier. I'm not quite… well…'

Her hand flew to her mouth. 'No, it is I who should apologise. I had not made allowances; they told us you were ill.' She fished a radio from her voluminous jacket and gabbled into it. The radio barked back. 'One second, pleases. They will send a cart.'

Hartmoor's knuckles were white on The Stick. 'You are very kind to meet us, Ms Jakobson.'

Passengers from the flight continued to brush pass them. Lynch felt an unreasonable urge to dash on, to push through the throng and be first to immigration. Her jacket was open and yes, she did have curves.

They heard the peeping of the cart before it rounded the corner. Hartmoor sat gratefully, Lynch and Anna behind him.

They made their cacophonous way through the terminal.

Anna twisted around in the front seat of the people carrier. 'So you have timed your visit to Estonia perfectly to enjoy some of our nicest weather. There is a snow storm now, it is six degrees below zero outside and the weather is forecast to get worse tomorrow night. It is lucky your government loves you, your hotel is a famous boutique hotel in the centre of the Old Town. We will take you there and I will leave you to freshen up, then we can have dinner. There is no rush for any action tonight, the aeroplane is most certainly not going anywhere and we have it under close surveillance. The pilot is staying in a hotel in Hiiumaa and we have him under surveillance too. You will meet the man in charge of this operation tomorrow, his name is Anders Väljas and he is in charge of the Western Region. We are organised regionally. I report directly to the deputy director general, Kristina Kuusik and I am responsible for liaison between our services for this operation. Also for liaison with you.'

'What about Kallas?' Lynch watched the wipers packing snow on the windscreen.

'We have him under close surveillance with a large profiling team. We're being very careful not to spook him, clearly. We also have electronic surveillance on him.'

Lynch was impressed by her manner. Channing had assured him the Estonians had highly sophisticated online surveillance and countermeasure capabilities. 'See how many minutes it takes them to tell you they invented Skype,' he had thrown sourly at Lynch. 'It's usually no more than twenty.'

Hartmoor was gazing dreamily out of the window, his eyelids dropping. Lynch shifted in his seat. 'And what do we know about this Mr Kallas?'

'I thought you might ask. Here. Try not to lose it.' She handed back a tablet. 'It's a secure device, it'll give you Internet access and I'm in there as a contact if you should need to get hold of me. Most of Tallinn has free wireless. Broadly, we know a great deal about the public Kallas and very little about the other Kallas.' She grimaced. 'To tell the truth, we weren't looking until very recently.'

'What about his background as a Soviet Ministry of Defence official?'

'What we know is in there,' she gestured at the tablet, 'but it is patchy. Any records regarding his military service are in Russia and getting them out of Moscow is not easy. Many of the records held here about such people became conveniently erased after the revolution. Mr Kallas is a very wealthy individual who owns a number of companies, particularly in the freight and logistics business but also in mining and oil shale, chemicals and technology. Frankly, we had not considered him to be involved in organised crime until your colleagues contacted us. We will meet tomorrow with the head of CERT, our military electronic intelligence unit.'

'Sounds impressive.'

'They are,' Anna turned back to face the front. 'Technologically Estonia, what do you say, bats above its weight? We invented Skype, you know.'

The hotel was sumptuous, contemporary décor dominated by charcoal walls, chequerboard brown floor tiles and ornate crystal chandeliers. Anna was sitting on one of the charcoal sofas in the lobby when Lynch arrived, duly freshened up. He had showered and shaved before exploring the luxurious room and its well-stocked minibar, which he had lightened by a beer and some nuts. He was joined by Hartmoor, who had spent the hour sleeping and still looked wan.

She stood to meet them. She was wearing a figure-hugging woollen dress, black patent boots and a scarlet Pashmina.

Hartmoor bent to kiss her hand. Lynch shook it.

She tossed her blonde hair over her shoulder and gestured behind them. 'The restaurant's here. Shall we go in?'

They followed her into the Restaurant Tchaikovsky, joined by a smiling waiter who showed them to a table at the back of the ornate room. They took their seats, the waiter speaking rapidly to Anna in hushed Estonian. Lynch took it all in: white linen, glass and shining tines, dark walls and gold frames with embroidered chairs and a domed glass ceiling.

'Can I suggest Martinis?' Anna broke into Lynch's reverie. 'Fine by me.'

Hartmoor hesitated. 'Actually, just water for me. I'll perhaps have a sip of wine with my meal.'

The waiter departed, leaving them menus. Anna leaned on the table. 'We can talk safely. I took the precaution of booking all the tables around us. I have arranged a briefing and liaison meeting with all the concerned departments at our headquarters tomorrow at eleven. I think it might be wise to do some shopping before then, it doesn't look like you both have clothes to suit our weather.'

'I don't want to be rude, but I hardly think we have time for shopping.'

She threw her head back and laughed, her eyes lively and her hand over her mouth. 'Oh, I am so sorry Mr Lynch. I had forgotten you are a man of action, are you not? As I said on the way from the airport, there is no action right now. We have surveillance in place to cover all of the players in this, we have investigations underway. We are taking this very seriously indeed, but the players aren't moving and the weather will stop anything like an operation to unload an aeroplane in the open right now. It is only sensible to relax and enjoy the downtime.'

The waiter arrived with their drinks on a silver tray. It was the largest Martini Lynch had ever seen. He raised his glass to her. 'Okay, so. You're the boss, it's your country. Maybe I'll just take your advice.'

'You're a fast learner, Mr Lynch.'

She ordered for them. A dish of little filled dumplings floating in a rich stock to start, venison with a rich berry sauce and Estonian cheese with cloudberry jam. Red wine for them, Perrier for Hartmoor. The food was exceptional and Lynch enjoyed her company. Jason Hartmoor was quiet throughout the meal and then announced he wanted to turn in. A quick glance passed between them. Hartmoor's illness was a topic the conversation had skirted.

Lynch and Anna stood, but Hartmoor waved them down. 'Oh, stop fussing. What time will we meet in the morning?'

'Nine? I'll bring the car and we can hit the shops. If your government loves you so much, mine might as well join in.'

'Nine then. Thank you, Anna, it has been a magical evening. Goodnight, Gerald.'

Lynch watched the retreating back, the hand wobbling on the hated Stick Hartmoor was using constantly now. He wondered how much time the man had left. The restaurant had filled while they were there, but the pair of tables adjacent to their own stayed empty.

Anna called the waiter over and ordered coffee, the bill and two double whiskies on the rocks.

'So tell me, Gerald, about this Jason Hartmoor.'

Lynch shrugged. 'What's to tell? He studied Arabic in Beirut in the '70s but had to leave when we shut down our language school there. He left a girl behind, but never went back to Beirut. He wrote to her for years. When he realised his time was up, he went back for a last trip to find her. He got lucky, or not as it turned out, and she was visiting at the time. Which is how he found out she wasn't writing to him, the CIA was. We've got people working on the backtrack but it's really of historical rather than operational interest. They were smart, the CIA boyos. They developed her character, made her the smart, interested player Hartmoor's wife wasn't, so he opened up to

230

her. To a shocking degree. He blew everything he was involved in, basically.'

The drinks arrived. Their glasses clinked together. Lynch waited for the waiter to depart. 'So why would the CIA want to spy on the Brits, you might ask. Well, for a start it gave them a useful check of our stated positions and intentions. It also helped them cut us out of a few opportunities, including some large telecom and defence contracts in Saudi Arabia and downplayed our role in the Oslo Peace Accords. And it gave their man in Beirut, a guy called Frank Coleman, a useful source of career-enhancing information to pass on to his tame Russian Joe. The guy was codenamed Dmitri, but you know him as Jaan Kallas.'

'Yes, I read the briefing.'

'Right. Hartmoor turning up in Beirut and threatening to uncover the whole operation by meeting up with his old girlfriend was Kallas' nightmare. So he tried to cover his tracks by having Hartmoor murdered. Didn't pan out that way.'

'How does he keep going?'

'Hartmoor? He might be stupid, but he's brave, I'll give him that. In my book that counts. He's taken some pretty big knocks on the chin and he's still standing.'

'So have you.'

Lynch glanced sharply at her.

'I'll survive. It's no…' He sighed. 'We were very close, yes. It was a long time. She took me under her wing when I first arrived in Beirut as a young man. It was just at the end of the Civil War. Probably the most dangerous time in some ways.'

'I understand, at least I try to. I have never lost a partner or a… friend in that way.'

'I can't recommend it, sure I can't. I try not to dwell on it too much but it has a habit of sort of staying with you. I'm only glad I killed that Estonian bastard.' A shadow passed. 'Sorry.'

'No, it's okay. We have many organised criminals. We do our best to keep them down but it's an ongoing battle, as I am sure you know. They are called the Ühiskassa here, the umbrella organisation. I am truly sorry that one of our thugs killed your girlfriend.'

There was a silence as they both tried to think of something to say. Lynch was first. 'Shall we call it a night? I have a feeling tomorrow might be busy.'

'I think you might be right.'

They left the restaurant, Lynch having insisted on signing the bill to his room. In the lobby, Anna called for her coat. He shook her hand and she smiled and kissed his cheek.

Lynch went up to his room and peeled off his clothes, popped a miniature from the minibar and switched on the adult entertainment channel he was assured would be billed as 'information services' when he checked out.

The meeting room was warm and Lynch could smell the newness of his clothes. Last night's storm had abated, a winter wonderland greeting him when he had looked out of his hotel window that morning, the yellow, blue and salmon-painted frontages of Tallin's old town buildings capped in white. The sky was sultry; the clouds hung low over the city. The vignetted sky deepened to a graphite horizon.

They had, indeed gone shopping that morning, Hartmoor had been too tired to join them so Anna had taken his sizes and bought a duplicate set of clothing which she had asked the hotel to send to his room. She had waited for Lynch to dump his things, then ferried him to the bald-looking, yellow building with a grey blockhouse tacked onto it, the home of the Estonian Security Police. This was to be the first of many planned meetings, she had assured him. Lynch quailed at the prospect, but managed to hold his peace.

Anna returned with coffees for them both, followed by a tall, donnish-looking man with round spectacles and close-cropped white hair. 'So, Gerald, I introduce Anders Väljas, the head of

232

the Western Region at the Estonian Security Police.'

Lynch reached across the meeting table to shake. 'Pleased to meet you.'

'And I you. An interesting operation you have brought us to.'

'You could say that,' Lynch smiled.

Anna put the cups down. 'Mr Hartmoor decided to stay at the hotel, he is tired. In any case, I do not think we see him playing active operational role.'

Lynch nodded. 'I thought it highly likely he might be useful when it comes to defining Mr Kallas' past career and current affiliations. Mr Kallas is keen to ensure Hartmoor doesn't link him to the CIA. So Hartmoor could be a valuable bargaining asset.'

Väljas took a seat.

'We are waiting for the head of CERT, who should be here, oh, just now.' Pushing the door shut behind him, a corpulent young man wearing a black jumper and jeans glanced nervously around the room. He was carrying a tablet. 'This, Gerald, is Juhan Eskola, the head of our computer emergency response team.'

The prematurely balding head bobbed, a wisp of hair dislodging itself to be brushed back into place by its owner. Eskola grinned and sat at the table. He fiddled with the projector remote.

Väljas cleared his throat and removed his glasses, waving them at Lynch. 'So let me fill you in, Gerald. We have a team watching this plane that's parked at Kärdla Airport. It's a provincial airstrip and doesn't usually play host to international flights. In fact, it's barely able to accept a plane the size of a 737, but this charter flight has been there several times before. The locals tell us it is usually on the apron for one or two days at the most then just flies out again. No passengers, no cargo. This is backed by the official paperwork. The pilot, a man called Nimr, I believe, is popular with the airport staff. He brings them gifts.

He is flying for an eccentric billionaire, apparently. The plane is always to detour to Kärdla in case it is needed. The billionaire has an estate on Hiuumaa.'

Lynch sipped his coffee and grimaced. Anna flicked two sachets of sugar across the pale wood. 'Anna tells me Kallas does, indeed, have an estate on the island.' Lynch noted the sharp glance his interruption earned him.

'This is so. The staff, as I was saying, like this Nimr and believe his story.'

'I'm sorry,' Lynch interrupted again. 'But isn't there a strong likelihood that someone on this staff is compromised and involved in this operation and is enabling their access to the airport to unload the cargo?'

Väljas' barked laughter startled Eskola, who dropped the remote. 'My dear Gerald, they don't need to be compromised. Every night at five pm they lock up the airport and go home. The complete staff numbers seven people. Kärdla is hardly your Heathrow.' Lynch tried not to be irritated by the man's whinnying and failed.

Looking around the room for approval, Väljas wiped his eyes, 'Oh dear me. *Compromised.*'

Anna appealed to Eskola. 'Do your guys have any updates, Juhan?'

Eskola smiled, a sickly effort. 'Well, we don't really get involved in everyday *criminal* investigations, as you know. But we have access to Kallas' email and we are analysing this. His phone records are clear, but there are relatively few international calls between Estonia and Beirut, so we are tracing them all. We have been looking at Kallas' involvements in the Hiuumaa Island. So we know he has this estate, but it is more of a working estate than a pleasure one. There is a logistics company he owns and has a facility there. Often trucks stay overnight at this place. So it is easy for them to arrange the distribution of the load from the plane. In fact, there is convoy of eight trucks on the way to Hiuumaa right now. The ice road is open today. We can assume these trucks will be used for the transportation of the load to the mainland.'

Lynch paused as he sipped coffee. 'Ice road?'

'Yes.'

Lynch shrugged at Anna who was holding back her grin. 'Juhan, I don't think Gerald has many ice roads in Beirut.' She turned to him. 'Hiuumaa is connected to the mainland by ferries. In the winter sometimes there is ice road. The Baltic freezes in the cold months, so thick it can be used as a road.'

Lynch craned forward, the veins standing out on his dark-haired hands as he gripped his cup. 'So they're moving. They'll unload the plane tonight.'

'Now calm yourself, Gerald,' Väljas was polishing his glasses. He put them back on his nose and peered at Lynch. 'We have a forecast of bad weather to factor in. Added to this, the ice road is closed at night. So they are highly unlikely to be going anywhere tonight except perhaps to their depot. Tomorrow the storm will have passed. It will be tomorrow they act. And then we shall be ready for them and swoop down on them like the avenging angels.'

Väljas collated the papers in front of him. He got to his feet and snapped a tight smile at Lynch, peering over his spectacle rims. 'We are most pleased to have you with us Mr Lynch. Most pleased.'

Lynch watched the door close. He wasn't sure whether to be bewildered or furious. He turned to Anna. 'This can't be right.'

'It's his call. It's his region.'

'It's dangerously complacent is what it is.'

Eskola cleared his throat. 'Actually, Anders has a point. The ice road does close at night and it is speed restricted. From the ice they have to make a landing at Rohuküla. Once we know they are loaded and moving, we can assume we are able to intercept them at any time.'

'I've always stayed alive not believing in assumptions.'

'Ah, you live in a different world to us, Mr Lynch.' Eskola

snapped his attention to the tablet, swiping with his fat finger. 'Oh. Wait. This is interesting. A number of Kallas' companies are losing money more than they make. The analysts are working on confirming this, but it looks like they are a network for money laundering. We have a guilty man, I think.' He peered up at them, beaming. 'Approximately a billion dollars this year alone.'

Jason Hartmoor lay on his bed, his head turned to idly stare at the strip of Roxanol tablets on the bedside table. The sunlight glinted on the foil edge, the little silver blisters each reflecting the light like domes on an endless plain. He imagined himself skating between them, a tiny figure skimming along the brilliant foil surface, surrounded by ordered lines of great shining domes.

He dozed for a while. He woke to a moment's disorientation. He was in Estonia, of course. He propped himself up on his elbows and gazed around the opulent hotel room, the snowy rooftops outside the window. His eyes were crusted and he rubbed them clear.

His daughter was dead. He had a daughter. She had lived, breathed, laughed, loved for all he knew. An only child born to strict Christians, Jason had grown up lonely and envying his friend Michael who lived in a warm, bustling house full of laughter and noise. The youngest of seven, Michael was more worldly and confident than Jason. He knew more about the latest music and his vocabulary was always more colourful than Jason's book-read, proper English.

Jason's parents had met during the war, at a Toc H gathering. The tick of the grandfather clock in the hall and the smell of polish came back to him. As did the memory of his father's smile coming home from the printing press and his mother baking on Saturdays.

They had been kindly people, if worthy. Jason had longed to rebel but found his escape in academia instead. He had so wanted a family of his own to give the warmth his own childhood had lacked. Lesley hadn't wanted children. There had been arguments about that, bitter towards the end. Everything had been bitter towards the end.

Yet along, all these years, he actually had a daughter. His own flesh and blood. Born to Mai, the woman he had loved and left behind. The tears came to him, his face crumpling as his throat burned and he squeezed his eyes shut against the world. They coursed down his cheeks. Dana. She had been called Dana. Dana Hartmoor. Half Lebanese, half British. And this is my pretty wife, Mai. Nice to meet you. So you met in Beirut? How interesting!

And then there was Estelle. His granddaughter. Mai's image. Wiped out. Erased in a moment of horrifying violence that descended from that innocent blue sky.

Dana's husband. What of him? Elie. Their lives together and their love for each other. What had he said when they told him his wife and daughter were dead? What can his grief have been like, assuming of course they had let even him, untainted by this affair, live. It was too much to bear, Jason felt he would explode with the enormity of it all and the sense of responsibility for all this carnage. He cried out, then, refusing to accept it as the tears flowed and mucus ran onto his upper lip.

How had he allowed his life to be steered like this? He gripped the white duvet and feebly battered the bed. Why hadn't Mai told him there was a baby? Those first letters, before the gap and Frank Coleman. They had been real, had been her. She could have let him know. Of course he would never know now. He could only suppose her family had forbidden it. And Fadi, the stupid cook, waiting in the wings to take her away from him. The woman he loved and the daughter he had so desperately wanted. Fadi's revenge, helping Coleman to turn Jason's life inside out for a pitiful trove of supposed secrets.

Ah, the secrets. Jason grabbed a handful of tissues from the box by the bed and staunched the flow from his nose. He dried his cheeks and dabbed at his eyes, his body still racked with sobs.

Jason had sat with Lynch and gone through everything he could remember, the Irishman prompting him with a timeline of Middle East history he had drummed up from Wikipedia or somewhere. It had all come back and Jason had gradually been overwhelmed by the enormity of what he had given away. He had judged her trustworthy and believed his judgement stood above the rules, the practice of his profession. As his masters trusted him, so he had trusted Mai. She she had been sympathetic, supportive, well-informed (Oh God, so well informed) and her views had helped shape his own.

As they walked together through Middle East history, Jason had painstakingly outlined every indiscretion, every discussion on policy he could recall having. Right up until Benny Livitz. Lynch had quickened then. Tell me more. Go around again. More detail. How did you feel. Tell me about that bit again. Exhausted, Jason walked through the story again and again as Lynch urged him on.

Benny was probably the only Israeli Jason had met who wasn't hostile to him. Word had got around quickly that he was an 'Arab lover,' and few people he had encountered in Givat Ram hadn't clearly demonstrated they'd known it when they first met him.

But Benny had been different. A press attaché with the Ministry of Foreign Affairs, Benny had gone out of his way to put Jason at his ease. Over time, the hostility around him had waned, leaving Jason able to work effectively, but also with a feeling of deep gratitude to Benny for his friendship when he felt so very alone.

They would go for drinks at the end of each week, sometimes just one after the working day but occasionally, particularly on the increasingly frequent occasions when Lesley was away for some reason or another, they would settle in for a longer session. Benny was an accomplished raconteur with a wicked sense of humour and, rare for an Israeli, he was almost frighteningly candid.

Benny smoked like a chimney. In his late forties and balding prematurely, the top of his head shone in the bar lights. His permanently crumpled suit was two sizes too big for him. Benny was on a diet that never seemed to Hartmoor to extend to any form of restraint. His face, creased in amusement, was oily. The laughter lines around the shrewd brown eyes etched deep, folding as Benny grinned at Hartmoor, his drink raised.

'To Ariel Sharon. A right old horse's arse.' Livitz finished his pint and called the barman for another. He had been in a fury all evening, arriving late and cursing the Ministry of Defence and all in it, professing himself fed up of 'clearing up the diplomatic fallout from Sharon's constant and insane pursuit of Arafat.'

Jason was shocked. 'You simply cannot say things like that in public, Benny. You are a scandal. They can't possibly let the PLO continue to operate the way it has been from Lebanon.'

'There are other ways, Jason, than a full-scale invasion of the country.' Livitz leaned forwards, poking his two yellowed cigarette-bearing fingers at Jason. 'Horse's arse. I'm telling you. The man's dangerous. You know what his latest cock-and-bull scheme is? Hmm? Operation Peace for bloody Galilee. Know how he's going to do it? This "peace" of his?'

Jason popped a peanut from the bowl on the bar and shook his head. 'Obviously not. Why would I know what Sharon's planning any more than the next man?'

'Well, I'll tell you. The maniac is pushing for an invasion of Lebanon. Our Glorious Minister of Defence is going on the attack. He wants the PLO wiped out once and for all. You know with him it's personal? This isn't about peace for anywhere. It's about crushing the cockroaches.'

Livitz' new pint arrived and he pulled at the drink like a desert traveller, the cigarette once again waved at Hartmoor.

'Big Pines. That's the plan. The IDF is going in right the way through to the Damascus highway. They want Syria out, the PLO crushed and Lebanon a vassal state. That's how Sharon's going to win his "peace for Galilee". It's fucking insane.'

The Damascus highway! That meant the Israelis would take their war up the mountain, past Choueifat, Bchamoun and up to Shemlan. Jason drained his Stella but tasted nothing.

'Why would he do that, Benny? Come on, that's just tittle tattle. At best sabre rattling. Even Sharon wouldn't commit Israel to a prolonged ground offensive against the Syrians.'

Livitz waggled his cigarette at Jason's glass, twisting to catch the barman's attention. 'Another one here.' The precarious ash fell on Livitz' trouser leg. 'Sharon's original operation was rejected by the Cabinet last year. Now he's going to implement it anyway by provoking the Arabs into responding to attacks across the border. Bit by bit he'll escalate until he gets what he wants. And that's the plan – the Syrians out, the PLO crushed and Gemayel on the throne. He's in cahoots with the bloody Maronites and they're loving it. He's a mad dog. And, by the way, a horse's arse, to boot.'

Jason couldn't stop thinking of Mai and the tiny village on the hillside. His drink came. He felt stone-cold sober, despite the evening's heavy drinking. If Israel invaded, Syria would send its troops over the mountains. The Chouf and Bekaa would become a battleground, the little villages clinging to the mountainside above Beirut would be torn apart in hand-to-hand fighting between the factions that had already ploughed Lebanon's fields with their tithes of dead.

'And you know what the beauty of it is? You know, Jason? They've laid it all out, right on the Ministry of Defence meeting room table. They know what they're going to do, operation by operation. They're totally ready for it. They could go in tomorrow. Everything's lined up. And they'll go in next month.' Livitz waggled his cigarette again. 'The sixth of July. You mark my words. Sharon will find his provocation just in time for the sixth of July.'

Taking his leave of Livitz, Jason sat in the taxi home thinking of Shemlan caught up in fighting between the Israelis and their Maronite allies against the Syrians, the Druze and the PLO. He felt sick and it wasn't the drinks he'd had with Benny.

Jason had warned her, of course. He had written to her and confirmed Operation Mole Cricket 19 to Coleman and, by inference, to the Russians. The Israeli invasion of Lebanon, handed on a plate by Jason Hartmoor to every player in town.

Lynch's eyes were shining excitement, but Jason had finally run out of steam, his head lolling as he fought to stay awake. The next morning they flew to London and Jason was forced to repeat his story to many faceless men in many grey rooms. Their questions were draining, constantly testing him from every angle. He had pleaded for respite in the end and they had finally left him sleep.

Dana. My daughter. Jason gazed up at the ceiling and tried not to count the number of people who had died because of him. No, because of Frank Coleman. Jason had created none of this, it had been Frank's doing. All apart from the most important moment of all, of course. The moment when Jason had left Beirut behind and walked away from the woman he was supposed to love and the little girl he had put in her belly.

There were no more tears to shed. Jason had let the pain come back for too long and now it was making his muscles ache. He reached across for the Roxanol and pushed one out of the strip, then shrugged and took two. He was tempted to carry on popping them.

It wasn't the first time he'd had the thought. He could join Estelle, Dana and Mai. What would they say to him?

Jason got out of bed and went to shower. He regarded himself in the gold-framed bathroom mirror. He was horribly thin, his ribcage stark in the halogen light. Just a sad, naked old man with red, watery eyes.

Hartmoor had dressed and was gazing out of the window at the fairy tale sight of Tallinn in the snow and the growing dark smudge on the horizon when the suite's doorbell rang. He hobbled over and opened the door. A well-at-heel man stood on the threshold wearing a Crombie jacket and red scarf. He smiled, his hand held out.

'Mr Jason Hartmoor, I believe. It is a privilege to meet you, sir. I am Dennis Wye. I'm a long-term colleague of Frank Coleman's.'

'He's dead.'

'I am aware of the fact, sir. I deeply mourn his loss. May I come in?'

'By all means,' said Hartmoor, standing aside to let the man past. Strong hands gripped his arms and a pad was held to his face. He struggled, a reek of alcohol and esters before the world shut down.

Lynch and Anna stood together at the reception desk at the Estonian Security Police headquarters. He had spent much of the day in seemingly endless meetings and briefings. He was, if the truth be told, feeling itchy. People bustled around them, their quiet efficiency impressive, despite his frustration with the results they were getting.

Anna turned as a woman beckoned. 'Okay, we can go in. Gerald?'

'What?' Lynch stopped smacking his fist into his palm.

'Behave. Kuusik is not someone you want to fuck with.'

Lynch would have been irritated, but Anna's smile was only lovely. He followed her into the lift up to Kristina Kuusik's office.

It was a big, minimalist space, a mixture of steel and natural woods that screamed expensive design and perfect taste. There was an open fireplace with a brass chimney over it. A step up led to a brushed wood conference table with white shelves to the side and a picture window at its end. There were coffee table books and knick-knacks sparsely arranged on the surfaces around them, a camel bag on the wall and a series of grainy, artily composed black-and-white photographs of cities around the world.

Kuusik rose from her desk as they entered, coming around to meet them. She was in her fifties, peppered short hair and a pince-nez. She wore a baggy jumper that made her look smaller than she was and a pencil skirt split to show more leg than Lynch had been used to from figures of authority. She caught Lynch looking and frowned at him. He beamed back at her and held out his hand. 'Gerald Lynch. Anna says I'm to behave.'

Kuusik took his hand, her grip firm and dry. She regarded him over the rims of her glasses. 'And so you are. Take a seat, Mr Lynch. You've had a dry day, I gather.'

Lynch sat at the conference table, joined by Anna and, carrying her mug of coffee from her desk, Kuusik.

'There have been quite a lot of briefings and so on, yes. Can I speak frankly?'

'Of course. I was rather expecting you to after reading your file.'

'A document I have never myself had the privilege of reading. I'm worried, Kristina. There's nothing happening and I understand conditions right now mean everyone's more or less pinned down, but I met with Anders,' Lynch didn't even try and pronounce the man's name, 'the head of the Western Region, earlier. I think he's being complacent about the situation. I know the pilot of that aircraft and he's a highly capable individual. If the stakes are as high as we think they are, these people will go to extraordinary lengths. And I think they're being regarded as ordinary criminals.'

'You mean Anders Väljas.' Kuusik frowned. 'A highly respected member of my team, Mr Lynch.' She fixed him again over the rims and this time he knew, from the twitch at the corner of her mouth, his fast-formed regard for her was reciprocated. And she had nice eyes. 'But I agree. We have a very large problem on our hands. We didn't know quite how large until your Mr Channing called. But we have been busy and we have a better idea now.' Kuusik leaned back in her chair. 'Ready for a last briefing for the day, Mr Lynch?'

'Fire away. Sure, I'm hardly going anywhere.'

'We have a problem, a major and growing one. Large quantities of very cheap high-grade heroin have been flooding the Russian market for the past eighteen months. Recently the Russians have been accusing Estonia of being the source, but they were unable to provide little hard intelligence, just bellicose assertions. It is,' again, a twinkle in those blue eyes, 'their style when dealing with us, despite our long history together. Or perhaps because of it.'

'But you investigated those assertions.'

Kuusik nodded. 'We certainly talked to our friends at customs and they ramped up their efforts and we tried to look at obvious routes here, putting on extra patrols in key border points, but without any leads it was something of a haystack. And then your Mr Channing called.'

'I take no pleasure in the ownership.'

Kuusik beamed at him. 'Here is the result of that call.'

She picked up a remote from the conference table and the lights dimmed and curtains descended over the window overlooking the city. The projector whined as it warmed up and an image of a man in a suit started to resolve on the wall. He was large-framed, a strong face with short hair, mostly white but with a peppering of virile darkness. Lynch guessed he was in his seventies, but whether early or late was beyond him.

'Jaan Kallas.' Kuusik tapped the remote on the conference table. 'We had no idea he was anything other than a highly successful businessman who had profited cleverly from the transition. An oligarch.'

Lynch studied the figure. There was a hardness to Kallas'

jaw, a sense of power to him. He was wearing a dark suit, head turned to the right. An associate was explaining something to him. Kallas didn't seem best pleased by it, whatever it was. 'You had no form at all on him?'

'Marked clean all the way. He had been in the Russian army. He returned home to Tallinn after the Singing Revolution and, of course, the collapse of the Soviet Union. It took him two years to come home, but this was a time when many people found themselves rearranging their lives, no? Kallas settled in quickly, had clearly got Russian backers and knew what he wanted. He bought businesses, but he wasn't alone in that. Others were also helping convert the state enterprises into private ones.'

The slide advanced. A woman, in her fifties. 'His wife, Alina, originally Glinka. A Muscovite. He had always maintained they met in Moscow but our researchers now believe she was on active service with military intelligence in Syria and he met her there.'

Another advance. A white-haired, corpulent man in a beige corduroy jacket and jeans. He had a young dark-skinned woman on his arm and a cigar in his hand. He wore a moustache and was grinning, but didn't strike Lynch as particularly genial. 'His business partner when he arrived in Estonia after Russia. His name is Genady Orlov. He was a co-signatory to many early documents and business transactions, but gradually faded into the background. We've asked the Russians for more on him, but they're not being particularly efficient at getting back to us. They want results from us, but they don't like us rushing them. It's history.'

'We had not connected Kallas with the *Ühiskassa*. Our operations against organised crime had been particularly successful and by the time we joined the Euro, we had thought the *Ühiskassa* no longer represented a significant threat.' A click of the remote. 'This man was found dead two days ago. His body had been frozen, we are not entirely sure when he died.

His name is Hillar Mark. He was the owner of a number of night clubs and a casino in Tallinn. He had most definite past links to the *Ühiskassa*. His business ventures appear to be under new ownership – a perfectly legal transfer, it appears, which took place some weeks ago. His widow confirms it. Grief has apparently rendered her very nervous and prone to shaking fits. We're keeping her in custody for now in the interests of her own safety.'

Lynch rubbed his chin. 'Let me guess the new owner.'

'I think you'd be right. It's odd that Kallas should be so careless at this critical stage of his operations, if our conjectures regarding this flight from Beirut are proved right. But we have a number of other links now that confirm he is perhaps not as squeaking clean as we thought him to be.'

Lynch nodded, enjoying the rare error in her English. The slide clicked forward. 'There are obviously many photographs of business events and the like over the years, which we're still trying to analyse and cross-match, but we're about 80% through and nothing has matched yet. This shot was taken yesterday, but we don't know who this one is. We thought you might.'

The image showed Kallas sitting at a café table, talking to a man in a greatcoat and scarf. The man had turned, allowing the photographer a side view of his face, blurred with movement.

Lynch sat back in awe. 'Oh God, yes. That's a man called Dennis Wye.'

Kuusik twisted around to face him. 'And he is? The shot wasn't good enough to run through facial recognition.'

'Head of station for the CIA in Beirut is what he bloody is. So the bastard's in Tallinn all of a sudden. Because it's his heroin, isn't it?'

'So your Mr Channing tells us. It makes sense, this man, now. We placed him under surveillance following this meeting. This operation is now rather straining my available resources, by the way, Mr Lynch. We tracked him to a warehouse on the outskirts of Tallinn, owned by a logistics company called

FastFreight. It is, of course, one of Kallas' companies. It specialises in sending frozen goods into the Latvian and Russian markets. It seems reasonable to assume the heroin comes by sea from Hiuumaa and is transferred to FastFreight to make the border crossing to Russia. Clever, isn't it? Frozen heroin doesn't smell, so the dogs wouldn't pick it up. And although we had stepped up our customs activities, we're hardly going to tear apart every road shipment of frozen Baltic herring to Russia.'

'So now you have your pipeline.'

'Now we have our pipeline. So we have the heroin, the pipeline and the mastermind. I should feel happier than I do, Mr Lynch.'

'What happens on the Russian side?'

'That's not our problem. The Russians can work on that. I'm more concerned at the mess on our side of the fence.'

The slide advanced again to show a complex organogram. 'As of this morning, we were able to redraw this. We were surprised at how out of date it was. It is the organisational chart of the *Ühiskassa*. As I said, we had been successful against them and probably you could accuse us of complacency. They have seen a resurgence in recent years we now learn. This is hardly surprising, they appear to be under new management. And at the top sits a man called Jaan Kallas. You have no idea how irritating I find the idea that he is a CIA asset obtaining his heroin from American sources in Afghanistan.'

'Oh, I think I could give it a try,' Lynch stared wide-eyed at the chart. 'Poor old Hartmoor really did kick a hornet's nest, didn't he?'

Kuusik grimaced. 'You could say that.'

'And the CIA boys must have helped Kallas to the top, same way they helped him to the top when he was working with the Russians in Syria. Christ, but they've looked after their joe.'

Kuusik squeezed the remote. The projector flicked off and the blinds rose to let in the light. 'So there we have it. Your friends are running billions of dollars of heroin into Russia through Estonia and we didn't know a thing about it until we got your call. We are in your debt, Mr Lynch.'

'Sure, that's okay. I drink whisky at Christmas.'

Kuusik paused then her face cleared with understanding. 'I shall pack the consignment personally myself. Meanwhile, Anna will be your liaison and we will work with you in every way we can to ensure a successful outcome to this operation.'

'Thank you. I appreciate that.'

Kuusik walked around the table, her hand held out. 'Is there anything you need from us right now, Mr Lynch?'

'Yes,' Lynch had replied, emboldened by the clear rapport they had quickly struck, taking her cool skin in his grip. 'A Walther P99 and a holster.'

'Anna, would you arrange that please? And he'll need ammunition too. Obviously he is too polite to ask for it.'

Back at their hotel, Lynch called Hartmoor's room on the kitsch, faux old-fashioned hotel phone but there was no answer. He raided the minibar, then tried again. He checked with reception and yes, Mr Hartmoor was in residence. The operator tried. No answer. Perhaps he's sleeping? Perhaps, Lynch agreed.

He took the stairs to the floor below and knocked on Hartmoor's door. No response.

Lynch was gripped with an awful premonition. Jason had been so tired the night before, had looked awful that morning when he had come to call on him for breakfast. Hartmoor had been getting weaker since Shemlan, leaning more heavily on The Stick, pausing more frequently to catch his breath and eating Roxanol like it was going out of fashion.

'Jason? Jason. It's Gerald. Can you hear me?'

He knocked again, twice, hard and loud. Nothing.

Lynch moved down the corridor to the lift and stabbed at the button. He flexed his fingers and smacked the wall as he waited for the lift. It finally came and he waited an eternity for it to descend. He sprinted for the reception desk.

'It's Mr Hartmoor, the Samuel Morse suite. I think he may have passed away. Can someone please come with me?'

The girl at the desk cried out, her hand flying to her mouth. She scrabbled around behind the desk. 'Come,' she gasped.

She was stealing sly glances at him on the way up in the lift, a brunette with a ponytail, pretty eyes and bad skin. Lynch realised his jacket was open and zipped it up. The doors opened and he waved her through first. She swiped the master key on the door and held back. Lynch dashed into the room.

'Hartmoor? Jason?'

He checked the bedroom, the bathroom. He stood in the middle of the suite.

It was empty.

Back in his own room, Lynch called Anna. 'Hartmoor's gone. I don't know where to. His stuff's still in the room, but not his stick or his pills. My room's been entered while I was out.'

'Nice timing. Kallas is on the move. His helicopter has put in a flight path request to Hiuumaa from Tallinn International via his holding company's office building. It'll be picking up at the company's office helipad in about three minutes. We're watching.'

'We have to go to Hiuumaa, Anna.'

'I agree. I got a helicopter arranged myself. Sadly we don't have a private helipad, so we have to go to the City Hall. I'll be with you in five minutes. The weather's bad, be warned. This will be a horrible ride.'

'Yeah, whatever.'

Anna drove quickly through the whirling snow, the wipers thudding against the packed ice on the windscreen. They passed the Linnahall. Lynch had expected a grand old building not the huge grey blockhouse surrounded by high, snow-covered banks. The sea's black expanse was in front of them and to their left as they rounded the corner of the long, low building to the back of the Linnahall, the outline of a helicopter visible on top of it. The roadway was dusted white. Anna pulled the car up and they got out. A blue sign on the building read 'Copterline,' a glass-encased iron stairway doglegged up to the helipad. They ran through the door of the terminal building and raced up the steel stairway. The Sikorsky's blades were slicing the air, its engine idling.

Lynch jogged doubled up towards the chopper, the snow flurries stark in the powerful floodlights. Anna was ahead of him, pulling open the passenger door of the Sikorsky. The wind bit at his face. Snowflakes whirled around the bird, lashing at his exposed skin. He thrust up into the doorway, thankful for the respite from the wind and the sharpness of the flakes whipped by the rotors. She handed him a helmet. He strapped in and pulled it on.

'You alright, chap? You took your time, I must say.' The pilot's accent was distinctively London. It threw Lynch as the engine note started to rise.

'Sure, never better. You're *English*?'

'Did me degree at London University. I'm as Estonian as they come. You strapped in? Anna?'

'Roger,' Anna's voice, her accent flattened by the radio's squawk.

'Okay,' Lynch confirmed.

'This'll be rough. There's a bag in the pocket in front of you. Use it, wouldja? I hate having to sluice this thing out.'

The helicopter swayed, lifted, then lurched up into the air. The snow whirled around them for a second before they left the floodlights and rose into the inky darkness. The wind took them immediately; Lynch watched the pilot wrestling to control the chopper. 'I didn't get introduced,' he shouted. 'What's your name?'

'Toomas. Call me Tom. That's fine.'

The Sikorsky reeled in the strong wind; the spatter of snow against the windows audible even through the helmet and above the rotor noise. Anna yelled at him over the radio, 'We can't land at the airport in case the weather's too bad to take off again, so we're going to try and get down outside the Kärdla police station. The car park's just big enough for us to land.'

They banked and levelled off. The engine note varied constantly, the wind a persistent howl.

'What about Kallas? Has he landed?'

'Not yet. He's about twenty minutes ahead of us, so any second now. He's lucky, we're getting the worst of it behind him.'

They sat without speaking, the helicopter in a constant fight against the unpredictable gusts. The turbulence provoked a relentless juddering; occasionally they plunged into air pockets. Lynch clamped his lips tight shut and tried to think about anything other than the storm outside and their little aircraft being tossed about by the momentous force of those huge, roiling clouds.

The Sikorsky yawed, twisting to pitch them on their side. Toomas' voice burst into the radio in Estonian.

Anna caught Lynch's hand and squeezed hard. He glanced across at her.

'He called to God for help. If Toomas uses language like that, I'm officially scared,' she bawled. 'He's a Christian.' Lynch's face must have betrayed his absolute bewilderment. 'We're the most secular country in Europe. We don't *do* Christian.'

Lynch tried to peer out of the window, but there was nothing but darkness and the whirling of snow lit by the flash of the helicopter's navigation lights. They were pitched over by another gust. The acrid stench of fuel filled the cabin. Lynch was thrown forward, his torso straining against the straps.

Countless shards of ice smattered against the aluminium skin in bursts, the wind's howl rising above the straining engine. They were flying into the wind now, the airframe juddering against the force of the gale. The snow smashed into the glass in front of the pilot. The wipers struggled to clear it. There was a moment of near-silence. A sickening lurch upwards brought bile into Lynch's throat. He swallowed. The wind returned, smacking against the helicopter's shell. *Like getting hit by a rhino*, flashed through Lynch's mind. They lost altitude, their nose hard down. Lynch feared the worst.

Another burst of Estonian on the radio, the tension in Toomas' voice clear over the squawking link.

Anna shouted, 'Okay, we're there. They've cleared the car park for us to land, but it's tight. He's scared of their communications mast. Visibility's very bad. Hold on, we're coming in to land.'

The rolling motion was powerfully emetic. Lynch grabbed onto his seat as they levelled out, Toomas correcting the yawing of the aircraft and slowly descended. A gust caught them and tipped the helicopter, earning a barked expletive from Toomas. A few seconds later the wheels bounced on concrete, a hard landing that slammed Lynch against his seatbelt, then back into his chair.

He grabbed at the chinstrap, his hands shaking. Anna pulled off her helmet, ruffling her hair and laughing. 'I don't want to do that too often.'

Lynch put his gloves on. 'Ready?'

'As I'll ever be.'

Lynch got down and held the door for Anna, following her at a crouch through the biting cold wind towards the blue-roofed building, the snow compacting in crunches under his feet and flakes flying around him. They burst red-faced into the warmth and light of the police station.

Lynch shook himself down, stamping the snow from his boots. He ripped off his gloves and wiped his face. The blue and grey carpet tiles were dusted in snow from their shoes, the room functional and sparse with grey vertical slat blinds on the windows. There was a hint of heating fuel in the warm air.

Breathless, Anna waved at a tall man waiting by the reception desk. 'Gerald, this is Inspector Georg Vaino, he's heading the police team here.'

Vaino was in uniform, dark blue with a yellow high-visibility vest with a radio handset and other gear packed into its pockets. He was perhaps in his late thirties and sported a short beard. There was a dash of grey around his temples and humour in the brown eyes. Lynch found his hand in a firm grip.

'Welcome to Hiuumaa. I'm normally based in Pärnu but we've moved over here for this operation. They've called it Operation Draakon, dragon in English. Smart lads, the boys in Tallinn. So we're chasing the dragon, yes?'

'Several tonnes of it.'

'Come on in, we'll fix you a coffee and I'll tell you how we're set up here.' Vaino gestured into a side room with a light wood meeting table and steel-framed chairs. 'Take a seat, dump your jackets. Anders Väljas doesn't think anything's going to happen tonight but I'm not so sure. We've got men stationed at the airport and I've sent a team down to Kallas' logistics and warehouse complex with orders to stay low but monitor traffic movements. I have twenty men here in the station house, all firearm trained and armed. There are three all-terrain vehicles for transport. We're in good shape.'

Lynch wriggled out of his overcoat but kept his leather jacket on. 'Where did Kallas land?'

'At the airport. Our team called that in a few minutes ago and air traffic control in Tallinn confirmed it. The staff went home hours ago. The way the weather is right now, nothing's flying tonight. I'm surprised you guys made it through.'

Lynch jumped as Anna shook him awake, her face

253

concerned. Georg Vaino stood behind her. He fought for a second to regain his sense of place.

'What's up?'

Vaino answered. 'Our team at the airport, two men. They haven't called in. They're about half an hour late for their scheduled check-in.

Lynch rubbed his face. 'How long have I been asleep?'

Anna checked her watch. 'Two hours.'

'What about the team at the logistics centre?'

'They're on schedule and report no movement.'

Lynch was already on his feet, pulling on his overcoat. 'They went direct, is all. They didn't stop at the depot. We need to move.'

Vaino nodded. 'Come, we'll take my jeep. The team can follow. They must be planning to use the ice road at night. It's insane. I will let Heltermaa Port know. They have security and border-crossing teams there. They'll lock down the approach to the ramp onto the ice.'

'Is there any possibility they've made their own ice road? Must they go through Heltermaa?'

'I will not think about that. Let us find them first.'

TWENTY-FOUR

Hartmoor woke to find himself strapped into a seat in some sort of executive jet. He resolved the noise from the engines, a helicopter. Hartmoor felt sick. The stench of pear drops was still in his nostrils and he struggled to sit upright. His mouth was dry. Slowly coming into focus, facing him was Dennis Wye, the man who had abducted him. The man next to him was bigger, older and had a cruel smile.

The interior of the executive helicopter was compact but plush. Four black leather seats faced each other across a polished black table. Dennis Wye was observing him, his elbows on the table and his straight fingers tented in front of his mouth. There was a tablet on the table, its dark screen reflecting Wye's chin.

'Welcome back. I apologise for the unsubtle transition, but it was necessary to remove you from your location.'

Hartmoor parted his dry lips painfully. 'Why?'

'Operational.' Wye smiled. 'Why didn't you stay in Wales and retire like any normal man?'

'It's a shame Frank is dead, it has rather deprived me of the pleasure of wishing him so.' Hartmoor croaked.

'She's dead because of you, Hartmoor. Not Frank.' Wye reached into a cabinet set by his seat and pulled out a plastic bottle of water. 'Here.'

Hartmoor fought to sit up straight. He struggled to twist open the lid. He drank and another wave of nausea washed over him. 'She's dead because you killed her with a drone. And my daughter, too.'

Wye blinked. 'Daughter?'

Hartmoor's laugh was hollow. He shook with rage. 'Oh, did

Frank forget to tell you that? The whole pretty deception was made possible by the man who married her to avoid the shame of her child conceived out of wedlock. With me. Only your "operation" meant she never did get my letters, never did learn I still loved her and had not in fact abandoned her. So she married him and together they brought up my daughter and she had a child in her turn. My granddaughter. And I learned who they were just in time for me to see them for a few seconds before your bloody agency blew the whole family to bits.'

Wye shrugged. 'Collateral damage. Happens. So you're here with Lynch? Still chasing Dmitri, is he, the old soak?'

'Yes. He hopes the Estonians have records that can help identify the man. He was talking about giving up this morning, they haven't been terribly helpful.'

'So why did he drag you along for the ride?'

'I am the only person who can identify Dmitri, apparently. I met him once at an embassy reception.'

The man next to Wye laughed. 'Not so useful, then. I am Dmitri, Mr Hartmoor. I am Jaan Kallas. It has been a long time.'

Hartmoor would never have picked the man from an identity parade. Thickened by age, dressed in an expensive suit, his carefully groomed grey hair swept back, Jaan Kallas carried an air of power about him.

Kallas' bleak smile was fleeting. 'How much does your government know about me, Mr Hartmoor?'

'What is there to know?'

'Please do not play with me. I have little time and am not inclined to spare the rod.'

Hartmoor believed him. The thought of physical violence meted out on his failing body was horrifying to him. 'They know about your career as a Russian spy, that you were a double agent for the Americans. Beyond that I'm not sure what I can give you. Lynch doesn't confide in me.'

Wye took a call, turning to murmur into the handset.

Kallas sat forward. 'Has anyone mentioned me in connection

to a man called Abbas Ali?'

'No. Who is he?'

'It need not concern you.'

'Then why ask me then?' Hartmoor said with some asperity. Kallas' jaw tightened and Hartmoor thought he could go to hell. His anger grew as he confronted the arrogance of the men behind his lifetime's betrayal. It had all been to benefit this man, Kallas/Dmitri. Even the deaths of the family he had never had and the fact he had never known them.

The helicopter juddered as the wind outside strengthened. The seatbelt light came on and a disembodied voice announced 'Turbulence ahead. Seat belts please.'

Wye finished his call. 'You left a mess behind you in Beirut, didn't you?'

'I presume you mean your man Goldman? Lynch killed him. I must confess, I rather enjoyed that.'

'Lynch will pay for it, I can assure you.' Wye's smile was not pleasant.

Kallas leaned forwards. 'Mr Hartmoor, I understand you are not well man. You face death and, if I may say so, you are braver than many I have met. But sometimes a brave man and a fool are the same thing and I counsel you reflect on this, because I have little time for fools. They are best snuffed out.' He clicked his thumb and second finger and Hartmoor managed not to flinch at the snap. Kallas' smile was grim and his eyes as cold as the white flakes spraying the helicopter's windows. 'You must ask yourself, which death you face. You want to die in sleep or you want to die screaming for mercy? You choose.'

'The histrionics are hardly necessary. I can see little I have to give you in any case.'

Kallas sat back, his fingers tapping on the polished stone surface of the table between them. 'Lynch killed one of my men in Aleppo. Why he was there instead of babysitting you?'

'I had two SAS men guarding me. Your other thug took care of them.'

'Why Lynch went to Aleppo?'

'To see a man called Bashar. An army man.'

Kallas leaned forward, his face set hard. 'Bashar? Junaidi? Did he make contact?'

'I don't know. I think so.'

'How you think so?'

'Lynch doesn't make a habit of confiding in me, Mr Kallas.'

Kallas turned to Wye. 'Persson was supposed to take care of Junaidi. You said he did. If he didn't get to old man before Lynch did, we are blown.'

The helicopter veered in a powerful gust. Wye's tablet slid across the table top. Hartmoor's bottle of water dropped to the floor. All three men reached wordlessly for their seatbelts, Hartmoor's movements slower than the pair opposite him. The tannoy coughed into life. 'Hold on. It will get rough.'

The wind hit them with a sickening concussion, lifting the helicopter and twisting it. Hartmoor's stomach, already upset from the after-effects of the anaesthetic they had used on him, rebelled. He cast about for a bag, found one in the side pocket and scrabbled to pull it out and unfold it as the bile burned his throat. It came up powerfully. He leaned into the bag just in time, managing to hold onto it as the helicopter lurched in the vicious wind and spasms racked his body. Finally there was no more and the dry heaves abated. He looked up from the bag to the contempt on both Wye and Kallas' faces. He pulled a tissue from the box in the side pocket and wiped his mouth. It felt as if his teeth had been etched. He retrieved his water from the seat next to him.

'Two minutes' came over the tannoy as the juddering briefly eased. They started to lose altitude. Hartmoor folded the top of the bag over so he could open the bottle. He sluiced his mouth out with little option but to swallow. To his surprise it stayed down.

The helicopter fought against the churning wind, the engine note rising and falling rhythmically. Sleet pelted the windows.

They landed heavily. The engine died, the din of the rotors slowing. The door was pulled open by unseen hands to let in a blast of frigid air. A hail of icy flakes stung his face. Half blinded by the cold air and its sharp payload, Hartmoor reached for the doorframe and descended painfully, without a glance back at his fellow passengers. He realised he was still holding onto the bag. Its contents were warm. He threw it aside.

He stood in the cold, uncertain as to what to do. They had landed on tarmac, a runway by the parallel bars that ran across the width of the strip. He couldn't see the stretch of asphalt beyond a few yards in the dark and snow. His jacket was pitifully inadequate against the biting cold, his hands were blue.

'Come,' Kallas urged him. They walked to a black four-wheel drive. Wye sat in front. The driver edged along the runway, his visibility limited by the thick curtain of flakes. The heat in the car was a glorious relief. Hartmoor put his hands under his armpits to warm them.

Kallas leaned forwards and said something in Estonian. They gained speed. The driver's knuckles were white on the wheel.

The shape of a plane loomed up ahead of them, picked out by the floodlights on the opposite side to their approach. They circled around behind the tail.

A cargo unloader was pulling back from the plane, which had a large hatch open on its side. There was a line of trucks parked on the apron, one of which had been turned to present its rear to the plane. The unloader wheeled around, its platform dropping. It contained a large, odd-shaped load. They drove to the terminal building, light blue in the edge of the floodlighting.

Kallas was first out of the car and into the building, Wye taking care to walk behind Hartmoor. A burly man with a cigarette stuck into the side of his mouth saluted Kallas.

'Boss. We got trouble. Picked these two up on the perimeter.'

Hartmoor noticed them, then, sitting back to back on the floor, their hands tied with nylon ties. Uniformed policemen.

'How long until we finish loading?'

'About twenty minutes should do it.'

'Good.' Kallas motioned at one of the policemen. 'Have him brought upstairs. Dennis, you can wait here with Mr Hartmoor.'

'Sure, Jaan. It's your show.'

A few minutes later the policeman on the floor jerked, wide-eyed as a scream came from upstairs. It was hoarse and high and just kept coming, battering Hartmoor with its unrelenting horror. There was a bump and it was cut off.

The burly man came downstairs and dragged the other policeman to his feet. 'Your turn.'

Hartmoor shut his eyes, but the screams came nevertheless. This time they only lasted a few seconds and then there was blessed silence broken only by the building creaking in time with the gusts of wind outside.

Kallas was wiping his hands as he came downstairs, his face grim. 'Dennis, we have a problem. We have been blown as I thought and we must move quickly. These two were part of a surveillance operation mounted against us by the Kaitsepolitsei. The yard is under surveillance and there is a significant detachment of armed police stationed at Kärdla. We have to move fast.' He turned to Hartmoor. 'Your friend Mr Lynch has been busy, Mr Hartmoor. I am going to very much enjoy his death, I can assure you.'

They moved out in fifteen minutes precisely: Hartmoor, Wye and Kallas in the four-wheel drive, the trucks falling into line behind them. The snow battered the car windows, the road ahead carpeted in white and the trees around them looming. The corona of lights was swallowed in a few yards by the expanse of white framed in darkness. Kallas urged the driver faster.

Before they left, Hartmoor shuffled up to Kallas. 'Why not let me go? Just leave me behind here? I'm hardly a threat to you.'

Kallas laughed. 'The only reason I have not kill you is because you are doing this job for yourself. You might even become chip for bargaining. No, I keep you here, thank you.'

Hartmoor gazed out of the window at the snow for a time. A thought formed in his mind, a recollection of something Wye had said. It nagged him and he kept going back to it, forcing away the onionskin layer by layer until he had its heart in his hand. He turned to Wye. 'You wanted to know why I didn't stay retired, didn't you?'

'It would have been simpler all round.'

'I'm sure it would. It was you people who retired me, wasn't it? You know in Khartoum, that whole incident with the girl? That was Frank cleaning up after his operation was over. The Soviet Union had fallen, Estonia gained its independence. There was the little coup around Oslo, so Frank was finding me useful even without Dmitri to support, Kallas I suppose I should call him now. But Mai finally stopped writing just before the millennium and I wrote a series of increasingly intemperate and silly letters to her threatening all sorts of things. So I had to be removed, didn't I?'

'That's classified.'

'Oh, do stop playing soldiers, Mr Wye. Just tell the truth for once in your miserable sneak's life. Coleman had me burned.'

'Okay. So Frank burned you and you got retired. So what? He put you down. So why didn't you stay down?'

Hartmoor didn't reply. The thought had occurred to him that if he had, indeed, just died quietly in his house in Newgale, his daughter and granddaughter would be still alive.

And Mai. All of them. Even Fadi. With every reason in the world to hate the man who had betrayed him all those years ago, Lynch only remembered the pallid youth in cooks' whites who had slunk around the kitchen door when he and Mai had stood in the darkness kissing.

He turned his head so Wye wouldn't see the tears. To people

like Wye, tears just meant weakness.

Lynch came down the stairs of the airport administration building with his hand over his mouth. Anna caught his expression and went to move past him but he held out his arm to stop her. 'Believe me, you don't want to go up there.'

Georg Vaino wandered over. 'What's up?'

'Your two men. They're up there. You'd better call the medics in to clear up. They're both dead. They were tortured. It's not pretty. So the game's up. They know we're on their tail and presumably will know how many men you've brought in.'

'Yes, we made no secret of briefing the whole team.' Vaino grimaced. 'Estonian egalitarianism.'

They had found the floodlight switch, illuminating the 737 standing on the apron where it had been unloaded, the snow around it churned up with the passage of the lorries. The cargo unloader they had used had been abandoned on the tarmac. Vaino's men had found a ladder and brought it up to the plane. The dogs were just going up the steps. The snow was still falling in gusty sheets.

Lynch went outside and heard the dogs barking and men shouting. Anna joined him. 'What do we do now? Call the mainland and have them picked up on the other side?'

'It's too chancy. They might have cut their own road, or taken a detour. We'll have to try and find them. This weather's fucking annoying, we can't even call in air cover.'

'I—I found something.'

Lynch was staring up at the plane. He turned to face Anna. She held a little foil strip in her hand. It was empty; every one of the pills had been pushed through.

'Hartmoor. So he's with them.'

'It may be just coincidence. But on the balance of things…'

He pushed open the door to let her inside and followed. Vaino was looking worried, toying with his radio.

'They have Hartmoor with them. What's the problem?'

He brandished the handset. 'This. It's down. We must have lost the mast back at the station. This storm's just getting worse and worse. Try your mobile?'

Lynch had no signal. Vaino frowned. 'I feared as much. The snow density is too much. We're in the dark. We can only really go in pursuit of them now. I'll send two of the boys back to bring a medical team and also try and contact the mainland to raise a welcoming committee for our friends.' Vaino tilted his head at the stairs. 'Is it really that bad up there, Mr Lynch?'

'As bad as I've seen. I'd really spare yourself the nightmares.'

Vaino nodded. 'That is kind of you, but they're my men. I feel I have a responsibility. Give me one minute and then we can move.'

A short while later, the sound of Vaino throwing up echoed down the stairwell.

They were barrelling along the icy, snow-capped roadway at breakneck speed. Vaino was squinting through the windscreen as he drove. The road was straight with gentle curves but they were going way too fast to stop in time if anything came up.

'You want to take it easier?' Lynch was gripping the driver's seatback. 'If this thing slides we're going to lose a whole lot more time.'

'Snow tyres,' Vaino explained. 'Have you not noticed? All cars in Estonia must have snow tyres in the winter months. It is compulsory. They are studded. It does not eliminate skidding, but it improves the grip. It will help on the ice road, too, if it comes to this. Don't worry, Mr Lynch.'

'How does this ice road work?'

'There are several of them between the islands. In the winter, the Baltic freezes over. We've always used the ice this way. The road's good for loads up to 2.5 tonnes, you'll notice they had eight trucks. We got a briefing over from Tallinn on that 737, it's a conversion. It's designed to take eight pallets. So eight two tonne trucks. One pallet each. Neat, is it not?'

'So why a road at all? Why not just drive across the ice any which way?'

Vaino nodded. 'Good question. It is possible, but the road is maintained, it is ploughed so the snow layer is taken off. This thickens the ice. If you are on the road, you are on safe ground. Leave it and you're maybe in deep snow. Snow is funny. It essentially warms things up. It is an insulator. Ploughed ice is colder and thicker than unploughed ice. So off the road can be very uncertain. When you are driving over the sea on ice, certain is always preferred.'

Anna leaned forward between the two front seats. 'And it is forbidden to wear a seatbelt on this road.'

'Why?'

'Because if you get in trouble and the ice breaks, you want to be able to get out of your car fast,' Vaino explained. 'It is also forbidden to stop. Because this puts pressure on the ice. If you stop and the cars behind you stop, you create massive weight very quickly. Vehicles are allowed onto the ice every three minutes and must maintain a 250-metre distance.'

'Right,' said Lynch. 'Right.'

'It would be better we catch them before the ice road. I think we can. They didn't have such a head start on us and we can drive a great deal faster than a convoy of trucks. I am seeing their tracks already, you see this rutting?'

Lynch stared out at the furrowed snow on the road but didn't see any difference. The headlights reflected off the myriad brilliant specks of the blizzard. Propelled by the gusty wind, the flakes spattered against the windscreen like handfuls of wedding rice.

The gateway to Heltermaa Port was a scene of absolute chaos. The entranceway to the port was a red-roofed gantry with two manned positions. One kiosk had been raked with gunfire and a police car had driven into the gantry, its windows starred and broken and holes punched through its bodywork. The gantry was upright still but one end was twisted. The darkness was punctured by streetlights. White road markings glistened on the tarmac. An ambulance stood by, its flashing lights colouring the snow driving through the air. Another police car had been hit by heavy machine gun fire, its tyres shredded and its bodywork crumpled by the impacts. Beyond the gateway, a security van was on its side, the chassis facing them. Men in high-visibility jackets were running between the damaged vehicles. Lynch glimpsed two covered bundles on the wet road, fast being covered by the snow.

Georg Vaino glanced across at Lynch. 'This is crazy. We're losing men to these maniacs.'

Lynch nodded. He glanced back at Anna, watching the scene in front of them wide eyed.

Vaino brought the Audi to a halt. A police officer in a heavy jacket ran over to them, his hand held up to shield his face from the snow. Vaino wound down the window and the warm air inside the car was whipped out. There was a sharp exchange in Estonian. Vaino patted the man's arm in thanks and raised the window.

Lynch stared out at the broken cars and grim-faced policemen. 'Well?'

'We've lost four dead. Two hurt, one bad. They opened fire as soon as they were in range, apparently. The guys weren't ready for an all-out assault. Every one of those trucks is packing an automatic weapon and opened fire as they passed. The lead car was a Range Rover. Three pax and a driver. That's it.'

'When? Not long ago from the look of it.'

'Less than five minutes. We can catch them if we go alone but our teams are likely to be a while behind us. It would be unwise to proceed.'

'Yeah, sure an' it would. So we go. Come on.'

Vaino nodded, grim-faced. 'Yes, I think this might now be a little personal. Anna, could you wait for the teams to catch up?'

'No, Vaino. I'm weapons trained. I'm in.'

Vaino twisted around to face her. Lynch caught her expression in the mirror. There were tear tracks down her cheeks, which had reddened in the cold. But her blue eyes were steady and her expression was hard. Vaino nodded. 'Then could you reach the guns forward?'

She nodded and Vaino turned the car to the right, away from the port gateway to a side road, which led down to the ice. The gates guarding the ice road hung crazily on their hinges. The kiosk at the entrance to the road was in darkness, the red-and-white barrier in pieces on the snowy ground. They bounced down onto the ice, the road muddy at the margin. They passed signs reading 10-25 and then 40-70.

'What's that?'

'Minimum and maximum speeds. You can create a wave under the ice which will resonate with it. I forgot to say. It is also forbidden to drive the road at night. It is very dangerous. You should be aware of this; we may be in some danger. Undo your seatbelt.'

'No shit,' said Lynch who, despite himself, was quite impressed. Unclipping the seatbelt felt oddly liberating.

They drove on into the rutted white carpet of snow, the wind a constant moan. Picked out in the big car's headlights, the sides of the road were mounds of packed snow. The tracks led away into blackness. The snowy plain of ice stretched around them, infinite white swallowed up by the dark. Occasional tracks left the road, always returning after a few hundred feet. In places the roadway converged into a single pair of ruts, in others it widened and flattened out, shining ice burnished by the passing tyres.

Lynch stole a glance at the speedo. Vaino passed 25 and he waited for the cracking as they entered the forbidden zone, but nothing happened. They passed 40 and then 70. Vaino topped out at 100 Km/h and kept the speed steady there. Lynch noted how much effort it was costing Vaino to keep the wheel steady at that speed, constantly battling against the rutting in the road. Visibility was down to a few yards, the wipers compacting snow on the margins of the windscreen. A shape loomed out of the darkness, a dead branch jammed into the snow either side of the road, their twigs pointing to the inky sky. Vaino slowed as they hit a curve in the road, the pairs of branches set in the packed snow either side of the road every few yards acting as guides. The road straightened and Vaino accelerated, the ice once again bare and level, the ruts ahead of them stretching into the darkness. Vaino accelerated again, the snow lashing past them, the big car's engine booming.

Two branches set in the margins whipped past them. Vaino snapped a curse in Estonian and hit the brakes too late. The car slid as another set of branches passed and dark shapes materialised from the gloom ahead of them. Vaino struggled to control the car. The studded tyres scraped the ice surface. The car shuddered as its tail started to drift. Lit by the car's headlights, the shapes became wooden pallets set across the track, branches marking their location. Lynch braced as he realised they were going to hit them.

The car impacted the pallets at an angle, the rear now out of control and sliding. The front tyres threw the wood up to smash against the bodywork, the car's angle jamming it into the pallet and bouncing as wood splintered. They swerved crazily, spinning out of control. The car's wheel stuck in the pallet. It came free with another impact on the body as they sideswiped the edge of the jagged snowy trench. Vaino screamed as the steering wheel spun and smashed into his hand.

They slid to a halt, Vaino cursing. The engine ticked over. Gusts of wind buffeted the car.

'You okay?' Lynch touched Vaino's shoulder.

'No I'm fucking not.' Vaino was gripping his wrist, the fingers on his left hand already starting to swell. His thrown-back face was stretched in lines of pain. He let his head drop. 'Sorry, Lynch. Sorry. It's my fault. They put those pallets out to cover cracks in the ice and I should have known when I saw those markers on a straight stretch. It was a stupid mistake.'

'That's okay. Will I drive?'

'Better Anna. I'll sit back.'

Lynch was about to protest and then bit his lip. Vaino and Anna swapped and she turned the big car easily into the track. 'It's okay, Lynch. I've driven before. I'm more used to these conditions than you.'

Lynch composed himself and closed his mouth. 'Sorry, I just…'

'It's nothing,' she replied. 'Georg, can you pass Mr Lynch a gun?'

Vaino reached from the back and handed a carbine over Lynch's shoulder. 'Advanced Police Carbine. You've used these before?'

'I have.'

Lynch took the bulky firearm and slid his hands over it to locate the safety. He thumbed it off and on again, checking the action. Anna drove at the same speed as Vaino had. The twig markers sped by. Anna's movements on the wheel were lighter and defter than Vaino's, he noted.

The snow thickened. Anna switched off the beams and drove on sidelights. It barely made a difference to the visibility and Lynch's eyes started to acclimatise to the darkness. She turned off the sidelights and they drove on in the gloom, the sinuous curve of the ice road a shadow in the shadows ahead of them. The flakes were black motes now against the faint blue-white moonlight.

Lynch peered into the gloom. He turned to Vaino, who was cradling his left hand in his right. 'Is it worth trying the radio? If we can't get to the mainland, maybe we can pick them up. They've got to be using radios.'

Vaino nodded. 'It's worth a try, if they're using the same

system. Here. You've got more hands than me.'

Lynch placed the carbine in the footwell and took the handset from Vaino. It was familiar to him, a Motorola TETRA unit. He scanned the channels. The airwaves were remarkably empty of signals. He tried again, picked up chatter. He turned up the volume. 'Estonian?'

Vaino leaned forward straining to listen. 'Yes.'

'It's them.' Anna said, slowing the car as another pair of pallets came into view. They slid again. They hit the wood hard but straight and she controlled the bucking wheel. 'We must be close to them.'

'How far have we come?'

Anna checked the speedo. 'About twelve kilos.' She paused, her lips moving as she calculated. 'So they're sticking to the lower speed limit, then. It's hard to keep a convoy together out on the ice by day, you have to keep the separation. And they dare not increase speed unless they can guarantee to go above forty. That's too hard in a truck in these conditions. Visibility is bad. Really bad. And it's dark. We have them. Maybe a minute and we will have contact. What's the plan?'

'Shoot out their tyres,' urged Lynch. 'We can take them out one-by-one.'

Vaino's voice from the back of the car was grim. 'Roger that.'

Anna cried out. 'There! Tail lights.'

The truck had slowed for one of the pallets the road managers had laid across a crack in the ice. Its pursuers hit it hard, the dark shape directly ahead of them. Lynch set the APC to single fire and opened his window. Leaning out, using the wing mirror as a tripod, he fired. The snow-laden gusts whipped at his face, his eyes screwed up against the icy flechettes. He directed his fire as best he could but the truck ploughed on. He groped for the APC's fire button, setting it to automatic. The gun jumped in his grip, muzzle flashes reflected in snowflakes, the ground behind the lorry's rear tyres erupting. The magazine emptied and Lynch pulled his head in, tore the used magazine out and pushed a new one in place. This time around his fire found its mark, the truck's rear tyres exploding in a gout of ice and snow. The truck slid in a slow-motion dance across the ice and its tyres bit into the side of the ice road's furrow. It toppled, side-on to the road ahead of them. Anna cried out as they slid inexorably towards the fallen truck, twisting the wheel to try and avoid slamming into it. The heavy car responded, taking them right and over the edge of the furrow into the raw snow beyond the ice road. They ploughed through it, the engine screaming.

Anna's hair flew as she wrenched the wheel left, trying to get them back onto the road. They pitched over the side of the trench, the wheels bit and she brought the wheel under control.

'One down,' Lynch shouted, closing the window. His face was raw from the barrage of icy particles.

'We have to find another way,' Vaino's urgent voice was tight with pain. 'That was too close for comfort and we'll burn all our ammunition.'

Anna gulped for air. 'We can take the other lane; it's about fifty metres to the left. Pull alongside them and take out the first one. If the road is blocked they won't make it on the raw ice, the snow's deep now. They'll have to stop.'

'Okay,' Lynch agreed. 'But that gives them a clear shot at us as we pass.'

Anna shrugged and stamped on the accelerator. 'It'll be on your side.'

They jumped the side of the channel and drove through the raw snow overlaying the ice spanning out from the black lines of the road, ploughing a line through the white carpet. The Audi's engine strained, their momentum gradually eroded by the weight of the snow. Lynch was beginning to fear they'd bog down as the other lane of the ice road came into sight, a dark sinuous line in the grey expanse.

They pulled alongside the convoy within a minute, the headlights of the trucks barely visible.

Lynch counted them off. 'Okay, I make that seven.'

Anna accelerated to pass the line of trucks until they breasted the lead truck. Lynch saw the flashes but heard no sound above the wind as the drivers of the trucks in sight fired at them. Two impacts thudded against the car's bodywork.

'They're speeding up,' Anna called out. 'Hurry up.'

Lynch pulled the window down and aimed the APC. He heard the window behind him open and Vaino's cries above the gunfire as he used his broken hand to steady his bucking gun. Lynch saw a headlight flicker out. He pulled back into the car to change the magazine.

Anna cried out. 'Lynch, they're in the danger zone. We're travelling at thirty kilos. Look how close together they are. They're mad.'

Vaino waved the TETRA handset at them. 'It's Kallas. He's directing them. They're in a four-wheel drive ahead of the lead truck.'

The trucks were closer now; the weaving lanes of the ice road were converging. Lynch snapped his magazine in place and fired out of the window, the APC butt jerking against his armpit. He hesitated as a strange bass roll joined the moaning wind. It built in intensity until the echoing rumble was deafening. The car bounced on the heaving roadway. Lynch pulled back into the car to switch magazines. Anna was tight lipped, fighting the wheel as the ice sheet juddered.

She shook her head. 'It's too dangerous; they're going to break the ice. We have to stop.'

Lynch shouted over the din. 'No way. I have a clear shot.'

Lynch sighted and fired as Anna braked. Frustrated, he kept his finger pressed on the trigger until the magazine was spent, but the trucks were swallowed in the darkness. He whipped around to Anna but the rebuke was knocked out of him as the ice lifted beneath them, a rolling wave that shot snow into the air, the noise making Lynch cup his hands over his ears. She turned on the headlights.

The trucks were lifted by the ridge as edges started to appear on its summit. The enormous cracking explosion shook the car. The surface split open, a crevasse opening up and great chunks of grey ice thrown in the air by the force unleashed by the wave below. The trucks slid, careening into each other. The car slid to a halt as the trucks smashed into the shattered ice, their rear wheels lifting as their momentum drove them down into the broken surface and the roiling water beneath.

TWENTY-FIVE

The sky above the dazzling carpet of snow was azure, the air clear and bitterly cold. Sunlight bathed the flat white plain and glinted from the mirrors of the cars around them. Lynch stood with Anna and surveyed the scene in front of them. Off to one side Vaino was directing his men, his hand bandaged.

The ice had sealed around the trucks in various stages of immersion. Just the rear portion of one truck was visible. Others were buried up to the side of their cabs. Vaino's men had opened the back doors of the most exposed truck, cut open the pallet and started to hand out sacks.

Lynch's hands were hunched in his pockets. 'You know, when you consider that's pure heroin, that's a pretty impressive sight.'

Anna nodded. Vaino crunched up to them. 'So, you had a good night's sleep?'

'Thanks, but you could have woken me. When did you guys start work out here?'

'We got here at around half nine. There was little point in trying to do anything before sunrise and none of this material was exactly going anywhere. I had men here through the night in any case.'

'What about the surviving drivers?'

'We're holding them both at the police station back at Heltermaa. To be honest it was all I could do to stop the Heltermaa boys from lynching the bastards. We've lost four good men and another's in intensive care. Thank God the storm broke or he wouldn't have made it. We got him to the mainland just in time.'

Vaino's mobile rang and he took the call with a little grimace of apology.

'This'll take a while to clean up.'

She nodded. 'It's a mess. And we've no way of knowing if Kallas got away or not.' Anna's hands were on her hips. Lynch wondered where she'd found the time to paint them with red varnish.

'A million dollars says he got away. He knew what he was doing, getting those trucks to close up and drive at the resonant speed. Their weight was all it took to finish it all off. I bet he was hoping the Baltic would swallow all the evidence. We'd best get back to Tallinn, no?'

Anna sighed. 'Yes. We'll see if Georg will lend us his car.'

Vaino raised his index finger as he finished the call, 'Sure. Will do. Thanks.' He cut the line. 'Okay, so the warrant for Kallas' arrest has been issued. There are witnesses in Rohuküla who say a four-wheel drive and a truck passed through town. The gate to the ice road has been broken open. All airports, ports and border crossings have been alerted. They want you back in Tallinn double quick. There's a chopper on the way to Heltermaa for you, you'd best take my car. If you drop it off at the hotel car park, I can pick it up from there.'

Lynch grinned at Anna. 'Ain't it only lovely when a plan works out?'

'Come on. We've got work to do.'

Lynch held out his hand. 'Thanks, Georg. It's been fun working with you.'

'In the nicest possible way, Mr Lynch, please don't come back in a hurry. You have a marked tendency to bring trouble with you, I think.'

They walked to Vaino's car. It sported three bullet holes in the right-hand door pillar, door and rear panel. Vaino had been lucky the night before.

Despite the dash back to Tallinn, by the time they had

reported to Security Police Headquarters, the trail had gone cold. And cold it stayed for two days of enforced inactivity during which Lynch received a stern call from Channing telling him to calm down and leave the Estonians to their investigation. Now they were back in Kristina Kuusik's artily minimalist office. Lynch was having a hard time containing his frustration. Anna sat to Lynch's side wearing a low-cut baggy jumper dress and, Lynch noted as she crossed her legs, black tights.

Kuusik gazed at Lynch over her half-rims, her steady blue eyes amused. 'Well, Mr Lynch. You appear to have brought a certain amount of chaos to our shores.'

Lynch acknowledged the charge with a dip of his head. 'Not more than your citizens brought to my quiet life in Beirut.'

'Quiet life? I very much doubt that.' She removed her glasses. 'I thought you might like an update on the operation against Jaan Kallas. You have been a tourist for, what, two days now?'

'Yes. And very pleasant it has been, too. Tallinn is a very special city.'

'You are too gracious. Anna has been telling me how you have been finding your enforced break frustrating.'

'I didn't realise it was so obvious.'

Anna snorted. 'Obvious? You—'

'Never mind.' Kuusik was openly amused now. 'You will soon be in action again. Let me share an update with you. We have now recovered all the heroin, bar one container. Sonar confirms two trucks on the seabed, so one truck had, indeed, escaped the breakup of the ice. But we have nevertheless made a haul of some fifteen tonnes of heroin. Our public relations people are extremely excited. An announcement will soon be made to a grateful press. The case against Jaan Kallas has been filed with the public prosecutor and his companies and assets have been traced and frozen. He is, essentially, a man on the run.'

'He'll have other assets. They always do.'

'We have been quite thorough, but I would tend to agree there is that possibility. As to the Central Intelligence Agency and their involvement, I think I can tell you that this is the subject of some considerable dialogue between our governments. We await its outcome with…' She searched for the right word and gave a cold smile. 'Interest.'

'And Hartmoor?'

Kuusik smoothed her dress down over her knees as she stood and came around the desk to offer Lynch her hand. 'Bear with us, Mr Lynch. We hope to be able to bring Kallas to justice and find your friend. We believe he is still alive.'

'What makes you so sure?'

'There was a robbery at West Tallinn Central Hospital last night.'

Lynch blinked, then grinned. 'Roxanol?'

She nodded.

Lynch was meeting Anna for dinner at the restaurant next door to his hotel. He checked himself in the mirror before going downstairs: a Jaeger jacket and a blue shirt with silver cuffs testament to an earlier trip to one of Tallinn's funkier boutiques for the discerning male. She was waiting for him in the lobby, wearing a black dress that accentuated her curves, a shining black mink coat and high-heeled black boots tied knee to toe. Her dark eye make-up accentuated the brilliance of her eyes and her pencil-thin brow was raised at him.

'You'll draw flies.'

'I'll do what?'

'With your mouth open like that. You'll draw flies.'

He closed his mouth. She took his arm in hers. She was giddy. 'Come on, buy me a drink. I've got news.'

They walked across the cobbled side street that lay between the Telegraaf and the restaurant. Cream tiled floor, black tables and chic minimalism greeted them, the warmth of the interior welcome after the cold outside. Even the short walk had Lynch shivering.

They sat and ordered Martinis. 'It's a weakness of mine, the Martini. But they're bad for me. They make me indiscreet.'

'I'm sure. So what's this news?'

'We have to wait for the Martini before I can be indiscreet. Otherwise I have no excuse.'

Lynch growled at her and she laughed at him. It was early but the restaurant was already busy, getting a table at the last minute had been no mean achievement, Lynch reflected as he watched a waiter turning away a party at the door.

The Martinis came. They clinked glasses and sipped. 'So. The news,' Anna said, placing her glass carefully down on the table. Her tongue darted out to lick her lips.

Lynch resisted the urge to strangle her and waited patiently.

'Jaan Kallas has contacted us. He was clearly running out of options. He has requested immunity for turning state's witness and also for Jason Hartmoor's safe handover. He has asked for protection and rehousing with a new identity.'

Lynch sat back. 'Wow. Okay, so that's a result. Have your people decided?'

'It's not just down to my people. Your people need to have their say, too. Especially they'll have to handle the protection program. Kallas has turned his truckload of heroin into more options for his retirement, it seems.'

'Right. So he gets away with it, really, doesn't he? The fat cats always do. It's a dirty deal, sure enough.'

'Do you think they should do it? The deal?'

Lynch considered it. 'Yes. Yes, they should.'

She put her hand on his. Her fingertips were cold from the Martini glass. 'I'm so glad Gerald. Because they've agreed to it. Kallas will meet us tomorrow at midday at Suurtüki, it's parkland, near the old city wall. There he will hand over Jason Hartmoor.'

They presented themselves at Kristina Kuusik's office at nine.

'Sit down, both of you,' barked Kuusik. 'Jaan Kallas has requested a handover to Mr Lynch personally. Following the safe delivery of Jason Hartmoor, Kallas will give himself up into our custody. There are to be no handcuffs, which is a condition we have reluctantly agreed to. Are you willing to take charge of Mr Hartmoor in this way?'

'Yes, of course,' Lynch murmured.

'The area Kallas has asked to meet in is problematic from a security standpoint, but he is insistent. It is close to the old city walls, near major tourist attractions, such as St Olaf's Church. So a large security operation is out of the question. We will bring in resources from the Special Operations Force. Principally, there will be cover provided from the ramparts, surveillance of the approaches by plain clothes teams and covering fire on the ground. We are very keen for this to be as discreet as possible.'

'Are you expecting trouble?'

'Let us just say I am reluctant to entirely trust Kallas.'

'And he gets to walk away a rich man.'

Kuusik nodded. 'That is quite possible. As we believe, one truck got away with him. If it was carrying the same as the other trucks, it would have been a cargo with a street value of some 140 million dollars. We have seized his known assets but as you pointed out when we last met, Mr Lynch, we cannot guarantee to have unearthed everything. So it is likely Jaan Kallas will indeed enjoy his retirement.'

She put her glasses on and peered at them both. 'That is the price we pay to ensure this operation is terminated throughout the chain and does not come back. The smuggling of heroin into Russia through Estonia is a major embarrassment for us and a trade we are particularly keen to minimise, if not terminate entirely. It would appear this particular route was responsible for an incredible amount of that trade, possibly as much as forty tonnes of heroin over the past year. It's a vast amount of misery. We are already working on rolling up the networks this artery fed and so far have uncovered routes extending into Latvia, Lithuania and Finland as well as Russia. Kallas was not alone in this, there is a whole network of organisations who have been feeding from this cargo.' Her face wrinkled in disgust. 'Like carrion.'

'Do we know what is happening at the other end of the supply chain? The raw product, the refinery operation?' asked Lynch.

'The Lebanese have not arrested Abbas Ali. Apparently there is a technicality that would prevent his prosecution under the charges as they stand. But I understand a number of maintenance staff at Rafiq Hariri International Airport have been arrested in connection with heroin smuggling. The pilot of the 737 is the subject of a Lebanese extradition request we are reluctantly meeting. I cannot say I admire the justice in your part of the world, Mister Lynch.'

'And Afghanistan?'

'That's in the hands of the British. I believe there is a considerable amount of inter-governmental dialogue regarding this operation. The Americans can hardly have been more embarrassed.'

TWENTY-SIX

Lynch was wearing a heavy jacket against the cold, careful to have a thick jumper underneath. He walked with Anna along the cobbled street. Fifteen minutes to go. They turned left onto Suurtüki, a map of the park to their left. The area Kallas had requested for the handover was close to the edge of the park, a lightly wooded area arranged around a circular flowerbed.

They were early. Lynch turned and started to walk back towards the ancient city walls. The sky was deep blue, the sunlight dazzling off the snow on the ground, slush in the stone drains that lined the cobbled streets, the red roofs of the stone houses ahead of them showing through the snow. The weather had been clear since the storm and Tallinn was starting to show through its snowy layer.

'Are you nervous, Gerald?'

'Jesus, yes. You never get used to this sort of thing.' He turned on the radio, the earbud cracking into life. He made sure it was set to mute.

'This is the first time I have been involved in a handover. It is more like the Cold War, no?'

Lynch chortled. 'Or any hostage situation.'

The radio burst into Estonian then, in English, 'Target has embarked a taxi on Rannamäe tee.'

They turned and made their way past the tall stone tower that marked the city gate to their right. Lynch led their way into the park. They stood in the allotted place, their backs to the road.

They waited. Lynch took his gloves off and undid his jacket. The holster was a comfort to him, his nerves jangling. His hands quickly got cold. He dug them deep into his jacket pockets.

'Target in the park. Moving slowly. Two pax.'

Lynch gazed up at the high ramparts of the ancient city walls of Vanalinn. Somewhere up there would be snipers, modern knights populating the ramparts of their Hanseatic kingdom.

'You okay?' he asked Anna. She nodded. Her nose was red.

'Target in sight.'

Lynch saw Hartmoor first, moving deliberately through the trees. Kallas was supporting him, coming into view as they turned towards the flowerbed. Hartmoor was leaning heavily on The Stick and looked deathly pale even against the snow. He was dressed, as usual, in black, his white hair partly covered by a woollen hat pulled down over his ears.

Kallas was confident, smiling. He was talking to Hartmoor. Kallas drew to a halt facing them.

Lynch's heart was drumming in his chest, sweat pricked his armpits. He hated these handovers. He raised his left hand slowly and carefully in greeting. Kallas did the same.

Nothing happened for a second.

Kallas gently impelled Hartmoor, who picked his way on the snowy ground, his knuckles white on the bent handle of The Stick, the walking aid he had hated so much and now depended on. Its black rubber foot left little holes in the snow.

Lynch murmured to Anna. 'Good luck. Just make sure you move slowly and predictably. And by the way, you are totally gorgeous.'

Anna smiled back at him as she started to walk towards Kallas, who stood with his hands open at his sides. She passed Hartmoor, who lifted his head and smiled at her. The bare trees reached blackly for the sky. A crow in the distance. A child laughing. Blood in his ears. A figure appeared behind Kallas. Lynch recognised Dennis Wye and found himself thinking idly what the hell Wye was doing here.

Hartmoor was still smiling as he called out, 'Gerald Lynch, I believe.'

Lynch started forward. The crack of a gunshot reverberated

from the high city walls. Kallas crumpled. Only now did Lynch make out the pistol Wye held straight at arm's length. Wye wheeled around to face Lynch and Hartmoor. Another two shots rang out from farther away, their report slapping back from the high city walls. Wye jack-knifed backwards to crash on the snow. Anna stood by Jaan Kallas' body, frozen in tableau as white camouflage-coated figures carrying guns started to appear from the sparse woodland around them.

Lynch ran to Hartmoor, who batted the air with his free hand. 'Don't fuss. I'm fine.'

There was to be no more talk of arresting Hartmoor. He was free to return home. Lynch had brought him the news the next day and Hartmoor numbly accepted it. He had elected to take the first available flight and Lynch took him to the airport in a hotel car. Anna met them there and walked them through immigration and security.

'It seems like a lifetime ago we came through here,' Hartmoor's said weakly. His face was lined.

'I got you a buggy without having to be asked this time.'

'Thank you, Anna.'

Lynch got in behind them, riding silently through the corridors, the orange light flashing and the warning tone beeping plaintively. *Hardly James bloody Bond, are we?* He thought savagely. They eventually pulled up at the gate and Lynch helped Hartmoor to a seat near the boarding desk. Anna left them to talk to someone she knew on the security team.

'You're making love to her.'

Lynch raised an eyebrow. 'What if I am?'

'Just that you are. It's been interesting meeting you Mr Lynch. I can't say I have enjoyed every minute of it, but it most certainly has not been what I expected.'

'Well, we try and keep it real, you know yeself.'

'I'm sorry about Marcelle. We both seem to have lost quite a lot. Please believe me when I say I am genuinely happy you have at least gained something.'

Lynch stood, his hand out. 'Goodbye, Jason. No, don't get up. You need your energy. But all the best to you.'

Hartmoor took his hand and smiled.

TWENTY-SEVEN

Jason Hartmoor wakes. His pillow is dry: no nightmare disturbed his sleep. He lay, luxuriating in the light seeping through the curtains. It's a spring day outside. He knows the long beach is laid out for a mile and more, the tide is out.

He has survived another night. It's a source of constant amazement to him. But he feels the pressure on him now. There's literally nothing to look forward to. He has nothing left. She is dead. Lying in the bed, he feels the weight of the loss again, as raw as when he realised what that cloud of smoke rising above the Chouf represented.

He lets his memory take him back to the day he first met her back in 1978, when he was a young man and the world was a younger place. He had escaped from the school, from the constant procession of word cards containing vocabulary to be memorised, each little card bearing English on one side and its Arabic counterpart on the other.

He had been *salaamed* by a Syrian tank crew on his way down to the restaurant down the road from the school, his Boccaccio in hand. Still smiling at the encounter, Jason walked through the open door of the restaurant; a marble plaque set into the threshold read '1936.' He smelled coffee, an odd aroma paired with it which he was to find out later was cardamom. He paused to survey the vaulted sandstone walls of the rich interior, a round stone window seat to the rear capped with richly Arabesque cushions around a brass tray, *argileh* pipes to the sides.

To his right was an open room lined with long tables, the big sliding windows pulled back to open it out to the hillside. He stood looking out at Beirut stretched far below him, the Mediterranean beyond shimmering in the afternoon light.

Jason heard a footstep and turned, smiling. A young woman stood by the doorway from the vaulted area of the restaurant. She wore a black skirt and a white blouse that was revealed, as she ducked out of her apron, to be slightly too tight across her chest. Her hair tumbled down over her shoulders, her curls enriched by the light shining off them. She folded the apron.

'*Marhaba.*'

'*Salaam.*'

Jason's Arabic exhausted, he could only respond to her next words with an embarrassed grin and a shrug. She paused and then spoke again in English.

'Can I help you?' Her English was coloured with a faint accent Jason couldn't place for a second. He realised it was French. Her voice was light.

'Is it possible to have some coffee?'

'*Bien sur.* Turkish? Nescafé?'

'Turkish please.'

'Medium?'

'I'm sorry?'

'You would like sugar in it? Medium sugar?'

'Oh, yes, yes please. Medium. Can I sit outside?'

'Of course. I will bring your coffee.'

Jason sat in the sunlight, feeling the warmth on his skin. He opened his Boccaccio. Luxuriantly, he lit a cigarette and settled back to read, his body in the hills above Beirut, his mind in the hills above Florence.

He blinked as her shadow passed over him, the little coffee cup clinking as she placed it on the blue and green patterned plastic that covered the table.

'Thank you.' He waved. 'It's a beautiful view.'

She stood back to share his viewpoint across Beirut, the airport runway almost immediately ahead of them. 'Yes, we command the city.' She gestured to the East, to a tendril of smoke rising from the rooftops. 'But will there be anything left for us to command when they have finished?'

Jason stubbed out his cigarette. 'It's peaceful up here in Shemlan, for sure.'

Standing at the wrought iron railing at the balcony's edge, she turned away from the cityscape to face him, the sunlight splashing across her cheek and the mound of her breast as she crossed her arms. 'Peaceful? There are soldiers here, Palestinians with guns. The fighting is everywhere, inside every heart. There is no peace any more, Mr...'

'Hartmoor. Jason Hartmoor.'

'Mr Hartmoor.' She smiled and offered her hand. It was cool when he took it, slim. 'I am Mai Khoury. Welcome to Shemlan.'

Jason nodded gravely. 'Thank you. It is a beautiful village. Is this your restaurant?'

'My father's. He is on holiday, the first he has ever taken. My mother nagged him, but it is quiet here now in the week, busier at the weekends. It is almost the autumn, you see.' She frowned. 'And then the fighting...'

The fighting is bad for business, Jason finished for her in his mind. She darted him a tight smile. 'I should leave you to your coffee.'

He had hardly gathered his wits to protest when she pirouetted and swung back into the restaurant. He sat watching the smoke gathering over the city. A muffled crump sounded far away and a black puff rose, a steady column soon following it. Jason sipped the hot, strong coffee and lit another cigarette. A burst of heavy arms fire echoed in the hills from below and then silence reigned. After a few seconds, the cicadas started again.

Later, he had taken his cup and ashtray inside. She handed him a wallet with a hand written bill for fifty Lire. He handed it back with the note.

'May I come back tomorrow?'

She fussed, business-like at the till. 'Of course. I shall order more coffee.'

He left, smiling at her sarcasm. On the way up the road towards the school, glancing furtively around, Jason remembered her cool touch and lifted his hand to his nose.

Jasmine. Faint, but unmistakeable.

It's there in the room overlooking Newgale beach, impossibly. The scent of Jasmine. He is crying now, for the loss of his daughter, his granddaughter and the lover he betrayed unwittingly and who, in turn, unwittingly was the instrument of his own betrayal.

A whole life he could have had. They could have had.

The pain comes back in slow waves, lapping at his oh so tired body. He reaches out for the pills and pushes one through the foil. Then a second. He doesn't stop until the strip has been harvested clean. He reaches out to pull open the drawer of his bedside table, his hand shaking, and finds another packet. He has to take care not to spill the little cache of pills floating on the white sea of the duvet. He pops the next strip. It's oddly therapeutic, a little like popping bubble wrap.

TWENTY-EIGHT

Elsie walked up the steps to the house with its blue painted window frames. It was a lovely view back down the beach, especially on a day like today when the sky was so blue and the sun taking the spring chill out of the air.

Mr Hartmoor was back from Beirut, but she hadn't missed a day's cleaning since he had left. The call had come as a huge surprise, for some reason she hadn't ever expected him back at all. Jim had taken it. He had come home but didn't have his house keys with him for some reason. Jim had arranged to meet him at the house. He would call as his taxi passed the village of Roche so they'd have time to get to the house. Elsie felt a bit strange seeing him, a bit like a servant welcoming home the master of the house. He looked awful, thinner and more haggard. There was something broken about him, something lost.

Elsie had made him a cup of tea. She had thought to stock up on some basics, eggs, milk, bread and the biscuits he liked. He had complemented her on the way she had kept the house and she had blushed. He was so gentlemanly, a sort of old world dignity you didn't see much of these days. People didn't understand respect these days.

She twisted the key in the lock, pushing the door open and pausing on the step to glance at the view, the long beach being swept by the waves, the spray and the little black stick figures of the surfers and swimmers. She called out to him, but he didn't seem to be in. She pulled the bucket of cleaning things from under the sink and hefted it onto the kitchen table.

She didn't know what it was, she told Jim later after the police had left and they had gone back down the hill to have a much-needed G&T. She just had a queer feeling and went up to the bedroom.

He looked so peaceful lying there, Elsie had said as Jim handed her glass. Smiling, he was. That was the funny thing, see, he was smiling. And the room smelled of flowers.

Fin

Nota Bene

MECAS, the Middle East Centre for Arab Studies or 'the British spy school' located in the mountain village of Shemlan between 1948-1978 was very real, although I have clearly fictionalised its inhabitants. Today the MECAS building still stands in Shemlan, just as Jason Hartmoor found it upon his eventual return, made into an orphanage since the centre closed its doors due to the Lebanese Civil War. Likewise, The Cliff House Restaurant *Al Sakhra* in Shemlan is also very real and I have similarly populated it with a fictional family who, I hasten to point out, have nothing whatsoever to do with the proprietors of the real Cliff House. There are four main families in Shemlan – the Hittis, Tabibs, Jabbours and Farajallahs who have lived in the village since the year dot. I invented the fifth one. Do go and eat at *Al Sakhra* if you can, by the way, because it's a magical restaurant.

The Aleppo Souk was utterly destroyed in 2012 during the Syrian Civil War, an event that occurred after I had originally written the scenes set in its sinuous Ottoman alleyways. I had a clear enough set of choices – rewrite them to omit the souk entirely, re-set them in the ruins of the souk or preserve my souk, the one I spent many happy hours walking around soaking in the relentless bustle and glorious diversity, snapping photos (including the one that decorates my blog) and generally snooping around. I decided to keep my souk which, sadly, you will never see unless you had gloried in its rich sights, sounds and smells sometime before the conflict swept it away. The C14th Armenian church, in which my friend Lena was married to Krikor, was a Byzantine marvel and its loss is tragic, but of course only an infinitesimal part of the greater tragedy suffered by Syria and its people.

And yes, the ice road running on the frozen Baltic Sea from Hiuumaa to the Estonian mainland is real. It's seasonal, opening for as many days a year as the Estonian roads and transport authority decrees it is safe to travel on the ice. And all the restrictions are real, too, including the 'no seatbelts' rule!

While we're talking of Estonia, I cannot commend highly enough the work of Estonian composer Arvo Pärt. His 'Fur Alina' was playing as I wrote the last chapters of this book. It is a magical, haunting piece.

Thanks

The usual criminals: Maha Mahdy who first 'discovered' Shemlan with me; Sara Refai, Micheline Hazou and Eman Hussein for their treasured friendship and the pleasure of their company at the Cliff House as I painstakingly researched this book by luxuriating in the afternoon sun drinking *chai bi na'ana* after long Almaza-laced lunches. This writing thing can be so hard…

My thanks also go to The Grey Havens Gang for their constant companionship and shoulders to cry on and to the book's beta readers, Bob Studholme, Bren MacDibble, Philippa Fioretti, Micheline, Derek Kirkup, Mita Ray and Peter Morin for their insights, eagle eyes and general, well, *stuff*. Of course a thank you goes to my editor, Gary Smailes at Bubblecow, for all the extra work he created for me, but his insight has been invaluable. Katie Stine's exceptional proofreading has spared me legion blushes.

Duncan Campbell-Smith was not only a student at MECAS through the last days of the school but is a contributor to *The*

PS_BX03396508

CreateSpace
7290 Investment Drive Suite B
North Charleston, SC 29418

/08/2014 10:56:47 PM
der ID: 53489048

j.	Item
	IN THIS SHIPMENT
	Shemlan 1493621939

Arabists of Shemlan: his input is greatly appreciated. Some of his story of leaving MECAS sneaked its way into some of Jason's. Similarly, former MECAS student and latterly the centre's director Leslie McLoughlin also read a draft of the MS and made valuable suggestions – any remaining absurdities are entirely my responsibility.

The cover image is by Australian artist Gerrard King and you can find more of his wonderful things at www.gerrardking.com.

My biggest thank you of all goes to Barry Cook, whose ten year battle with terminal cancer ended inevitably, but whose spirit, humour, valour and sheer humanity were an inspiration and a delight when he shared part of his last journey with us. He was most certainly not Jason Hartmoor, but he planted the seeds of an idea in my mind when he stayed with us in the Emirates on his last trip to the UK from his and Breda's home in Australia and this book is the eventual result of that seed.

@alexandermcnabb

www.alexandermcnabb.com

Made in the USA
Charleston, SC
08 January 2014